D1527247

COZY HALLOWEEN

COZY MYSTERIES

ADDISON MOORE

HOLLIS THATCHER PRESS, LTD.

ADDISON MOORE

MURDER
IN THE MIX

Bobbing For
Bodies

DESCRIPTION

Love your books with humor, sass and murder? You'll devour the Murder in the Mix Series!

*each book in the series can be read as a standalone novel.
XO Enjoy!

y name is Lottie Lemon, and I see dead people. Okay, so rarely do I see dead people. Mostly I see furry creatures of the dearly departed variety, who have come back from the other side to warn me of their previous owner's impending doom.

So, when I spot an adorable, fuzzy, little squirrel skipping around at the grand opening for my new bakery, I about lose it, until I realize it's a perky little poltergeist only visible to yours truly. But there are so many people at the grand opening it's hard to discern who exactly might be in danger— that is, until I follow the little creature right out the back and straight into another homicide. It's horrible to see your friend

lying there vacant of life. Honey Hollow will never be the same.

LOTTIE LEMON HAS a brand new bakery to tend to, a budding romance with perhaps one too many suitors, and she has the supernatural ability to see dead pets—which are always harbingers for ominous things to come. Throw in the occasional ghost of the human variety, a string of murders, and her insatiable thirst for justice, and you'll have more chaos than you know what to do with.

Living in the small town of Honey Hollow can be murder.

My name is Lottie Lemon, and I see dead people. Okay, so rarely do I see dead people. Mostly I see furry creatures of the dearly departed variety, who have come back from the other side to warn me of their previous owner's impending doom. But, at the moment, I'm not looking at a ghastly phantasm. No, this is no ghost, and as much as I hate to admit it, she very much feels like a harbinger of ominous things to come.

The tiny metal newsstand that sits in front of the Honey Pot Diner has Merilee Simonson's face staring back at me from behind the glass. It was just last month that Honey Hollow had its very first homicide, and I was unlucky enough to discover the body. Merilee, my old landlord, was even unluckier to *be* the body.

I shake all thoughts of that hairy scary day out of my mind as I step out into the street to admire the newly minted bakery which Nell, my best friend's grandmother and my boss by proxy, has put me in charge of.

"The Cutie Pie Bakery and Cakery," I whisper as I take in the beauty of the divine little shop that I've gleefully been holing up in the last week solid while baking up a storm for today's grand opening. It's the beginning of October, and autumn is showing off all of its glory in our little corner of Vermont. Honey Hollow is famous for its majestic thickets of ruby maples, liquidambars, and bright yellow birch trees—all of the above with leaves in every color of the citrine rainbow. The sweet scent of cinnamon rolls baking, heady vanilla, and the thick scent of robust coffee permeate all of Main Street, incapacitating residents and tourists alike, forcing them to stagger down toward the bakery in a hypnotic state. I'm pretty sure I won't need business cards to pull in the masses. I'll opt for the olfactory takedown every single time. Not even the heavy fog that is rolling down the street this morning has the power to subdue those heavenly scents.

Hunter, my notorious ex-boyfriend's cousin, stretches to life as he stands from where he was crouching by the entry. Bear and Hunter have been working out in front for the last three days trying to repair cracks in the wall that divides this place from Nell's original restaurant, the Honey Pot Diner. Inside, a nice opening has been made in the south-facing wall so that patrons of both establishments can meander from place to place. And I'm glad about it, too. I've been a baker at the Honey Pot for so long I would have missed seeing the inner workings of it daily even though it is right next door. Not to mention the fact my best friend, Keelie, is the manager at the Honey Pot, so this guarantees I'll still see her smiling face each and every morning.

Hunter strides over and rests his elbow over my shoulder as we take in the sight together.

"Don't forget that part," he says, pointing to the smaller sign below the words I just read. "Fine confections, gourmet coffee, and more!" he reads it just as enthusiastically as the exclamation point suggests.

We share a little laugh, never taking our eyes off the place. Otis *Bear* Fisher—the aforementioned and somewhat infamous ex—and Hunter spent all last week getting the furniture for the bakery painted in every shade of pastel. Bear bought out all of the chairs and café tables he could find at his friend's chain of secondhand stores, and the end result is so sweet and cozy it's hard for me to leave this place at night.

"Thank you for all your hard work," I say, looking up at Bear's lookalike cousin. After Bear shattered my heart into shards as if it were a haunted mirror, it was Hunter who offered up his support and suggested I leave town for a bit to clear my head. I took his advice and hightailed it to New York—Columbia University to be exact—and, well, let's just say my heart was shattered ten times harder in the big city than it ever was in Honey Hollow. "You know, I've probably never said this before, but thank you for your friendship, too." I can't help but sniff back tears. "You really have been a rock in my life. I'm sorry I didn't get a chance to tell you sooner." I offer a quick embrace to the surly blonde with the body of a brick building. Both Bear and Hunter look as if they're primed to be lumberjacks with their tree-like muscles, but lucky for me their chosen profession just so happens to be construction.

"Whoa, easy, Lottie. Don't shed a single tear for me." He laughs at the thought. "I know this day is an emotional one for you. This bakery has been your destiny for as long as I can remember." He nods back to the place where his tools are strewn all over the sidewalk just under the scaffolding he's had set up for days to assist him in the exhausting effort. "Let me clean this mess up so you can get your party started." He jogs back to the sprawl of tools, and I quickly follow him under the canopy of this skeletal structure.

"It's not bad luck to stand under a scaffolding, is it?" I tease. I'll admit, my nerves are slightly jangled just thinking about the festivities about to ensue.

He barks out a short-lived laugh. "Nope, that would be a ladder. But you're not allowed to have any bad luck, period. This is your big day, Lottie Lemon, and I promise you not one thing will go wrong." He gives a playful wink, and something about that facial disclaimer sends me in a jittery panic ten times more than before. He winces. "I think I left something out back."

Hunter takes off, and no sooner does he leave than I press my hand to the window of the bakery, a no-no as far as Keelie is concerned. She's been helping me scrub and scour every inch of this place to get it ready for its big debut, but I'll gladly wipe away my own fingerprints in a moment just to garner one more look inside before we open. It's all there—the café tables and chairs look as sweet as confections themselves, the refrigerated shelves that line the front are fully stocked and loaded with every cookie, brownie, and delicious dessert you can think of, and the walls are painted a decadent shade of butter yellow. My sister, Lainey, came by yesterday to help me decorate the place for Halloween with ghosts, witches, and scarecrows set in every free space. Autumn leaves carefully line the counters, and tiny orange pumpkins dot each table with gold and red maple leaves blooming out from underneath them. To think that in just a few short hours this place will be filled with family and friends—with Everett and Noah. Noah who—

A horrible creaking sound comes from the scaffolding above me, and I look up in time to see the gargantuan structure rocking back and forth. My entire body freezes solid as it careens toward me, and before I know it, I'm hit from behind by a warm body, pushed to safety as the entire scaffolding crashes into a pile of dust. That metal newspaper stand is lying on its side, and Merilee's grinning face is staring back up at me in replicate.

"Oh my God," I pant as I struggle to catch my breath.

"Geez, lady." A man with dark curly hair, a lantern jaw, and eyes the color of espresso pats me down by the shoulders. "You okay? You almost got crushed to death." His eyes widen a notch at the thought as do mine.

"Yeah"—I glance down at my body, thankfully still intact —"I'm fine. You saved my life!" My hand clutches at the thought of me dying, right here in front of my own bakery on opening day of all occasions. How horrible that would have been for me and perhaps for all of Honey Hollow, considering there is a stockpile of sweet treats in there to feed the entire community for a month if need be. I'd hate to think that anyone would let all of my hard work go to waste just because I met an untimely demise, but I suppose seeing my body splattered like a dead fly might kill an appetite or two. "You have to come inside." I grip him by the sleeve, and he quickly frees himself with a shake of the head. "Please, let me give you a cake or something. You're a *hero*!"

"I'm no hero." He glances past my shoulder just as Hunter and Bear shout their way over. "I gotta run. I got a kid waiting for me at home." He jogs across the street and is swallowed up by the fog within two seconds.

"*Wait*," I call after him. "Please bring your family by later! We're having a party!"

"Lottie!" Bear pulls me in tight, and I struggle to breathe for a moment before inching away. "You could have been killed!" He turns his attention back to the carnage. "*Hunter*"—he barks —"how many times have I told you not to put heavy crap on top of the scaffolding?" he riots over at his cousin, and poor Hunter looks just as shaken as I do.

"I didn't. I swear." He kicks one of the hefty looking bags that almost crushed me right along with the planks on that scaffolding. "I'd never put bags of quick-set on there. I'm not that *insane*," he riots right back.

Keelie appears from nowhere and pulls me into the safety of the Cutie Pie Bakery.

"Don't you worry about a thing, girl." She slings her svelte arm around my shoulder as we take in this magical place, and somehow the trauma of what I've just been through begins to subside. "It's a good thing to get all of the bad luck out of the way up front." She bites down on a ruby red lip as if it isn't. Keelie and

I bonded at an early age, and she's felt every bit like one of my sisters. Her blonde curls are pulled back into a ponytail, and her bright blue eyes glow as if someone lit a match behind them. Keelie is as peppy as she is sincere, and I love every attribute about her. "This is one of the best days of your life, and I never want you to forget a single moment of it. It's nothing but good luck from here on out."

"Right," I say, looking past my bubbly bestie, and with everything in me I want to believe her. "Nothing but good luck."

I glance back outside as Hunter and Bear work to clean up the debris. It's so windy those newspapers have come apart and are floating through the air like ghosts.

Then with a slap, the front page of one of those papers seals itself against the glass, and there she is, Merilee Simonson and her unnatural grimace looking right at me like a dark omen as if to say *there will be nothing good about this day*.

There is not one part of me that believes Keelie's kind words. There will be no good luck today.

Something tells me it will be bad, bad, bad.

CHAPTER 2

Fall in Honey Hollow has always been a mainstay as far as the tourists are concerned, and seeing that it's early October I was expecting my fair share of leaf peeper foot traffic, but the number of bodies that have been passing through the Cutie Pie Bakery is enough to fill a cemetery.

I frown at my morbid analogy. I can't help it, though. After I nearly lost my life this morning when that scaffolding came down, I've been more than a bit shaken. I feel downright lucky to be alive and you'd think that thought alone would have me in a good mood, but there are cookies to be baked, cookies that are being *eaten* at a breakneck pace, thus the aforementioned hustle in the kitchen. Thankfully, both of the chefs from the Honey Pot, Margo and Mannon, have been helping out these past few days as we pump out batch after batch of delectable treats. The entire town holds the scent of vanilla and sugar at this point.

"Lottie!" Lainey comes at me with a death grip of a hug. Technically, we're not blood-related since the Lemons adopted me when I was just a few hours old, but Lainey and I have the same caramel-colored waves, same hazel green eyes. Even our features hold the same open appeal. Neither of us seems to go too long without offering the world a friendly smile. "I can't believe we pulled this off!" She takes a step back, and we admire the place together. Yes, it's Lainey's finishing Halloween touches that really make the bakery feel homey and well, a bit haunted. "Wasn't it a great idea to hang those witches by their pointy hats? I just love the way they're spinning over the refrigerated shelves!"

I glance to the stuffed witches as they twirl effortlessly in a circle. "They're great, and I love the pumpkins you brought in even more. They're adorable and really make it feel like fall." Lainey wanted to put up fake spider webs in every free corner, but since spider webs in general hold an unhygienic appeal, I opted out of that decorating disaster. I don't want the first impression of the Cutie Pie that the world sees to look as if I've never cleaned the place.

Keelie heads over with an empty tray and hands it to one of the many workers from the Honey Pot who is graciously helping me out today.

"We really need to get you a staff of your own. This grand opening is straining the Honey Pot. But don't you worry. I'm discerning just the right people to populate the bakery with." She leers over at me suggestively. "Guess who I saw pulling in across the street?" She bites down on a cherry red smile, a sure sign she's up to no good. "Everett and Noah just showed up."

"Together? In the same car?" I'm a bit stunned by this. I may have just met them both a few weeks back, but I know enough about their history to understand they're not the best of friends. They were stepbrothers for a time while they were both in high school, and it didn't end well between their parents—and, apparently, not between themselves either.

Keelie shrugs. "Who could tell. There are so many people out front, a spaceship could have dropped them off and I wouldn't have noticed." She gives a wild wave at someone coming in from the Honey Pot, and I look to find Keelie's grandmother, Nell, weaving her way over.

"Hello, girls!" She offers us both a spontaneous embrace. "How are two of my favorite granddaughters?" She pinches my cheek with vigor. Nell is a sweet little ninety-two-year-old powerhouse who happens to own her fair share of real estate in Honey Hollow. The Honey Pot Diner and the Cutie Pie Bakery happen to be two of them.

"Fine and dandy." Keelie kicks my foot as she answers for me. "Should we tell her about the surprise?" She nods at her grand-mother as if trying to get her to agree.

I glance to Lainey with wild eyes. Neither my sister nor I can fathom that life could get any better.

"What surprise?" I shoot Keelie an accusing glance. She knows I don't like surprises, and she knows I'm the last person on Earth I want anyone fussing over. The last time I got a surprise I was in a courthouse down in Ashford County when Everett took the stand as the judge presiding over the small claims court the Simonson sisters dragged me off to. Everett and I had just had a physical altercation of sorts, to put it delicately. We tripped and fell—and, well, I might have inadvertently used my head to hammer down over his crotch. It was not at all what you might think. It was totally accidental and not at all sexual even though his nickname Mr. Sexy was employed within the same hour. Everett *is* sexy, but then so is Noah. I let out a dreamy sigh just thinking about that man's lips. Noah's, not Everett's.

Nell clears her throat while shooting Keelie with venom herself. "It was going to be a true surprise if you hadn't said a word." She looks my way, and her features soften. "But, since the cat is halfway out of the bag, just know that I'll have to ask you to leave the shop a little early one night later this month, and when you get back in the morning, there will be something special waiting for you."

I gasp at the thought. "You are one naughty lady, Nell Sawyer." I elbow Keelie. "You're pretty naughty yourself. You know I don't need a single thing." I glance back at the gleaming stainless appliances—it was Noah who helped purchase them with the money his father stole from unsuspecting people, but I didn't know it at the time, and that marble island that sits in the middle of the kitchen was a surprise enough. I had ordered a simple counter constructed of stainless steel, but Nell canceled the order and had a beautiful stone island put in instead. Trays and trays of sandwich cookies, peanut butter bars, cream cheese swirled brownies, and chocolate macaroons sit upon it waiting to be brought out to the front for residents and tourists alike to enjoy. "Trust me, I already have everything, and if you continue to spoil me, I might just morph into a monster."

"You, a monster?" a deep voice strums from behind, and I'm greeted with a handsome Noah Corbin Fox looking just as vexingly good-looking as his surname suggests, and next to him stands Judge Essex Everett Baxter—who humbly goes by Everett. Noah is an intense man with a dangerous side that has a way of looking at me as if he were about to take me to the nearest bedroom and do amazing things to my body—all of which I wholeheartedly approve of. I've been in one serious sexual drought ever since the New York debacle, and Noah is just the right kind of trouble to alleviate me of all my frustrations.

Everett is dark and intimidating. He rarely, if ever, smiles, keeps his words to a minimum, and oozes testosterone to the point of demanding the attention of every female of every *species* to the forefront of his majesty.

"You're here!" I shout while throwing my arms around each of them at once. I hop back and take them in once again—Noah in a navy corduroy jacket and jeans, and Everett in his traditional three-piece inky dark suit. "Can you believe all of the people who are streaming through this place? I swear, it's all of Honey Hollow and then some have come to visit."

Noah takes in the crowd. Both Noah and Everett have the same dark hair, with the exception Everett's is jet-black and Noah's has a touch of red in the sunlight. Noah has the dreamiest marbled green eyes, and Everett's gaze is more of a blue heated flame. Both men are handsome in their own right, but it was Noah I took a bold step with a few weeks ago. We've been fused at the mouth pretty much ever since. And how I can't wait to fast-forward this day just to pull him into the walk-in like I did last night and shower him with all the affection I can. Who knew having a boyfriend could be such a stress reliever?

I touch my fingers to my lips a moment as if I had spoken those words out loud.

Noah and I aren't anything official. I shouldn't even be thinking the word *boyfriend* lest I accidentally pepper it in casual conversation. I'd hate to chase him off over some silly verbal blunder.

Noah winces. "I'd say you've got all of Vermont in here and part of New Hampshire, and Connecticut, too."

Everett chuckles at the thought. It still amuses me to see him smile. He wasn't at all friendly for at least the entire first month I knew him. It's a miracle we're friends at all.

"It's more like the Western Hemisphere." He nods to the feast out front. "I don't know about the rest of you, but I'm loading up."

Noah brushes a quick kiss to my cheek, and I can feel my skin heating to unsafe levels. Never have I had anyone show me physical affection in Honey Hollow before. Not even Bear, and we dated on and off for about three years in high school. I shudder just thinking about that time in my life.

"I'd better go with him." Noah frowns at this once-upon-a-stepbrother. "I'll make sure he leaves enough for the rest of us." He takes off after him just as I spot my mother circulating in the crowd, and I can't help but groan at the sight of her.

"She's here," I hiss to my sister.

Keelie bumps past us with a tray full of Honey Bars. "Don't sweat a thing!" she calls out as she heads to the front.

"I can't help it," I say, pulling my sister in close. "I don't trust this new guy Mom is dating."

Lainey scoffs. "You don't trust any guy Mom ever dates."

"I know that, but he's not culled from the usual bunch. The fact our mother is openly deviating from her usual pool of suspects makes me think that she might be serious about this guy." It's true. My mother has dated the same four men for as far back as the year after my father passed away. Oh, how I loved that man. And not just because he was the fireman who found me swaddled in a blanket on the cold floor of the firehouse. As much as I've struggled with abandonment issues sponsored by my birthmother, at least she didn't leave me in the woods to freeze to death. Joseph Lemon was a saint. I don't think I can say the same for the four clowns that my mother has switched out like a crop rotation since his untimely demise. But this new man, with his steely silver hair, his tall sturdy frame, his unyielding handsome features, he seems a lot more sinner than he ever does saint.

"Who cares?" Lainey's phone rings and she pulls it out of her purse. "Mom really likes this guy, and so should you. I've met him, and he seems pretty decent. You're going to love him." She holds out her phone, and my younger sister, Meg, waves manically our way on the other side of the screen.

"Congratulations, Lottie!" Meg laughs wildly as she looks past us into the room. "Can you believe it? All of your dreams have finally come true!" Meg looks a bit jarring with her harshly dyed jet-black hair teased every which way, and those signature yellow contact lenses of hers makes it feel as if Halloween were already upon us. "I gotta run, but eat some cookies for me, would you?" she roars menacingly into the screen, mostly to entertain us and quite possibly to get her in the mood for the rest of the night. Meg is a superstar on the Vegas female wrestling circuit. When she first started, Mom, Lainey, and I took a road trip to Nevada to see her in action. Seeing my little sister in that ring was the most frightening and yet empowering thing I have ever witnessed. Suffice it to say, Madge the Badge put on one heck of a show.

I spot Mom near the entry to the Honey Pot and glower at the man she has plastered to her side. Just as I'm about to bring up the boyfriend grievance to my sister's attention once again, a watery-eyed woman steps in front of me, and I blink a few times trying to process where I've seen her before.

"Micheline?" I take a half-step back just taking her in like this. I've known Micheline Roycroft for the better half of my life. She dated Hunter off and on while I dated Bear. I used to tease that we were clawing for the same life raft while on two different sinking ships. Her hair is longer, darker, her eyes a touch red and glossy, and she looks a bit forlorn. "My goodness, I've missed you!" I wrap my arms around my old friend. "Where have you been? Welcome to my new bakery!"

Her lips tremble with a smile. "I was living in Hollyhock for a while, working at the bank. I just transferred to Honey Hollow Savings and Loans. I moved back about a month ago." She gives a side-eye to the crowd. "Have you seen Hunter? I thought he'd be here since he helped with the construction."

"Oh, he's here somewhere. Are you two trying to work things out again?" I'm almost sorry I asked, considering the fact she seems on the verge of tears.

Micheline cranes her neck into the crowd and mumbles something about *later* before threading herself into the thicket of bodies.

Mom dances her way over with open arms. "Here you are!" She offers a firm embrace before pulling forward the man of the hour—more to the point, the man of my discontent. "Wallace, this is my middle daughter, Lottie. It's her special day, and I can't believe I'm alive and breathing to witness it!"

"Gee, thanks for the depressing endorsement. It's nice to know you believed in me so strongly."

She swats me. "You know I do."

17

It's true. I do.

Her gentleman caller extends his hand, and I can't help but frown at the over-sized mitt before I give it a shake. "Wallace Chad." His voice is warm and deep, and yet despite the equally warm twinkle in his eyes, I can't help but distrust him. "My pleasure to finally meet you. You have an amazing mother, as you both know." He nods a quick hello to Lainey.

Mom lifts a finger as if a thought just came to her. "Lainey, I've been meaning to tell you to make sure that garage of yours is locked up tight at all hours of the day. We heard Becca Turner just tell a crowd in the Honey Pot they've had a rash of burglaries right here in Honey Hollow." She taps her fingers over her lips as if the thought were unspeakable, and it is. That homicide we had last month was pretty unspeakable, too. It's just too much to wrap my head around. My heart still bleeds for Merilee.

Mom tugs at her new beau's lapel. "We'd better work the room. I'd hate for my friends to miss the opportunity to meet one of the kindest men on the planet."

Wallace leans toward Lainey and me. "I'm a financial planner by trade, so if there's anything I can ever do for you, it would be my pleasure to be at your service. Free of charge, of course."

Mom squeals as if we just won the lottery. "*Free!*" she shrills, making crazy eyes at both Lainey and me. "Isn't that something? You never get anything free these days." She looks to her silver fox of a boy toy. "Now you're just far too generous to me."

"Only because I can't begin to repay how generous you've been to me."

They blend back into the crowd, and I turn to Lainey and gag.

"I don't even want to think about how generous our mother is being. If you'll excuse me, I need to check the ovens and make sure nothing's burning. God knows I've been a little distracted today."

I take off for the back, and the scent of fresh devil's food cupcakes cooling on the rack has me swooning. Those delectable delights have been flying off the shelves—or trays as it were, so I've been baking them nonstop. It was Nell's idea to have an all-you-can-eat dessert bar. She said that would be a surefire way to get everyone addicted to my tasty treats, and when the shop officially opens for business tomorrow, I'll have a line out the door. She was also gracious enough to pay for all of the ingredients I'd need to pull off a feat such as this.

Lord knows I wouldn't be anywhere without Nell in my life. She's the one who gifted me my precious cat, Pancake. She happens to own Pancake's brother, Waffles, and our shared affection for the adorable, yet severely aloof, Himalayans is just another facet of our inextricable bond. I'm pretty bonded to Pancake, too. In fact, I'm going to collapse on my bed with my arms wrapped tight around him tonight.

Technically, it's not my bed. I'm still holed up in Lainey's guest room, but once I get a little time on my hands, I'll be back to apartment hunting so I can get out of her hair. We get along well enough, but we've never made good roommates.

The back door is open, and I meander over for a quick breath of crisp autumn air. The fog is still rolling in thick, unfurling like batting, and I'm momentarily drawn to it. No sooner do I get to the back porch than I'm stopped in my tracks by the sound of shouting voices escalating to my left. Not far off in the alley, I spot Bear and Hunter going at it, both men red-faced and angry. It looks pretty volatile, so I quickly step back into the shop. I know for a fact Bear blamed Hunter for that scaffolding incident this morning, but I wish he wouldn't hammer into him like that. It was an accident, and everybody involved survived.

I head back into the bakery, picking up a tray of creamy white cake pops swirled to look like mummies, complete with chocolate chip eyes. The kids especially love those and, sure enough, every last one of them is snatched from me before I have a chance to set the tray down.

Everett comes up and bumps his shoulder to mine as we

inspect the wild crowd. "That went fast. But then, so is every-thing else. Bear's brownie bar is a pretty big hit, too."

"Don't I know it. At least I can count on the fact they'll love my brownies." It was in honor of Bear that I put up the brownie bar to begin with. It turns out, he put this project at the top of his construction roster just so he could complete it as soon as possible.

"They'll love everything," Everett assures before nodding to the entry that leads into the Honey Pot, and I hike up on my tiptoes to see what he's motioning to.

I suck in a quick breath at the sight of Cascade Montgomery, Merilee and Mora Anne's cousin. And here I thought she was the one who stabbed poor Merilee in the back, but actually it was her sister, Mora Anne.

"Well, I'm glad she's here. Actually, I'm glad everyone's here."

I take in the crowd again and spot Holland Grand, who owns the orchard, speaking with Ken and Molly McMurry, who own the pumpkin patch. Next to them stands Naomi Turner, Keelie's twin sister. But, unlike Keelie, Naomi has decided to eschew her naturally blonde locks and dye them a gorgeous shade of ebony much like my own sister. Her eyes are a startling shade of blue, and I must admit the combination looks stunning. Both Naomi and Keelie are stunning in general. Next to her stand her best friend, Lily Swanson, and her newly minted beau, Travis Darren. I can't help but scowl over at him since he was dating both Simonson sisters at the very same time just last month.

Past them stand Becca Turner, aka my second mom, Naomi and Keelie's mother, speaking with Eva Hollister, the woman who runs my mother's book club, and Chrissy Nash, the mayor's ex-wife. And seeing that Mayor Nash himself is here mingling amongst the crowd, I'd say Chrissy is finally past the point where she can't stand to be in the same room with him.

To their left, Collette Jenner postures for the attention of every male in a three-mile radius. Apparently, she's one of

Everett's many exes, and I can't help but grunt at the sight of her. Sure, she's a perky redhead who makes it a point to brighten any room she's in with that obnoxious witch-like cackle, but there's something about the fact Everett used to date her that has made me unsure of how I feel about her anymore. It's not like we were friends to begin with.

Just as I'm about to tempt Everett with one of my wickedly delicious devil's food cupcakes, something small and furry scurries across the floor, and I gasp as if trying to suck all of the oxygen out of the room.

"A *rodent*," I hiss to Everett, suddenly regretful I said anything at all. God forbid word get out that I've got rats or bats or whatever that thing was that just skipped into the place.

"What? Where?" Everett looks to the ground right along with me.

The tip of a fluffy little tail threads through the crowd, and my jaw unhinges. "It's not a rat after all. It's a squirrel." I'm only a touch relieved by that fact. It's still a menacing rodent, *vermin* if you will. And I certainly don't care to have it in my shop. I would have said all of that out loud, but I'm terrified of starting a stampede for the front door.

"I don't see it."

"It's right there." I point as the brazen little beast comes forward and stands on its hind legs right in front of my mother. Dear God, she's going to stomp it to death with those four inch stilettos she's stuffed her feet into. My mother is notorious for stomping out the life of a vermin or two, mostly mice and rats that found their way far too close to her killer clogs. She would do anything to defend her daughters, and a spontaneous homicide has never been off the table.

"Right where?" Everett leans in toward the spot my finger is poised to.

"Are you blind?" I tease as the creature takes a few ambling steps in our direction, and I freeze solid. That silver bushy tail, that fuzzy gray coat is suddenly translucent in nature, and I can see the floor right through its body. This isn't your run-of-the-mill woodland creature. This was once somebody's loveable, and well past its prime, pet.

"I'm beginning to question your vision." Everett looks stymied by what it is I'm staring at.

"Oh"—seeing that this beast is for my eyes only, I think it's best I ditch this entire conversation with him—"you're right." My cheeks flush pink as I stand straight as a pin. "It must have been a scarf someone dropped momentarily. It's about freezing outside already." A thought occurs to me, and I jolt to attention.

Dear God! The last time I saw a dearly departed beast it was Merilee's orange tabby and look what happened to her! Merilee, not the tabby. The pets that skip over from the other side of the rainbow bridge are *always* a prequel to some horrible event in their previous owner's life. The trouble used to range from skinned knees to broken bones, but in Merilee's case, that cat might as well have been dressed like the Grim Reaper. I've seen the ghost of a person just twice before, as well, and I'm darn glad I haven't seen one since. The squirrel comes up and holds its tiny paws up in my direction, just looking at me with those big brown eyes, that bushy tail hiked at attention, and I can't help but coo at it.

"Oh my goodness, you are the sweetest little thing," I whisper as I give it a quick scratch over the back.

"Lottie?" Everett sounds more than worried for me.

I straighten once again as the tiny creature scuttles past me, making his way to the kitchen.

Everett's dark brows bounce with concern. "Are you feeling okay? Who were you talking to?"

"You!" My voice squeaks. "I was talking to you. You're just the sweetest thing." I bite down hard over my lower lip. Lying is something I'm loath to do. "Say! If anyone in this room were to once have had a squirrel as a pet, who would you think that would be?"

"*Me.*" A warm, masculine voice buzzes in my ear as Noah wraps his arms around me, and my heart lurches inside my chest.

"Please tell me you're kidding," I say, spinning around in his arms to take in his gorgeous face. I couldn't stand it if anything even remotely bad happened to Noah. My heart hurts just thinking about it.

That tick of his cheek spells out concern. "I am kidding." He opens his mouth to say something else just as the McMurrys come upon us.

Molly smiles at both Noah and me. "I hope we're not interrupting." My eyes flit to that shoulder-length bob of hers with its cute, vertical curls. I've been envious of everyone who can pull off that hairstyle. I've wanted to try it myself this summer, but I never had a free moment. And now with the bakery, I'm afraid my hair will be set in a messy bun permanently. Her husband, Ken, is classically tall, dark, and handsome. He always has a toothy grin at the ready and a piece of straw tucked behind his ear that gives him a scarecrow-esque appeal.

"Not interrupting at all," I say, fully relieved to steer all conversation away from that poor deceased squirrel.

"Good," Molly says, holding up a purple frosted devil's food cupcake with a tiny meringue ghost spiked into the top. "Ken and I were wondering if you'd be up for baking about twelve dozen or so of these for the Fall-O-Ween Fest down at the pumpkin patch? Of course, we'll pay you and be happy to do it. Each year we like to offer a refreshment table, and these would be a perfect treat to go along with it."

"*Yes!* Of course, I would." A rush of adrenaline bursts through me all at once. "I would love to furnish any and all of the treats you need for the Fall-O-Ween Fest. It happens to be one of my fondest memories growing up."

"That's perfect." Molly's entire face brightens as if my cupcakes had the power to make her day, and I'd like to think they did. "I'll get you a firm number of how many we'll need, then email me with an estimate of the cost, and I'll come by next week and leave a deposit."

"I sure will," I say as they weave their way back into the crowd. Collette crops up in their place and immediately begins asking Everett ridiculous questions in a clear effort to pry him away.

I look to Noah. "I'll be right back. I'd better refill those cupcakes so that Molly and Ken can see firsthand how much the locals love them."

Noah ticks his head toward Nell. "Sounds good. I'll head over and say hello."

I take off for the kitchen, and just as I'm about to steal a fresh chocolate chip cookie off a cooling rack and pop it into my mouth—there is nothing like a warm chocolate chip cookie straight from the oven—that bushy silver tail garners my attention once again.

A horrible feeling of foreboding comes over me as I follow the wily beast as he makes his way out the back door. Carefully, I take a step out into the chilled autumn air. The maples from across the way have blown their golden hand-shaped leaves all over the ground as the tiny squirrel scampers over them and right over a body.

A scream gets locked in my throat.

Flat on his back lies Hunter Fisher with one of my devil's food cupcakes in his hand and a bullet wound through his chest.

Hunter isn't ever going to finish that cupcake. In fact, he won't be eating anything at all ever again.

He's dead.

CHAPTER 3

The echo of my own screams riots through the tiny alleyway as a crowd amasses from nowhere, and soon it seems as if the entire bakery has drained of all its patrons to gawk at poor Hunter who lies motionless, his eyes still opened to the sky. Judging by that sizable pool of blood beneath him, Hunter Fisher is most certainly no longer with us.

Noah grabs ahold of me and pulls me back while Everett shouts into his phone for help to arrive.

"Lottie, what happened?" Noah weaves us through the tangle of bodies, and I can finally catch my breath. "What did you see?"

The crowd whispers Hunter Fisher's name until it sounds like an ominous chant.

"I didn't see any—" That squirrel! "Well, I guess that mystery is solved," I say under my breath. It's clear the adorable creature belonged to Hunter at some point in time.

Noah runs his hands up and down my arms as I startle back to life. "You saw something. What did you see?"

Everett comes up before I can answer. "The sheriffs are on their way. They want you to stick around for questioning."

"Sadly, I know the routine," I say as Bear comes running out of the back of the bakery just as a fire truck rolls onto the scene.

"What's going on?" He pushes his way through the crowd. "Oh God!" He dives onto his knees toward his poor cousin lying helpless on the asphalt, and I barrel through the knot of bodies to be with him.

"Who the hell did this?" The veins in the sides of his neck distend like cords as his face turns an instant shade of red. I've never seen him so filled with rage and grief.

I fall next to him, and Bear lets out a mighty roar as if he had some primal capability to morph into the beast from which his nickname was hewn. Bear loses it, cussing and shouting at anyone and everyone before leaning over his lookalike. Poor Bear just sits there stunned, red-faced and angry as if he were ready to kill whoever was responsible for this. And I have no doubt he would. If I never knew it before, Bear loved Hunter like a brother.

Before long, sirens saw through the air, and the dim alleyway is lit up with spasming red and blue lights. Most of the crowd has dissipated, and as soon as Captain Turner gets out of his vehicle, he instructs anybody who didn't witness the event to please leave their names with the attending officers before they head home. Not long after, an all too familiar coroner's van pulls up behind the brigade of patrol cars, and my blood runs cold.

It's happening again. It's already happened.

Captain Turner helps Bear up and pulls him to the side for questioning, and it's just me staring at my old friend as tears of my own stream down my cheeks.

"It's not fair," I say to no one in particular.

Noah materializes from out of nowhere. "You're right, Lottie. It's not fair. Murder never is." He helps me to my feet and holds me as I do my best to pull it together, but I can't seem to stop shaking, can't stop the tears from streaming like a wild river with no end and no beginning.

Keelie and Lainey head this way, shaken and pale themselves.

"Here," Lainey says while dabbing my cheeks with a wad of tissues. "I'm going to get you home. Captain Turner knows that you're staying with me. You shouldn't be here, seeing him like this."

"No." It comes from me like an abrupt protest. "I need to be here. I need to be here for Hunter and for Bear. You go ahead." I spot Tanner Redwood behind her and can't help but frown. It shouldn't be Tanner making sure my sister gets home safe. It should be Forest Donovan. Forest and Lainey were high school sweethearts who dated for a small eternity. But then, they hit a bump in the road last summer, a boulder if you will, and, well, Lainey thought it would be cute to make Forest jealous with Tanner. One date led to another, and they've been joined at the hip ever since. Not literally. And as far as I know, ever. Just the thought makes me want to gag.

Just as Lainey is about to protest, Forest comes over all decked out in his firemen garb, heavy yellow coat, loose tan pants, and thick black boots. Forest is every bit the hot firefighter with his chestnut waves and those crystal gray eyes.

Tanner looks more like your typical playboy—which everyone knows he is. My sister is so fooling herself if she thinks he's being loyal to her. I spotted him speaking to three different girls just this week alone. He happens to be the head of Parks and Recs for all of Honey Hollow. He's got a tanned surfer look about him, hair that's short in the back and longer in front so he's forever doing that annoying head flip to get it out of his eyes.

"Lainey"—Forest offers her a partial embrace—"thank God you guys are okay. When I heard it was the new bakery—" His voice breaks, and he ticks his head to the side as if working hard to keep his emotions in check. "Let me take you home."

Her mouth opens as she looks to Tanner.

"Dude." Tanner gently removes Forest's hold on my sister, and my heart breaks for my sister's one true love. That would be

27

Forest, by the way. "I'm taking her home." He does that annoying hair flip thing three times in a row, and I'm starting to think it's a tic. "And I'll stay with her all night long."

"No thank you," I'm quick to interject, and my sister makes wild eyes at me as if to say thank you herself. "I'll be home as soon as I can, and I'll take over from there."

The three of them say a quick goodnight as Lainey and Tanner take off in one direction and poor Forest in the other.

Everett gives my shoulder a quick squeeze. "Are you okay? Did you see anyone taking off when you came out here?"

Noah's chest puffs up on cue. "I already asked her that. What did you see, Lottie? Did you hear anything?"

"No." I shake my head, bewildered. "I mean, he was shot, right? I certainly didn't hear a gunshot."

Noah nods. "They most likely used a silencer. Did you see anything at all? Anything?"

"No, I mean, yes. I was just following that sq—" My fingers land hard over my lips, and I shoot a quick look to Everett.

"Detective Fox," Captain Turner shouts as he motions him over.

Noah looks from me to Everett. "I'll be right back. Don't go anywhere."

Everett wastes no time leaning in. "You were going to say squirrel, Lemon. Don't deny it. We may not be in a courtroom, but I don't think it would be beneficial for you to perjure yourself in my presence regardless."

"Please." I avert my gaze a moment. "I would never lie to you —willingly." I wince as that last part comes out. "Besides, it's not important. What's important is that they catch whoever did this. And I can promise you, Essex Everett Baxter, that it was not me," I hiss out that last part, and to my surprise a tiny smile twitches on his lips. "*What?*" It comes out annoyed, as has been my go-to emotion with him in the not-so-distant past.

He straightens a bit, and his jaw squares out, making him look irritatingly far more handsome than ever is fair. Which reminds me—I know firsthand they label his java cup *Mr. Sexy* down at the coffee shop next to the courthouse. "You're not telling the truth."

A breath hitches in my throat. "How dare you insinuate that I'm a liar."

He leans in with those serious eyes. "I never called you such thing. I just so happen to be very good at reading people—and I have my ways of getting information out of just about anyone. It's my gift." His brows twitch. "You saw that squirrel again, didn't you?"

My hand clamps over my mouth, and I hop back a step in the event I need to bolt from this human lie detector machine. There's no way I'm telling Everett about my gift—or curse as it were. And at this point, I think it's a little too late to convince him that there was a real squirrel in question. The best thing to do is drop it.

Noah heads over and wraps his arms around me, dotting a gentle kiss over my forehead, and I take in his spiced cologne, allowing myself to relax over his rock-hard chest. I'm so exhausted from everything that's transpired tonight—this entire last week. The nonstop baking alone is enough to make anyone delusional. I'm hoping I'll wake up tomorrow morning to find my sweet cat Pancake curled up in my arms, and this will have all been one long nightmare.

Noah gently lifts my chin with his finger. "Captain Turner wants us to speak with him."

No sooner do I look over than Jack, Captain Turner as he's known to everyone else, is upon us. Jack is Keelie's dad, and since I've grown up with him as a second father, I've only ever called him by his proper name. Next to him stands a tall woman in a dark pantsuit. Long amber hair parted straight down the middle hangs over her shoulders. Her face is pale and offset morbidly by dark crimson lipstick. On anyone else it would look like a disaster, but she looks every bit the supermodel and pulls it off effortlessly.

Jack nods to me. "Lottie, this is Detective Ivy Fairbanks. She'll be asking you a few questions." Someone calls for him from behind, and he gives a quick bow. "I'll be right over here if you need me."

"Detective Fairbanks." Noah extends his hand, and she glares at it as if it were a rodent. Noah drops his hand. "My name is Noah Fox. I'm a private investigator myself, licensed in the state of Vermont."

She gives him a quick once-over. "Did you find the body?"

Noah turns to me. "No, actually—"

"Then you're dismissed." She tips her nose toward Everett and me. "Which one of you found the body?"

I clear my throat. "That would be me. And if you don't mind, I'd prefer we address him by his name, Hunter." My gut wrenches just hearing his name sail from my lips. "He was my friend."

"Very well." She pulls out a notebook, looking perennially bored. "What happened?"

I quickly relay the chain of events, sans any mention of Hunter's pet squirrel. For a moment, I wonder what Hunter had named him. He was so cute and fluffy. It was obvious anyone could have fallen in love with the tiny creature. I bet it was something cute and clever like Acorn. Hunter always did have a soft heart.

"So, that's it?" She blinks up at me with those dark coffee-colored eyes, and a chill runs through me. Sure, she's beautiful, but she's equally intimidating, and it has nothing to do with her beauty.

"That's it."

"You were just coming out for some air?" She glowers over at me. "With a bakery full of people and six batches of cookies in the oven? Hmm." Her lips crimp into something that looks like a smile while she simultaneously stares me down. It's an unnerving feat, and coming from her, it feels like a mental interrogation. "I'll be speaking to you again soon. Hopefully, something else will come to mind."

Noah wraps his arm around me. "I'll try to jog her memory. If anything new crops up, I'll let you know as soon as possible."

Detective Fairbanks straightens a moment, looking at him as if he were a vagrant who wandered onto the scene. "Have the Fishers hired you for your services?" There's a mocking undertone in her voice, and instantly I don't appreciate it or her.

A breath expires from him as he relaxes against me with an air of defeat. "No, they haven't."

"Then stay out of my investigation." She stalks off, and my jaw roots to the ground.

"How dare she speak to you that way," I say as I give his chest a light scratch. "I'm going to have her fired."

A deep rumble of a laugh lives and dies in his throat as his eyes sparkle my way.

"Don't worry about her. She doesn't have the power to slow me down." He glances to our left a moment. "Hang tight. I'm going to talk to Bear and see what I can glean."

Everett pops up just as Noah takes off. "Now that we're alone, I think you owe me an explanation regarding that squirrel you claim to be chasing."

An incredulous laugh strums from me. "I owe you no such thing, Judge Baxter. Like I said, it was nothing."

Everett folds his arms across his enormous chest, his suit drawing tight around his elbows. "It was something, Lemon. And if you don't tell me, you'll have to tell Noah or Detective Fairbanks. Like it or not, whatever you saw led you straight to the scene of a homicide. You don't want to be guilty of withholding evidence, do you?" His tone drops several octaves when he says that last part, and you would think he were fifty years older than me rather than simply half a decade.

"Withholding evidence?" I practically mouth the words.

31

"That's right. People get sent to prison for it all the time."

A dull laugh expels from me in a powder white plume. But Everett isn't laughing. He's dead serious.

"Prison." I gulp at the thought of being forced to wear orange for years at a time. That alone sounds like a punishment. "Everett"—I plead with him—"I can't—"

"You can and you will," he says it stern, and a moment of thick silence bounces between us. "Fine. If you don't tell Noah or Detective Fairbanks by the time the night is through, I'm afraid I'll have to bring this information to light. I hope you don't take offense to it. It's simply my civic duty. My duty for justice doesn't end when I leave the bench."

My heart strums wildly in my chest. My entire body slaps with heat from embarrassment. I can't imagine me ever telling Everett something that sounds so insane. Something that *is* so insane.

My mouth opens and not a sound comes out. I glance over to Noah as he's comforting Bear, and my heart aches for the both of them. For Bear because he lost someone he loved like a brother. And for Noah because he's about to wish he never met someone as certifiable as myself.

"Hey"—Everett leans in with heavy concern in his eyes—"I don't want to upset you any more than you already are. I can see this is hard for you."

"Oh? Because you're good at *reading* people?" I can't help but smear it with sarcasm.

"Yes." He frowns. "Okay, here's the deal. You don't have to tell Noah or Detective Fairbanks for now. I'll come by the bakery some time this week, and you can fill me in once you've had a moment to relax. I wouldn't pry so hard unless I thought it was important. A man died, Lemon. Believe me when I say even the smallest shred of evidence can help put away whoever did this."

"Fine." I swallow hard, trying to push the next words out. "I'll tell you. Sometime this week." Maybe.

"You will." Everett looks every bit as intimidating if not more than Detective Fairbanks could ever hope to be. "And, Lemon?" he says as Noah heads back in this direction. "I'll know if you're not telling the truth."

"Yes, sir, Judge Baxter." I look up at him sternly from underneath my lashes. "I promise to tell the truth and nothing but the truth." I'm not crossing my fingers. I'm crossing my *soul*. I hope to God I don't accidentally spew the truth his way at any point during this next week or ever.

"Good. I'm counting on it."

We look back at the crime scene just as the area is cordoned off with caution tape, a blinding shade of yellow in this dim light. A photographer circles poor Hunter as men with plastic gloves begin to comb every inch of the alleyway.

I will tell Everett the truth.

Just as soon as I come up with some other truth to tell.

Poor Hunter is dead. And I'm more than positive that feral, long-dead creature won't add anything worthwhile to the investigation.

There's not a ghost of a chance.

CHAPTER 4

$\mathcal{H}$oney Hollow is robed in fog this early Monday morning. All of Main Street is blanketed in cardinal maple leaves, a red carpet fit for royalty, and yet here we are, grounded common folk blessed with the honor. It might still be early in October, but the Halloween spirit is alive and well with every last nook and cranny of this tiny town dotted with bright orange pumpkins in every shape and size. Just down the street in the town square, there's a heap of pumpkins surrounding Honey Hollow's enormous three-tiered stone fountain, and just beyond that, Founders Square Park has a friendly looking scarecrow staked at the entry that every tourist stops by to take their picture with. That's the thing that I have always appreciated about Honey Hollow. It's a warm, comfortably cozy small town that makes any and everyone feel right at home. I used to add that it was safe—that I felt much safer here than in the big city, but after everything that's transpired, I'm not so sure about that.

The day wears on, and I've been at the bakery now for hours. I've made it a practice to show up at five in the morning just to get everything started. Keelie said she'd help me hire my own staff since most of the staff working alongside me is on loan from the Honey Pot.

Margo and Mannon, the chefs next door, have been a godsend, utilizing their five-star superpowers to help streamline my baking and create a few marvels of their own in the process. I just finished with three dozen hazelnut bars, a dozen cutie pies, the famous, or perhaps infamous caramel apple treats that were served at the Apple Festival last month. I've filled the cupcake shelves with red velvet, French vanilla, and a devil's food variety frosted in colors of green, purple, and orange, each with either a black tarantula made from licorice, a meringue ghost, or a tiny chocolate cookie cut out in the shape of a wizard's hat, complete with candy stars. I kept the sign for Bear's Brownie Bar and moved it into the casing where I have a variety of brownies and blondies to choose from. I made up an entire tray of cheese and raspberry Danishes, along with fresh croissants for the morning crowd, in addition to a couple loaves of crumb cake.

When Keelie helped me order the coffee equipment for the bakery, I nearly passed out at the expense, but she promised it would be worth every robust drop, and once I learned to navigate my way around the steely beasts—and more to the point, now that I consider us friends, that beast is producing something magical that I never thought coffee could be. Suffice it to say, the bakery smells divine. I have no doubt the scent of rich, roasted java beans, coupled with the scent of fresh pastry dough baking has thoroughly permeated Main Street. I had the cinnamon rolls in the oven at about seven when we opened, and that's what truly brought in the heavy morning rush. But now that most of the crowd has dissipated and my molasses spice cookies and pumpkin cheesecakes are still in the oven, I've decided to pull my laptop out and sit in the café among the customers while my poor, tired feet do their best to recoup.

The bell on the door rings and in comes Lainey along with

another small crowd. One of the girls from the Honey Pot motions for me to stay put while she takes their order.

"Hey, hey!" Lainey takes a seat across from me. "How are you doing? I'm surprised you're here. I thought for sure you would have at least taken a day off after last night." She ticks her head toward the back where Hunter's body was found.

"It's my official first day." I make a face at the thought because yesterday felt far more official. "And there are no days off when you're running the show. Nell expects me to be here. This is my baby as much as it is hers, and I'm going to make sure it succeeds."

Lainey waves me off. "That's a given. But you need to take care of yourself, too, lady." She peers over at my laptop. "Whatcha looking at? You weren't serious about setting up a kitty cam, were you? Because if my house is going to be under surveillance, I want to know about it. The last thing I want you to see is me dancing around in my leopard print robe. It's short, you know."

"Oh, I know it is." I avert my eyes at the memory of it. "Which reminds me. I know what to get you for Christmas. The rest of that robe."

"Ha-ha." She scowls as she leans in further. "What is this? Online classified? The real estate section?" Her voice pitches with the epiphany. "You're not thinking about moving out so soon, are you?" Lainey whines in that adorable way only she can. My sister looks every bit the Kewpie doll with her bowtie lips and perfectly coifed curls. She's head to toe in eggplant today, wearing a deep purple dress with a matching cardigan. Lainey always makes it a point to dress up for work. Nobody loves working at the library as much as my sister. Books are her passion as much as baking is mine.

The bell rings behind us again and in strides Noah Fox clad in a suit, that naughty smile twitching on his lips just for me, and my stomach bisects with heat at the sight of him.

"Hello, ladies."

Lainey pulls up a seat for him. "Please talk my sister out of looking for a place of her own. She's hardly home as it is. Paying rent wouldn't make sense at this point."

I can't help but shoot my sister a disparaging look. She's right, and I happen to hate when that happens, especially when I'm disagreeing with her.

"You looking for a place?" Noah spins his seat around and sits on it backwards, and something about that boyish move tugs at my heart.

"Yes," I say it low as if Lainey couldn't hear. "And you look extremely dapper and handsome, might I add." I can't help but bite down a naughty smile of my own. "Where are you off to today?"

"The office for now." He ticks his head in the direction of the bank. Noah's office is right next door to that financial institution. Actually, that's how we met. I thought he was a part of the loans department and started right in on why I needed a loan for kitchen equipment. It turns out, Noah gifted me the money without me realizing it and copped to it once everything was firmly purchased and installed. The finances came from the money he received from his father's estate. And since the money wasn't earned with integrity—he pilfered Everett's poor mother while during their short tenure together—he wanted to donate it to a good cause. Both he and Everett agreed the bakery was a good one.

Noah's cheek rises on one side as he sheds a crooked grin. "After our hand in Mora's arrest last month, the calls started pouring in. I've got a few investigations going."

"*Ohh.*" I lean in, intrigued by this sexy detective seated before me. "Anything juicy?"

"Yeah." Lainey leans in as well. "Who's having an affair with whom? Are you doing any stakeouts?" She jumps in her seat, practically foaming at the mouth wanting answers.

Noah holds out a hand, his chest thumping with a laugh. "I

can't divulge the details of my cases. And, believe me, they are far from juicy. But I can say a few of them involve those garage burglaries." He points to Lainey. "Be sure to keep a good lock on that thing. Most of these thefts occurred by way of garage doors that are operated with an electronic remote."

She gasps, "That's all I've got. So not fair. It's as if the thieves of this world are always one step ahead." She looks at her phone in haste. "I'd better hustle. I've got to be at the library in a few minutes." She glances my way as she rises. "Any recommendations on what I should have for breakfast?"

"I put in a few chocolate croissants that—"

"Ah-ah!" She holds up her hand and stops me. "Say no more. Sold. In fact, I'll take two and have one for a snack later," she sings as she makes her way to the counter.

I give Noah's sleeve a quick tug. "Any leads on who killed Hunter?" Thankfully, I'm not a suspect in this one despite the fact I found his body. A thought occurs to me. "I'm not a suspect, am I?"

He winces as he warms my hand with his. "It's routine. But I promise, the captain doesn't think you had anything to do with it outside of the discovery of the body."

"Oh, cheese balls," I hiss as I snap my laptop shut. "Anyone else? Anyone who could have feasibly done this?"

"There's Bear."

"*Bear?*" I screech a little too loud, and a few women at the next table turn this way. They're tourists and most likely have no idea what carnage took place here last night. "That's terrible. Bear wouldn't hurt a fly. That's nothing but another dead end."

"Well"—Noah tugs at his collar—"he didn't shed a tear last night, but he did look upset. In fact, if I had to guess, he looked fighting mad."

That argument I witnessed between Bear and Hunter just a few minutes before I made the gruesome discovery comes to mind, and a breath locks in my throat at the thought of it.

"Lottie, what is it?" Noah leans in close, the tip of his head just an inch from mine, and his warm cologne permeates me with its warm scent.

"I—" A part of me can't do it. I know for a fact Bear would never kill Hunter. Why arm Noah with false evidence? "It was nothing. I'll do whatever I can to prove Bear's innocence. It's the least I can do after he moved heaven and earth to open this place in record time." Even if it means keeping his dark, *angry* secrets.

Noah squints into me as if prying into my thoughts. As if he could. But then, if I can see the dearly furry departed, and on occasion those once robed in flesh, maybe he can pry into my thoughts? I straighten in fear.

"I've got a juicy tip for you."

"Oh?" I'm right back to leaning in and swooning into those key lime green eyes, those kissable lips just inches from mine.

"I know of a couple of houses for rent side by side on Country Cottage Road."

"Ooh, that's a nice neighborhood. It butts right up to the woods. I just love that— *Hey?* Isn't that the street you live on?"

He nods, and that naughty grin is right where it's supposed to be.

"If you decide to take a look, call me and I'll join you. In fact, I can have my realtor set up an appointment if you like."

My mouth falls open at the thought of living in such close proximity to this alarmingly handsome man who has stolen my heart so quickly.

"I am more than interested. Let your realtor know we'll take a look as soon as we can." *We.* A content sigh expels from me. Deep down, I've always wanted to be a happy we. Although, we haven't actually spoken about the fact we're dating. Heck, I don't even know if you could call what we do dating. We're pretty good at kissing, though. My lips can't help but curve up at the sight of his.

"Good." He pats his hand over mine as he stands. "I'll follow up on some leads I've got concerning—" He tips his head toward the alley. It's probably wise not to shout Hunter's name after what happened. The last thing I want is for my bakery to be a landmark for murder, or a place too sad to visit. "Text me when you hear anything."

"Will do," I say as he takes off with a wave.

Oh shoot. I forgot to feed him and give him coffee. Everyone knows the way to a man's heart is through his stomach. Looks like I'm failing Boyfriend 101 right out the gate.

Speaking of boyfriends, I need to find a way to clear my ex's name.

Micheline and those teary eyes she had at the grand opening come to mind. Hey, wait a minute. She looked like she was grieving before poor Hunter ever bit the big one.

I head back to the kitchen to pull out my cookies and cheesecakes. I think in a couple of hours I'm going to make a deposit down at the bank. And while I'm there, I'll bring Noah a dozen fresh-baked chocolate chip cookies that I'm about to whip up just for him.

Look out, Noah Fox's stomach, I'm gunning for you.

I cringe at my own analogy considering the fact Hunter was shot to death.

Regardless, I hope Noah's heart is quick to follow his stomach.

I'm falling for him.

I just wish I knew exactly how he felt about me.

CHAPTER 5

I was right.

The thick, sweet scent of the Cutie Pie Bakery and Cakery can joyfully be inhaled all the way down the street where I'm currently standing outside of Noah's office cradling a box of freshly baked chocolate chip cookies. But to my dismay, I'm not staring into the sea green eyes of that tall, dark-haired, and handsome private investigator. I'm staring into a cold hard sign that reads *closed* in glaring red letters.

And since Noah isn't here to partake in this warm batch of ooey gooey goodness, I decide to do the very next best thing with them. I don't waste any time trotting them into the bank.

The Honey Hollow Savings and Loans isn't too spacious inside, but it's always offered a warm, comforting feeling with its maroon carpet patterned with leaves, its brightly lit foyer filled with coffee urns, and a box of donuts open for any willing customer to enjoy. Just ahead of me, I see a hole in the wall and construction materials strewn about. I know for a fact Bear put this job off until the bakery was finished, and I feel a bit guilty over it.

I give a quick glance around. A handful of customers are being tended to at the teller windows, but I don't see Micheline.

A woman in a yellow pencil skirt and cashmere cardigan walks by with an arm full of files. "Can I help you?"

"Yes, actually. I was looking for Micheline Roycroft, but I don't see her. It wouldn't be her day off, would it?"

"Oh no, she's right next door in the loans department."

"Loans department. Right. Thank you," I say, scuttling my way back out. I know all about the loans department. That day I met Noah comes crashing back to me, and I can't help but smile just thinking about it. The day I met Everett comes barreling back, too, and I cringe at how up close and personal my entire head came with his nether regions. Both introductions were equally awkward, and yet they both led to what feel like genuine friendships. A part of me hopes that what Noah and I have blooms into so much more. After that New York debacle, I had sworn off men. Silly, I know. But here I am. Hoping to make it official with the cute boy down the street. And if I end up loving one of those rentals on Country Cottage Road, he will literally be the boy down the street two times over.

I head into the small, boxy room and spot Micheline and a couple of other people seated in makeshift cubicles. She's the only one without a customer at her desk, so I happily head on over.

"Hey, girl!" I say brightly and am suddenly mortified because the love of her life was just gunned down brutally less than twenty-four hours ago.

Micheline looks up with bloodshot eyes, her mouth pulled back in horror, and then just as quickly she softens as she stands and offers me a seat.

"What brings you here?"

"I come bearing gifts," I say with a grimace as I set the pink box in front of her. "Chocolate chip cookies." A lull of silences cuts through the air. "I know this is hard for you. It's hard for all of us. I'm really sorry. Hunter was my friend, too."

Her face pinches as if she might cry, and she snatches a few tissues out of the box in front of her and pushes them to her nose. "I know. I know it's hard for you, too." She offers a commiserating nod. "How is Bear?"

"He's with family. I texted him last night after I left, and he mentioned they'd be busy making arrangements today."

"I figured so." Fresh tears pour from her as she dabs them away with that growing wad in her hands. "I suppose it's for the best. Get that part over with." Her eyes congeal thick with tears. "How are you? How's the bakery?"

Micheline slouches over herself, her body looking far more fragile than I remember. If I didn't know better, I'd bet she was grieving far longer than a day.

"It's great. It's doing well. I mean, it's a few hours into the first day of business and the tourists and the townspeople really seem to enjoy it." I tug on a loose curl near my shoulder. "Can I ask if you had a chance to speak with Hunter last night, you know, before it happened?"

Micheline sighs as she looks to the ceiling. "I did end up finding him, but he was having a pretty heated debate with someone and I didn't want to interrupt. In hindsight, knowing how awful everything turned out, I wish I would have interrupted."

"I bet you had a lot to say." I tip my ear her way without meaning to. It's a natural tendency I have when I want to do my best to listen to someone. My mother says it's hardwired in me to do that.

"Oh, I did." She cocks her head as if none of it were good. "He had some troubles, and I wanted to help him as much as I could."

"Troubles?" I lean in. Micheline really is beautiful. I remember how close we grew while we dated the Fishers. I used to think she could have any guy she wanted, and I still stand by that statement. Of course, Hunter was a looker himself, as is Bear. But Bear's problem was that he knew it. And, if I'm being honest, Hunter knew it, too.

"Not dating troubles." She shakes her head as if ready to dispel any rumors from the start. "We were getting close, though." Her voice wobbles, and she adds another tissue to the collection in her hand. Her eyes hook to mine as she gives an exasperated sigh. "He had come to me asking for a loan. He didn't get it."

A loan? Micheline had to turn him down for a loan? That must have really put a pin in his ego.

"Is that why the two of you were having trouble? You looked pretty upset last night when I saw you. I didn't want to say anything, but you looked like you could have used a tissue then, too." My heart drums into my chest because I can't shake the feeling Micheline's walls are about to crumble, and all of the dark secrets she knows about Hunter are going to topple out.

"I could have. That's for sure." She cracks open the box and politely offers me a cookie first.

"No thanks. They're all for you." The rich scent of vanilla and chocolate permeates the air between us. It's too strong and far too delicious to ignore, so I don't blame her for diving on in.

"Mmm," she moans through a bite, her eyes rolling up toward her forehead. "I'm sorry, but this is bliss. I haven't eaten a thing all day. And, of course, I couldn't even think about dinner last night. You're a saving grace, Lottie. You always were."

"You're welcome." This is the part where I should probably wrap things up and leave, but I just feel so close to getting the answers that I need—answers that I didn't even know I wanted. "I hope you don't feel like I'm pushing, but is it true? Did the two of you have a disagreement? I mean, if you did, I want to be here for you. I can't imagine what that would feel like to leave things off with someone." It's true. I'm still her friend, and I would do anything to support her through this.

Micheline swallows hard and looks out the window to her left as an older surly man with silver hair loads drywall debris into his truck. I'm guessing he's one of the construction workers next door judging by the dirty white tee and matching pants. He has a tool belt on without anything attached. He turns slightly while wiping the sweat from his brow, and I note how ruddy his complexion is. I suppose hauling building materials in and out of the back all day would give anyone a great workout.

"Hunter and I had a lot of disagreements. But in the end, we were close to getting ourselves back on track." Her chest bucks, but she keeps her gaze firmly directed out of the window. "He didn't qualify for a loan from the bank, but I know he was asking Chuck for money, too." She nods toward the surly man outside.

"Chuck? Does he work for Bear, too?"

Bear has his own construction company, and Hunter was his second in command.

"No, that's the replacement Bear called in to finish up some of his overflow work. Chuck has his own construction company. Popov Construction." No sooner does she say it than he slams the door, and I see the oversized lettering across the door that reads *Popov Construction. We build it to last for life.*

"That's right. They were so busy with the bakery."

"Yes, exactly." She takes a deep breath, relaxing somewhat for the first time since I set foot in here.

"Did Chuck give Hunter the loan he needed?"

She shrugs as if she weren't certain of it. "Not that I know of. And if he were going to do it, well, it's too late for that now, isn't it?"

There's a note of anger in her tone, and it can't be denied. I've never seen Micheline so all over the place with her emotions. Not that the occasion doesn't call for it, but something is definitely off. First of all, she was upset before Hunter was brutally gunned down. I suppose a rocky relationship can do that to you, but still. So odd.

My brief wedding engagement comes to mind, and I quickly

push it away. Curt and all of the grief he caused can stay in New York forever as far as I'm concerned.

"Hunter sounded pretty desperate," I whisper mostly to myself. "Hey, Micheline? What do you think made him so desperate for money?" I lean in, ear tipped her way in the event she feels an innate need to fill it with words—hopefully, the right ones.

Her features harden a moment as she looks right at me.

"I guess"—her mouth opens and closes as she quickly scoops up a stack of files over her desk—"I really need to get back to work." She hops out of her seat. "Thank you for the cookies, Lottie."

There's that. She takes off down the hall, and I hightail it out the door and into the icy autumn air just as Chuck Popov is about to climb into his truck.

"Excuse me, Chuck?"

He does a double take my way and lifts a bushy gray brow.

"You wouldn't have happened to have any dealings with Hunter Fisher, did you?"

A garble of unintelligible sounds emit from his mouth as he climbs into his truck shaking his head. The engine fires up in a moment as the truck expels a plume of smoke and drives off down the street.

And there he goes.

"Looks like I'm two for two."

"Two for two?" a female voice calls out behind me, and I turn to find freakishly tall, redheaded Collette Jenner standing before me on what appear to be stilts, i.e., expensive red-bottomed stilettos. She's donned one of those power pantsuits she's prone to wear in a deep shade of burnt orange. Collette works at some fancy PR firm in Ashford, and I'm guessing she's through for the day. Lucky me.

She leans in with her nose twitching. "I bet you're two for two as in one man too many. I don't know who you think you are all of a sudden collecting boyfriends like they were playing cards, but stay away from mine." She sneers before speeding off in the opposite direction.

"And who would that be?" I call after her. I couldn't help it. Everett has told me countless times they are and will remain exes. Okay, so he may not have included the bit about remaining so, but he emphatically implied it.

"You know who he is, Lottie Lemon!" She turns around with fury in her eyes. "I'm warning you. Stay away."

I watch as she hops into her shiny black sports car and zooms off without so much as turning the ignition. Everything has always fallen into place for Collette—the looks, the cars, the careers, and the men.

Three out of four ain't bad.

She can't have Mr. Sexy. And not because he's mine.

It's because he doesn't want her.

I find myself standing in front of the window to Noah's office and touch my hand against the glass.

And I wonder if Noah wants me.

One thing is for certain—Micheline Roycroft knows exactly why Hunter was so desperate for money.

And I'm going to make sure I know exactly why, too.

CHAPTER 6

$\mathcal{T}$he first few days at the bakery have been more than hectic. Usually when I finish up for the evening, I head straight home to Lainey's where I happily crash on the bed in the guest room and Pancake is happy to crash right along with me. He's made it no secret how much he's missed me these past few crazy weeks. But I plan on making it up to him soon with a trip to Just for Pets. For the last few months, each time I head over to stock up on his Fancy Beast pet food, I've brought him along. I always bring along his carrier, too, in the event a large dog decides it's hungry for *pancakes*. But so far, the need hasn't arisen, and Pancake seems to be more than content to peruse all the goodies. I'll admit to purchasing him a few new toys each time we're there. But I did manage to resist the cute cat costumes they have on display. When I presented the idea to him, along with an adorable little tutu, he shot me with death rays. I'm pretty sure he knew where that was going.

Noah and I have been hit-and-miss all week partially because I'm so busy with the bakery, but he too has been so very busy with all of his new cases, it makes me wonder if the best of what we were to have is already in the past. I would never want him to slow down because of me. I totally get not having time to do all the fun things. Hopefully, it's just a passing phase. A part of me was hoping he'd at least ask me on a date, but on this mundane Friday night, I've decided to take myself out.

Mom called an hour ago and asked if I would meet her at McMurry's Pumpkin Patch to pick out a few of the happy squashes and gourds for her bed and breakfast and, of course, I was more than happy to oblige. Nothing makes me happier than a cool fall night spent at Honey Hollow's famed questionably haunted pumpkin patch. The McMurrys play up the Halloween angle every year and wisely so. Their haunted hayrides are so famous you need to buy tickets weeks in advance before they sell out. They have a haunted maze, a haunted house, which is more of a series of trailers that have been welded together, and, of course, there are a ton of family activities for the younger set—games, petting zoo, bounce houses. It's a real party the entire month of October, and usually I'm here every single night soaking it all in.

The pumpkin patch is festooned with scarecrows in every shape and color all around the enormous farm, and they stand illuminated against the backdrop of a glowing purple night sky. There's a traditional pumpkin patch lot, and then there's the pick-it-yourself version, which leads you out into the acreage the McMurrys own. As far as the eyes can see, the cheery orange globes dot the landscape, and the surrounding trees have all shed their colorful leaves as stacks and stacks of hay are strewn about with people sitting on them, climbing on them, and taking an endless array of selfies. The air holds the slight scent of cinnamon, and I spot a cider booth not too far off from here. Nothing pairs better with a crisp, fall night than a steaming cup of cider. My feet are already headed in that direction when I stop dead in my tracks and gasp.

Standing next to the cider booth is a tall, lanky, hair-flipping two-timer that I'd know anywhere and yet loathe to see just about everywhere I spot him. It's Tanner Redwood handing some bleached blonde a cup full of apple cider goodness. His free hand is pressed into her lower back, and they're laughing it up as if they didn't have a plus one in the world—or more to the point, at how bamboozled he has my sister. As much as I want to boot scoot in that direction, and dump that scalding cider over his head, I don't feel like racking up assault charges for accidentally blistering the blonde next to him. Him I might consider doing a tiny stint in the slammer for. A misdemeanor in exchange for getting him out of Lainey's life for good seems like a reasonable exchange. But I think better of it and do the next best thing—take a few clandestine pictures.

A pair of hands gives my ribs a quick tickle from behind, and I scream as I bounce my way to safety.

I turn around to find my mother laughing her head off.

"You about gave me a heart attack. Don't ever do that again."

She's quick to wave me off. She's donned her favorite denims and is swaddled in a flannel printed down jacket. My mother is forever the fashionista and would never miss an opportunity to dress for pumpkin picking success. I've donned my favorite knee-length boots, denim, and flannel as well, and I can't help but think I got the memo from my mother, but a quick look around the vicinity proves everyone in Honey Hollow got the memo. A flannel and jeans are your typical uniform around these parts anyway.

"Well, I didn't know how else to break your spell. You looked like you were intensely doing something on your phone. Texting the good detective, perhaps? Or if the rumor mill is correct, was it the good judge?" That smile of hers is quickly replaced with a pinched frown, her fists digging into her hips with disapproval. "Lottie Lemon, how could you keep the fact you have two budding romances away from me? And I had to hear it from the grapevine no less!"

A horrific groan comes from me as we make our way toward

the pumpkin patch. "I'm not even sure if I have one romance, Mother. Besides, who is busy spreading rumors about my love life? Please tell them I think they can use something constructive to do during waking hours. The bakery is hiring, by the way, so feel free to spread that rumor. It happens to be true."

"You know I will, honey," she says, grabbing one of the free wagons they offer to help haul your load.

When my sisters and I were little, we used to make our mother push us around in circles until we were dizzy and fell right off those red wagons. I've often wondered if that's where Meg got her love for tossing herself about so violently. She's at the top of her game, though. I've heard people place more bets on her matches than any other female wrestling pairing, so there's that.

Mom holds up a pleasantly plump, light peach Fairytale pumpkin for me to inspect.

"I love it," I say, taking it from her and setting it into the wagon. "Get at least three of those. There's something magical about them, and women especially just love them. You want to make sure your visitors feel good about every aspect of the B&B. In Business 101, I learned that depending on how you made your customers feel was ninety percent the deciding factor on whether or not they came back. Although, in my case, I'm sure the tasty treats have something to do with it. I hope."

She chortles at the thought. "I know so. That's all anyone's talking about is that grand opening of yours." She winces as she says it before picking up a few small pumpkins tiny enough to fit in the palm of your hands.

"Get at least thirty of those," I say, taking in a lungful of the earthy soil beneath us. "And you don't have to hide it. I know exactly why my grand opening was the talk of the town. Poor Bear hasn't even responded to my messages. He's really broken up about losing his cousin like that. And who wouldn't be?"

Mom shudders as the evening grows dark and sinister around

us. "I just ran into Dee Fisher at the florist. She said poor Hunter didn't have anyone but them. I didn't realize his parents had passed away a few years back."

"Wow." I'm stunned to hear it. "I didn't realize that myself. I bet that's why he had no one to turn to for the loan," I say that last bit under my breath, mostly to myself.

"Loan?" Mom startles. "Come to think of it, he did speak to Wallace extensively about his finances."

"Hunter did?" I take a few steps toward my mother in haste. "What did he say? Was he looking for a loan? Why did he need the money?" Who knew it would be my mother of all people who had the potential to crack this case wide open?

Mom scoffs while leading us over to the gourds. "Wallace and I don't make it a practice to mix business and pleasure." She hikes her shoulder my way suggestively. "We much more prefer the pleasure."

"Mother! I'd cover my ears if my hands weren't filled with acorn squash at the moment."

"What? You should be happy for me that I've found someone so handsome and eager to please me. Just like I'm happy that you found two someones looking to occupy your time. You don't know how thrilled I am to know you won't really grow to be some old cat lady. You need a man in your life to spice things up." She rocks her chest my way, and I'm quick to avert my gaze. "Someone to heat the sheets with on those cold winter nights. Speaking of winter, I need to have a new heating system put in at the B&B."

A thought comes to me, and I can't catch my next breath I'm so excited. "We should double date!"

"What?" She blinks at the curveball I've just thrown at her. "A double date?" Her eyes expand to the size of baseballs. "Why, that's a fabulous idea! We could bring Lainey and Tanner in on the fun. I couldn't think of any better way for the Lemon women to kick off their brand new love lives than together."

"No, not Lainey." I glance to the area where I spotted Tanner with his optional plus one, but they're no longer haunting the vicinity. "I think she and Tanner are on the rocks. But don't tell her I told you so," I'm quick to warn. My mother would spoil the surprise before I ever got home as far as Tanner's inadvertent exit strategy to leave my sister goes. "Just the two of you and Noah and me."

I couldn't think of a better way to do a little inadvertent strategizing myself. I've been chomping at the bit for a date with Noah, and I don't see why I shouldn't ask him on one myself. I did ask him to that football game in Ashford last month, and that totally counts even if we were secretly spying on Coach Hagan. But nonetheless, this will be another easy excuse to get together with him. Once he sees the potential value in gleaning all we can on Wallace, he'll happily go along—and hopefully be happy to spend time with me at the same time.

"In fact, I'll text him right now and see when he's free."

I step a few feet away while my mother busies herself filling that wagon to the brim. Just as my thumb is about to float over my screen, I spot an all too familiar scene at the cider booth, only this time it's not Tanner laughing it up with that bleached blonde of his—it's Noah and a leggy redhead who looks all too eager to snuggle up next to him. Her hand is on his arm, and her shoulder edges toward his chest as if she wanted far more of him than she's touching at the moment.

I've suddenly lost the urge to discuss Hunter's murder with Noah Fox.

Instead, I'm entertaining two new potential homicides.

CHAPTER 7

A cold autumn night like this one usually requires a cup of cider or two to warm my bones, but the sight of Noah Fox two-timing me with some leggy redhead has my blood boiling enough to thaw the poles and cause apocalyptic devastation.

Mom chatters on behind me, and soon she's dragging that wagon we filled with pumpkins and gourds of every shape and size toward the cashier. I'm just about to join her when Noah looks my way and does a double take. He sidesteps away from the cackling hussy so fast you would think she were an official carrier of an airborne STD.

"Lottie!" he shouts with a wave, and I pretend not to see him as I scuttle my way to my mother. It's murky out. The purple sky has darkened to a rich shade of navy, and the stars spray out overhead in their brilliant multitude.

Mom is busy chatting away with Ken McMurry, and I land shoulder to shoulder with her just as Ken offers to load our haul into the back of my mother's car.

"Lottie." Noah jogs up, out of breath. His cheeks look piqued as if he had exerted himself, but we both know it's because he's morbidly embarrassed because he was *caught*. "What are you doing here?" He sheds an easy grin, and it only makes me angrier.

How dare he be unaffected by the fact I saw him pawing over some redhead, even if she was the one doing the pawing. It matters not. He allowed it.

"I'm here with my mother. We were picking out pumpkins for the B&B. What are *you* doing here?" I tip my head his way, good and ready to listen in on whatever he has to say. I'm curious if this two-timer is also a liar. Most are.

"Thanks to Captain Turner, Detective Fairbanks invited me to help out with the investigation. You know, nothing official, but she thought it would be beneficial to exchange information."

My heart sinks because that's exactly what I was hoping to do with him. "And? Did you get anything useful?" My bruised ego has quickly taken a back seat to my need to have my curiosity quenched. "Do you know why Hunter needed a loan?"

"Hunter needed a loan?" He leans in, and the heady scent of his cologne makes me feel dizzy. Just thinking about those kisses we've exchanged so freely has my head spinning and not in a good way. I feel like such a fool. I had no idea I was in some kind of an open relationship—some cheap fling that involved a lot of heavy kissing. Not that I minded the heavy kissing. That was sort of my favorite part.

"I don't know." I decide to play coy. "Did he?" I lift a brow his way. I am so not above playing these head games right along with him.

Mom bounces over breathless from the trek to her car. "Oh my goodness, we meet again, Detective Fox. Has Lottie mentioned the double date yet? Saturday night works for us. I just checked with Wallace." Her shoulders do that annoying shimmy thing again. Note to self: Buy this woman a lead coat for Christmas—and a *muzzle*. "Anyway, I have to run." She wrinkles her nose my way. "I just realized I'll need to ask one of my strong boarders to help carry all of these pumpkins out of my car. The last thing I need is my interior ruined. I've seen the way those things liquefy seemingly overnight." She presses a quick peck to my cheek. "Let me know what you decide. The two of you can pick the time and the place!" She wiggles her fingers at us as she's swallowed up by the night.

"Are we going on a double date?" Noah is back to sporting that crooked grin once again. There's an innate cockiness about him that's just too smug for me to handle at the moment, and I'm half-tempted to jump into my mother's trunk myself.

"I am. I don't know about you." I pluck my scarf out of my purse and wrap it around my neck. "So, were you enjoying clinking your cider with Detective Fairbanks?" I don't see why we should ignore the redheaded elephant at the pumpkin patch.

The scent of a floral perfume envelops us, and I turn to find Detective Ivy Fairbanks, stone-faced and staring me down.

"Carlotta Lemon." There's a smugness in her voice when she says my formal name. Funny, smugness seems to be catching these days. "I might be by your bakery sometime soon. I have a few questions we need to go over." She looks to Noah, equally as bored, and now I'm shocked he got her to laugh at all. "I'll see you in the morning, Fox. We'll start back here first thing." She takes off, and neither of us says anything. I might be a little smug myself at the thought that Noah didn't even bother saying good-night to her, but then someone as confident, and let's not forget intimidating, as Ivy isn't insecure enough to let the absence of a goodbye mean a single thing. I wonder if Noah has been smooching with her, too, and as much as I don't want to go there, I can feel the word vomit ratcheting up my throat.

"Have the two of you kissed yet? You looked mighty friendly." Stupid, stupid me. I hate that I let my insecurities get the better of me. But I'm not surprised. It's practically my MO. No wonder all of my exes cheat on me. They can't get away from me fast enough to break things off properly.

Noah rumbles with a dark laugh as he swoops me into his

arms and gently lands his lips to mine for a good ten seconds. Those soft, delicious lips sealed to mine feel like heaven. It feels like bliss with Noah, his mouth warming mine, his body solid against my own. Everything about him is pushing me over the edge. It takes all of my self-control not to dive my fingers into his thick hair.

He pulls back just enough for his *ivy* green eyes to glow my way, and I can't help but smile despite all of my lunacy.

"I save all of my kisses for you, Lottie Lemon."

My insides disintegrate, and every last cell in my body is swooning hard for the handsome fox with his arms wrapped securely around me right now.

His dark brows do a quick waggle. "Did I score an invite to that double date?"

"Maybe." I shrug. "I guess it depends if you're up for exchanging a little info on the case." It comes out hopeful. "I just have to clear Bear's name and get to the bottom of whoever killed Hunter. It feels like it's killing me as much as it's killed him."

Noah stiffens as he glances in the direction of the parking lot. "I can't, Lottie. I'm sorry. I promised Detective Fairbanks that I wouldn't share any details from the case. That was the deciding factor in allowing me to work with her. She doesn't want anything or anyone tainting the case. I get it. And"—he winces—"I know we already talked about this, but I want you safe. And if you're investigating this case, then I won't be able to stop worrying about you. There is a very real killer out there with a gun, and he or she is not afraid to use it."

I can't help but frown as I gently remove his arms from my person. "I get it." I shrug as I head over to the cider booth. I certainly don't need a man to make all of my cider dreams come true. Before I can toss a dollar into the basket, Noah beats me to it.

"It's on me." He sheds a pained smile. "Just like dinner will be Saturday night."

"Fine, but just know that I'm thoroughly annoyed that you're so unwilling to share details about something that's so important to me. How would you like it if a good friend of yours was gunned down right in the back of your own bakery on the night of its grand opening no less? You wouldn't." I don't hesitate answering for him. "You would resent the fact that I chose to keep Everett as my confidant instead of trusting your abilities to keep things quiet."

"Everett?" He balks with a laugh. "I don't think my former stepbrother would be too interested investigating a homicide." He pulls me in again gently with his arms. "You're not involving Everett, are you?" He's right back to wincing as if the idea pained him. I happen to know firsthand that Everett is an easy way to push his buttons. In that sense, it wasn't fair of me to go there.

"Not yet." I shudder just thinking about the fact he threatened to interrogate me over a dead squirrel no less!

"How about it? You, me, your mother, and her date, Saturday night?"

A tiny giggle works its way up my throat. "Fine. Just know that I'm the reason you'll be seated across from Wallace Chad that night. My mother mentioned that he and Hunter spoke about finances."

"You mentioned he was looking for a loan." He sighs, and a white plume blooms from his lips. "So, you know he was having trouble with money?"

"I'll tell you what I know if you tell me why you need to meet Detective Fairbanks here tomorrow morning. You do realize that a person can get lost for weeks in that haunted corn maze if they're not properly caffeinated before noon."

He barks out a laugh, and his teeth glisten like a string of glowing moons. "Yes, I do realize that. I guess there's no harm in telling you he was looking for employment here. Just helping out at night. Ken was busy, but we'll speak with him more in the morning about it."

"Oh. No, I didn't know that." I glance over to Ken and Molly who are helping organize a hayride. Not the terrifying one that they sell tickets for, but the run-of-the-mill kind you can take your toddler on and not fear nightmares for the next six years. "I guess he really was having trouble with money. I'll talk to Bear and try to find out how much he was paying him. I can't believe it wasn't enough."

"No, no, no." He tips his head back and moans mournfully before holding my gaze once again. "If you talk to Bear, and we talk to Bear about the same topic, it might spook him. Let me handle the investigation, and you worry about how many brownies to bake for the next day. Sound fair?"

I open my mouth to protest, then quickly close it. Working with the Ashford Homicide Division could be a big break for Noah. I'd feel terrible ruining it for him.

"Fair," I say it short and sweet, all the while crossing my fingers behind his back. No use in worrying him over something so silly. Bear is used to me asking all sorts of prying questions. And honestly, I might be the only person he feels comfortable opening up to. "So, Saturday night—Italian or Mexican? Or, of course, there's always the Honey Pot."

"I'm not above trying something new. Italian sounds a bit more neutral as far as the heat level goes."

"Sounds perfect." I lose myself in those evergreen eyes. "I've missed you."

A warm growl comes from him. "I've missed you, too. But I've been talking about you all week. Have your ears been burning?"

"No." I'm pleasantly surprised. "With Detective Fairbanks?"

"With Imogene Cross. She's the realtor who helped me find my own rental. She said she can let you into both houses on Sunday. And that happens to be my day off."

"Tell me the time and I'll arrange to be there." I'm giddy over the thought of moving to such close proximity to him. "So, this whole keeping secrets from each other thing isn't really going to last forever, is it?" My stomach cinches as soon as I get the words out. Regret thy name is Lottie Lemon.

"I'm not keeping secrets from you, I promise." He dots a sweet kiss over my lips, and I can't help but dig my fingers into the back of his thick dark hair. "No offense to you, Lottie. It's just business. As soon as anything can be made public, you will be the first to know."

A conciliatory sigh escapes me. "In that case, I wish both you and Detective Fairbanks luck in catching the killer quickly."

"Thank you." His finger swipes gently over my lips. "So, a double date, huh? Does that mean we're dating?"

My smile expands into the night. "I guess it does."

"I like that."

"I like that, too."

Noah bows in for another kiss, and we share something deeper, with far more meaning than a simple kiss could ever convey. My mouth opens for him, and what comes next spells out he's all mine more than words could ever hope. Too bad Ivy has pressured him into not sharing any details of the case with me, and sadly my aforementioned insecurities suggest I take this seriously. If Noah's not up for sharing details about the case, then neither am I. There's no way I want to help Ivy get a leg up on something only to have it backfire in my face. I'm sure she wouldn't hesitate to humiliate me in the process. I'm pretty sure I read that body language of hers loud and clear. She's interested in Noah Fox for more than just a few leads.

And that's exactly why I'll be investigating the rest of this case on my own.

No offense to Noah.

It's just business.

CHAPTER 8

$\mathcal{T}$he next day, the bakery is still bustling well into the late afternoon. I blame those warm cinnamon rolls I just pulled out of the oven. I swear, each time I do that, all of Main Street empties out and floods into the Cutie Pie. Not that I mind. Actually, I cannot believe how much money we've made in less than a week. But as Lainey gently reminded me, the bakery is still in its honeymoon phase, and this is my chance to prove to my customers time and time again that our goods are as delicious as they smell. I need repeat business. I need for it to be this swamped and bustling a year from now. The last thing I want is to disappoint anyone. That, in fact, has always been my downfall.

It's almost five. The bakery is only open for one more hour and still no sign of catty Ivy wielding her badge in my face. Worse yet, she'll probably come in wielding my boyfriend at me. *Boyfriend.* There's that word again. We haven't fully discussed being exclusive, but he did say quite emphatically that he's saving all of those heated kisses for me. And, my God up in heaven, what sexy, smoldering, die-on-the-spot kisses they are. My insides do a cartwheel just thinking about them.

The bell to the bakery jingles, and my heart stops cold once I spot that all too familiar face. It's not Ivy or Noah. It's—Hunter?

"Hey, Lot." His voice strums my way as his features sag, and I come to.

"Bear." I rush over and wrap my arms tight around him before motioning to the staff that I'll be taking a break. "For a second I thought you were Hunter." I shake my head up at him, my eyes flooding with tears. "I'm so sorry about everything you've been through. I can't imagine the pain you're in right now."

His cheek flinches. "Thanks. I appreciate it." He looks around, and a sigh expels from his enormous chest. "This was the last place I saw him alive. It feels like five minutes ago. If I try hard enough, I can imagine that he'll walk right through that door grinning at me."

My heart breaks just hearing it.

The bell chimes again, and we turn to find Everett striding in, clad in a midnight-colored suit, his dark hair slicked back, and he twitches the slightest smile when he sees me.

Just as I'm about to greet him, a stunning brunette strides in behind him, thin as a rail, and stilettoes that practically make her touch the ceiling. Her chestnut-colored hair is taut in a bun, and she's wearing gold-rimmed glasses. A briefcase sits tucked under her arm. She wastes no time in striding over along with Everett.

Bear leans in. "Hope you don't mind, but I decided to meet with my new attorney here."

I suck in a quick breath as I look to Everett's female companion, and now that I think about it, I recognize her from that day the Simonson sisters took me to court.

"Fiona Dagmeyer." She's quick to shake Bear's hand. "Why don't we take a seat."

"Oh, sure," I say, pointing to an empty table by the window. "I can bring you coffee and some apple berry cobbler I just pulled out of the oven." I tip my head toward Bear. "I'll bring a few brownies to get you through it as well."

"No thanks." Bear picks up my hand carefully. "Just sit by my side. That's all the help I need to get me through this."

"I'll do whatever you ask."

"No, you won't," Fiona corrects with a curt smile that says something nasty far more than it ever does something nice. "I prefer to speak with my clients alone. I find when they're around family or friends they seem to want to embellish to save themselves of embarrassing truths. I don't have time for any of that."

"That's fine." I shake my head at Bear. "The two of you take a seat there, and Everett and I will sit at another table. I'll still be here for you."

Bear and Fiona head to the table near the window, and I'm slow to take a seat with the handsome judge in front of me.

"I'll get you some coffee," I say, batting my lashes up at him nervously. "In fact, I'd better check on those pies I have in the oven. There's so much to do before I close up for the night. I'm sure you understand."

I try to take off, and he quickly steps in front of me, blocking my path.

"Lemon." He points to the empty table near the door. "It's time."

I frown up at him. "I don't want it to be time. Can't you see I have nothing to hide? This little interrogation of yours is completely uncalled for."

"Lottie." His brows knot up. "You're incriminating yourself with your uncharacteristic behavior. You do realize I'm not going to hurt you. And I'm not turning you over to the police."

"It's not the police I'm worried about." It's men with nets that scare me. Ever since I was old enough to realize my gift was far from normal, I was petrified I'd end up in a mental institution somewhere. Just me in a straitjacket and a thousand critters from yesteryear. It's enough to make me go mad just thinking about it.

Everett lands a warm hand over my back and ushers us to the table as we take our seats.

He leans in, and the warm scent of his cologne tickles my senses. It's a bit spicier than the one that Noah wears but equally intoxicating. There's just something about cologne that does it for me. It might as well be a love potion—I respond that aggressively to it. A part of the reason is that my father wore his Old Spice liberally. Mom gifted my sisters and me each a bottle a few years back for Christmas, and we called it Dad in a Bottle. I guess that's why I love musky scents on men. Suddenly, everything just feels right with the world.

Everett takes a breath as if he too were girding himself. "What are you really afraid of?"

"You judging me." That, and psychotropic medications being force-fed down my pie hole. I would be the worst patient ever. They really would need to tie me to a bed.

A warm laugh bounces from him—a rarity in and of itself. "That's what I do by trade. I judge." His features harden. "But I won't judge you as a person. Now, walk me through it. You thought you saw a squirrel coming in through the front door."

"It was getting pretty warm in here with all of those bodies." Speaking of which, my body heat index spikes twenty degrees, and I can feel a bite of sweat erupting under each arm. "I hadn't eaten all day. Can you believe it? All of those fudgy brownies right in my face and not one bite." Truth. "Anyway. I guess it wasn't a squirrel after all. I'm just too embarrassed to tell you what it really was." A flare of heat rips through me as I spew an entire catalog of lies.

"What was it?"

Everett looks every bit the concerned friend. It's amazing to me that just a month ago I was swatting his behind with my forehead, and boy did I ever annoy the living heck out of him with those fancy face maneuvers. And yet here we are, chatting in my brand new bakery—about the curse that's finally about to take down my life.

I clear my throat. "It was a dust ball." It comes out lower than a whisper.

"A what?" He shakes his head in disbelief.

"You know, a little mini dirt devil. A tiny tornado of unhygienic fun. My mother always called them squirrels. They just come in and whip right through the house, embarrassing the socks off my mother and me." My face heats to unsafe levels. I'm positive you could light a cigarette right off of the tip of my nose. In fact, if Noah were here, I'd give him one big red-hot kiss just to get away from his snooping ex-stepbrother.

Everett sinks back in his seat. That look on his face is locked somewhere between anger and disappointment, a sure sign he's not buying the dirty load I'm trying to sell him.

"A dirt devil." He nods. "And you expect me to believe that a whirlwind of dust and debris—less than a foot tall—had the power to maneuver its way through a forest of bodies and make its way out the back—in a bakery with virtually no breeze." He cocks his head to the side as if volleying the dirty ball back in my court.

"Yes?"

"Lemon." He closes his eyes a moment, and for a second I contemplate running out the door. I can always cite female troubles. Men never like to hear the word *menstruation*. Actually, it not only might scare Everett off, it might clear out the bakery in record time. Of course, that would be another lie. And now that I'm dancing on a ball of flat-out lies, I'll have to keep adding to them just to keep myself from falling. Soon I'll be an astronaut who needs to check on the space station. A secret assistant to the President. My den of deceit knows no bounds.

"Let's try this another way." Everett sounds exactly as stern and in command as he did that day in court. "What do you think the repercussions would be if you told me the truth?" He gives a slight shake of the head. "Please don't bother elaborating on the dirt devil. I've already determined that was simply a cover in hopes I'll leave right this minute and buy you a broom."

A tiny laugh bubbles from me. There's just something about Everett that puts me at ease. "Fine." I swallow hard, knowing full well it's not fine. "But first, I have to tell you that what you're about to hear, only one other person on the entire planet is apprised of." I'm hoping that alone will give him pause.

"Go on." His finger calls to me as if beckoning me to get to it already.

"Not even my best friend, *Keelie*," I whisper in hopes he can see the severity.

"That's fine. I won't tell her. I promise I won't tell a soul without your permission." His gaze remains secure over mine.

Bear and Fiona head over, and I'm flooded with relief. Every last molecule in my body has just exhaled. I bolt up, and Everett is slow to follow.

"Well?" I ask the two of them. "What's the verdict?"

Fiona rides her gaze over me from head to toe, and judging by that nonplused look on her face, I gather she's not too impressed.

"Mr. Fisher"—she nods to Bear—"I'll be speaking with you soon. Think about the things I said and implement them."

Bear scratches at the back of his neck. "Will do."

She looks to Everett, and something akin to a genuine grin blooms on her face. "Essex, I'll be up late." She gives a sly wink before heading out the door.

"Up late?" I gawk as I give him a slight shove on the arm. "Don't tell me you're still dipping a toe into Dagmeyer infested waters."

"Not a toe." A dirty grin blooms on his face. "And not any other body part either. We're exes, Lemon. When I say something, you can count on the fact I'm telling the truth."

I suck in a quick breath and swat him over the arm once again.

Bear offers me a spontaneous hug. "I've got to run. It's been a long day."

"Yeah, sure." I bite down hard over my lower lip because there are still so many questions I want to ask him. "Hey, Bear? What kind of things did Fiona ask you to implement?" I'll start easy. Warm him up a bit.

"I need to buy a suit in the event this escalates any further. I'm innocent, but she said people are hungry for answers. I guess she's heard enough rumors that Hunter and I weren't exactly on friendly terms the last few weeks."

"Did he ask you for a loan?" I regret the words as soon as they sail from my mouth. So much for warming him up.

Bear ticks his head back as if it were ridiculous, but there's something in his eyes that says it's not. "Yeah, he asked. But I'm tapped so he didn't get it." He pinches his eyes shut a moment.

"Do you know if he asked Chuck Popov for a loan?" Micheline already suggested as much, but I figure square one is the best place to start as far as this conversation goes.

Bear winces. "How do you know this?" he whispers before rolling his eyes to the ceiling. "Yeah, he asked. The kid asked everybody. Nobody gave him anything, Lot. Especially not Chuck." He glances over my shoulder a moment at Everett before leaning in. "I asked Chuck not to give him anything, and in exchange I told him I'd make sure he got the bids when I backed out."

"At the bank?"

He nods. "And other jobs. I didn't want anyone feeding Hunter's need for green speed."

"Why?" I'm suddenly ravenous to know the answer.

He shakes his head. "Because nobody needs that much money, Lot." Everett clears his throat, and Bear's chest expands with his next breath. "I'll talk to you some other time, Lot. Funeral's on Sunday. I'll text you the details."

"Please do," I say as he speeds out the door.

Everett takes an enormous breath, and I swear I can see the judgment ready to pour out of him. "How did you know that kid needed a loan?"

"Never you mind." I look past him for signs of Ivy whom I've quickly adopted as my nemesis. Technically, that would be Naomi, Keelie's twin, but since Naomi isn't trying to staple Noah to her side, she's been evicted from the coveted position.

"Lemon, are you investigating Hunter's murder? Both Noah and I don't think—"

I hold a hand up between us. "I don't care what you think. Hunter was my friend, and Bear still is—sort of. Anyway, I'm being cautious so no need to worry."

He rocks back on his heels. "If you don't care about what I think, then you shouldn't have a problem letting me know what had you running out the back door that night. You found a body, Lemon. And to be honest, I think maybe you're too close to the situation or you'd see that there might be some importance in your own timeline of events leading up to the gruesome discovery."

"Ugh. You are relentless, you know that? And you're just as obnoxious as you were that day I met you in the coffee shop. If I recall correctly, you wouldn't tell me your name. Your *name*. And you're asking me to divulge something extremely private and quite painful to admit."

"What are you talking about?" His voice hikes an octave to match mine. "You said you saw a squirrel bolting through the place and followed it to a dead man."

"And you didn't see it!" I smash a finger into his granite-hewn chest. So not fair. Everett has the face and the body of a god. Lucky for me, so does Noah.

"You didn't see it either," he barks, and my adrenaline hits its zenith.

"Yes, I *did*," I spit the words in his face. "I saw a dead squirrel that once belonged to Hunter Fisher himself. A dead *pet*. It's what

I always see before something very, very sinister happens to its previous owner. Are you happy?" I snip as I whip off my apron and speed through the kitchen. I tell the staff I'll be back to close up as I snatch my keys off the rack and race to my car that just so happens to be parked right over the spot Hunter breathed his last breath.

"Lemon, wait," Everett riots as he barrels out after me. But it's too late. I'm already racing off into the night.

I've never seen Everett so full of emotion—his heated anger matching mine. And then I remember him mentioning that he had his ways of getting information out of just about anyone. It was his gift.

I shake my head as a dull laugh pumps from me.

Everett wasn't angry with me. He was manipulating me to get what he needed.

Well played, Everett. Well played.

I pull out of the alley and spot Ivy Fairbanks heading into the bakery with a dutiful Noah by her side.

But I don't stop. I drive all the way to my sister's. There's only so much torment I can take for one night.

Everett promised he wouldn't tell a soul.

I kept my end of the bargain. Let's see if he keeps his.

*I*n keeping with this seemingly new tradition of having my sanity disband at some point in the latter half of the day, my mother and her questionable suitor are seated across from Noah and me at Mangia, Honey Hollow's premier Italian restaurant which has write-ups in three national newspapers.

Noah picked me up from Lainey's, looking exceptionally comely tonight with a dark inky suit and a slick black tie to match. His hair is thick and glossy as if it were still damp from the shower, and the musky scent of his cologne made me want to grab him by the tie and trail off into the woods with him. Under no sane circumstances should we be waiting for our meals to arrive while discussing politics of all things with my mother's formidable boy toy. Sure, he's handsome for a silver fox, but there's a hint of something wily in his eyes that I can't quite pinpoint. His movements are too fluid, and his face is peppered with white hairs that look decidedly like a briar patch. Side note: Both Everett and Noah have a comfortable amount of dark stubble on their blessed by God faces, but it looks soft and inviting. Wallace here looks like a prickly cactus. I don't see how my mother could stand to make out with him.

Oh my *God*.

I bolt upright as if I had just been shot. She's not making out with him, is she?

Mom gives me a slight kick from under the table. "So Lottie, why don't you tell us all how it feels to finally run the bakery of your dreams? You've been waiting for this moment all your life." She offers a crimson-lipped smiled to both Noah and Wallace. "My daughter has been obsessed with baking ever since she got her hands on an Easy Bake Oven when she was three. Of course, all the girls used it." She grimaces at the memory. "Meg would toss a little mud in for flavor. But not my Lottie. She only uses the finest ingredients."

She winks my way, and I can feel my face heating. I've never done well with compliments in general. Truth be told, there's nothing more that makes me want to duck under this table and bury my face in my purse. It's been a long-standing problem of mine. My therapist, back in New York, suggested it was a byproduct of the fact I far more prefer rejection. She claimed that I don't actually believe the generous statements offered my way, that, in fact, I infer it to be mocking and satirical. My God, she is so right on the money. But this is my mother, and I know for a fact she would upsell me to a tree if she had to. So I take my therapist's sage advice on how to handle any kind words slung my way and say a simple thank you.

"Speaking of the bakery"—I start in on a perfect segue to Hunter and his financial woes—"I still haven't quite gotten over the trauma of having a homicide occur on day one."

The waitress comes with our dishes, and I grunt at the fact she's just ruined my momentum. Wallace isn't even looking at me right now. He's practically salivating over the chicken Parmesan they've set in front of him. I can't help but twitch my nose at the sight. My father once said never trust a man who orders chicken when there is steak on the menu. Noah moans approvingly as his steak Toscano is set before him, and I brush my shoulder to his, proud to have him by my side. Both my mother and I opted for the lighter fare, angel hair with Alfredo and shrimp.

Noah looks tenderly at me, and if I didn't know better, I'd swear we were having a moment. "I'm sorry you had such a dark event the night of the grand opening." His dimples press in, and I'm openly swooning at the king by my side. Why are my mother and her prickly pear here again? Oh, right.

"Yes." I take a deep breath, looking to Wallace. "It was quite a trauma. Did you know him very well?" I ask at the precise moment he indulges in a mouthful of chicken. He didn't even wait for my mother to place her napkin on her lap. I'm guessing his table etiquette is indicative of every other aspect of his life. He will always come first. And anyone who won't put my mother first is last in my book. She might as well give him his walking papers tonight, because judging by the way he's plowing through his meal—

Noah leans over, his mouth set directly over my ear, and my insides melt like butter on a griddle. "You're glaring."

I look up at him wild-eyed before bouncing in my seat and composing myself once again. "Your food looks wonderful, Wallace." Take two. "I came this close to ordering the chicken myself." Lies, all lies.

"Mmm." He lifts his fork as he swallows down a mouthful.

"Did you know Hunter Fisher?" I look right into his eyes, and my mother gasps, waving her hand at me as if she were gunning to swat me.

"Lottie Kenzie Lemon. You do not speak of the deceased while others are trying to enjoy their meal. It's bad enough you brought it up at dinner." She shudders, her narrowed beams of disapproval still set my way. "Noah, I promise you that I brought her up better than that. Lottie is always so rife with sparkling conversation. I don't know what's happened to her tonight."

Noah's chest bounces with a quiet laugh. "It's quite all right. I've already been treated to Lottie's sparkling conversation. And I rather enjoy her natural curiosity." He tilts his head while giving me the side eye, and I'm betting he's onto me. Crap. This was going to be my great find. My very own sparkly new suspect.

Noah reverts his gaze to Wallace. "So answer the question," he spits it out with a friendly grin. "Did you know Hunter Fisher?"

Wallace gives an eager nod while washing down his food.

Figures. I pry and nothing happens. Noah asserts his male prowess, and suddenly Wallace is so eager to speak he's practically choking on his food.

"I tried to work with the kid." His eyes flit to the depths of the room, and something about that ocular move raises my suspicions. He's thinking about something, and I want to know what. "The kid didn't have two dimes to rub together. It's a little tough to put a portfolio together when you're broke." He barks out a laugh while toasting us with his wine, and my mouth falls open, incredulous.

Anger is usually not my friend, but in this instance, it might be all I need.

"*Hey*"—I play up the affronted angle—"Hunter was a great person. Sure, he wasn't as financially savvy as yourself—" A good ego stroke always works with narcissistic men like Wallace. "But you could have helped him out, you know. Maybe got him started by giving him a loan?"

"*Lottie!*" Mom's fire engine red lips round out in a perfect O.

"It's fine." Wallace lifts a finger. "I actually looked into a loan for the kid." There's a bleak look in his eyes as if it didn't go so well. "Sometimes these things don't pan out."

Ha! Knew it. There is a connection between Wallace and Hunter's incessant need for green.

"So, how does that work? I mean, the loan process. If I needed a loan for the bakery, would I just go to you?"

Noah cuts me a quick look and gives a slight nod as if to say good work, and I can't say I'm not gloating a bit at the moment.

Wallace blows out a breath as if considering this. "It's not an easy process, but since I know you"—he leans in toward Mom —"and I *know* your mother..." Eww. "I can see about pulling a few strings."

Mom coos and chortles as if those strings were directly connected to her body. Double *eww*.

Noah clears his throat. "What's the name of the financial institution?" There's a hardness in his voice that has Wallace stiffening, so I give his knee a knock with mine, hoping he'll take a hint. "I mean, I'm looking for office space, and I can certainly use a leg up."

"Martinelle Finance," Wallace is quick to answer. "I've used them for several projects." His demeanor darkens.

We finish up with our meals, and soon Wallace and my mother are off to the late showing of some action adventure film at the Cineplex. I'm guessing that was not my mother's pick. He is so into pleasing himself it sickens me to think what goes on behind closed doors.

Noah and I take an inadvertent casual stroll down Main Street and end up at the huge fountain in the middle of Founders Square. He's held my hand every step of the way, and it's all I can do not to pull him into some dark alcove and have my way with him. To say Noah gets my heart pitter-pattering wouldn't be skimming the surface of what this man does to me. Parts of my body are quivering that haven't quivered in a good long while, and if I pant any faster, he's going to think I need a medic.

Noah pulls me in, and my fingers glide down his tie as the moonlight washes him silver. The air is icy, and the wind blows the oak leaves around us like glittering confetti.

"Lottie Lemon." He doesn't smile when he says my name. In fact, there's a note of suspicion buried there somewhere. "You're investigating Wallace, aren't you?"

"Aren't *you*?" I tease. "I mean, professionals like Detective Fairbanks and yourself certainly must already have a bead on Wallace Chad by now." I can't help but flutter my lashes up at him. I might as well soften the blow to his ego with a little flirtation, and I do plan to spend the rest of the evening indulging in every flirtation possible with this shining moon god. The fountain rushes behind us, and the scent of night jasmine still clings to the air despite the fact autumn is well underway.

His affect darkens as his expression turns serious on a dime. "We do," he deadpans. "We also know that Martinelle Finance has a reputation, and they may be dealing in dicey waters. We found that out two days ago." He brushes a stray hair from my cheek tenderly with his thumb. "I know this is going to be hard for you to hear, and just because you hear it doesn't mean you'll listen—but we don't need you in this investigation, Lottie. You're right. We are professionals," he says it sweetly enough, but it puts a pin in an ego I didn't even know I had. "You keep baking pies, and brownies, and every cookie under the sun. You're good at it. That's what you do. This homicide investigation is what I do. And I'm good at it. So please, trust me to catch the bad guys and don't go looking for them yourself. And I know you don't care to hear that, but I couldn't live with myself if anything happened to you."

Every last ounce of me sighs with defeat. A part of me wants to push aside the investigation for the night, push aside our differences in how that investigation should be run, and by who, and just take in the splendor of this god before me. I want to do a million carnal things with this beautiful man, but I can't run away from this. Hunter meant something to me, and just because I've been bested doesn't mean I'm going to let it go.

"Okay, you are a professional, and my time and talents are better served mixing up cake batter and putting your favorite chocolate chip cookies in the oven." I give a cheeky smile, and it's genuine. "And thank you for sharing that tidbit with me. I know it's not easy for you to share information, especially now that Detective Fairbanks has taken a blood oath from you." I glower at the mention of her name.

"Good." His hand presses into my lower back, closing the distance between us. "If we weren't having such a big day tomorrow, I'd invite you to my place right now." There's a glint of something decidedly naughty in his eyes, and I'm suddenly ready to eschew anything on my calendar tomorrow to explore the night in the *Fox's den*.

Then it hits me, and I tip my head back and groan.

"I forgot all about the funeral in the morning."

"And I hope you didn't forget about my real estate agent."

I suck in a quick breath, hopping up on the balls of my feet with excitement. "The rentals! I did forget all about them. But now that you've reminded me, I'm thrilled about it." I cringe a moment. "It feels so wrong to be excited about anything tomorrow."

"I know." He brushes a quick kiss to my lips, and my heart slaps hard against my chest as if it were trying to get out and get a kiss for itself. Noah Fox has pillow-soft lips, and I could eat them for breakfast, lunch, and dinner.

I'm not sure why, but there is a very real soul-crushing need for me to ask him about us, who we are, what we mean to one another. It sounds so silly, so schoolgirl to ask something as ridiculous as *are you my new boyfriend?* But inquiring minds would like to know if he's interested in something more than just a few kisses.

"What are you thinking?" he whispers into my ear, his lips softly outlining my temple, and the sensation alone has me outright moaning.

"I'm thinking if you keep doing that I'll need to take a dip in the fountain to cool off." I pull back and look into his heated gaze. Noah is feeling something primal for me, and every last part of me is right there with him. "And I was wondering if"—my mouth remains open, but the words get lodged in my throat—"um, maybe we could grab lunch tomorrow. I really do enjoy spending time with you."

"That sounds like a perfect plan."

Lunch? That's the best I could do? I frown over at him without meaning to. At least I'll get to eat one of my favorite meals, and if Noah takes me to his place, I might get to take a bite out of something else my mouth is watering for.

Noah cups my cheeks and pulls me in gently while landing those magic lips over mine. There is a sweetness to Noah's kisses, a willingness to linger, and we do. Noah and I kiss in front of that fountain as if we were offering up a nonverbal proclamation to the townspeople of Honey Hollow. We are saying here we are, together, and that's how we'll remain. We are real. We are falling hard for one another. The only thing I can't say with certainty is whether or not we're officially together. I've never felt this way about anyone before, and seeing that I've been engaged before, that's saying a lot.

Noah has blown the doors off any expectations I might have had for the opposite gender. He's blown the doors off what I thought I knew about the boundaries of my feelings, and that closed door to my heart has been taken right off the hinges.

Yes, I will give Noah his space as far as the investigation is concerned, but only so he doesn't bump into mine.

Noah mentioned that Martinelle Finances may be dealing in dicey waters. And if he's not looking to assist me in delving in further, I know a certain judge who owes me a favor for wrangling out the deepest, darkest secret from me.

Noah is right. He can ask me a lot of things, but it doesn't mean I'll listen.

And when it comes to solving Hunter's murder, I sure as heck won't.

CHAPTER 10

*H*oney Hollow Covenant Church is packed to maximum capacity as the entire town shows up to bid farewell to one of its own. The funeral is brief, and both Bear and his mother offer up moving eulogies. But once they roll that video montage of Hunter's beautiful life, there isn't a dry eye in the house. Then just like that, the service is over.

Keelie threads her arm through mine as the bodies disappear and the sanctuary begins to drain. "That was beautiful, Lottie. If by chance I happen to die before you, please make sure to vet any photos my mother is willing to toss into the pictorial. That picture with Hunter's bedhead made me cringe. Rest assured, if anything untimely should happen to me and things at my funeral do not go as instructed, I'm not above ditching paradise to commence a good old-fashioned haunting."

"Duly noted, and, might I add, more than a little morbid considering the venue."

Keelie openly scowls at someone seated near the back, and I crane my neck to get a better look. "Can you believe he brought her?"

"Who brought whom?" No sooner do I say it than I spot them, and my heart lurches in my chest.

Noah offers a quick wave, along with what looks to be an apologetic smile, as a very unimpressed Detective Fairbanks stands dutifully by his side.

"That's funny. He didn't mention anything about her last night."

A light tap lands on my shoulder, and I turn to find the good judge nodding solemnly my way. Keelie spots her sister and takes off singing hello in such an alarmingly cheery tone half the congregation turns to inspect her. But that's Keelie. Nell always says you can't keep a good Keelie down. And she's definitely right about that. Knowing Keelie, she'd come back to haunt us just to say hello.

"Everett! What a surprise." And as quick as the joy of seeing him comes, it dissipates once I realize what he knows. My cheeks heat on cue.

"Lemon." He bows slightly. "My condolences."

"Accepted." I frown up at him because a part of me is waiting for him to whisk me away to some psychiatric facility for a prompt and necessary evaluation.

"Collette asked me to join her. She was extremely distraught so, of course, I couldn't say no."

"I bet she was." That woman never had a kind thing to say about Hunter. She's simply using his funeral to get into Mr. Sexy's pants. "So? How are you doing with the news I shared?"

He pulls back with confusion, and regret takes over his features. "Honestly, I don't know what to make of it. And, that's why I was hoping to talk to you this afternoon. I think I need you to elaborate."

"So you can firm up the case against me to have me committed? No thank you." I glance back to where Noah and his date were just a few minutes ago, but they've done a disappearing act. Probably outside inspecting the casket for clues before they bury poor Hunter. "But since you pulled something so intimate from me—a feat no other human has ever achieved before—" I told Nell myself, and that was willingly. Everett offers the hint of a smug grin. "I'd like to ask a favor of you. I need you to meet me in Ashford sometime this week."

"Stepping out for a clandestine meeting behind my stepbrother's back so soon? I'm intrigued. Where are we meeting? Just a heads-up. I prefer hotels to motels."

"Ha-ha. You're not funny. I'll text you with the details. Do me a favor, though, and try not to look so official. You're downright intimidating in a suit." He breaks out into an outright grin. "We'll have to pretend to be a couple going in for a loan. And it has to be believable."

"A couple looking for a loan?" Gone is any trace of a smile, and he's right back to being his intimidating self. "It sounds like you're investigating. What's in this for me?" He folds his arms across his chest as if we were suddenly in the boardroom going over hostile negotiations.

"This is a prepaid venture. I handed you the secrets of my soul on a silver platter, remember?"

He leans in, stern. "I want more. A full and thorough examination from A to Z. I need to know when this began, how often it occurs, and if you're hearing voices."

"Oh? Is that what the psychiatrist you contacted suggested you look for?"

A twinge of guilt erupts over his face. Everett knows I've got his number, and I'm petrified that I ever gave him mine.

Noah crops up and saves both Everett and me from any further hostile aggression.

"What's going on?" Noah looks to the two of us with an affable smile, and I suddenly want to shake it right off his body.

"Where's the good detective?" I ask, looking past him and coming up empty of one redhead. "Off to interrogate the family, I suppose? She is a professional. I don't see why the funeral should be off-limits."

Noah's brows pinch together in the middle, forming a perfect V, and suddenly I'm hungry, but it isn't for food. "She left. It's not uncommon for a homicide detective to pay his or her final respects at a public memorial. Besides, you never know who might show up."

"Like you," I muse, pulling him in and dotting his lips with a kiss. "I was just telling Everett about my little house hunt this afternoon." I shoot a death ray over to the nosy judge. "I'm looking at two houses, and they happen to be side by side. You wouldn't know anyone in the market for a rental, would you?" If Everett knows what's good for him, he'll go along with it. When he promised he wouldn't tell a soul, that umbrella undoubtedly covered Noah. But in the event he needs a reminder, I covertly stomp my stiletto over his shoe.

"Yes," he says it curt and directed right to me. "I do know of a few people looking to relocate." He looks to Noah with a glaring grin. "Lottie was kind enough to invite me to tag along. I'm ready as soon as you are."

"Great." Noah glances around the vicinity. "My realtor gave me the combination to the lock boxes. Why don't I meet the two of you out front and we'll head on over?"

"Perfect," I say. "I walked from the bakery, so if I can catch a ride with one of you, that would be best."

Noah nods to his stepbrother in the way you do when you're about to have an altercation. "You'll ride with me," he says before gifting me a kiss and speeding off in the direction of daylight pouring in from the front.

"What are you doing?" I hiss to Everett as soon as we're alone.

"I collect payment prior to delivery of the goods. If you want me to go on some asinine undercover op, then you need to spill it, Lemon. I'm worried about you, and I don't like that feeling."

"Why? Because you've never worried about anyone else

before?" I'm betting not. But it's sweet of him to venture into unchartered territories for me so soon into our questionable friendship.

"Because I'm frightened for you." It comes out kind, softer than any other words he's ever spoken to me. "I'll meet you out front." Everett takes off, and I stand there trying to process how I landed in a vat of boiling emotional oil and how Hunter Fisher ended up in a casket.

I step out into the straggling crowd and note a woman hunched over near the front. She looks about my age, for sure a romantic contender as far as Hunter was concerned. A young man about the same age wraps his arms around her in an effort to comfort her. Although, judging by the way she's batting him away, she looks far more hostile than she ever does grieving. But that man, there's something about that dark head of curly hair that seems more than vaguely familiar, and then it hits me.

"It's him," I say under my breath as I speed on over.

The girl is pretty, long, dark, wavy hair and long, thick lashes that are most likely not from nature, but she's able to pull it off. Her lips are painted a bold shade of red-blue that my mother keeps trying to push on me, but I've tried it and, believe me when I say, it just makes me look like a clown, and a scary one at that. There's something theatrical about the girl in general, like she just stepped off a runaway to attend the funeral.

I hasten my way over, clearing my throat as I close in on them. "Excuse me," I say as I step in close. "I remember you," I say to the young man, and his expression irons out. "The bakery. You saved my life about a week ago. The scaffolding?"

He ticks his head back. "That's right. That was a close call. I'd say it was your lucky day." His skin is slightly pocked around his cheeks, and he's got a tattoo on his neck of a bird in flight that I didn't notice before.

"Well, it wasn't really. Hunter was gunned down behind my shop later that night. So it was a terrible day, actually."

The girl looks to her phone and flicks on her sunglasses. "I gotta run." She pushes past the crowd without so much as a goodbye.

"I'd better get her home. Glad to see you're safe." He takes off after her, and I'm left in their wake.

"But I didn't get your name!" I shout and suddenly feel like an idiot. I don't need his name. Most superheroes prefer it that way.

Everett and that first encounter we had come back to mind, and a quiet laugh bubbles from me.

He's going to be my superhero, all right, and Noah isn't going to know a thing about it.

COUNTRY COTTAGE ROAD is just as cozy as its moniker implies. The streets are narrow and heavily lined with liquidambars and oaks in every spectrum of the citrine fall color spectrum. Each house has a cluster of pumpkins festooning its porch, and wreaths filled with fall leaves and acorns sit proudly against each and every door.

Noah parks in front of two gorgeous homes, one with white siding and a wraparound picket fence porch and the other a blue split-level with a balcony off the second story just above the front doors.

I take a step toward the white house and fall immediately in love with its bright red entry. "That *door*!" I coo. "And the banisters on the porch railing make it look as if it has a white picket fence. I think there's a clear winner."

Everett scowls at my quick assessment. "The only practical thing to do is look at both of them."

"That's just the logical side of you speaking," I say as I look across the street. "So, which one is yours?" I ask, threading an arm around Noah's waist.

"Second from the left." He points to the cabin-like home adjacent to the one I like.

"Perfect. I'll set my binoculars to look right into your living room window. I am prone to spy on occasion. I can't help it. It's the investigator in me." I give his side a quick pinch, and he laughs.

"Why do you think I brought these to your attention?" He waggles his brows. "I'm prone to do the same. I can't help it. It's the investigator in me."

We share a warm laugh before heading up to the white house, and Noah punches the combination to the lock box to let us inside. Immediately I'm taken.

"I am head over heels instantly in love," I say. "And that's my logical side speaking, Everett." I skip right out into the spacious living room with a custom cutout in the wall for a television that could fit the one I own perfectly. A large fireplace sits underneath with a stone hearth, and the room opens nicely to a decent-sized dining room. Then there is the pièce de résistance, a spacious kitchen with light granite countertops with enough white glazed cabinets to house everything I own in, an island with a genuine slab of white marble, and behind it sits a commercial grade high-end oven. "Where do I sign?"

Noah rumbles with a laugh. "Let's check out the bedrooms and make sure it's exactly what you want."

"Are you kidding?" Everett balks. "She's not signing anything until she thoroughly investigates option two. Never sell out before you have to, Lemon."

"I'm not selling out." I'm quick to roll my eyes. But, my God, how I would sell out in a second if I had that contract in front of me. Noah already ran the numbers past me on the way over, and both are within my reach.

We sail from room to room, and each inch of this cavernous well-lit place screams home to me.

"Pancake is going to love this place. There's so much for him to explore, to see, to do!"

"Pancake?" Everett looks as if I'm about to divulge the news of yet another supernatural wonder.

"Her cat," Noah is quick to divulge.

"My friend. My very *best* friend. But don't tell Keelie I said that. Pancake has been the dutiful man by my side ever since I brought him home." I shoot a quick look to Noah, hoping he might offer up his services in that department. I'm not looking for a proposal for Pete's sake. Just something to affirm how he feels about me.

"He sounds lovely," Everett says, pointing the way to the door. "Shall we inspect house number two?"

The three of us head over, and I'm pleasantly surprised to see a far more spacious home than the one we just left, with an extra bedroom and bathroom attached.

"It's amazing."

"Told you." Everett rocks back on his heels. "Always keep your options open, Lemon. You never know when you might be standing next to something better than what you have in hand."

Noah growls as if he were rabid. "What's that supposed to mean?"

"It means exactly what it says." He cuts him a sharp look. "I'm taking off. Thanks for letting me tag along for the adventure." He nods my way. "Lemon, text me when you're ready to claim your prize."

My mouth falls open as he strides out the door, and I'm fuming he left us with such a cryptic remark.

Noah ticks his head to the side. "Prize?"

My mouth opens once again, and I beg for anything to stream out of it. I'd settle for a not-so-white lie at this point.

"*Coffee.*" I shrug. "He bet I couldn't go through the funeral without bawling like a baby, and I managed to hold it together well enough, so he owes me coffee."

Noah inches back at the thought. "That's a terrible bet." He wraps his arms around me, and I rock steady in his arms.

"Everett's a terrible person." I'm only half-teasing at this point.

He belts out a laugh. "Go easy on him. He's only rough around the edges because he was raised to be."

It never occurred to me that Everett's tough persona was something inbred into him.

"Fair enough. I guess you're looking at your new neighbor. How fast do you think I can get the keys?"

"I'll talk to my realtor and find out asap. But let me be the first to welcome you to the neighborhood." He lands a heated kiss to my lips, and a moan works its way up my throat.

I pull back, nibbling on his lower lip playfully. "I'm thinking about hosting a housewarming party once I settle in, but since I'm on a strict budget, I'm only able to invite one person. Any idea who that should be?"

A dark laugh rumbles from him as he presses me against his chest. "I have an idea." His lids hood as he gets that naughty look in his eyes, and then just like that, he looks suddenly downcast. "But I have to ask. Are you and Everett hiding something from me?"

"No, not at all. I promise. It's not like that."

Did I just lie to Noah's face? Oh my God, this is all Everett Baxter's fault. If I lose the one good thing that's happened to me in a long time—aside from the bakery, of course—I'm going to wring Judge Baxter's illegally gorgeous neck.

"Good." He touches his forehead to mine. "Because I think we should start things off with open communication and one hundred percent honesty."

"Start things? Are we starting something?"

His eyes bear hard into mine, and my stomach does that roller coaster thing that makes me feel about thirteen-years-old again.

A crooked grin breaks out over his devilishly handsome face. "I think we've already begun."

"I think we have, too."

Noah crashes his lips to mine, and we indulge in a kiss far more daring than any of those shared before. Noah rides his arms up and down my back, along my hips before securing me tight in a warm embrace. Noah and I have started something. We are at the beginning of something that I predict will be spectacularly beautiful.

Noah wants open communication and one hundred percent honesty.

I can't help but sigh as I indulge in everything he's willing to give me.

One out of two isn't bad.

*I*t turns out, Martinelle Finance isn't located in your routine run-of-the-mill bank, nor is it located in an offshoot due to the fact the loans department is under construction. As fate, a heck of a lot of googling, and utilizing Everett's connections would have it—the two of us find ourselves seated in a holding room that happens to be in an underground gambling casino hidden behind your average strip club—if indeed the scandalous venue Everett and I walked through to get here was average. That's yet to be determined, and not by me. I held Everett's hand the entire time we were whisked through the place, and as soon as the bras came off those heavily made up dancing girls, I closed my eyes and let Everett lead me blindly through that den of depravity. Red Satin is a dicey establishment that I never want to set foot in again, let alone have an entire string of catcalls shouted at me as I strutted my way through it. Although, in hindsight, those catcalls were most likely for the topless girls dancing for their dinner.

"We're going to get shot," I whisper directly into Everett's ear.

He pulls back and rolls his eyes as if it were an asinine

thought while a man in a white suit clicks away at a computer monitor in front of us.

If this seedy locale, and this dizzying cube of a room they've stuffed us in, didn't ring any alarms, then his glaring fashion faux pas should have sent us running.

The heavyset man seated in front of us chokes on a cough. His nose sits crooked on his face as if it were broken at one time and someone didn't set it right. "You're in luck, Mr. and Mrs. Essex. We've got a special lending program for folks such as yourself."

Yourself. That fake grin on my face expands once he lets that grammar offense fly.

I give Everett's hand a firm squeeze, and he gives a slight squeeze back. And in no way and at no time did it feel at all sexual holding Everett's hand—more like self-preservation. I'm sure Noah would forgive me if he knew the circumstances. And yet, Noah can never ever know the circumstances—which, of course, completely dismantles all that whole open communication and one hundred percent honesty clause we hammered out the other night. But there are simply some things that need to be done for the greater good of the people—even if that particular person is dead. Hunter needed justice, and I'm not sitting on my hands—or baking a cake as Noah would have it—until Ivy Fairbanks decides she's going to solve this mystery.

"What are the terms?" Everett leans in, that serious expression still pinned on his face. He decided to eschew my fashion advice and wore a suit anyhow. And now that we're in this hot box, I don't mind at all that Everett looks so intimidating.

The man in the white suit twirls the pencil in his hand while staring Everett down. There is definitely some male testosterone showdown going on that I want no part in. Thank God I dragged Everett down here with me. I can't imagine how terrifying this entire experience would have been if it were just my butter knife and me. I really do need to up my game in the weapons department. The least I can do is carry around a bottle of pan spray so I can blind a perpetrator or two.

"Now"—Mr. White Suit tosses his hands over his desk—"in no way am I a loan shark. This is a short-term small industry loan."

"Numbers," Everett grumbles. "I need numbers."

"Okay, okay. I'll give you the full amount due on signing. Ten points for a six-month window with each month compounding. In other words, it would behoove you to pay it off in a month." He blinks a quick smile. "It would behoove me for you to pay it back in six months or never—collateral being the house once you sign. Until then, I'll hold the spare keys to the two a yous vehicles. You can bring those in when we do the exchange."

I lean in and clear my throat. "How fast can we get the money?"

His chest bucks a few times with a dry laugh. "Honey, I got the money here today. Getting the money isn't a problem. You'll have your bank account filled legally. We write cashier's checks. And lastly, we do a drive-by twice a week past your residence. Consider it an added layer of security you didn't know you needed."

"We won't skip town," Everett notes, and I jump in my seat.

My God, I didn't even connect the mafia-inspired dots! And here I thought these nice men were looking to keep our shiny new neighborhood crime-free. Ha! And *they're* the criminals!

My entire body heats to unsafe levels, and suddenly I'm itching to get out of here. But what about Hunter?

I glance around and spot a file cabinet that looks rusted shut, then another quick sweep for any evidence of security camera and an idea comes to me. That computer he's tap-dancing on is my best bet.

"Excuse me"—I lift a finger weakly as I interject—"would you mind giving us a moment together so we can process this? It's a lot to take in and uh…" Boss Hog here looks as if his patience with me is dwindling. "Well, I'm just a little ol' baker, and I need my big, strong husband to translate all those daunting numbers for me." As if. I shed a wide smile. That was one lie I didn't mind at all imparting.

He gives a sober shake of the head. "Oh, I get it."

And I figured you would.

He struggles to rise before hitting the door. "I'm gonna run next door and grab a cold one. Can I get you anything?"

Both Everett and I decline his offer. No sooner does the door shut behind him than I bolt over and seal my body against it.

"What are you doing?" Everett hisses, his eyes bulging with horror.

"I'm shielding the door while you look for any files on Hunter Fisher on that computer!"

"Geez." Everett looks as if I've just threatened to run over him with a semi. "I'll hold the door. I am not violating anybody's privacy. I happen to make a living off of other people trampling over one another's constitutional rights."

He trades places with me, and I bolt to the desk where a screensaver of a scantily clad woman with her thighs split open jars me before I hit a key and the dashboard loads before me. I click into finder and begin scanning for anything that might remotely get me to where I want to be. There's a file marked *Open Cases*, and I quickly scan an entire roster of names, only to realize there's enough to fill a phonebook.

"I'll never get to the end of this," I hiss.

"Get to the end of it now," Everett hisses back. "I'm giving you less than thirty seconds to get back in your seat."

"Fine." I shut the file down and note one with the name *Closed Cases*. "Maybe it's here."

There's a rustle outside the door, and both Everett and I freeze solid. Everett is glaring at me as if I had accidentally dragged him off to ground zero just before a nuclear warhead were to drop out of the sky. And, honestly, that might have been more painless. The rustling subsides, and I get back to clicking. My entire body breaks out into a sweat. I can hardly steady my breathing as I scan the list all the way to the letter F.

"Hunter Fisher!" I practically screech his name out.

"*Sshh*," Everett hushes me just as loud.

"Okay, let's see what it says." I whip my phone out and snap a few pictures of the screen before reading over it quickly. "Two loans for the amount of three thousand dollars each. Both paid off in full. Ten points on pick up. March of last year and July. The foot note says—" I scan over it myself and can hardly believe it.

"What does it say?" Everett flicks his hand through the air, signaling for me to speed it up.

"It says money for girlfriend. Money for kid." Huh.

The sound of a belly laugh coming from down the hall proceeds to get louder, and I'm betting it's Mr. White Suit.

I quickly shut down the file, and both Everett and I slide back into our seats.

The door swings open. "So, what's it gonna be, kids? You in?"

"On second thought"—I rise out of my chair as does Everett—"I'm going to ask my mother one more time."

Everett nods. "But if she says no, we're coming right back. Believe me, she's the last person I want to deal with."

Mr. White Suit laughs it up before giving Everett a commiserating slap to the back. "Sounds good. Go get yourself something good to eat. I've got a pastrami sandwich in the microwave. You let yourselves out." He leaves the door open as he takes off, and I spontaneously wrap my arms around Everett.

"Way to go, Mr. Sexy. You really lived up to your name." I pull back to get a better look at him. "Hey, if I didn't know better, I'd say you were blushing."

"I'm not. It's about two hundred degrees in here. We literally sweated this one out." He presses his hand into the small of my back as he ushers us to the door. "But I think we make a heck of a team, Lemon."

"I know we do. And we make a pretty cute couple, too. You were brilliant. I could just kiss you."

We share a laugh before speeding our way through the strip club. Everett tries to turn his head toward the stage, and I don't hesitate to swat him.

As soon as we hit daylight, we hightail it to the fast food restaurant across the street where Everett parked his car. I met him at the coffee shop in Ashford as planned, and once we get back, I plan on caffeinating myself back to the land of the living after that near-death experience with the underworld.

"What do you say we blow this one cow town and I buy you a cup a joe, Mr. Sexy?" I tease. Way back when he refused to give me his name, I hung out at the coffee counter and snooped to see what the barista would scrawl onto his cup. It turns out, she had the aforementioned hot-to-trot moniker picked out just for him.

"Mr. Sexy?" a female voice bleats from behind, and we turn to find a haughty redhead tucked in a black pea coat.

"Detective Fairbanks." I'm so stunned to see her I keep blinking in hopes she'll evaporate like a bad vision.

She ticks her head to the side with a husky laugh. "Heard it all. The two of you really do make a cute couple."

My mouth falls open. "You did hear it all, didn't you?"

She strides our way, her affect hard as flint. "It's called surveillance, sweetie. The place is tapped. The entire conversation was on blast."

A thousand scenarios run through my head at once, and all of them involve Noah. The world sways beneath my feet, and I can hardly catch my next breath.

"I swear it's not what it looks like. You can't tell Noah."

A shadowed figure steps out from behind her, and into the light emerges Noah Corbin Fox.

"She doesn't have to tell me, Lottie." His voice is calm yet strained. "I heard every last word."

GAH!

He didn't hear the part about Mr. Sexy, did he? Because I totally did not mean that. It's simply a fact that baristas the world over most likely agree upon.

"Noah…" I try to take a step in his direction, but my toes feel as if they've screwed themselves into the ground. "I'm so sorry. I—"

"Don't." He holds up a hand and glares at Everett. "You took her right into the armpit of danger. You could have gotten yourselves killed," he growls out the words as the cords in his neck distend. Noah charges at Everett and slams him against his SUV before I can process any of it.

"*Whoa!*" Ivy Fairbanks riots and does her best to pluck Noah right off. "You do not get to screw up my investigation. I'm taking you off the case, Fox." Her icy stare never leaves his. "And if I see any of you diving back into it, I'll have you all arrested." She glares over at Everett. "I expected more out of you." She looks to Noah. "I'll give you a lift back to the station if you need it."

"I accept," he says, his hard gaze still penetrating mine.

We watch as Ivy Fairbanks and Noah disappear around the corner, and it feels as if my chest implodes, crushing my heart completely.

"I've ruined everything," I whisper, my entire body numb to the world. "It's over."

Something tells me, Noah and I will never recover.

CHAPTER 12

*D*ays drone by, and no matter how much I text, visit his office, or stalk at his house, Noah Fox always has a seemingly good reason why we can't meet up.

Apparently, his cases have given birth to baby cases, and he's up all night with those, too. He doesn't have a free moment to spare for me it seems. I can't blame him. Here he was giving me the best his lips had to offer and how did I repay him? By doing exactly what he kindly asked me not to do—with his sexy step-brother no less.

Darn Everett for having such an adorable and frighteningly accurate moniker. Not that this is all Everett's fault. As it turns out, he's not so pleased with me either. Everett has been busy these past few days, too, and for that I'm feeling thankful. I'm also thankful that the bakery has been filled to the brim at all hours of every day. At least this way I'm too busy baking up a storm and eating my feelings to digest what a dumpster fire I've managed to turn my life into.

An ear-piercing cackle comes from the large group near the window. Apparently, Naomi Turner has started up a naughty book club for the pre-menopausal—her word choice, not mine, and the who's who of said non-hormonally challenged age bracket is all present and accounted for.

Lily Swanson, Naomi's mean and bitter bestie, sits dutifully by her left side. And ensconcing the queen of mean on her right is my bestie, Keelie, who apologized through the roof for not getting their sleazy read to me in time to participate. But she did politely point out that while they were doling out the bawdy book, I was up to my eyeballs trying to solve poor Merilee's murder last month. Speaking of Merilee, her cousin, Cascade, is here cackling right along with the rest of them. With that long, dark hair of hers and her penchant for crushed velvet, she seems to be carrying on the legacy of the Simonson sisters nicely. Ellen Rawlings from the bank showed up. She hasn't stopped showing off those illuminated teeth of hers since she sat down. Funny, I've never once seen her smile during our banal monetary transactions. Nice to know she's capable. Darlene Grand, whose family owns the apple orchard, and Janet Darren, Travis Darren's lookalike sister, sit attentively as if there will be a quiz later—and knowing Naomi, and her need for dominance, there might be. Travis Darren was the one dating Merilee and Mora Anne at the very same time—thus driving Mora Anne to the brink of insanity. He's basically the primary reason Merilee was stabbed to death by her sister. Some men are heartbreakers. Travis was quite literally a heart taker in a roundabout way.

Collette Jenner shoots me a sharp look from over her shoulder, and I can't help but snarl at her slightly. Collette can't seem to keep her paws off of her legal eagle ex, and, yet, Everett has said a thousand times he's not interested in pursuing anything romantic with her again. Some people just can't take the hint. Speaking of which, it reminds me. I need to text Noah again at some point today. You never know when his schedule will free up.

Lainey waves me over, and I can't help but think she's a little traitor. I'll admit, it stung a bit not to be included on this innovated literary effort that just about every woman from Honey Hollow in my age group seems to be a part of. I grab my carafe and head on over. Lainey is seated next to Molly McMurry, so I'll hold any snippy comments for later. I'm still blown away by the fact Molly wants me to provide all the cupcakes for the Fall-O-Ween event next week, and the last thing I want is for her to see me sporting a bad attitude.

"More coffee, ladies?" I hold up my carafe, but they're all too engrossed in the steamy passage they're dissecting to notice me, so I do a quick round of refills anyhow.

The bell tied to the door chimes and in breezes a pale Micheline Roycroft with her copy of *Fit to be Tied* in her hand as she breezes to the seat next to my sister.

"Did I miss anything?" Her entire face brightens as she smiles up at me. I'd swear her smile just warmed the whole place. The last few times I've seen Micheline she's looked miserable beyond recognition. I guess she's coming to terms with Hunter's death, as she should.

I shake my head. "I don't know. But they've been here for an hour and there have been lots of spontaneous outbursts of—" I'm about to say *laughter* just when the room explodes with wild cackles once again.

Chrissy Nash and Eve Hollister amble in and give the younger sect the stink eye.

I head over and take their orders, two lattes, two chocolate-filled croissants, an order that's quickly becoming their usual.

Eve leans over to Chrissy. Eve's salt and peppered curls are certainly looking more salt these days than pepper. "I suppose our blood pressure is too high to be a part of that club," she huffs, indignant.

Chrissy, a fit blonde whom the mayor dumped because, well, let's face it, he's an idiot, chortles away. "I'm guessing you're right. I guess it's a good thing that our book club meets at the B&B this month." She looks my way. "Your mother is hosting a haunted high tea."

"Sounds delightful." I know all about it because my mother has put me in charge of providing all the petit fours for the aforementioned event. "And what book will you ladies be reading? A steamy historical romance, perhaps?"

Eve smirks as she waves me off. "You know us all too well, Lottie. *The Duke's Haunted Bedchamber* has been steaming up my glasses for weeks."

Chrissy's mouth falls open. "Since when does it take you weeks to finish a book?"

"It doesn't. I'm on my third go-round. Some books are so hauntingly delish they deserve a reread or two. Besides, with my house in shambles, I've nothing better to do than read by the fire."

"Still working on the remodel?" I ask. It's a well-known fact that Eve Hollister's retrofitting of her mansion has been going on for a small eternity.

"There's no end to it, Lottie. For the love of all that is holy, do not invest in a fixer."

A dull laugh thumps in my chest. A fixer to Eve would be a model home to most.

I hand them their coffee and croissants and sigh dreamily at that house across from Noah's with its white picket railing. I haven't heard word back, but a part of me wonders if Noah has told the realtor to forget it. There's no way he wants to live in close proximity to me after that fiasco down in Leeds. Face it, I'm the fiasco he wants no part of.

The book club concludes, and all dozen or so of them stand at once.

Naomi claps the murmuring crowd back into submission. "The next book we're reading is *The Thankful Subservient*. I think it will tie in nicely with Thanksgiving."

"Get it? *Tie* in?" Lily guffaws right in her bestie's face, but Naomi is quick to brush her off.

Collette Jenner pulls on a black pea coat, and her bright orange curls cascade off the back. The black and orange give off a Halloween vibe that I'm sure she wasn't going for, but she is scary. I'll give her that.

"You never let us pick our next read. We should take it to a vote." Collette dares defy the head witch of this unholy coven.

But Naomi doesn't flinch. "We don't need a vote. The books I pick are fantastic. Did I let anyone down with this month's selection?"

A round of approving giggles circles the small crowd before it officially disbands.

I waste no time in picking up a platter of fresh oatmeal cookies with adorable iced spider webs over the tops and head over to Micheline, but Lily Swanson gets in my way.

"The sign in the front says you're hiring, and I want in." Her large, glossy, green eyes look as if they're about to pop with anticipation. "Rumor has it, that hot judge keeps hanging around. And, seeing that I'm newly single"—so another rumor is true, she's up and dumped Travis—"I can use a handsome man with a hefty paycheck."

I can't help but frown. I'm about to shut down the gold digger in front of me when—although I have no doubt she's attracted to Everett—she is right, he is a rather hot commodity—Keelie bubbles her way over.

"Yes!" Keelie threads her arm through Lily's. "The bakery is running off fumes from the Honey Pot, and we so need our staff back. Can you bake?"

Lily shudders as if the concept offended her. "No, but I can run a register like it's nobody's business."

"You're hired." Keelie doesn't waste a moment as she whisks her away. "I just need you to fill out an application, and then I'll assign you some hours."

So much for discerning the right people to populate the bakery with.

Micheline whips on her jacket, and I quickly dash in front of her before she has the chance to leave. I just have to know if she's aware of any girlfriend Hunter might have had who happened to be a mother. I've been racking my brain trying to think of anyone in Honey Hollow who fits the description but come up with blanks.

"Oatmeal cookie?" I hold the platter in front of her, and she's quickly overcome by the heavy scent of cinnamon and vanilla.

"My God, these smell divine." She snaps one off the tray and indulges in a moaning bite. "So good. I'd say you really should sell these, but you beat me to it." A tiny dimple imbeds itself into her cheek as she grins.

As much as I loathe to ruin her good mood, Hunter's murder investigation is growing colder by the moment, so I dive right in. "Hey, I heard a funny rumor about Hunter, and I wondered if you heard it, too." I wrinkle my nose while playing up the chagrinned angle. "Was he dating someone with a kid? I mean, it's no big deal, but Hunter and I were pretty close, and he's always liked kids, so I wondered why he never mentioned it."

Her naturally pasty complexion turns a bright shade of pomegranate, and I can't help but think I've stumbled upon something big. Either that or I've just shocked her so badly there won't be enough spider web iced oatmeal cookies in the world to revive her.

"He"—a croaking sound emits from her throat as if she were deciding which lane she wanted to get into—"he was seeing someone." She closes her eyes a moment and shakes her head as if she couldn't believe she had to go there—as if she couldn't believe *he* had to go there. "It was stupid. Some stripper from Leeds."

I suck in a quick breath, trying my best to think on my feet. "The one from Red Satin?" *Brill!* Suddenly, I'm thankful for my minute knowledge of all things scantily clad.

"No"—she bats her eyes to the ceiling as if trying to remember the name and, dear God, I pray she remembers the name—"it was Girls Unlimited." Her lips purse with disgust. "Anyway, that was a bigger deal than he intended it to be. You might even say it was the nail in our casket." She winces. "Sorry. I don't mean to be disrespectful." Micheline's whole affect shifts, and suddenly she looks crestfallen. "I'd better get going." She snaps another cookie off the tray. "Thanks for being such a good friend, Lottie."

"No problem." A good friend who pumps a grieving girl for info. Some good friend I am.

Lainey comes up, and I manufacture a smile for my sister. "Are you free tonight?"

"Yeah, why?" Her brows dip as she sinks her suspicion my way.

"You might want to let your hair down and leave your reading glasses at home. We're headed to a strip club in Leeds."

Naomi and Collette Jenner scuttle over with their eyes agog.

"I'm in." Naomi doesn't miss a topless beat.

"Me, too," Collette gruffs it out as if she's angry about it before stalking to the door. "Naomi, text me with the details. I've got a board meeting all afternoon, and God knows I'll need to unwind." A salacious grin rides up her cheeks. "I'm all for an appetizer before I sink my teeth into Judge Baxter's neck." She bares her fangs as she speeds into the chilled autumn air.

"She's quite the vampire," Lainey notes. "So, what's with the strip club? Two men not enough for you, lady?" She shakes her shoulders in a suggestive manner. Good Lord, Lainey really is in training to become my mother.

Keelie shuffles over, nearly tripping over a chair. "Did someone say strip club? Dear God up in heaven, you are not going without me. You'll need a tour guide who speaks the language and knows where to put the dollar bills!"

Lainey chortles. "I didn't know you speak banana hammock?"

The three of them share a titillating laugh.

Little do they know there won't be a banana hammock in sight at Girls Unlimited. I may not know which stripper Hunter dated, but I do know she's got a kid. That should narrow the field significantly.

I have a feeling I'm about to split this case wide open with a stripper pole.

Noah bounces through my mind. I know for a fact he wouldn't want me digging back into the investigation, but then we're technically not speaking so he doesn't really have a say.

Keelie and Naomi screech with laughter at something Lainey says, and I cringe.

Something tells me Girls Unlimited will be one banana hammock short of what they're looking for.

CHAPTER 13

"*W*hat do you mean every stripper in here has a kid?" I shout above the music to the bartender I've enlisted to help me find Hunter's mystery girl.

I shoot a quick glance to Lainey, Naomi, Keelie, and Collette who sulk at a table nearby. Not one of them is hooting and hollering at deafening decibels the way they threatened to on the way over. Suffice it to say, I'll have to bake a batch of banana hammock muffins just to get back in their good graces.

"That's what I said." The bald and brawny bartender tatted from the neck down continues cleaning out a glass with a dishrag. It's so dimly lit in this seedy establishment, save for the stage where the girls working hard for a dollar have an entire bevy of spotlights dancing around them. "They've all got kids. What else you got on her?"

Crap. The music is so loud it sounds as if a jet engine has suddenly decided to spit out rap tunes. Although, I'm slightly grateful for the scent of fries permeating the air. The first thing I did when we got seated was order a round for the table. Who knew they served appetizers here? *Hey*? Maybe I can work out a deal for weekly cookie deliveries? But, at the moment, I'm coming up short on what cookie goes best with beer.

"She was dating someone who works construction," I add.

He shakes his head, that dead look on his face lets me know I've hit another bump in the road with far too many options to choose from.

"He was from Honey Hollow," I shout the words just as the music hits a lull, and someone from the back whoops *Honey Hollow* right back.

The bartender's mouth opens as he cocks a squinted eye to the ceiling. "Yeah, I know of one."

Lainey comes up and gives my sleeve a quick tug. "The girls and I want to go. We gave you your five minutes, and they were up ten minutes ago. Collette is threatening me with kidnapping if I don't get back on the road soon."

I avert my eyes at the thought. I knew bringing Collette and Naomi along would be a big mistake, but then I reasoned it might work out if we were surrounded with a tough crowd. That way we'd have someone to feed them while the rest of us made our escape. Besides, Naomi and Collette have the power to scare off any thug who has the nerve to mess with us.

"Five more minutes, I swear. I'm just getting to the good part!" I hiss before turning back to my tatted-up friend. "What's the girl's name?"

"Stella." He nods to the stage. "That's her up front."

My heart thumps wildly in my chest as I spin on my heels. There are at least six women on stage, each one wiggling and jiggling to the soothing sounds of a slow song that's currently melting over the speakers. The girls all look too beautiful to be real with their long, glossy hair, their showy curves, those sparkly pasties catching the light and arresting our vision. Then I see her. A woman with long, dark, wavy hair and long, thick lashes, and a familiar deep red lipstick that makes me suck in a lungful of stale French fried scented air.

"It's *her*," I hiss, and Lainey pulls me over to our table.

"Her who?"

"The girl from Hunter's funeral. I think I just found out who Hunter's mystery girlfriend was."

"Which one?" Naomi looks bored as she stares at the scandalous show before us.

"The girl up front—dark hair, purple pasties." I guess I do have a lot to be thankful for when I realize that no one will ever point me out in a crowd by way of the color of my nipple coverings.

"That's Sparkling Cider." Keelie gives a mean whoop her way. "You want me to make it rain over her? I've got some serious cash burning a hole in my pocket and not a lot of prospects."

"*No*," both Collette and I say at once.

I glance to the irate redhead who looks as if she's itching to bolt.

Collette sneers at Keelie. "Save the dinero. There's a place down the street called The Ladies Lounge and, trust me, there's not a purple pasty in the place. I wouldn't lead you astray, unlike some people." She takes a moment to glare my way. "And what would Everett think if he knew this was the kind of place you preferred to frequent?" Her lips twitch with a malevolent smile. "I'm pretty sure that would take you out of the running to fill his heart."

"Believe me, that man is not looking to fill his heart." It's yet to be determined that he has one. "And, fine, we'll leave—but not before I see the end of Sparkling Cider's act. As soon as she steps off that stage, I'm going to ask her a question."

I know for a fact once the girls are through they trot down and mingle with the masses. I'm betting those personal lap dances are where they make the real money. I can't imagine Hunter frequenting this place, but I know both he and Bear have amassed some serious frequent flyer miles at places just like this. For a second I envision Noah seated in some secluded booth and

Sparkling Cider shaking her baby maker in his face. My stomach sours at the thought.

The girls finish up their tantalizing tease, leaving their G-strings and pasties right where they belong, and that alone makes me want to tip them. All six of them make their way down the stairs to the left of the stage, and a raucous rock song starts in and another set of temptresses in hot pink satin robes strut out as if they were about to teach us all a lesson.

"We're out," Naomi knocks back the rest of her drink before pulling Keelie to her feet.

Lainey and I stand, as does Collette, but Collette isn't putting on her coat just yet. She's grinning ear to ear at something behind me.

I turn my neck just enough before doing a double take.

"Oh God," I whimper under my breath. For the life of me I just can't catch a break.

Striding our way, shoulders back, clad in his signature sexy suit, those piercing blue eyes of his slotted to angry slits is a stone cold, chest wide as a linebacker judgmental Judge Baxter.

"*Everett.*" I try to sound cheery as if this were any other venue I might have bumped into him in. "You're looking grand tonight. Have a pocketful of Benjamins just begging for a pair of panties to stuff themselves into?" I couldn't help it. He so had it coming.

The good judge doesn't so much as a flinch. "What are you doing here, Lemon? When Collette mentioned you dragged her off to a strip club, I didn't believe her."

Collette wastes no time in snuggling up next to him, doing the worm over the left side of his body, but Everett doesn't even notice. "That's right. I sent him a picture of you loading up at the bar. Can you believe it?" She cackles into his ear. "Honey Hollows not-so-sweet baker showing her true colors. And, as it turns out, there's a *rainbow* involved."

"Oh stop." I lunge at her and she's quick to cower.

"All right." Lainey holds up a hand. "Let's get to The Ladies Lounge and banana hammock it up. It's almost my bedtime."

"I'm not going." I do a quick scan of the room and spot Sparkling Cider bouncing on the lap of some mussed hair businessman. "There's someone I need to talk to. I have unfinished business, and I'm getting to the bottom of it." My God, this might just be the most unhygienic conversation I've had with a person yet.

"I'll be with her." Everett nods to Lainey. "And I'll give her a ride back," he says it stern my way. And why does it sound like I'm about to be punished? "We have an unfinished conversation of our own we need to tend to."

My entire body seizes. I'm not sure which is worse: grilling a stripper about her dead boyfriend or diving into the deep end of dead pets with Everett.

Lainey, Naomi, and a seething mad Collette pluck a whooping Keelie from climbing on stage and hit the door for far more testosterone-laden pastures.

It's just Everett and I glaring at one another.

The glint of a purple pasty hits my eye, and I gasp.

"Here she comes." I wave over at her, and she struts on over with those long doe eyelashes tipped with glitter, those ruby red lips looking at Everett as if she too were ready and willing to take a bite out of his neck.

She moans as she caresses his tie, "You need a lap dance, big boy?" She bites down on her lip while her just about naked girls smash over Everett's steely abs. And really? Why does this feel as if I'm in a bad nightmare that's about to get porny?

"Actually, it's me that called you here."

Gone in an instant is that gleam in her eye as she inspects me head to foot. "Fine. Take a seat on the chair."

I do as I'm told, and before I know it, her backside is bouncing in my face and I try my hardest to slap her away.

Everett averts his eyes as he helps the poor girl off.

"I don't think she really wants to play the bongos." His demeanor is downright serious as he pulls out a seat for the girl. "You're up, Lemon."

Sparkling Cider looks as if she's about to lose her effervescence and hightail it over to the bar, so I get right to the chase.

"Hunter Fisher has a message for you." My entire body spikes with heat at the lie.

Her mouth falls open, and she jumps in her seat. "But—but Hunter's dead."

Ah-ha! So she does know him!

"Yes, he is, unfortunately. But before he died, he asked me to give someone he was seeing at Girls Unlimited a message."

"That's me!" Her eyes expand to the size of silver dollars. "What is it? Am I in his will?"

My gut wrenches at the thought of poor Hunter having a will at such a young age.

"Um—" I glance to Everett, completely unaware of where to go next with this.

Everett takes in a deep breath, and she looks his way, practically drooling over how wide that man's chest can get in a single lungful.

"Hunter had a certificate of deposit made out for you, but it was damaged and it can't be replaced. His attorney offers his apologies but—"

"That stupid, *stupid* idiot. Screwing up finances right up until the end." Her eyes gloss over with tears, and as upset as I am that she was calling him names, I can tell she cared a lot about him. Or the money. It's debatable at this point.

"I agree." I shrug over at her. "Hunter was always broke, and I couldn't figure out why. He mentioned something about you having a kid. A boy, right?" Just a wild guess. The worst she could do is correct me, considering it's a fifty-fifty split.

Stella freezes stiff. Her eyes slit to nothing as she looks past me out into some unknowable horizon. "I prefer to leave my son out of this." The music dies down as the applause picks up and Stella rises out of her seat. "Besides, I don't need anything else from Hunter." She hightails it into the crowd before disappearing into the back.

"That was abrupt." Everett helps me out of my seat.

"I agree. You know that underground source you used to help us find Martinelle Finance? Do me a favor and have them find out everything there is to know about Sparkling Cider, aka Stella. I have a feeling that's not the last we'll see of her yet."

"Will do," he says as he steps in close. That towering presence of his makes me feel about as big as a shoe. "But first, you're going to tell me all there is to know about you."

I take a deep, exasperating breath, girding myself for the inevitable.

"I guess my moment of reckoning has finally come."

"That it has, Lemon."

Everett presses his hand against my back as he navigates us out of the seedy club, and I can't help but think I'm walking to my doom. And in a way, I am.

I'd rather trade places with Hunter than try to explain my supernatural superpowers with someone as logically minded as Everett.

This will not end well.

But I'm guessing it will be the end of our friendship.

CHAPTER 14

The McMurry Pumpkin Patch gleams like a crown filled with amber jewels on this late October night. Everett offered to take us out for something warm to drink, and I opted for cider. There seems to be a theme tonight. And Everett, being the gentleman he is, opted to hold off our chat until we each had a warm cup in our hands.

The moon shines down from the east, casting long shadows across the fields laden with enough pumpkins to create a pie for every person in North America. We settle on a couple of bales of hay and look out at all of the families enjoying the festivities. There are pumpkin carving stations, three oversized bounce houses sagging and rocking in rhythm, and a petting zoo filled to capacity with both humans and animals—and the sight of the furry creatures sours my expression because it's a harsh reminder of why we're here.

"So I've done some research"—Everett begins—"within the community of people who believe in those kind of afterlife phenomena. Seeing dead pets is not entirely uncommon."

I make a face at his attempt to put a quasi-scientific spin on things. "And what's your verdict? Are you going to lock me up in a psychiatric facility for life, or do I get the electric chair?"

"Neither." His shoulders sag as he scoots in another inch. "Tell me your history. When did this begin? What exactly *is* this?"

My eyes close involuntarily as I try to summon the right words, in the right order, but they won't come.

"Okay, I'm just going to blurt this out." I take a quick breath, my gaze pinned to those blue flames that are ready to torch my world down. "When I was a kid, I started seeing creatures that happen to be missing a tangible body—little see-through cute and furry ghosts, if you will." I sigh at how ridiculous it sounds coming from my lips. "Anyway, one day I saw a little turtle floating near Bear's ear, and later that afternoon he broke his arm. So the next time I saw a little disembodied beast, I held my breath and, sure enough, it happened again—and again, and again, and again. And then, of course, there was Merilee's orange Tabby, which I saw on the same day I met you. That was the first time anyone actually bit the big one. But now that I think on it, everything that's ever transpired has been pretty awful."

He ticks his head back, just trying to absorb it all. "How about your family, your mother, your father? Do they share the same gift?"

"I was adopted by the Lemons when I was just an infant. There's no telling who my real family is. Like I mentioned before, the only other person on the planet who's aware of this is Nell Sawyer. She's my best friend, Keelie's, grandmother, and well, mine by proxy. She didn't judge me." I glance out to the pumpkin patch for a moment as a truck filled with bales of hay and a happy load of passengers goes by. "But you'll judge me." It comes out lower than a whisper. "You can't help it. It's what you do for a living."

"I don't judge like that." He bounces his hand over mine a moment. "Lemon, as strange as it sounds, I believe you. I don't claim to understand everything about this universe. And if that's what you say happens, then I accept that as the truth. And I can tell that you're telling the truth. I'd like to ask your forgiveness for prying. I just needed to be clear that in no way this would've impeded on the case."

"And what have you decided?" I'm almost teasing, but you never know with Everett.

"You're in the clear." He takes a sip of his cider. "You want me to take you home?"

"Actually, now that you know all about my family history, I was hoping you could share something about your own. Noah mentioned that his father took your mother to the cleaners. I feel just terrible about that—especially since I ended up turning her misfortune into appliances for the bakery."

Everett pumps out a dull laugh. "Well, he didn't exactly clean her out. He did, however, put in a darn good effort. Despite the fact, my mother is still a wealthy woman. She still lives in Fallbrook. Still cautiously single. She's a hotel heiress. My grandfather owned a chain of five-star hotels across Europe. I've got a sister, Meghan. She works for an insurance company. She's still back in Fallbrook as well. Single, no pets." He smirks over at me, and I pretend to sock him on the arm.

"And you?" I lift a shoulder his way as if I were being coy. "How are you possibly single? I mean, I get that whole exes thing. I've met them. But why haven't you settled down yet?"

Everett turns toward the fields and takes a deep breath. "Guess I haven't found the one."

"You will. You'll be off the market soon enough, believe me. And there will be a body count, too. Women are going to war over you."

He winces. "Coming from you, the body count sounds like a threat."

"Sadly, coming from me, it might be."

"And you?" He touches his shoulder to mine as if to prod me. "Are you off the market?"

My stomach sinks because I can't seem to find the answer. "I thought I was. Noah and I seemed to be going pretty strong. I just—he never told me how he felt about me, and I was left questioning whether or not he wanted something exclusive with me."

"Did you want something exclusive with him?" He bears those ocean blue eyes into mine, and a shiver runs through me.

"Yes, I wanted it. I mean, Noah's a great guy. He just—I don't know. He doesn't want me tampering in what he refers to as his investigation. And I get that to a certain extent. But Hunter was my friend. I can't just let it go and hope for the best. There's a bona fide killer out there. And if he or she isn't caught soon, they might just strike again."

"I get that. But I also get where Noah is coming from. You're a great person, Lemon. And at the risk of losing a friendship, I have to say I agree with him. He doesn't want to see you get hurt and neither do I. I'm sorry, but it's safety first. You said it yourself. There's a bona fide killer out there who might be looking for another victim. We don't want that to be you."

"Neither do I." I sag into the words. "I don't really fault Noah for wanting to keep me safe. Or you." I knock my knee into his as an entire gaggle of kids run for the pick-up area for the next round of hayrides. "Say, you wouldn't happen to know if Noah has any hang-ups about relationships, would you?"

He cocks his head to the side. "I know his ex was a pistol. I'm sure that made him more than a little cautious. But that's his story to tell. If he's smart, he'll commit to you soon. He's not a player anymore."

"A player, huh?" I can't help but giggle at the thought. "Did you take the baton from him?"

He groans as he cringes. "I might have taken a page out of his playbook. Both he and his brother were a bad influence on me back in the day." He glowers toward the pumpkin patch as if he were having a bad memory. "You know what? How about we hop on that hayride real quick? It'll be a nice palate cleanse before we head on out."

"*Judge Baxter.*" I laugh as I hop up and dust the hay from my jeans. "You really do know how to have a good time."

We finish up our cider and board the tractor-trailer, seating ourselves near the back, a safe distance from the howling masses. Everett and I laugh during every inch of that bumpy, twisted, and jerking good time. And once the tractor comes to a stop, we're the last to get off. Everett exits first. It's so murky and dark in this area of the pumpkin patch it all feels like a dream.

"This night sure took a turn for the—" I'm about to say *better* when my foot glides right off the hay bale that's acting as a stepladder and Everett catches me in his arms.

"*Whoa!*" he says as the momentum sends us spinning, and I laugh as we come to a complete stop just shy of the petting zoo.

"Looks like fun," a masculine voice calls out from behind, and Everett swings me back around, only to have my heart stop cold.

"*Noah?*" I squint into the darkness, hoping against hope it's just Ken, the owner, wanting to give me the final count on how many devil's food cupcakes to bake for the Fall-O-Ween Fest— but this is me we're talking about. That handsome brick wall of a man glowering at us is in fact Detective Noah Corbin Fox.

"I"—he hitches his thumb over his shoulder, his face looking morbidly long—"was just asking the owners about Hunter. They were kind enough to show me the application he filled out just a few days before he passed." His jaw squares out. "And yes, I was going against orders and investigating. I guess I'm not too fond of the rules myself." His eyes hook to mine before he traces out my body with his gaze.

"Oh, no, no, no," I say, caught off guard that I'm still tucked high in his stepbrother's arms.

Everett lands me safely on my feet and takes a deep breath. "It's not what it looks like."

"It's not?" Noah twitches his head at us incredulously. "Of

course, it is. The two of you were enjoying one another's company." His voice dips low, and if I didn't know better, I'd say he was struggling with the words. "I guess I'm okay with that."

"You *guess*?" My heart slaps wildly against my chest. "You either are or you aren't." There. I said it. If Noah has any feelings for me whatsoever, this is his moment to speak now or forever hold his peace. Didn't those kisses mean anything to him? Although, to be fair, he could say the same to me.

My phone bleats in my pocket before he can answer, and I quickly scan over it.

"Oh no," I say, looking up at both Noah and Everett. "It's my sister. She says she thinks her garage may have been broken into."

Noah leans in, rife with concern. "Tell her to call the police and get back in her car. Do not go in the house. I'm on my way. Everett, you keep Lottie here until I give you the all clear."

He takes off, and I choke on my next words before taking Everett by the hand and hightailing it to the parking lot.

"Come on, Everett. I don't care what he says. You're taking me to my sister's."

"But Noah—"

"Noah will have to live with it."

Just like I might have to live without him.

CHAPTER 15

e find Lainey perched by the open mouth of the garage, the police already there with two squad cars. It's a horrible sight to see your sister's house lit up with blue and red strobing lights in the night.

"*Lainey,*" I say, lunging at her with a hug. Everett sped just as fast as Noah did to get here, but Noah still managed to beat us. To be honest, it felt like I was caught up in some testosterone-fueled game as they kept trying to outrun one another. I'm not sure what happened between the two of them, way back when, but this screams unresolved childhood issues.

I spot Noah already deep inside the garage speaking with a member of the sheriff's department.

"Tell me what happened?" I ask my sister as I quickly inventory all of the boxes from my old apartment, a few of which have toppled to the side.

My sister wraps her arms around herself as she turns to look inside. "Well, I came home and the garage door was ajar. I couldn't figure out why, so I figured it must have been that rash of break-ins we've been having."

Everett strides up next to me. "Is anything missing?"

Lainey shrinks a bit in her oversized plaid coat. "I can't tell. I mean, it's all your stuff, Lottie. How would I know if anything was gone?" She threads her arm through mine. "Does anything look as if it's missing to you?"

I take a step inside, and Noah tips his head over at me, the look of grief slightly veiled in his eyes.

"Actually, it looks as if everything is present and accounted for."

"Look at this"—Everett points over to a couple of bricks that are bucking in the driveway and a loose one tossed to the side —"it looks like your door may not have shut properly."

"Oh no." Lainey tips her head back. "I had it open before I left, looking for a bin of books I've been meaning to donate." Lainey is forever donating books to the library. She once told me that working at the library felt as if she were visiting old friends. And she would be, considering half the books are donated from her private collection. "I guess it was a false alarm."

"Not to worry." The sheriff standing next to Noah comes over. "Better safe than sorry. It's an odd thing, but those robberies seemed to have come to a stop abruptly a couple weeks ago. Whoever was doing it has either been caught or killed." He nods our way. "Goodnight, folks. We're heading on out." He takes off, and my mouth falls open as a thought comes to me.

I glance over to the spot Noah was standing in, but he's gone.

The sound of a car purring to life ignites behind us, and I turn just in time to see him taking off with a wave.

Everett huffs at the sight, "Don't take it personally, Lemon. It's me he's ticked off at. I can promise you that." He offers Lainey and me a slight bow. "Enjoy the rest of your night, ladies. I'm glad it was nothing."

We watch as he takes off, and my sister lands her head on my shoulder.

"You really showed up with the cavalry. Have you settled on one yet?"

"Yes, I've settled on one. It's just that he can't seem to settle on me."

"Option B isn't so bad himself. Honestly, there are no wrong choices here."

"There's a wrong choice, all right," I say, turning back around and looking into the cozy little garage—"and that choice would be me."

"Oh, *you*." Lainey is quick to swat me. "So, I guess those garage thieves moved on after all."

"Or died." I can't help but think it's the latter. "I'm starting to wonder if I knew Hunter Fisher at all."

THE NEXT FEW days are maddening with nonstop baking as dozens upon dozens of devil's food cupcakes are frosted in festive Halloween hues of orange, purple, and green, festooned with meringue ghosts, bright blue wizard hats, and licorice spiders.

But my mind is far from the task at hand. I can't help but mull over the case while I pour batter into another batch of cupcake molds. As far as I'm concerned, Bear isn't at all a suspect, but then, I guess I can't really take anyone off the list just yet. Then there's Chuck Popov, who as Bear suggested didn't lend Hunter a dime. Although, Hunter could have borrowed money from Chuck behind Bear's back. And Chuck did seem a little rough around the edges that day when I mentioned Hunter's name. Perhaps he was just a disgruntled colleague? However, if Hunter owed him money, people can get unfriendly real quick when a little cash comes between them. Not that I'm assuming it was a small sum Hunter borrowed. But, as for now, that's just my imagination running wild. Until something solid comes up, Chuck isn't really on my radar. Then there's Mom's new boyfriend, Wallace, who said he tried to get Hunter a loan but failed. That actually penciled out. And interestingly enough, led us to evidence of Hunter's stripper ex-girlfriend, the one with the kid. And, of course, there's Micheline Roycroft. She didn't do it. I'd stake my life on it. Although, she was useful in tipping me off as far as where I could find Stella. Stella. I shake my head. She was so angry. For an ex-girlfriend, she sure as heck didn't so much as shed a tear. Come to think of it, she didn't look too torn up at his funeral either. Stella. Maybe once I recuperate from tonight I'll head back to Girls Unlimited and have another chat with her? I'm sure Everett won't mind one bit escorting me back to that flesh-fest. I roll my eyes at the thought.

Keelie helps me transport the multitude of boxes to the McMurry Pumpkin Patch with just minutes to spare before the Fall-O-Ween Fest gets underway.

The crowds have already descended upon the place with costumes that range from adorable to looking like they outright belong in a horror movie. Keelie and I lean toward the adorable end of the spectrum with Keelie dressed up as a fairy in a pale green tutu and sparkly leotard to go along with it. Her makeup looks as if a fairy herself showed up to apply the magical wonder, but Keelie being Keelie has decided to vamp the look up a bit with some heavy eyeliner for dramatic flair. And have I mentioned that her leotard is low-cut in the front and that tutu hardly covers her rear?

"You're going to freeze to death," I say, shivering myself.

"I told you. I'm determined to find my fae prince who will wrap me in his strong arms and return the feeling to my s-s-skin." Her teeth chatter as she says it. "You're no better yourself."

I glance down at the short blue dress and my tall black boots with their cute crisscross pattern running down the front. That badge on my chest is proudly glinting in the light, and the patches that read *police* over my sleeves look official. Keelie lent me a pair of official handcuffs she swiped from her father, and I'm terrified I'll do something dumb like lock myself in them, so

I'm letting them dangle from my belt for now as a flashy accessory.

"I *know*." I shiver. "But I couldn't help it. There's some irony to it. Besides, when Lily said she'd bring in one of her spares for me, I had no idea it would be so suggestive."

"*Please*"—she tips her head back and laughs openly at the thought—"everything that girl does is suggestive."

"Amen to that," I say as a giant mass of humanity fills the pumpkin farm as far as the eye can see. The entire grounds are decorated with scarecrows and skeletons, witches and ghosts. The nonstop screams from the haunted hayrides can be heard for miles despite the fact they have speakers set up and are blaring Halloween-themed music on a loop.

"No, no." Keelie shakes her head at something behind me. "Do not turn around." Her hands grip me by the shoulders. "Say, I really want to try that blue cotton candy. How about we each get one and see who can finish up the fastest?"

"We already know it's going to be me. We do that every year, Keelie," I say, straining to turn around. "What is it that you don't want me to see?" I break free from her hold, and as soon as my eyes snag on a horrible sight, the wind gets knocked right out of me.

"Well then." It comes out with a contrived sense of strength. "I guess we really are over."

Off in the distance, standing in line for the coveted haunted hayrides are Noah and Ivy Fairbanks. Her long, red hair glimmers like copper as she laughs at something he said, and my heart breaks just witnessing the event.

I stagger backward until I end up at the petting zoo and spot a familiar stripper dressed as a scantily clad bunny—far more than she wears most weeknights. She's on her knees helping the little child in her arms pet a baby goat, and I gasp when I see the little boy's face. That dirty blond hair, that olive skin—sure, a lot of people have those physical attributes, but that face looks a little too familiar. I've seen that face a thousand times before, and it wasn't on him. A dark-haired man steps in front of the boy, blocking him from my view, and I glance up to find the man who was comforting Stella at the funeral, the same one who saved me from the scaffolding the day Hunter died.

A crowd moves in between us, and I lose them in the happy chaos of the evening.

Kids shout into the night at the trunk-or-treat lot next to me, and suddenly this entire farm is nothing but a cacophony of sounds.

Just as I'm about to pull out my phone and call Noah, I suddenly remember we're not exactly on speaking terms, and he just might be having the time of his haunted life with Ivy on that spooky hayride.

I glance over and spot the haunted corn maze and frown. That about sums up my life. Everywhere I turn there's a dead end —or a dead pet. And right about now, I'm not crazy about either.

"*Lottie!*" a cheery voice calls out, and it's Molly with Ken trailing by her side. "You did a fantastic job on the cupcakes! You really are a genius in the kitchen."

"And you're far too kind. It was really—" I'm about to segue into an entire litany of self-deprecating thoughts when I spot Micheline Roycroft standing next to Bear, and the two of them seem to be having a heated debate while they each hold one of my genius cupcakes in their hands. I'm betting they're not anywhere near the topic of my IQ. "I'm sorry. I see someone that I need to speak with. I'll be right back."

I speed over just as Bear and Micheline hit a lull in their argument.

"Happy Halloween," I say, looking to the both of them without the aid of a smile. Truth be told, there's not a hint of anything cheery in my voice either. I'm a bit peeved at them at the moment, because it's becoming clear the two of them know more than they're letting on.

"You look great, Lot." Bear frowns while craning his head past me.

Micheline is dressed as a vampire with trails of fake blood running down her chin. She looks past me as well, and I follow her gaze to where Stella and the little boy were just a moment ago.

"That's him, isn't it?" I look back to the two of them accusingly. "Hunter had a son. That's why he had to keep borrowing money." A slap of shock detonates over me all at once as the pieces to the puzzle fall into place. "And the two of you knew about it." I shake my head incredulously. "Why? Why keep it a secret?"

"*Lottie*," Bear moans. "Hunter didn't want anyone to know."

"Why? It's his kid! Hunter loved children. He would have made a great father."

"I agree." Micheline nods, but those wild eyes are saying something else entirely. "But you don't know Stella. She's a nightmare to deal with."

"Was she threatening him?" I step in front of Bear as I demand the answer. "Do you think Stella or that creepy boyfriend of hers did this?"

Bear's face hardens to flint, and he takes off into the crowd without warning.

"*Bear!*" Micheline calls after him. "We're not finished," she shouts before threading through a thicket of people, and she too is gone before I can stop her.

"Oh my God," I whisper as I pull out my phone once again. A part of me demands I call Jack, Keelie's father, the captain of the Ashford Sheriff's Department, but my fingers find another name, and I put in a call to that number instead. But Noah doesn't pick up. I bolt into the crowd in the same direction Bear and Micheline took off in and run for what feels like half a mile before I head away from the crowd to catch my breath. From the corner of my eye, I spot a dark-haired man looking at me just as he ducks into the haunted corn maze, and hot on his heels are Stella and that sweet baby who bears a striking resemblance to his father.

My heart drums up my throat as I head on over.

Corn Maze, I hit send before I realize I sent it to Noah and not Bear.

But I don't waste time rectifying the error. Instead, I head over to the haunted corn maze myself and step on in.

It's time to confront the mother of Hunter's child, and maybe his killer as well.

CHAPTER 16

$\mathcal{T}$here have been moments in my life that I've been morbidly afraid, frightened out of my mind for far lesser reasons. But at this moment, entering into a dimly lit maze —haunted at that—I'm riding the zenith of terror. I'm so far outside of my mind with fright it almost feels sublime.

The corn maze is a walled-in wonder filled with erroneous twists and turns—and don't forget a horror around each corner. I should know, I've been once before—ironically while I was dating Bear. I screamed until my vocal cords went out and finally closed my eyes and made Bear get us the heck out of there. I swore I would never subject myself to the terror ever again and, yet, here I am. My feet move brazenly at a quickened clip in hopes of catching up to Stella and her man.

The sound of a child crying can be heard at a distance, and my pace picks up. No sooner do I round the next corner than a zombie-looking creature jumps out at me with a tiny zombie baby doll in her arms, and I snatch it from her without thinking.

"Hey, lady"—the zombie woman calls after me as I take off —"where you going? That's a part of my bit! Ah, geez."

Her voice fades to nothing as I bullet past vampires jumping out of caskets, monsters and maniacs, werewolves and space aliens. I pass a small crowd of teenagers who scream their heads off as I bolt past them with the zombie baby still in my hands, but I'm a woman on a mission, and I'm not stopping until I get the truth out of Stella.

The violent sound of a power tool grows in ferocity as I propel myself from one dead end to the other, and I pause, holding onto my knees, panting so hard I start to feel light-headed. The glint of something small and furry wraps around my ankle, and a shrill scream unleashes from me as I try my best to stomp the life out of the creature. But the tiny beast only lifts its cute little face at me and appears to chatter out a laugh.

I suck in a quick breath as I bend over and give the ghostly little cutie a scratch over his back.

"You scared the living daylights out of me." Another breath hitches in my throat as an idea comes to me. "Take me to Hunter's killer! I've got an entire fleet of deputies I can employ to wrangle them to justice. Wouldn't you love that?"

Its bushy little tails whips back and forth, and it takes off without so much as a wink.

"Here goes nothing," I say as I follow along after it.

It leads the way straight to a split in the road, and for the life of me I can't tell which direction the sound of that buzz saw is coming from.

"Just FYI," I whisper to it. "I'm practically allergic to spooks. If at all possible, I'd like to avoid anyone who's even remotely near a chainsaw.

The tiny fuzzy creature chirps up at me, and I'd swear I was just laughed at by dead vermin. It leads to the right where the maze opens up to a clearing, and I spot a couple with a baby up ahead.

"Good job, little guy," I pant as I do my best to blend in with corn stalks.

Stella turns and spots me before pulling her boyfriend to the left, and just as I'm about to follow, they come right back to where they started.

"Dead end?" I can't help but chide them.

The poor baby has his head tucked into his mother's neck, too afraid to look at his surroundings, and I don't blame him. Stella looks on fire as if she thrived on the adrenaline, but her boyfriend has a stiffness about him as if he were trying his best to get them out of this situation at any cost. And that's what I have to fear the most.

Bear must be on my trail by now. Both he and Micheline were after them. They'll be here soon. I have to believe it. I step forward, and they back their way into another offshoot as it opens up to a large octagon-shaped space that's—

Out jumps a man in a hockey mask wielding that horrifically loud chainsaw, and the three of us howl in unison.

Stella and her boyfriend hightail it to the back of the octagon, entrapping themselves with nowhere to go. Instinctually, I block the exit, holding my hands out like a goaltender with the zombie baby dangling from my wrist.

"That's Hunter's baby boy. Isn't it, Stella?" I shout up over the roar of the motor. The man in the hockey mask does his best to jump and jive while wielding his weapon, but not one of us pays him any mind.

"What do you care?" she shouts back, cradling the back of the baby's head protectively. "This isn't any of your business. But you've been putting yourself where you don't belong right from the beginning." She jerks her head toward her boyfriend. "Get me out of here, Jonas."

The man with the chainsaw growls and shakes his weapon but to no avail. He got the reaction he wanted out of us the first time, and now we're onto something far more frightening —ourselves.

"*Jonas*—" I call out, and he looks up at me with a steady gaze as if he were calculating how to burst right through me, and then a thought occurs to me. "Oh my God." I straighten as I come to an epiphany. "You rigged the scaffolding, didn't you?"

He looks to Stella, and they exchange a steely glance.

"You wanted Hunter out of the picture—but why? You had Stella. Hunter didn't."

Stella lets out a riotous groan, and the man with the chainsaw tosses a hand in the air in exasperation.

"Aw, come on," the masked man growls. "I'm supposed to be the scary one here," he whines, and yet we continue to dismiss him.

Stella takes a few brazen steps my way. "He didn't have a problem with Hunter. *I* did." The baby in her arms whimpers, and she takes a moment to soothe him. "Hunter was supposed to give me enough money to live off, and instead, I was stuck at that dive bar dancing for dollars. You think I wanted to twirl around that pole all night? But Hunter didn't care. All he wanted was to take my son away from me. He wanted him. He was trying to steal him away."

I shake my head in disbelief. "I'm his good friend, and I didn't even know he had a kid. That can't be true," I howl over the whirl of the chainsaw.

Jonas snatches her by the elbow a moment. "I told you he wasn't out to get you. You're paranoid, and you have been ever since you had the baby."

"*Enough!*" Stella raises her foot and shoves it into his stomach before whipping past me and out of sight.

I'm about to dash after her when my feet are knocked out from underneath me. The zombie doll goes flying, and my hands slap down over the ground before I inadvertently kiss damp Honey Hollow soil. I scamper to my knees as Jonas tries to leap over me, and I reach up and grab ahold of the bottom of his jeans.

Jonas falls to the side, knocking down the man in the hockey mask with him. The chainsaw bounces wildly behind them as I scramble to my feet.

And just as I'm about to hightail it out of there, Jonas snatches up the roaring weapon and jabs it my way.

"Don't move!" he shouts at the top of his lungs, and every cell in my body is suddenly immobilized. "This isn't about you. Leave us alone. Stella needs help. She's been a different person ever since she had the kid."

"You've been with her as long as she's been with Hunter? I don't get it. How did that not strain your relationship? You must really love your girlfriend."

"*Girlfriend*?" His head ticks back as if I threw him for a loop. "Stella's not my girlfriend. She's my sister. I'm trying to get her the help she needs."

It's as if time stands still, and this entire night turns on its ear once again.

"You're trying to help her. She's not well." I shake my head. "You didn't kill Hunter, did you?"

The man in the hockey mask takes a swipe at Jonas, and he swings the weapon the man's direction. A part of me says run—and another far more logical part says he can outrun me even with a chainsaw in his hands.

I snatch the zombie doll off the ground and toss it in the air at him, and he slices its head off without hesitation. The man with the hockey mask knocks the chainsaw out of his hand and wrestles him to the ground. As much as my feet are twitching to bolt, those handcuffs Keelie gifted me catch the light, and an idea springs to life. Perhaps not a good one—in fact, one that can backfire spectacularly, but I pluck the handcuffs free and fall to my knees.

"What the hell are you doing, lady?" A muffled cry comes from our masked friend.

"This is a citizen's arrest!" I bark over the roar of the motor. Jonas continues to struggle, but he's effectively pinned to the ground. It takes two tries to leash his left wrist with the cuff. "Get his hands together!" I scream at the masked man, but Jonas is working hard to overpower him, and I don't have another moment to think about it. Instead, I cuff his wrist to the man in the mask and run like hell.

The maze goes on forever, spookier, darker, and with no sign of that useless squirrel. Instead, I wise up and follow a couple of screaming teenagers right out the exit. My feet stumble to a halt as I pant into the night while surveying the landscape.

To my right sits the open pumpkin field, to my left a midway with games and an entire legion of large round barrels filled with water. Apples bob lightly along the surface as they wait patiently for the nighttime festivities to fully commence. The apple bobbing competition is the one that crowns the night. It's a long-standing tradition that the McMurrys enjoy right along with their patrons.

A glowing beam of light twitches near the base of those apple barrels, and I can't help but give a weak smile as I spot my furry friend. It seems to tick its head for me to follow it as it scampers over to a mob of people in the thick of the midway and, low and behold, leaning on a post, I spot a head of long, dark hair, that curvy body. The sequin of her bodysuit gives her away like a disco ball spraying out a spasm of light in our dimly lit world.

Every muscle in my body propels me in that direction, and before Stella can bolt I'm on her. The child isn't anywhere in sight, and my heart thumps wildly, almost afraid to see what she's done.

Stella makes a run toward the barrels, and I'm right on her tail.

"You killed Hunter!" I scream up over the music, incensed that she had gotten away with it for so long.

Stella stops cold next to a barrel, her wild pants pumping from her in long, white plumes.

"He wanted to take Travis away from me. I was just some disgusting breeding factory to him."

"Not true. Hunter would never look at another human being that way. Especially not the mother of his child."

"He looked at me that way." A dark laugh strums from her as her eyes glisten like shards. Stella looks every bit like a woman unmoored. "He thought I was trash because of what I did for a living. Sure, it was great when he first met me, but once I had the baby, he didn't think I was fit enough to raise it."

"Is that why he needed so much money? He was giving it all to you?" I ask as I continue to cautiously inch my way toward her.

"*Ha!*" she belts it out into the night. "He wasn't giving it all to me. He was giving it to a fancy lawyer in Ashford. He was trying to get full custody. He wanted me permanently out of the picture. I had to take things into my own hands and make sure it was him who never got to raise our son."

My gut wrenches just hearing it. "You didn't want to shoot him, did you?"

A high-pitched laugh escapes her. "No, I didn't. I wanted to smash his skull in!" she riots into my face. "I went to that site he was working on early that morning. Sun wasn't even up. I hauled those bags of concrete mix up that scaffolding myself. My damn brother wouldn't help me." Her gaze disappears past me. "I had to do everything myself."

"They must have weighed seventy pounds apiece." And there were three.

She glowers over at me. "You'd be surprised what a mother would do for her son. It gives you supernatural strength just when you need it most."

"I can imagine." I come in so close I can reach out and touch her. "They'll go easy on you," I whisper. "Jonas said you've been having trouble since you've had the baby. I'm sure they'll give you a top-notch psychologist who can help you out."

Her eyes widen to the size of twin moons. "I'm not going to prison. I've killed once, and I'm not afraid to do it again." She glances to my neck a moment. "If I had a gun, I'd kill you. I'm sorry this won't be as quick."

In the blink of an eye my entire head is submerged beneath the water as she struggles to hold me under. I buck and seize as I wriggle my way back to the surface, catching an enormous breath as soon as I hit air.

Stella digs her knee into the back of mine, and I collapse toward the barrel once again. "You little bitch," she roars as she dunks me under so fast so hard it feels as if she has a bionic grip over me. Stella is right. She's got supernatural strength right when she needs it most. But so do I.

My elbow flies back into her gut, and she doubles over, loosening her hold over me long enough for me to rise back out, gasping and sputtering.

Stella yanks me back by the hair and tries to throw a punch at me, but I duck right out of her line of fire.

"Freeze! Hands up!" a voice thunders from behind, but Stella doesn't bother with protocol. Instead, she growls like a lioness, and I'm right back in that water, her body pressed over mine, heavy as if a building were lying over me.

The pressure releases, and I cork to the surface, only to find Stella being plucked off of me by none other than Noah Fox.

"No—" I struggle to say his name as the entire vicinity fills with men in uniform. Noah hands Stella off to the sheriffs before speeding my way.

"*Lottie.*" He runs his lips over mine, holding me tight as my arms collapse over him. "Are you all right? I need to get you to the hospital—make sure she didn't hurt you."

"I'm all right," I pant as if I just ran the circumference of the planet. "She didn't hurt me. I promise I'm fine." I cling to Noah as if he were a life raft, and he is. "Stella killed Hunter. She confessed to the whole thing. Where's the baby? Where's Hunter's son?" I struggle to crane my neck past him. I'm so exhausted I can hardly hold myself up.

"He's fine." Noah brushes his thumbs over my cheeks. "She handed him off to Micheline just a little while ago. Bear told me." Noah searches my features with his eyes as if it were the first time he was seeing me. "All that matters to me is you, Lottie. You're all I care about. You came into my life and upturned everything I thought I knew. All of those things I swore I'd never feel again, those things that I forbid myself from feeling—you didn't give me any damn choice. I'm yours, Lottie Kenzie Lemon, and every day without you is miserable. I need you in my life. I need you by my side. I've fallen hard for you, Lottie. Please tell me that you feel the same or I'll go insane."

A laugh bubbles from my throat as I bear hard into his pine green eyes. "*Yes*. I do feel the same." The world around us feels as if it slows down, as if all of time stands still just for the two of us. "I'm falling for you, Noah—and, I'm afraid." My affect falls flat as I spill that singular truth that I wish never crested my lips.

A pained smile expands across his gorgeous face. "Don't be. We're in this together. Through thick and thin."

"I'm pretty sure we've seen our fair share of thick." I bite down over my bottom lip. "Or is it thin that we've seen? Sorry, my head's a bit fuzzy." I tuck a wet lock of hair behind my ear.

Noah tips his head back, those glowing green eyes never leaving mine. "I don't know if it's thick or thin, but I do know one thing for sure. I'm never letting anything petty get between us ever again. Everett called the other night and let me know that the two of you were just friends. He says he's happy for me, for us. He doesn't want me to screw it up."

I cock my head playfully. "Neither do I."

"That makes three of us." His dimples ignite as he bows in for a kiss. Noah crashes his lips to mine, and we declare exactly how we feel for one another in front of every ghost and goblin, every vampire and werewolf Honey Hollow has to offer.

Noah blesses me with soft pecking kisses before pulling back to get a better look at me. His eyes ride down over my costume, and he growls with approval.

"I fully authorize you to conduct a pat-down any and every time you feel like it, Officer Lemon."

A naughty grin twitches over my lips. "Don't you worry, Detective Fox. I plan on conducting a thorough investigation of your person. I promise to leave no stone unturned." My hand glides over his chest like a threat. "I suggest you obey my authority and get those lips back to mine right this minute."

A dark laugh rumbles in his chest. "Yes, ma'am."

And he does as he's told.

*H*alloween in Honey Hollow has always been filled with its fair share of terrors, but on that night, there was also a genuine relief that Hunter Fisher's killer had finally been brought to justice. Stella was arrested and is currently awaiting trial. Jonas was booked as an accomplice, and Everett said that although he was a party to aiding and abetting a murderer, that because of the circumstances the legal system wouldn't go tough on him. Stella is getting the help she needs for her paranoia, and it was brought to light that a part of that paranoia was actually triggered from the birth itself. Baby Travis is with Bear's mother, and no one is more delighted to have an infant in her care than she is. In fact, in light of the new circumstances, we've decided to host a celebration of life party for Hunter, and I insisted on hosting it at the bakery. Keelie had the chefs prepare sandwiches while I baked an entire litany of every dessert I know that Hunter loved—and he loved them all.

The crowd is small, but the atmosphere is cheery.

The surprise Nell and Keelie had been hinting at ever since the grand opening arrived last night just in time for the celebration, and Bear and his crew worked well into the early hours of the morning to install it. When I arrived, they were just leaving, and I about had a heart attack seeing them here. Bear was the one who got to show it to me—and as soon as he flipped the switch, my heart burst like a piñata filled with love. It's an extension of that glorious oak tree staking claim in the middle of the honey pot with its branches elongating like tendrils all throughout the café portion of the Cutie Pie Bakery and Cakery. I called both Keelie and Nell and cried over the phone as I thanked them. Each branch is carefully entwined with twinkle lights, and it adds a flair of magic to this already enchanted piece of Honey Hollow.

Noah holds me by the waist as Bear heads our way.

"You've got a keeper," he scowls at Noah. "And you'd better keep her, because if you ever let her go, I'm taking her back." He winks my way.

"You're hilarious." I can't help but tease him. I've made it more than clear to Bear that the door to any intimate relationship between us is forever closed. "So tell us, Bear"—I pause to glance to Noah who offers a confirming nod—"was it Hunter that was behind all of those garage robberies?"

Bear takes a breath and sweeps his eyes over the vicinity. "All right. I found a bunch of crap in his truck one day, and he may have implicated himself." He closes his eyes, his entire body sagging with remorse. "He was pawning stuff and giving the money to Stella. She kept threatening to leave with the kid, and she had Hunter where she wanted him. The poor guy didn't see a way out."

Noah groans, "So, he was never trying to sue for full custody?"

"Nope." Bear gives a wistful shake of the head. "In fact, I was the one who threatened her with it. And that's exactly why I was so angry with myself when I saw him lying there in the alley. I had my suspicions it might have been her or someone connected to her."

I gasp at the revelation. "Bear! You should have turned her in. We could have avoided this entire mess."

"I know, I know. But Hunter made me swear on his mother's grave that I wouldn't do a thing to cause trouble in her life no matter what happened. I think he knew he was staring down the barrel of a gun. And, in the end, he did just that." Bear drops his gaze to the floor before slapping the back of his neck, something he usually does when he's trying to hide his emotions. "Excuse me. I think I need to step outside for a minute."

"Don't be too hard on yourself," I say, catching him by the wrist. "Hunter would never want that. And neither do I."

A soft moment bounces between us like a truce, and Bear gives a sheepish smile before heading out the door.

Nell steps over, her silver hair catching the twinkle lights from above and it gives her the ethereal glow of an angel.

"Well done, my dear." She cups my cheeks with her sweet wrinkled fingers and presses a kiss to my cheek. "Now when my time comes, don't you dare let them host one of those depressing tearjerkers down in the church's rec room. I fully expect the entire lot of you to celebrate my life."

I shudder against Noah at the thought. "Nell! Don't talk like that. You're miles away from going anywhere." She may not be, but it certainly felt like the right thing to say. "Besides, I need you." I look right into her crystal blue eyes when I say it, and they swell with tears in an instant. "Thank you again for this beautiful work of art." I glance up to the glowing branches above us. "It makes me feel like a princess every time I see it. It also makes me feel like family."

"Oh, Lottie, you are a princess." She offers my cheek a hearty pinch. "And I certainly love you as my own family." Her mouth remains open as if she were about to add something to it, but she lets out a sigh instead. "I'm afraid I'm through for the night. Each time you look at those branches, I want you to know that you are a part of my family tree." There's a pained look in her eyes, and I can't quite pinpoint why. Most likely because she feels sorry for me, for the way my journey in this life began on that cold cement floor of the firehouse. "Thank you for having me." She brushes another precious kiss to my cheek before threading her way back toward the Honey Pot.

I turn to Noah. "That was a little strange. Didn't you think so?"

But before he can say anything, Keelie bounds over with Lainey, and the two of them pull me in for a quick embrace, temporarily breaking the hold Noah has on me.

Lainey wags a finger in my face. "You are not allowed to scare us like that again. No more running toward danger."

Keelie leans in. "And no more dead bodies," she whispers. "It's not a good look on you. I'm just saying."

The four of us share a morbid laugh as Everett heads in this direction. I can't help but note Collette Jenner scuttling alongside him like a parasite he can't quite get rid of. Okay, so parasite is a bit harsh, but I've scanned my entire lexicon, and that's the best fit I could come up with on such short notice.

Collette rolls her eyes. "I will admit, those cupcakes at the Fall-O-Ween Fest were to die for. I must have eaten ten if I didn't eat thirty."

"Thank you." I'm taken aback by her kind words, and suddenly she's looking less parasite and a bit more human.

Lainey leans in. "Molly said every last one of them disappeared before eight o'clock."

Keelie bounces the curls off her shoulder. "In fact, they were so well sought-after that the calls have been pouring into the Cutie Pie for more large orders."

"They have," I affirm as I look back to Collette. "Say, don't you work for Endeavor PR?"

Her head ticks back a notch. "Everyone knows I work for the best PR company in the country." She smirks up at Everett. "I only go after the best in life."

I clear my throat as she tries to dive her mouth over his. "Anyway, they called this morning and asked if I'd cater the desserts for an awards ceremony they're having next week at the Evergreen Manor."

"VIP awards," she corrects. "And yes, Everett and I will be there with bells on. He's already promised to be my official plus one." She offers a strangulating hug to his arm, but Everett seems unmoved by her psychotic advances. "Oh, and, by the way, my boss is into pumpkin spice everything. Make it worth his while. You don't want to see him unhappy."

"Duly noted and I guess I'll see you there."

Everett gives an approving nod my way. "Everything looks great tonight. You did good, Lemon."

Lainey jumps beside me. "My sister always does good."

Noah tucks a kiss to my cheek. "That she does." He picks up my hand and gives it a squeeze. "I've got some good news for you." Noah sheds that signature cocky grin, and my stomach bisects with heat. "You got the rental house. My realtor called and said you can pick up the keys as soon as you're ready."

"I got the house!" I shout so loud the room breaks out into a cheer right along with me. I'm so excited, I wrap my entire body around Noah's as he spins me gently, and I'm dizzy with happiness, dizzy from the way he makes me feel.

He lands me back on my feet, and both Keelie and Lainey slap me five.

Collette snickers. "That's just dandy. It looks as if Lottie is off the market." She bats her lashes up at Everett. "I'm ready to get off the market myself, big boy. You got any idea of who can fit the bill?" Collette gives his tie a light tug, and it's all I can do not to groan in disapproval.

"No"—he gently removes her hand from his tie—"I don't." He sheds his killer grin—it's such a rare sighting that every girl in the room pauses to observe it. "But I do have some good news of my own that you might like." He winks her way before turning his attention to Noah and me. "I'm moving myself. It looks like I'm heading to Honey Hollow."

"*What?*" both Collette and I cry in unison.

"That's right. Being here reminded me of how much I hate living in the city. And I happened to get a great deal on a house myself. I paid cash in full, and they didn't argue. It's mine now. I'm a full-fledged homeowner."

"Congratulations!" we all shout at the top of our lungs.

The whooping dies down, and Noah gives his stepbrother a handshake. "So, where exactly will you be? I need to know what street to avoid." A grin spreads wide over his face as we laugh it off.

"Country Cottage Road."

"What?" Noah balks. "Really? I don't remember seeing a house for sale in the neighborhood."

"It wasn't. I liked the blue house we toured that day, and when Lottie didn't want it, I made my move. Let's just say the old owners were more than happy with how things worked out."

"We're going to be neighbors!" I give Everett a spontaneous hug and note that Noah is slower to congratulate him this time.

"Great." Noah's head bobs with an unconvincing nod. "Just great."

"It will be great." Everett tips his head back as the two of them stare one another down for a moment.

"It will be very great," I say, pulling Noah in close. "We're all turning a new leaf."

Collette wraps herself around Everett like a suckerfish. "To *new leaves!*"

"To new leaves," we chant back.

Things will undoubtedly be different with our new living arrangements, but I'm determined to make it work. After all, I couldn't imagine my life without either of them in it.

A gray ball of fur hops up onto the brownie tray, and I gasp as my entire body solidifies.

Noah leans in. "Everything okay?"

"Everything is just fine." My head turns toward him, but my eyes never stray from that bushy-tailed visitor.

Everett steps over and points down to the brownie bar as if acknowledging what I see, and I give a little nod. He doesn't hesitate picking up a dark fudge brownie and holding it over his open palm against the table. The tiny woodland spectral hops right over and does its best to nibble. I can't help but coo at the sight and offer an approving nod as Everett and I share a warm smile.

The party dwindles down, and Noah helps me close up shop long after everyone has gone home.

He pulls me into his strong arms as we step outside into the brisk autumn night and looks lovingly into my eyes. "It's official. I belong to you." He tucks a kiss to the nape of my neck. "We're official," he says, swaying back to get a better look at me.

"We're official?"

"That's right. I hope it doesn't sound weird for you to call me your boyfriend. I already called my stepbrother and told him all about my new girlfriend."

"You did? Will I like her when I meet her?" I can't help but tease him, and we share a warm laugh.

"You can't help but love her." His features smooth out as he says the L word, and my heart drums wildly right into my ears.

"You really called Everett?"

He nods, affirming the fact.

"You're a sneak. I love that." There's that L word again, and I suppose it means something even minutely that we both used it back to back. *Love.* That word circles my mind. It begs to be redirected toward him, but I'm afraid I'll scare him off if I do. And just like that, I shake the thought right out of my head. "You know what? I think I—"

Noah gently muzzles me with a lingering, sugar sweet kiss before pulling back with sleepy eyes.

"I want to say it first," he whispers right over my lips. "I need you to hear me say it. I want it to sink into your bones." He pulls back and gazes tenderly into my eyes. "I think I love you, Lottie Lemon. In fact, I know I do."

My lips part as I try my hardest to memorize this moment. "I love you, too, Noah. I do."

The moon shines a spotlight over us as if it were the final scene in some romantic black and white movie. But it's not the final scene for Noah and me. The two of us have just begun.

That crooked grin begins to bloom on his face once again, his eyes never leaving mine.

Noah gently tucks a stray lock behind my ear. "I have a feeling I've just entered into the best season of my life. And I predict that with you by my side every season thereafter will be better and better."

"They never stop getting better?" I bite down over a smile.

"With you in my life, that would be impossible. We're a team, Lottie. And we're building a solid foundation. No pretense, no secrets—filled with honesty and communication."

Noah lands his oven-hot mouth over mine, and we indulge in something richer, far more decadent and sweeter than anything I could whip up in the kitchen. Noah and I are building a solid foundation. No pretense, no secrets—filled with honesty and communication. But deep down, I know for a fact there is plenty of pretense involved. I am rife with secrets. I am not filled with honesty, not entirely—especially when it comes to my supernatural tendencies. And I will most certainly not communicate a single word about them. It's bad enough I've spilled the supernatural beans to Everett.

No, Noah Fox can never be apprised of that paranormal part of my life.

And because of this, there will always be a thorny secret nestled between us, creating a barrier, a buffer that will forever stand between us.

It's a division, and everyone knows a house divided cannot stand.

But Noah and I are different.

Aren't we?

And I wonder.

ADDISON MOORE

MURDER
IN THE MIX

Toxic Apple
Turnovers

BOOK DESCRIPTION

*This book takes place a bit later in the Murder in the Mix series but can still be enjoyed as an independent mystery. Happy reading!

My name is Lottie Lemon, and I see dead people. Okay, so rarely do I see dead people. Mostly I see furry creatures of the dearly departed variety, who have come back from the other side to warn me of their previous owner's impending doom.

Fall is in the air, the weather is crisp, the leaves are golden, and the atmosphere is ripe for murder. It's the first catering event of the season and I'm blindsided by what transpires at the outlandish party. Not only that, but I stumble upon the one person I would never want to see facedown in a flowerbed. And to top it all off, something wicked has rolled into Honey Hollow, and every dead spirit I have ever encountered is back to help me fight it.

∾

Lottie Lemon has a brand new bakery to tend to, a budding romance with perhaps one too many suitors, and she has the supernatural ability to see dead pets—which are always harbingers for ominous things to come. Throw in the occasional ghost of the human variety, a string of murders, and her insatiable thirst for justice, and you'll have more chaos than you know what to do with.

Living in the small town of Honey Hollow can be murder.

$\mathcal{M}$y name is Lottie Lemon, and I see dead people. Mostly I see furry creatures who have crossed the great divide, but right now I don't see anything. I'm being hand-fed one of my scrumptious light and crunchy mini apple turnovers, and it just so happens that its sweet, yummy goodness has blinded me to the world.

"*Mmm*," I moan right at Noah who happens to be the one helping me indulge in this little bit of heaven.

"Have another," he says with his lids hooded low, his voice dropping down one seductive octave.

Noah and I used to date pretty hot and heavy, but about six months back, I discovered he had a wife stashed away in another state. Technically, it was his wife hunting him down at my bakery, the Cutie Pie Bakery and Cakery, that tipped me off.

Noah is tall, has impossibly dark hair that turns red at the tips in the sun, and is hostilely handsome. He also happens to be one of the lead homicide detectives down at the Ashford County Sheriff's Department.

"Is this a party anyone can join?" a gruff and rough voice

147

booms from behind, and both Noah and I turn to find Judge Essex Everett Baxter, my official plus one—sort of.

"Get over here, Everett." I'm quick to motion this way as I hand him one of my crispy apple turnovers.

We're standing in the kitchen of my mother's spectacularly haunted bed and breakfast. She bought the place when my father died a little over a decade ago and renovated it to perfection.

The B&B is booked into the foreseeable future—but that has very little to do with my mother's hospitality skills and far more to do with the ghosts. You see, last January it was highly rumored that this place was haunted and, truth be told, it is. First, there was the ghost of a bear that started the *boo-ha-ha*, but eventually, I found a couple of willing spooks to fill the position permanently—Greer Giles, a girl in her mid-twenties who was murdered last winter, and her two-hundred-year-old boy toy, Winslow Decker, a farmer from yesteryear who is as adorable as he is frightening.

Greer couldn't be happier with her shiny new specter of a beau. And a few months back, they adopted a little girl named Azalea, Lea for short.

Lea is a mean axe-wielding six-year-old with a penchant for vengeance due to the fact her family was slain right over these grounds generations ago. But she's since toned down her scare tactics a bit and helps out with the rattling of bookcases and the misplacing of objects here and there.

Suffice it to say, my mother has profited nicely off the dead. She runs excursions right here at the B&B on the regular, which she's dubbed the Haunted Honey Hollow Tours, at eighty bucks a pop. And once her victims are through here, she sends them my way to the bakery for what she's dubbed as The Last Thing They Ate Tour.

Yes, the rumors are true. There has been a murder in Honey Hollow every month for the last solid year, and each and every time, one of my baked goods has been loosely connected. That thought alone makes me shudder.

I hand-feed Everett one of my delectable apple turnovers, with the light and crispy pastry dough, a gentle rubbing of turbinado sugar on top, and only the freshest apples from the local orchard.

"*Lemon,*" he moans hard.

I've heard that guttural evocation of my surname before, but it's been in far more intimate settings. Everett and I have been together ever since Noah and I abruptly broke things off. And now that Noah's divorce is official, it was Everett who suggested that Noah and I date once again just to see if it's still a direction my heart wants to pursue or if, in fact, it's time to give that old relationship its proper closure.

Closure is something Noah and I didn't get around to. As soon as his wife, Britney Fox, sauntered her blonde bombshell self into Honey Hollow, I pretty much gave Noah the boot.

Everett nods. "This is perfection, and so are you." He lands a simple kiss to my lips. "In fact, you taste sweeter."

I bite down hard on the inside of my cheek to keep from giggling like a schoolgirl.

Essex Everett Baxter goes by his middle name, Everett, to the masses, and Essex to the hordes of women he's bedded. I'm not sure why, but Everett isn't all too thrilled with his formal moniker, and yet it's been reserved as sort of a door prize for the women he's done the mattress mambo with—his mother and sister withstanding, seeing that they've called him that since birth.

Everett, too, is tall, dark, and alarmingly handsome, but he's a bit more stoic than Noah, slow to smile, and those Caribbean blue eyes are as sexy as is his demeanor. No matter where he is, females within the vicinity crane their necks just to get a better look at him. I've witnessed entire herds of women gasping at the mere sight of him, fanning themselves as he walks by. He's a lean, mean, well-oiled, mouthwatering machine that has the capability to pop ovaries at a single glance.

We met in his courtroom last fall where I was a defendant and he wisely sided with me for the judicial win.

Noah gently spins me around until I'm once again facing him. "You are perfection. And that's exactly why I'm so thrilled to be heading out on an official date with you this evening."

I glance to Everett and give a wry smile. "It is a date." I nod into the admission. "I asked Noah what he wanted for his birthday and this was all he came up with." Noah's birthday was last month, but things officially went sideways, so I thought we should have a do-over. And when I asked what he wanted most, his answer was me. Noah has been trying to diligently win me back ever since the marital mishap.

"Lottie?" My mother bounces into the kitchen of the B&B. The kitchen itself was recently renovated with an enormous gorgeous marble island and a plethora of white cabinetry dotted with brushed gold fixtures. As of right now, every inch of this island is covered with platters of my sweet treats ready to be delivered to the next room over where someone has rented out the conservatory for a ritzy engagement party.

My mother rolls her eyes at the sight of the three of us. "Lottie, please, stop playing with these boys—handsome as they might be." She gives a husky laugh as she bats her lashes at them. Miranda Lemon, the sweet angel that adopted me twenty-seven years ago, is a gorgeous woman who looks far younger than her biological age allows. She wears her blonde hair in curls to her shoulders, has high-cut cheeks that would make any model envious, and a smile that never leaves her lips. "Your sisters are here. They can help deliver all these goodies to the dessert table. The guests have all arrived at the very same time. It's a mob out there. Good thing the music is playing and the decorations are all in place. That Amanda Wellington sure knows how to throw a party."

"Did I hear my name?" A saucy little redhead in a hot pink dress and matching heels saunters in. Amanda is just as successful as she is beautiful. Not only is she a realtor at Redwood Realty, but she has a burgeoning party planning business, Make it Happen, that's taken off like a rocket. "I hope you're saying good things." She winks my way as she pops a mini apple turnover into her mouth and moans. "Oh, Lottie, you've outdone yourself. I just know the future bride and groom will love this. But we need to get these to the table."

My sisters, Lainey and Meg, zip into the room. Lainey is the head librarian at the Honey Hollow Library and recently married her longtime love, Forest Donovan, in July. We share the same caramel-colored long wavy hair and hazel eyes.

When I was young, I used to think since we looked so much alike that my parents were mistaken about my adoption.

And Meg is a blonde beauty who dyes her luscious locks a deep onyx, and when contrasted to her ice blue eyes, it's quite a striking look. She teaches strippers how to shake their stuff down in Leeds. For years, she used to be a female wrestler in Las Vegas, but she's been home since last spring.

She's officially in l-o-v-e with Hook Redwood (Amanda's boss) who happens to run his father's realty empire, Redwood Realty.

Lainey giggles as she glides on over. Lainey has essentially been walking on air ever since she came back from her honeymoon. "Did you get the invite, too?"

"What invite?"

She inches back as if affronted. "To the engagement. Meg and I both got one. Everyone did. It's some secret party that nobody knows the details to."

Mom nods as she does her best to quickly swallow the turnover in her mouth. "Hey? Maybe this is one of those murder mystery parties?" She waggles her brows like this would be a good thing—lest she forgets where she is and who I am.

Meg gags on a laugh. "It's always a murder mystery party with Lottie around."

The room breaks out into a warm laugh on behalf of both the dead and me.

It's true. In the last year alone, I've found twelve murder victims. *And* thanks to the help of those that come back from the other side, I've helped track down the killers, too.

I'm not clairvoyant, and I'm not a medium—I'm not any of those things. I'm transmundane, further classified as supersensual, which means I can essentially see the dead. When the dead first started appearing to me—it's almost always an adorable furry creature that has long since crossed that rainbow bridge—they would come back for someone they had a strong adoration for before they passed—usually their old owner—and almost always their earthly reprisal was a harbinger for that very person.

It used to mean nothing more than a scraped knee or a sprained ankle at best, but as of late it has consistently meant death. Only Noah and Everett are aware of my deep, dark secret—with the exception of my birth mother, Carlotta, who also shares the gift, or curse as it were.

"I don't remember getting an invitation," I say, sliding a platter of turnovers to my sisters and one to Amanda, too.

"I got one." Everett's brows pinch in the middle. "And you?" He looks to Noah.

Everett and Noah used to be stepbrothers back in high school when Noah's father married and proficiently financially ripped off Everett's mother. But they've since divorced and Everett's wealthy mother has recovered nicely. Noah and Everett? Not so much.

Noah gives a guilty look my way. "I did. But for the record, I'd much rather go out with you, Lottie. Are we still on for Mangias and a movie?"

Mangias is our favorite Italian restaurant, and we happen to be addicted to their pizza. I know for a fact we're about to pick up a pizza on the way back to his place tonight, where coinciden-tally the movie will take place as well.

"Yeah, sure." I shrug up at Everett. "I don't see why not, seeing that I'm not invited to this event. I'm sorry, Everett. I hate leaving you here."

"I'll be fine," he's quick to answer. "And I'll be home soon, so whenever your pizza party wraps up, head over to my place and I'll show you what a real good time looks like between two consenting adults."

Noah shakes his head. "As opposed to the adolescent good time I'll be showing her?"

Everett ticks his head to the side. "You said it, not me."

I hand them each a platter, and my mother and I grab the last two. Each mini apple turnover sits nestled in a pristine white pastry cup, and they look as elegant and formal as the occasion requires.

"Let's get these goodies next door," I say.

I'm the first one out into the generous foyer of the B&B, and just as I'm about to head to the conservatory, I spot Amanda in what appears to be a heated conversation with a blonde and a short brunette on stilts.

Everett leans in. "Everything okay?"

"Yes," I say, nudging him with my shoulder. "Let's get these put away."

In truth, I was expecting to see the ghost of Greer Giles, or Winslow, or Lea—or any of the other ghosts that have visited me in the last twelve months.

A very odd occurrence happened at the end of last month. Every single poltergeist that's haunted me in the last year showed up on my front porch. And Nell, my grandmother who was one of them, warned me that something very sinister was coming to Honey Hollow. And then, just like that, they all up and disap-peared. It was unnerving to say the least. I've been on edge ever since. I've made an effort to grill Greer about it, but each time I spoke about it she up and disappeared.

My mother leads the way to the conservatory, and Everett is right on her heels. I'm about to mobilize myself when a white-feathered bird dives right in front of me, and I nearly drop my turnovers onto the floor.

"*Whoa.*" Noah helps stabilize my tray with his. "You almost lost them there."

The bird zips by again, short and adorably plump, and it's not until it lands square on Noah's head do I see it's a magical looking snow owl.

"Oh my goodness." I take a step back with a laugh caught in my throat. "It must have gotten in through the side entry. My mother had that thing open for hours as they hauled in all of those massive decorations. Whoever is getting engaged today has spent some serious cash on this event." It's true. Crystal chandeliers in a smoky gray have been installed, white couches were brought in, and the entire conservatory is dripping with crystal and laden with blush pink roses. It's a feast for the senses, with the shimmer and heavenly shine, and now my mini turnovers will provide the piece de résistance. I came by earlier and witnessed the entire spectacle taking shape.

"What got in?" Noah ticks his head to the side. "I'd better put this down. It feels like I've got a brick sitting on my head." He ticks his head again, but the bird remains steady.

"More like an owl—a gorgeous snow owl with white and gray plumage and a dusting of gold around its bright yellow eyes. I bet he's a part of this circus next door and he got away from his handler. Let's get to the conservatory and get him where he belongs."

The beautiful beast tips his head back and lets out a bark-like howl. "I don't belong to the circus. I belong to one who will soon be dead." He flies off toward the ceiling, and a breath gets caught in my throat.

"Who?" I shout out after him, and he echoes the word until he disappears.

"Lottie?" Noah's dimples press in, no smile. "You saw another one, didn't you?"

"Yes, I did." My heart thumps clear into my chest.

"Someone is going to die," Noah says, looking to the conservatory with an apprehensive stare.

"Yes, Noah, there's going to be a murder in Honey Hollow tonight. And someone is going to die."

*N*oah and I speed into the conservatory, and no sooner do we put down our platters than the lights flicker on and off.

The entire room is bejeweled in the aforementioned crystal. It's cut shimmering glass everywhere you look, and the wall-to-wall guests all look equally as opulent.

I feel a little silly in my sweater and jeans with my cozy UGG boots adorning my feet in comparison to all the sexy heels prattling about. But in my defense, it's September in Honey Hollow, and our little corner of Vermont is notorious for turning into a virtual autumn wonderland overnight. The temperatures are already dipping into the low fifties during the day and the low forties at night. The sugar maples, oaks, liquid ambers, and sweetgum trees have already turned stunning shades of orange, gold, and bright crimson.

I spot Mayor Nash, my recently revealed biological father, having cocktails with Carlotta Sawyer, my recently revealed biological mother. Carlotta is supersensual like me, and at the moment that adorable fuzzy little owl just rematerialized on Mayor Nash's shoulder and it looks as if Carlotta is openly having a conversation with it.

Carlotta looks exactly like me if you added sixteen years and a couple of gray hairs. I see some resemblance of myself in Mayor Nash, too, but nothing to write home about.

Amanda Wellington saunters back into the room, dabbing her pinkies into her eyes as if she were drying up tears, and I watch as the other girls she was with melt into the crowd as well. Amanda makes her way to Cormack, and I can't help but frown.

Cormack Featherby is the ex-girlfriend of both Noah and Everett. She dated them both back in high school. Technically, she dated Everett first, then Noah swept her off her cheating feet and she left one stepbrother for the other, creating a rift in their relationship that has never quite recovered.

Cormack is an impossibly thin blonde with celadon green eyes and a wardrobe purchased straight off the runaways of Milan. She comes from money, a trust fund baby at her finest, which might explain why I haven't seen her work a day in her life. Unless, of course, you count her constant badgering to get Noah back as an amusing form of employment. In that case, she has a full-time job with no pay and no benefits. Noah isn't interested in getting back together with Cormack, not now, not ever.

She extends her left hand for inspection, and Amanda chortles as she looks down at the massive hunk of pressed carbon. And she should laugh at the delusion taking place before her. Cormack believes she's engaged to Noah. She's not. Last summer, she stumbled upon a ring in Noah's closet that he bought for me and, of course, she thought it was for her. I don't see why not. The entire planet revolves around her.

"There's your fiancée." I nudge Noah in the ribs. "She didn't happen to have an owl as a pet, did she?" Here's hoping.

Okay, so I don't wish a homicide on anyone, but let's call a spade a spade—I'm not a member of the Cormack Featherby Fan Club either.

"Of course, she's here." Noah sighs. Cormack has been a proficient stalker of his for the better part of the year. Noah leans in. "Hey, isn't that Landon?" He nods to her left and, sure as sunshine, there's another Featherby making an unwanted appearance— Cormack's baby sister. Noah sucks in a quick breath. "Those are Cormack's parents behind her. And that's her brother talking to Everett."

"*Huh,*" I muse as I take in the entire primped and polished Featherby clan. Honestly, they look like a walking ad campaign for Ralph Lauren. "They must be friends with the couple that's getting engaged. It's a small world, and it only seems to be getting smaller by the minute." *And snobbier*, but I leave that commentary out for now.

Cormack and Amanda begin frantically nodding to one another before Cormack slinks her way over in her pristine white lace dress, tight-fitted and short, but adorably stunning nonetheless.

"Pardon me, Lee-Lee," she says while taking Noah by the hand and sauntering away with him.

For reasons unbeknownst to me, neither Cormack nor Britney, Noah's official ex-wife, can get my name straight. I don't even bother correcting them anymore.

Speaking of Britney, I spot her wrapped in a little black dress in the corner with my newfound half-brother, Finn Nash. Britney is basically a blonde Jessica Rabbit, all va-va-voom, no thanks to her daily workout at the Swift Cycle gym she owns down the street from my bakery. She actually owns an entire chain of them and is quite the successful businesswoman. After she divorced Noah, she and my brother made their relationship official, which is a bit awkward. But, considering I didn't really grow up knowing that Finn was my brother, I don't mind all that much.

The lights go out once again—save for that ethereal owl glowing as if he has an entire solar system of stars trapped in his plumage. It used to be that I could only *see* the dead, but as my powers grew so did their abilities, and now they can not only move things in the material world, but as of late they can speak to me as well. It's a refreshing change of pace compared to the silent era of haunted days gone by.

The lights snap back on, and a giant felt sign at the front of the venue unfurls to reveal the words *Congratulations, Noah and Cormack* in large glittering letters.

"*Surprise!*" Cormack and her friends and family shout at the top of their lungs.

Amanda Wellington appears next to me. "Isn't this wonderful, Lottie? It's a surprise engagement party!"

My mouth falls open as I lock eyes with Noah—my sanity and my heart break at the lunacy exploding around us. Clearly, our date is off, too.

"It's something," I say as I shake my head. Soon enough, both Noah and Cormack are surrounded by well-wishers, and I suddenly want to be anywhere but here.

I turn to go, and Amanda catches me by the sleeve. "You have to meet my sister, Lottie. She's my new assistant, and I've told her all about your wonderful shop. The Cutie Pie Bakery and Cakery is officially the only bakery we'll refer our customers to."

Amanda flags down a petite redhead that's essentially her doppelgänger. "Hazel, meet Lottie. Lottie, this is my little sister, Hazel. She just finished up with grad school, and now she's come to work for me."

"Nice to meet you, Hazel." I shake her hand and can't help but note the adorable freckles dotting her nose and cheeks.

"I'm not working for my sister," she's quick to correct. "I guarantee in less than a year she'll be working for me. I graduated summa cum laude twice over, and I happen to hold the scholastic reins in the family. She might be able to lord over me the fact she's older than me by two years—and far more successful, but I plan on lording my degree over her head for a good long while." She gives a little wink, and Amanda laughs it up as if it were the funniest thing in the world. Truthfully, it might be, but Cormack just plucked both my funny bone and my heart out by way of her stiletto.

Everett rushes up to me, along with Meg and her boyfriend Hook.

Everett wraps a strong arm around my waist. "Let's get out of here, Lemon."

Meg grunts, her ice blue eyes set to kill. "And miss the fun? I say we start a good old-fashioned food fight. It's good to see you brought enough ammo, Lot." She glances to my poor innocent turnovers and I shudder.

"No way. I'm above that." Albeit just slightly.

The sound of an argument brewing behind me ignites, and I turn to find it's Amanda with that blonde bombshell and the brunette on stilts going at it once again. I'm about to look away when that gorgeous little owl lands smack on the brunette's head and I gasp.

I give Everett's arm a tug. "It's happening."

Meg snaps up a handful of my sweet miniature treats. "Darn tootin' it's happening."

"No, not that." I step in close to Hook. "Do not let my sister toss a single turnover into the crowd," I say as I yank Everett over a few steps. "I see a ghost! An adorable baby owl sitting right there on that brunette's head." I nod that way.

"All right." Everett gets that serious look in his eyes, the one he usually reserves for the courtroom. He walks us over to the bickering girls and is quick to hold up a hand. "I apologize for interrupting your conversation."

The tiny brunette, who is pretty to a fault but looks as if she's been injected, filled and stuffed with silicone from the chest up, brazenly gives Everett's silver tie a quick tug.

"You can interrupt me anytime, big boy. I've been watching you. I predict we'll be going home together in just under an hour. I've got plans for those blue eyes and strong hands."

The blonde bombshell groans, "Ignore her, Essex. How have you been?"

Every muscle in my body freezes when she spouts off his proper moniker. That's a dead giveaway that she's done the dirty deed with my boyfriend.

Speaking of boyfriends, I lean back to scowl at Noah who is still swimming in well-wishers. One of them is Detective Ivy Fairbanks, a leggy redhead who works alongside him down at the Ashford County Sheriff's Department. I've always suspected she's wanted more from their friendship, but as it stands she'll have to stand in line. First, behind Cormack, and then behind me.

Noah cranes his neck past her as if looking for someone, probably me. It looks as if our date has gone sideways once again. But that seems to be par for the course for the two of us.

"I'm Lottie Lemon." I look to the blonde who could pass as a body double for Marilyn Monroe. "I'm Everett's girlfriend."

"Fiancée." Everett bows into the lie. I'm not sure why he keeps perpetuating this myth. Honestly, he told his mother and sister he was engaged to some mystery woman before he ever met me, and I just so happened to fill that mystery woman's shoes. And then a few months back, his mother shoved a rock the size of Gibraltar onto my ring finger, her own mother's wedding ring, and I've been wearing it loyally ever since. I'm not really sure what else I'm supposed to do with it. Everett won't take it back, and I'm paranoid I'll lose it or it'll get stolen if I take it off for a moment. The only time I do take it off is when I'm at the bakery, and then I put it in the ground safe in my office along with the deposits ready for the bank.

"Fiancée?" Marilyn's look-alike's eyes bug out. "Allow me to introduce myself. I'm Janelle Hastings. I used to work down at the courthouse. I can't believe what I'm hearing." She turns to her brunette friend. "Connie, I would have thought he was a shoo-in to end up in your bed tonight. It looks like you missed out on the Baxter Express."

"We'll see about that." She winks. "Connie Canelli." She holds her hand out toward Everett, and he pauses a moment before shaking it. "Ha! I take it you've heard of my brothers."

Brothers? As in the Canelli brothers? Now it's me going rigid. Everyone has heard of the notorious Canelli brothers. They're essentially the mob that runs Leeds. I shudder just thinking of that seedy town south of us, and then I shudder harder at the thought of that illegal gambling ring they run—among other unsavory illegal dealings they have their shady hands in.

The owl lets out something between a hoot and a purr before disappearing into a sparkle of dust.

A lot of help he is. That is, if he's a *he*. I'll grill him on his name and gender the next time we're alone, and I have a feeling we'll be alone often. I'm just about to ask which of these lovely ladies once had an affinity for the pretty poltergeist when Cormack trots up in that lacy white number that should have given away her silly shenanigans.

"It's time, Amanda." She gives a cheeky wink as she picks up both my hand and Everett's and dances us to the middle of the cavernous room.

The lights blink on and off again, and this time another felt sign unfurls next to the first eyesore, and this one reads *Congratulations, Lolli and Essex.*

"Oh my God." All I can muster are those three words as the room breaks out into a riot of cheers around us.

Everett glances my way, his eyes wide with surprise. I have seen Everett in just about every situation, and not once has he been caught off guard the way he is now.

"Don't look at me that way. I had nothing to do with it."

"I'm not looking at you that way," he says and I follow his gaze behind me to find his mother, Eliza, and sister, Meghan, dashing over with their arms held wide.

"Congratulations!" Eliza shouts into my ear and blows out an eardrum. She's essentially another version of Everett, beautiful and cultured and all those good things. Meghan is a bit grittier, but she still bears the signature Baxter black hair and blue eyes, an intoxicating combo if ever there was one.

"Come here, sis." Meghan pulls me in and smothers me against her chest. "I just knew this day would come."

I pull free and gasp for air. "I certainly didn't expect it to come so soon." I lift my brows toward Everett.

Mom bounces over with her boyfriend, the new pastor of Honey Hollow Covenant Church, Pastor Stephen Gaines.

"Lottie Lemon!" Mom scolds playfully with tears in her eyes. "A surprise engagement party? I can't believe you managed to pull this off right under my nose!"

I glance to Cormack and frown. "Neither can I."

Noah comes up with his brother, Alex. You would think they were twins if you didn't know Alex was just a hair younger. Alex shares Noah's dark hair and serious green eyes, but he's beefier and looks as if he belongs in a heavyweight boxing ring. He's been dating my assistant, Lily, and her best friend, or should I say her *ex*-best friend, Naomi Turner. Naomi's twin sister, Keelie, is actually *my* best friend.

"Lottie"—Noah shakes his head, a sign he's filled with remorse —"I can't apologize enough."

Cormack is quick to swat him. "No apologies necessary. In fact, they've already thanked me by way of those dazzled looks on their faces. Of course, I myself put together the custom cocktails." She brays like a donkey. "The Lottie Toddy and the Gavel Buster—I threw in an extra for Essex, the Mr. Sexy Sangria. And for Noah and me, I have the Foxy on the Roxy and the *Cormapolitan*. Please feel free to enjoy! It's an open bar courtesy of Daddy."

I'd like to strangle both Cormack and her daddy right about now.

Mom accosts Everett's poor mother just as Meghan excuses

163

herself, something about needing to inhale all of my delicious desserts.

Amanda pops up again, and Pastor Gaines asks to speak with her in private.

I pull Cormack in by the elbow. "Are you *insane?*"

"Ugh," she grunts. "You hate the color scheme. I knew I should have gone with something more garish that was guaranteed to please you, but it's my special day, too, you know. Don't be selfish, Lonnie."

Her mini-me, Landon, comes by. "Congratulations, all! It wasn't that long ago we were all amassed right here for my fabulous divorce party. How I wish I had another upcoming matrimonial dissolution. Everett, you'll have to hook me up with one of your rich lawyer friends. No one under the thirty-seven percent tax bracket, I'm pleading with you." Her gaze hooks to someone in the corner, and I glance over to find a couple of men in suits—a tall bald man a little older than me perhaps, clean-shaven, an air of superiority about him, and next to him is a smooth looking dude with a dark inky suit and heavy lids.

"*Whoa.*" Landon wiggles her chest their way as if showing off her wares. "Come to mama!"

Amanda pops back up. "The one to the left is taken." She giggles. "That's Mark Russo, my fiancé."

Both Cormack and her younger sister inch back as if they were blown away by this news.

Landon chokes as she struggles to speak. "*The* Mark Russo?"

Amanda laughs. "The one and only. That's Chrissy Castaneda next to him. He works as a manager at one of Mark's plants by day, and he's a wedding singer by night. A darn good one, too. You should both consider booking him for your weddings."

"Chrissy?" I say under my breath as I inspect the man with dark curly hair and a prominent chin.

Everett leans in. "Odd name for a grown man."

Amanda waves it off. "Some nicknames never die. I've

known Chrissy forever." She makes a face as yet a third man joins them, a redheaded man who looks ready to kill in a sharp gray suit. "Chrissy is my brother's best friend." The smile glides off her face. "Excuse me." She takes off in the opposite direction.

"I'm betting that's her brother," I say, looking back at the redhead, this time seeing a family resemblance.

Noah takes a breath. "And I'm betting they don't get along."

Cormack slings her arm around his shoulder just as the music picks up in volume. "But we certainly get along, don't we, Big Boss?" She yanks him to the middle of the room and starts in on some sort of stripper moves as she shimmies up and down his body.

"I hate it when she calls him that."

Everett leans in. "You know what I'd like to hear you call me in about an hour?"

"My ex-fiancé?" I make a face.

"My first name." His lids hood dangerously low as a wicked grin twitches on his lips.

I may have called him by his spicy moniker a time or two when we've been in a compromising position, but only because the throes of passion practically demanded it.

"How about Mr. Sexy?" I'm about to lift my arms around his shoulders just as a brunette in a power suit glides between us.

"Essex, you dirty dog." She chortles, and it's not until I step around her do I realize it's Fiona Dagmeyer, a defense attorney slash ex-girlfriend of his. Okay, so girlfriend is stretching it. More like lady friend—of the night.

Yes, Everett was a dirty dog when you get down to it, or at least he was before he met me. Oh heck, he's still very much so to this day—and this time, it's exclusively with me.

She turns my way with her crimson lips twisted in a knot of dissatisfaction. The aforementioned power suit is poppy orange, her eyes are filled with a familiar fire, and judging by that scowl

ADDISON MOORE

on her face, she's not too thrilled with her ex's newfound disposition.

"Lottie." She smacks her lips with disdain, but I couldn't care less. A woman from Everett's past who actually has my name right is an impressive unicorn in my book.

I lean in. "This is the part where you congratulate the happy couple." A gloating smile twitches on my lips. I can't help it. Fiona Dagmeyer has always acted as if she were superior to me in every way. And in the past, she's always had the "Essex" upper hand.

She glances back at Noah and Cormack. "And I have." She turns back to Everett and starts rattling off something about a backlog of cases down at the courthouse, and my brain essentially shuts off to the conversation.

Instead, I turn to see if I can find that adorable little specter flying around here someplace. For once I'd like the heads-up on who is going to bite the big one. But I don't see the adorable fuzzy little owl. I see Greer Giles in her ghostly frame, glowing like the ethereal being she is, waving me over by the mouth of the entry.

I do my best to thread my way through the crowd and smack into a body.

"Oh, sorry!" I say, stepping back, only to realize I've just bumped into Holland Grand of Grand Orchards. "Holland! It's so nice to see you." Awkward to see you is more like it. Awkward to see anyone is astutely accurate. I didn't want an engagement party. I'm certainly not engaged. Am I? I glance down at that rock glittering on my finger as if it were contesting my protests. Everett's mother gave it to me months ago when she found out Everett and I weren't doing rings. It was once her mother's, and I'm sure it's worth more than all of the real estate in Honey Hollow combined.

"Lottie Lemon!" Holland offers a giant grin. Holland and I grew up together. He's a year younger than me. For a while he dated my sister, Meg, and that went south quickly. Rumor has it,

166

he's the very person who sent Meg running toward Vegas in the first place.

Just as he opens his mouth to say something else, an arm comes up over his neck and nearly flips him backward. I quickly recognize the face that the arm is attached to as none other than Meg herself.

"What the heck are you doing here, Holland Grand?" She spits his name out as if it were a curse.

Hook comes up behind her and helps poor Holland upright. His face is as crimson as his hair.

He coughs and sputters. "Meg, Hook." He nods their way with a look of extreme annoyance. "I was just about to ask Lottie if she'd like to bake for the Apple Festival later this month. It's our annual harvest kickoff, and your cutie pies were such a hit last year we'd love for you to cater once again. In fact, these miniature turnovers are not only delicious, but they're brilliant. It would be the perfect dessert to feed the masses."

"Yes!" It comes out enthusiastic and genuinely joyful, the first bit of good news it feels like I've had in a while. "I would be honored to bake for the Apple Festival. Send me whatever details you have. I'm super excited to do this."

"Lottie!" Greer's ghostly voice echoes from the entry as she tries her best to flag me down once again. Her long glossy dark hair shimmers with light, and she's still wearing that white ruched gown she was killed in. The crimson bloom over her heart looks like a flower or a brooch more than it does a bloodstain.

"I'm sorry. I think I see someone I know. Please excuse me."

"It's your night, Lottie!" Holland calls after me. "Congratulations!"

I thread my way through the mob, and Greer does her best to pull me into the quiet foyer.

"What is it?"

"Oh, there's trouble, Lottie." She shivers as she floats toward the entry of the B&B.

"Goodness." I avert my eyes. "Is it Winslow? Wait, let me guess. It's Lea." Winslow is far too docile to ever get into any real trouble. But little hatchet-wielding Lea? That girl is trouble on a stick.

"No, Lottie. It's not Winslow or Lea." She glides right through the thick mahogany door.

"Funny," I say. "Unlike you, I have to go through it the old-fashioned way." I open the door and make my way down the expansive porch where Greer, Winslow, and Lea all look somberly into a patch of lavender impatiens.

"What is it?" I trot forward and stop abruptly, a scream buried in my throat.

"Oh no," I gasp.

"Oh yes." Greer nods.

It looks as if our party planner extraordinaire, Amanda Wellington, just booked her last event.

Amanda Wellington is dead.

CHAPTER 3

*D*ead.

I sway back on my heels just as Everett and Noah come bounding down the stairs.

Noah checks for a pulse while shouting for us to call 911.

Everett pulls me to the side. His jaw is tense, just the way it is when he gets angry. "Lottie, why didn't you get me? I would have come with you."

"I should have." I shake my head back at Amanda. She's lying facedown, her bare legs sticking out of the border garden in a grizzly manner. "Greer was the one who called me out this way." I do a quick scan of the vicinity for her, Winslow, or Lea, but the three of them have vanished.

Noah comes our way while texting someone on his phone. "I just told Ivy to get out here. Lottie, what did you see? What brought you out to the front?"

"Greer Giles," I whisper her name like a secret.

Noah's eyes expand just as Ivy clip-clops her way over.

"Tell her you needed a breath of fresh air," Noah whispers frantically.

"Why?" I glance over at Ivy who goes straight to the body.

"Because ghosts make lousy alibis." He heads over to her just as a couple of squad cars scream in this direction.

"He's right about that." Everett shakes his head wistfully. "But he's wrong about the breath of fresh air. Your story is that we agreed to meet one another outside, five minutes apart, in an attempt to leave that circus without drawing any attention to ourselves."

I suck in my bottom lip a moment as I take in this handsome blue-eyed devil before me. "You don't know how much of a turn-on it is to hear you willingly perjure yourself for me."

His cheeks flex in an attempt to smile, but Everett is too stubborn to give it, dead body in the vicinity or not.

The light cooing of an owl goes off behind us as we head toward an overgrown maple dripping with bright orange leaves.

"I hear you," I whisper as I crane my neck, and sure enough, a sparkle of light refracts sharply as if it were a prism. The owl materializes with its wings spread out, and it's a magnificent sight. "It's here." I quickly take up Everett's hand. For reasons I have no control over, if someone touches me, they can hear the dead, too. "What's your name, and why in heavens didn't you warn me before someone shoved poor Amanda off the planet?" My chest bucks with emotion as I look to the radiant being.

The beautiful creature lets out a whirling sound as if it were clearing its throat. "*Owlbert* Einstein." It shoots off a couple of *who-whos*. "Manda's murder was not mine to interfere with—only mine to solve. Who-who are you?"

"My name is Lottie, and this is my boyfriend, Everett." It just felt so natural to say that. Unfortunately, I'm wondering if it will feel just as natural saying the same about Noah? "Did you see anything? Who in their right mind would want to kill Amanda?"

"I don't know, Lottie. But I'm determined to find out. I'm headed back to the party." He flies right through Everett and into the B&B as quick as a lightning bolt.

A dull groan comes from me. "I doubt he's going to find the killer at the party."

Detective Ivy Fairbanks walks over with Noah as the area floods with sheriff's deputies from both inside and the bevy of patrol cars pulling up on the scene. A fire truck just rolled up, and Forest dashes past us on the way to the scene of the crime.

"Another one?" Ivy shoots me a look that could make the *Mona Lisa* cry. She folds her arms over her chest in a show of judgment and, believe me, I'm starting to think I deserve it.

"I was planning an escape with Noah." I wince. "I mean *Everett*. And once I hit the bottom of the stairs, I saw her legs."

Ivy squints my way, and if I didn't know better, I'd say she were giving me the stink eye. "Fine. Did you realize she had a fistful of those mini tarts you were serving? Her mouth was full as well."

Oh heck.

I give a long, weary blink.

For whatever reason, every murder in this town has a direct correlation to my bakery. And as horrible as it is, I've already started calculating how to increase my order of ingredients to meet the inevitable demand from those Last Thing They Ate Tours.

I gasp as a terrible thought comes to me.

"This is horrible." I look to Everett. "People are going to think I'm planting my desserts around the deceased just to drum up business!"

Noah winces. "In full disclosure, it's often brought up on our tipline."

"Great." I collapse my hands to my sides. "So what do you think was the cause of death? Was she stabbed? Shot? Strangled?"

"None of the above." Noah's brows dip. "We'll have to wait for the coroner's report to come in. For all we know, it might have been natural causes."

Owlbert floats by, assuring me it wasn't.

I glance past him just as an entire herd of bodies pour out of the B&B.

Noah rocks back on his heels. "I'd better take care of this." He takes off, along with Ivy. "I want this exit sealed," he shouts to the deputies milling around the body. But it's too late to stop those already racing down the stairs.

A petite redhead with an all too familiar face crumbles when she spots the body, and a wailing scream emits from her.

A couple of men in suits pull her away from the scene as they try their best to comfort her.

"That's her sister, Hazel." Tears come to my eyes. "I can't bear to watch her pain, Everett. I can't imagine what it must be like to see someone you love that way."

"I can't either." He pulls me close. "The men look familiar, too. Amanda's fiancé, Mark, and his buddy."

"Mark looks more concerned for Hazel at the moment."

The three of them look our way at the very same time, and my heart thumps hard against Everett's chest.

I shake my head apologetically over at Hazel as I start to head over, but a swarm of deputies have descended upon them.

Mom and Pastor Gaines head our way. My poor mother's eyes are red and swollen, and she's gasping for air as if she ran the length of Honey Lake.

"Lottie! Oh, thank heavens." She wraps her arms around me tightly. "When I heard there was an accident—and then I couldn't find you—oh, I thought the very worst." She pulls back and rattles me by the shoulders. "You found another body, didn't you? Who is it? How did this happen?"

Pastor Gaines pulls his gaze from the murder scene. "It appears it was Ms. Wellington."

"*What?*" Mom squawks in disbelief before turning my way. "Who's Ms. Wellington?"

"Amanda." My voice breaks as I say her name. "She was the

party planner for tonight's fiasco, and it sure ended that way for her."

Mom gasps, "How on earth did she die? Oh, God! Did she fall and break her neck? I'm going to get sued, aren't I?" She looks to Pastor Gaines in fright. "That's a terribly callous thought to have while someone lies dead on my property. You'll have to forgive me. This is only my third body on the grounds."

Pastor Gaines' eyes bulge at the thought. "Mandy would understand. She was a kind soul."

"You knew her?" I don't mind donning my amateur sleuth hat and making sure it fits nice and snug for the indelicate occasion. I consider Amanda a friend—or at least I did—and I plan on getting to the bottom of this.

"Yes." Pastor Gaines sheds that perennial smile my way. Wow, it never leaves his lips, does it? "Mandy orchestrated many weddings at the church. We grew to be good friends in the short while I've been in town."

Everett nods. "Makes sense."

Lainey and Meg come upon us. Poor Lainey is red-faced, probably from crying, and I feel terrible for her. First, her wedding planner in July and now her realtor? I'm sure she's starting to feel cursed.

Lainey comes in close, and she's not crying at all—she's red-faced with fury is what she is.

"You are cursed!" She swats me on the shoulder with her purse.

"Hey"—Meg pulls her back—"go easy on her."

"I'm not going easy on her," she snips as she edges in as close as Meg will allow. "You found the body, didn't you? Lottie Lemon, I'm going to take you home and tie you to the kitchen table!"

My mouth falls open as both Meg and Mom try to calm her down.

"Lainey"—my voice wavers as I try to take a step in toward

her, but Everett holds me back—"I don't know what you're implying, but whatever it is, it's not true."

"It's true!" Lainey shakes her head, but it's not anger she's seething with. She looks darn right frightened for me.

Keelie and Bear make their way to our circle, and Keelie breaks out into spontaneous tears. "I can't believe it's Amanda. Bear and I just hired her to—" Her mouth falls open as she looks my way. "Oh, never mind. It's not like you never kept an engagement from me."

I gasp at the implication. "Keelie, are the two of you engaged?" It feels horribly wrong of me to feel a slight thread of excitement over the prospect given the present circumstances.

Keelie gives a sorrowful nod, and we all offer up a somewhat subdued congratulations.

"Come here, you two." I pull them both in for a hearty embrace. "Congratulations." Fresh tears blur my vision, for an entirely better reason.

I pull back, and just as I'm about to open my mouth and let them know all of their pastry needs are covered for the foreseeable future, a flicker of light to my right garners my attention and my vocal cords are paralyzed with fright.

The ghost of that tiny orange tabby I met up with a year ago blinks into existence before blinking right back out, followed by the ghost of that squirrel that was at the opening of my bakery. And as soon as he disappears, I see the ghostly frame of Everett's father, the original Judge Baxter. And just as quickly as he came, he too disappears.

"Oh my goodness," I whisper as I turn to Everett. "I just saw your father for a brief moment."

"What?" Everett glances in the direction I was looking.

Noah heads this way, his eyes wide, and there's a note of concern in his face that I usually don't see during any phase of an active homicide investigation.

He ticks his head at Everett and me, and we follow him to the side as my mother hollers for Keelie's mother so they can share the joy, now that the engaged cat is out of the bag. Keelie and I are not only best friends, but we found out last winter that we're related as well.

"What is it, Noah?" I clutch onto his arm. It's safe to say, after finding poor Amanda, after seeing the dead from my past in quick succession that way, I'm feeling more than concerned myself.

"Everett, I'm going to ask you to please take Lottie home." No sooner does he get the words out than an entire army of deputies drains from the scene as they race to their patrol cars.

Everett watches as a couple of them leap over the oversized pots my mother has staged at the mouth of the property. "What's happening, Noah?"

He shakes his head ever so slightly as he looks to his old step-brother as if he doesn't want to say it in front of present company—present company being me.

I give his arm the death squeeze. "Spill it, Fox, or don't bother speaking to me again."

He takes a deep sigh. "There's been a rash of break-ins reported all over Honey Hollow tonight. Five at last count."

"What?" I don't waste a single second. I head back to where my family is congregating with Keelie's, and I shout for them all to get home. "Something is happening. You need to get home quick."

Everett whisks me off into his car, and we speed all the way to Country Cottage Road.

And my eyes can't believe what they see.

CHAPTER 4

"*E*verett!" I cry out as I jump from his car before he ever pulls into my driveway. It's dark as pitch out, but I can see the disturbance just as plain as day.

The front door to my rental sits ajar, the window to the right is shattered, and there's glass all over the porch.

"Pancake! Waffles!" I scream for my sweet cats as I burst in through the front door.

"*Lemon!*" Everett roars like a lion as he snatches me and pulls me back to the entry. "The criminals could still be here. It's too dangerous."

Both Pancake and Waffles emerge from under the sofa table, their cream-colored fur fluffing out with fright. They're brothers from the same litter—Himalayans—both with the same gorgeous off-white fur and rust-tipped tail. I snatch up Waffles, and Everett picks up Pancake. Waffles was actually my grandmother, Nell Sawyer's, cat. Nell was Carlotta's mom, and I only discovered we were related once Carlotta revealed herself to me last January. It turns out, Nell was sworn to secrecy, but that didn't stop her from developing a lifelong friendship with me. Up until she died last January, she was the only one who knew of my supersensual standing, and it was Nell who passed the gift down to me.

"Let's go, Lemon."

I'm about to turn around when a peppy Golden Retriever bounds out of my bedroom and heads straight for me. Dutch was crucial in helping me solve a murder last December.

"*Dutch!*" I cry out as I bend over and give him some love while Waffles does his best to claw up the side of my sweater. "Oh, how I've missed you!"

He does his best to lick up a storm over my cheek, but alas, I can't feel a thing.

"And how I've missed you." His voice is deep and charming and exactly as sweet as I thought it would be.

I gasp as I pull back and meet up with his serious glowing crimson eyes, but he blinks out of existence before I can say a word.

"That was him! It was Dutch," I say as Everett helps me up. "He spoke to me before he disappeared." I swallow hard. "That must mean your father will be able to speak to us as well."

Everett closes his eyes and sighs. "That's exactly what I wanted to hear, Lemon. I can hardly wait." He navigates us out of the house and down the stairs right back to the driveway. "But for now, we're calling the sheriff's department. Let's take the cats to my place."

Last year, while Noah and I were still hot and heavy, I thought it was a great idea to rent a house across the street from his adorable little cabin. And Everett, who came along for the ride to inspect my new potential rental, bought the house next door to me. And that is exactly how we all came to live on Country Cottage Road.

We're about to head over to his place when I spot a light shining through Noah's cabin across the street.

"Everett," I hiss lower than a whisper. "You're right. They're still here." No sooner do I get the words out than a figure dressed in camouflage from head to toe runs out of Noah's front door and into the woods, to the right, just past where the cul-de-sac ends.

Everett hands me Pancake in haste before bulleting off in that direction.

"*Everett!*" I scream so loud, I'm positive I've shattered the sound barrier.

I head to the car and lock the cats and myself inside while calling Noah and spilling everything in one rambling sentence. The figure of an all too familiar man comes ambling back down the center of the street, hobbling badly. "I have to go. Everett's hurt."

I leave the cats in the car and run over to him.

"I'm fine." Everett holds up a hand, panting as if he ran a mile in two minutes flat. "I turned my ankle on a rock at the neck of the woods. It'll shake off."

"It might, but first we're going to ice it."

Everett and I pick up Pancake and Waffles on our way to his place, which thankfully is left unscathed. I try to get Everett to lift his foot up while I apply an ice pack, but the flashing lights of a patrol car cut through the darkness outside in a red and blue seizure.

Everett and I head on out, where we find Noah parked in haste in his own driveway across the street. Before he can jog over, my phone buzzes in my hand.

"It's a text from Meg," I say to Everett as I quickly read it. "It looks as if Hook's house was hit, too."

Everett exhales sharply as we make our way down the walk. "What in the hell is happening?" he barks at the deputies.

Noah instructs the pair to inspect my place for any signs of the thieves, and they take off running.

Noah is quick to wrap his arms around me, his heart beating erratically against my chest. "Lottie, I need you to stay with Everett tonight. I can escort you back to your place to get a few things once we sweep the house." He shakes his head at Everett. "We're not entirely sure what's happening, but it seems it's only affecting Honey Hollow. No calls from the surrounding areas, and nothing from Hollyhock, Leeds, or Ashford."

"Hook Redwood was hit," I say, pulling back to get a better look at him. Noah is warm and solid and feels so very safe. I can't help but note the gun protruding from the holster on his back.

Everett looks my way. "All this and a homicide? I guess this is the big event those visitors you had last month were alluding to."

Noah nods in agreement. "And it's not over. I'm not resting until I catch both the killer and these idiots who have pillaged our houses."

Everett glances back at my place. "If they're smart, they've skipped town—the killer included."

"They're never smart, are they?" I look to Noah, and he shakes his head.

"No, Lottie, they never are. But they are always dangerous."

And that's exactly what I'm afraid of.

I SPENT the night at Everett's. Pancake, Waffles, and I all managed to sleep on Everett's unbelievably comfy mattress and, I'll admit, it was a bonus to wake up in his strong arms.

Everett woke up with my alarm and made me a breakfast of scrambled eggs and bacon while I showered and dressed for the bakery. A part of me can get used to the idea of waking up in Everett's arms and having that wonderful breakfast rolled out for me each and every day.

It's Sunday, a very crisp Sunday in September, and already the fall leaves are doing cartwheels down Main Street. No matter how stressful life gets, no matter how many homicides I'm quasi-connected to, the Cutie Pie Bakery and Cakery always feels like home. The walls are painted a butter yellow, and the furniture is

ADDISON MOORE

a mishmash painted in every shade of pastel. There's a walkway connecting us to the Honey Pot Diner next door, and in that adorable restaurant there happens to be an oversized resin oak tree planted in the middle whose branches extend over the ceiling every which way and bleed right into the café portion of the bakery. Each branch is lovingly wrapped in twinkle lights, and it adds a magical appeal to both establishments.

Keelie and Lily came in early to help me bake up a storm and open up. They both said they felt bad I had to be here alone after last night's dual nightmare. Thank goodness I had enough fresh dough in the walk-in to make up several batches of croissants, chocolate filled and regular. Keelie insisted we make up some cinnamon apple muffins, and Lily put in a request for a pumpkin spice roll.

Now that fall has essentially hit Honey Hollow hard with its icy breezes, it's put us all in the mood for pumpkin spiced everything.

"So what did they take?" Lily's eyes are wide with a morbid curiosity. Lily is a stunning brunette who has spent most of her twenty-seven years hating my guts. She is or was Naomi Turner's best friend, but they've recently had a falling-out over Noah's foxy brother, Alex—an ex-Marine turned investment banker.

"My gun." It's true.

After an hour or so, Noah helped me walk through the shambles that was left of my house. It was ransacked in haste, but they still managed to make a decent mess in the process, and they took some costume jewelry, a small wad of twenties I had on the dresser, and the *Glock 26 Gen4* that both Everett and Noah teamed up to buy me a few months back. I've only fired it a handful of times, but as much as I hate to admit it, I felt safer knowing it was in the house with me. I had made it a habit of putting it in my purse and taking it with me everywhere but the bakery—and since last night's event was work-related, I didn't have it with me.

"You have a gun?" Keelie looks green around the gills.

"*Had*," I say, looking to the two of them. "It's gone now." Come to think of it, I feel terrible I didn't give the gun a name. It was adorably small yet powerful. I should have called it something cute yet spunky like Sophie or Zoey.

Lily shudders. "Remind me never to rub you the wrong way, Lottie Lemon."

A crowd of tourists hustles through the door, and Lily hops over to the register.

"I'd better get next door," Keelie says, tying on an apron of her own.

Keelie is the manager of the Honey Pot Diner. Both of these places, along with a fistful of major real estate, once belonged to Nell Sawyer. And when she died, she left the lion's share of her holdings to me. Of course, the will was contested—ironically by my new uncle *Will*. And it's been locked up in red tape ever since.

"Hey"—I pull her in and look into those big blue eyes of hers —"congratulations again. You owe me some details. I'm not letting you out of this so easily."

Lily scampers back after the rush dies down. "*Ooh*, me too! Give us all the dirty deets. When did he propose? Let's see the rock on your finger."

Keelie is quick to cradle her left hand. "No rock. We haven't set a date and we're not having a fancy engagement party." She glances to my bare finger. I put Everett's mother's ring in the ground safe as soon as I got here. Boy, am I ever glad I have a habit of wearing it wherever I go just to keep it from getting stolen. "We'll be shopping for that later," she sings it low and flirty. Keelie's entire face is lit up like a Christmas tree. I can't remember the last time I saw my best friend this happy. "He proposed the other night at Honey Lake. He took me out on his canoe and he asked to spend the rest of his life with me right there in deep water as the sun was setting. It was magical." She sighs, bringing her hands to her chest.

"Oh, Keelie, that does sound magical." And now I feel bad for ever sleeping with Bear in high school. But then, he was my official boyfriend—the one I gave my heart to, and then he turned right around and stomped on it. It turns out, Bear was cheating with anything that moved. But he's since reformed his ways. I hope.

Lily huffs, "I hope when Alex proposes to me, it will be a real flashy event in front of everyone in Honey Hollow—especially Naomi." She makes a face at Keelie. "No offense."

"No offense taken. She's plotting the same thing." She looks back my way. "And when were you going to tell me that you and Everett made it official?"

"Excuse me?" a light female voice chirps from behind, and I turn around and gasp.

Standing before us is Amanda Wellington herself with her red hair piled on top of her head in a messy bun, dark sunglasses on, and a plain pink sweater and jeans.

A croaking sound emits from Lily's throat. "I think I'm going to faint now," she says it weakly.

"Please don't," the girl is quick to implore. "I'm Hazel, Amanda's sister." She looks to me. "We met last night." She takes off her sunglasses, revealing cherry-stained eyes. "You're Lottie, right?"

"Y-yes." I can barely get it out. I'm so stunned to see poor Hazel here. "Can I help you? Amanda was a sweet girl. I'll do anything to help at all."

"Good. I hear you're the best private detective all of Vermont has to offer." She opens her purse and shoves a handful of bills my way. "Here's all the money I have—six thousand dollars. Find my sister's killer, Lottie. And do it yesterday."

CHAPTER 5

*N*ever before have so many been invited back to the scene of the crime just hours after the Ashford Homicide Department removed the caution tape.

First thing Monday morning, my mother sent out a series of spastic text messages inviting just about everyone she knows for an impromptu dinner catered by none other than the Honey Pot Diner.

Both Everett and Noah are still on their way back from work. No sooner do I arrive at my mother's B&B than I note a bevy of photographers amassed near the entry.

"How does it feel heading into one of the most notorious haunted houses in all the United States?" one shouts my way. A barrage of camera flashes go off as I jog my way up the stairs.

Another shouts, "Do you think you'll be the next murder victim? Entering through those doors ups your odds, lady. I'd think twice!"

I turn to glare at the sea of men and women hungry for a picture as I walk on in and slam the door in their faces.

It's calm inside. Soothing classical music plays in the lobby,

ADDISON MOORE

and I can hear the din of laughter coming from the dining room to my left.

The thick emerald carpet and dark wood paneling make it feel cozy inside. I spot a fire going in both the grand room and the dining room. My mother has always had a flair for playing hostess, and, lucky for her, she was able to turn it into a profitable business.

The sound of frantic whispering comes from my right and I step around the staircase, only to find Carlotta embroiled in a conversation with—

"*Nell!*" I shout her name out carefree as I wrap my arms around her ghostly frame. For whatever reason, the ghosts that visit can feel pretty solid when they want to. "Oh, am I ever glad to see you." I pull back, holding her by the shoulders as I pause to take her in. She's here, really here, and she looks better than I remember. Her sweet wrinkled face is just so for the sake of Carlotta and me.

Nell exposed herself as a young hottie the last time she was here, but she wanted to share with us the version we most recognized—the one we miss deeply. Her white hair is short around her ears and glows like a flame. Her pale blue eyes could light up all of Honey Hollow at night.

I take her in. "Nell, you have to tell me what's happening. Those horrible break-ins? Is that why you're here?"

"I'm afraid so." She cups my face with her palms. "Oh, my precious Lottie, how I've missed you so." She lands a sweet kiss to my lips, and an electric impulse bounces from her lips to mine, warming me from head to toe. "There will be more chaos by this destructive crew. Just know that we're here for a reason. I want you to trust your gut, Lottie." Her eyes bear hard into mine when she says it. "Don't be afraid to dig down deep and utilize this wonderful power you've been given."

"Nell"—I glance to Carlotta, my doppelgänger on any given

day—"I don't know what you're talking about. And speaking of talking, the animals, they can speak now."

A tiny giggle bubbles from her, and she sounds like a schoolgirl. "That's right, Lottie. You should expect wonderful things from here on out. And how is your heart? Have you settled on a suitor yet?"

"Yup," Carlotta answers for me. "She's taking a page out of her mama's playbook and she's settling on both."

My mouth falls open as I look to her. "Carlotta, you dated two men?"

"I'm talking about your other mother. She and Harry went out for dinner last night." Her upper lip twitches as if she were about to growl.

"I'm sorry to hear it." Really sorry. My mother was initially seeing Mayor Nash, but once she found out he was my biological father, it sort of put a damper on things, so she started dating Pastor Gaines. Then things really went south, and Carlotta decided she wanted another spin on the Nash Express. "Please don't war over him." This is usually that part where I say he's not worth it, but now that Mayor Nash and I have grown a bit closer, I don't feel that way anymore.

"Don't be," Carlotta snips my way. "He stopped by my place on his way home." She thrusts her shoulders back and forth in a lustful manner.

"Ew," I say at the visual. "Nell, please tell me what's going on with this destructive crew you mentioned."

Nell cocks her head to the side and looks up at me from under her glowing lashes. "I asked first. How is it going with Everett and Noah?"

"Wonderful," I say it flat and full of sarcasm. "Noah's divorce is final, and Everett stepped back to allow me to fully explore my feelings for Noah."

"Now there's a gentleman for you." Nell nods sweetly as she says it.

"Ha!" Carlotta belts it out like a verbal exclamation point. "Now there's an idiot for you. If Lottie falls for the Fox, the horny judge will live to regret it. Mark my words. He'll be filled with regret the rest of his days for sponsoring these please-sleep-with-your-ex shenanigans."

My insides cringe at the thought of putting Everett through that kind of pain.

I look to Nell and my heart fills with unmitigated joy once again. "Now that you're caught up to speed, what's happening, Nell? Is this in any way connected to Amanda's killer?"

The soft moaning of what sounds like a dove emanates from behind as that gorgeous white snow owl expands his wings in a three-foot span at least. Its glowing feathers land softly over Nell's shoulder, and she reaches up and gives it a pat.

"There, there," Nell sings softly to it. "You'll be assisting my granddaughter, Lottie, in the investigation. She's quite good, you know."

"Good evening, Owlbert," I say, mostly because I've been dying to say his name in general. "And what a clever name you have." I turn to Carlotta. "It's Owlbert *Einstein.*" A small titter of laughter bubbles from me. "Don't you love it?"

Carlotta is quick to mock my laughter. "He's here for a homicide. Don't you love it?"

"Oh, you." I swat her before turning my attention back to the bird. "Who do you think killed Amanda, Owlbert?" Again. So much fun to say.

He lets out a couple who-whos. "Those men who were at the party. I don't get a good feeling about them."

"Me either. I'll be sure to check each one out. And the girls, too." I wince. "But that sister." I shrug over at Nell. "She came by the bakery on Sunday and offered me six grand to hunt down her sister's killer. Of course, I turned it down."

Carlotta scoffs. "Of course, you're an idiot."

I shake my head, choosing to ignore her. "I told Noah and

Everett about it. They thought it was a clear act of desperation. In fact, Everett said he's surprised I haven't drummed up more business in that manner by now."

"No, no," Carlotta says, staring at the carpet deep in thought. "She's trying to throw you off her scent. She's your killer."

Owlbert shrieks. "Not my precious Hazel!" He flaps his wings, and the one closest to Nell's face goes right through her.

"I don't think so either. But I'll keep that in mind."

The sound of men talking as they enter the foyer gets my attention, and I glance back to confirm it's Noah and Everett. I turn back to say something to Nell, but both she and Owlbert have up and disappeared.

"Great," I mutter to Carlotta, who inconveniently never disappears—anymore, that is. She disappeared for twenty-six years, but something tells me I won't be that lucky again. Kidding. Sort of.

She leans into the direction of the dining room. "I hear Harry." And with that, she takes off like a greyhound at the track after a gunshot.

I step over to Noah and Everett who both look dashing tonight. Everett is in his signature dark inky suit, bright red tie, fitting for fall. And Noah is in his chinos and brown twill blazer, a white dress shirt underneath, as well as his pistol, which he never leaves home without. I'm starting to wish I never left home without mine. How I miss Ethel.

"Ethel!" I say in lieu of a proper greeting, and they each exchange a glance. "I think I just named my gun."

Everett ticks his head back, his lids hooded seductively low. "I've got a gun you can name."

My teeth graze over my bottom lip to keep from smiling. "Everett, behave."

Noah threads his arm through mine. "It's time you see him for the animal he is."

Oh, I'm intimately familiar with Everett's animalistic tendencies, but I don't dare say a word.

Noah looks to the both of us. "Speaking of animals, the coroner's preliminary report was filed just a few hours ago. Amanda Wellington was poisoned."

I take in a quick breath. "You mean? You don't think my apple turnovers were toxic, do you?"

He winces. "I'm sorry, Lottie. They found high traces of Conium, a hemlock alkaloid both in her system and in the bolus in her mouth. Someone tampered with your dessert—and either it was meant for Amanda or she was very unlucky."

"Oh my God. How could this have happened? And how did she end up outside? The last thing I remembered she was in the conservatory with us."

"True." Noah shakes his head. "But as soon as the poison started to work its way into her bloodstream, her lungs would have begun to seize. She might have gone outside for some fresh air."

"Or"—Everett takes a breath—"someone might have baited her and fed it to her there."

I nod up at him. "That would have given them plenty of time and privacy to tamper with my dessert without anyone witnessing the event."

Noah offers a dismal smile. "Don't worry about that tonight. Let's enjoy dinner with your family."

The dining room at the B&B is filled with both family and friends. Keelie and Bear, Naomi and Lily and Alex—I cringe at the unhappy trio. Mayor Nash and Carlotta. His daughters Kelleth and Aspen—two blonde beauties who happen to be my new half-sisters. They're talking with Lainey and Meg, and I'm betting Lainey is warning them to steer clear of me at all costs. I won't lie. It hurts my heart to think my sweet sister thinks I'm cursed. It hurts even more to know she might be right.

Mom is laughing it up with Pastor Gaines—that eerie perennial smile of his. I don't care if he is laughing at the moment, it never leaves his face. Chrissy Nash, Mayor Nash's ex-wife, is here. She's the mother of my half-siblings and my mother's bestie. Both Chrissy and my mother share the same blonde shoulder-length locks, the same rotten luck with men—with the exception of my adoptive father, of course, but admittedly Joseph Lemon is a hard act to follow.

"Too bad there aren't any suspects here tonight," I whisper to both Noah and Everett.

Everett leans in. "Feel free to take the night off, Lemon. You deserve it. But if you see my father, consider yourself on the clock again." He gives a sly wink. "I'll get us a couple of drinks." He takes off for the bar, and I navigate Noah over to the cluster of sisters I seem to have amassed.

"Lottie." Kelleth tips her straight blonde locks to the side while inspecting my proximity to Noah. Her lips are heavily glossed, but other than that she's more or less a natural beauty. Kelleth is tall and impossibly thin. I'm not her favorite person. She's still bitter because I helped land her fiancé behind bars for swindling the elderly out of their retirement funds. "I see you're wasting no time in stealing someone else's man. I guess that whole finding bodies routine is just another way to kiss up to the cute homicide detective." She gives a hearty wink to Noah, and my stomach sours at the thought of drop-dead gorgeous Kelleth tossing her Prada hat into the ring for his affection.

Aspen cackles before I can get the chance to respond. Aspen is a blonde version of Betty Boop, complete with the racy curves, bouncy curls, big eyes, and a luscious pucker.

"Lottie isn't as innocent as we thought, is she now?" She bats her false lashes my way.

Lainey's face turns a strange shade of purple. "You leave my little sister alone. Nobody talks to her that way."

Aspen rolls her eyes. "She's our little sister, too. We can talk about her however we want."

I'm not quite sure if I'm their younger sister, but I go with it for now.

Meg jabs Lainey in the ribs. "They're not that off base. Sure, she says she stumbles upon these bodies by sheer coincidence, but look where it's landed her. She's got the lead homicide detective wrapped around her little finger. And don't get me started on that judge she's got in her back pocket—and, believe you me, he's enjoying his time back there."

Everett pops up and hands me a glass of clear soda. "That I am." He gives a wistful shake of the head.

He's impossible.

I give a little wink as I take the drink from him. I'm a bit impossible, too.

Mom wrangles everyone through the buffet she's set up on the granite counters built against the north wall like a sideboard where an entire row of elongated silver chafing dishes sits filled with amazing goodness from the Honey Pot. Once dinner is through, she brings out a couple of delectable pumpkin cheesecakes I sent over with Keelie and Bear earlier.

The room breaks up again in groups as we mingle one last time before saying goodnight.

Alex comes our way with a greedy grin on his face, and Noah's chest bounces with a quiet laugh at the sight of him.

"See that face, Everett? That's the face of the one that's ready to dethrone you as the official playboy of Vermont."

Everett grunts, "I've long since abdicated the throne."

Alex comes up, and Everett slaps him on the back. "Go easy on the girls, would you? It's a marathon, not a sprint."

Alex laughs because he's guilty of sprinting with both Naomi and Lily. Personally, I'm getting tired of listening to Lily expound the details of their nightly dalliances. She pointed out that both she and I were officially on an even playing field having slept with both a Baxter and a Fox. She even went as far as to ask if I wanted to compare notes, and, of course, that was a hard pass.

Mom waves me over, and I excuse myself as Alex regales them with tales from the bawdy bedside.

I speed over to my sweet mother and Pastor Gaines who stands glued faithfully by her side. I wonder if he has any idea that she's been going out with Mayor Nash behind his back?

"What can I do for you, Mother?"

She frowns for the first time tonight. "You went to business school, Lottie. How did I do?"

"How did you do with what?"

"With the *shindig*? Carlotta said the best way to convince the public that this place was safe and sound was to have a great big party as soon as possible. I even asked every news affiliate if they'd cover the event. I had eleven room cancellations right after that poor girl died. And my insurance company called and threatened to cancel the policy I have on this place."

"They can't do that." I think. "And yes, Carlotta gave you sage advice. I'm sorry about the cancellations. I thought the haunted aspect of the B&B is what they liked most?"

"It's true. But it turns out they don't actually want to be the ghosts. We'll have to turn this around somehow, Lottie. This is all I've got. It's my livelihood."

"I'm sure the positive press will help."

Pastor Gaines offers a solemn smile—still there. Never leaves. So eerie.

"Any word on how the poor girl perished? That last step on the porch was slicked with dew—and she did have awfully high heels."

"Good speculation, but you would be wrong," I say. "Although I'm sure poor Amanda would have rather gone that way. Please don't say anything until it's official, but she was poisoned."

"What?" My mother shrieks so loud, half the room quiets down for a second.

"That's terrible," Pastor Gaines says it with a grin, and I can't stand that obnoxious smile for one more minute.

"It is terrible." A thought comes to me. "Say, you said the two of you were friendly. Did she ever mention anything that would set off an alarm? Did she have any unsavory characters she hung out with?"

His brows hike into his forehead. "That she did—the Canelli girl." He tsks as he shakes his head. "She came by frequently with her. Can't say I cared too much for that one. Potty mouth." His grin widens, and I shudder.

The sound of barking comes from the entry, and I turn to find Dutch bouncing in along with Cookie Monster—a great big black teddy bear of a dog, a Newfoundland—and they happen to be chasing that tiny herd of precious little Chihuahuas as they scuttle right past my ankles with a breeze. It's been a known fact for months that the dead can now move things in the material world. The first one to do so was that enormous bear that cropped up right here in the B&B for the very first—

A horrific inhuman howl comes from the entry, and I cringe when I see that outrageously tall bear on its hind legs before he falls to all fours and comes bounding in. Soon enough, the animals are on the table, the dinnerware is unsettled, one of the chafing dishes goes flying, and there's pasta primavera raining down on my mother's guests. In an instant, the room is cleared out as everyone is sent screaming for the doors, and the paparazzi my mother invited over are able to document the entire unholy event.

I stay behind to help clean up the mess—and to scold a poltergeist or two, but they dissipate as soon as I start in on them.

All the way home I think about Connie Canelli.

No sooner do I meet with Noah and Everett in my driveway to say goodnight than I say her name.

"*No,*" they both spit out in unison.

"No *what?*" There's a slight protest in my voice because I know where this is headed.

Everett shakes his head. "No investigating Connie. I'll do it. I'll track her down and have a drink with her."

Noah looks my way. "Lottie, her family is dangerous. We don't want you getting involved with a mafia princess."

"When you put it that way." I give a little shrug. "I'll stay out of it." I give a quick wink to defuse the lie.

We say a brief goodnight, and I head back to my place. Everett kindly boarded up the window for me and contacted my landlord to help order a new one.

I cuddle up in bed with Pancake and Waffles, and all night I plot a way to get to Connie Canelli.

I'll stay out of it, just like I told them.

Right after I have a few words with the mafia princess myself.

CHAPTER 6

"Two words," Meg says as she stands before me at the counter of the Cutie Pie Bakery and Cakery.

I may have called in the reinforcements once I saw that both Noah and Everett were putting the kibosh on any leads that might help me gain access to Connie. But I knew I didn't need either Noah or Everett in order to get to the underbelly of the mob. That's what I have my trusty sister for. You don't teach strippers their night moves for a living without learning a little something in return.

She nods as if she heard. "Underground bingo."

I take an involuntary breath and hold it. "Underground bingo?"

Owlbert whirs softly as if he swallowed a whistle. "I wouldn't do it, Lottie. The term *underground* clearly stipulates this is against the law."

I glance his way. "Anyone ever tell you you're a know-it-all?"

Meg squints over at me as if I had just challenged her to a dare —or she's thinking of smacking me—either or.

Owlbert chortles out a laugh. "My love, my name does say it all."

"*Mmm*," Keelie moans from behind as she takes a bite out of one of my crispy apple turnovers. "Good move adding the caramel dipping sauce as an option. And by the way? Nobody goes to underground bingo without me." She takes off for the Honey Pot just as Noah walks through the door with a dimpled grin blooming on his face.

"Quick," I whisper to Meg. "When and where?"

"Thursday night. In the basement of the Trattoria. One street up from Red Satin." She takes a step back and waves. Red Satin is the gentlemen's club where Meg just so happens to teach those raunchy moves. "Tootles!" She slaps Noah on the arm and he grips it as if it hurt. I'm sure it did. Meg knows how to pack a punch when she wants to. "See you around, Fox. Catch a killer, would you?"

"I'm on it." Noah's smile broadens as he steps close to the counter. "You up for a quick bite?"

"Are you playing hooky, detective?" I can't help but flirt as I say it.

"Actually, I had to come back to town on business. I interviewed Hazel this morning. She's staying at her sister's place. I had a chance to look around briefly."

"Ooh, I'll have Lily man the register for me. I think I'd love to share a pizza with you at Mangias." No sooner do I take off my apron than Lily comes up holding the deposit—it's a hefty one, too, no thanks to my complete sellout of crispy apple turnovers—fifty cents extra for caramel dipping sauce, and I'm running low on that, too.

"I'll take it, Lily," I say as she hands me the canvas bag. "The bank is just a hop and a skip down from Mangias and I'm headed that way."

"Thanks." Lily takes the apron from me and wraps it around her own waist. "Hey, Noah, how about you and Alex take Lottie and me out for a double date sometime? That way you get what you want and I get what I want." She gives a cheeky smile.

"Clear out Saturday night on your calendar." He looks my way. "If you're in, Lottie, so am I."

"I'm in. I still owe you a date from your birthday, remember?" I can't help but frown as I say it. "You don't think Cormack has a surprise wedding set for that night, do you?"

He closes his eyes a moment. "I suppose you never know. Stranger things have happened."

A shrill cry comes from somewhere near the ceiling, and I look up to find a glorious colorful macaw—the ghost of one anyway.

It's Macon—yes, Macon the macaw. He was here to help a few months back with another case, and how I've missed him. How I've missed them all.

Macon screams once again. "Lottie Lemon! Lottie Lemon!" He dives down quickly and flies right out the center of the window.

Stranger things have happened indeed.

THE SIGN for the Honey Hollow Savings and Loan looms up above, and I stop short, swinging Noah's hand between us as I look up at it with a sense of nostalgia. The cool September breeze swirls around, blowing the dry leaves off the maple trees and sending them down the street in a citrus-colored processional.

"You do realize this place has a rich history between us," I say.

His brows arch softly as a gentle smile tugs at his lips. "You thought my ratty old office was the loan department." He reels me in slowly until we're just a breath away.

"And you gave me the money to start my bakery anyway," I whisper, looking into those hypnotic green eyes of his. It's true. Noah inherited some money from his father —dirty money that was swindled from unfortunate souls such as Everett's wealthy mother—who by the way, did not want it back. Noah didn't want to keep it either. He wanted to use it for good. And I'm humbled he thought I was good in any way, shape, or form. "Thank you, Noah. A thousand times thank you for that. I could truly never thank you enough."

He leans in and lands a soft kiss to my cheek. "No need to thank me. All I ask is that you keep those chocolate chip cookies coming."

"As you wish," I sing as we make our way into the bank.

It's a touch warmer inside. The old carpeting they had last year has since been replaced with gray wood floors, and the walls are painted the softest shade of blue. The Savings and Loan has undergone extensive renovations this last year, and judging by the opulent chandeliers and marble counters, I'm guessing that they're just about done.

The bank is nearly empty, about six or seven people in total counting the tellers, so this should be quick.

Noah leans in. "While you make a deposit, I think I'll chat with the loan department if you don't mind."

"Not at all. This will just take a minute."

Huh—a loan?

I glance back at Noah as he speaks to a woman in a navy blazer.

What could Noah need a loan for? I certainly hope that generous gift he gave to the bakery didn't drain him.

No sooner do I step up to the counter and smile at the teller—a young woman by the name of Doreen whom I've come to know throughout the years—than a loud pop emits from the entry.

I turn to find several people dressed in black. Each one has donned a mask with the face of a cute little pig, and in each of their hands is a not so cute little black gun.

"Everybody on the floor!" one of them shouts—a male according to his gruff deep voice—and the room explodes in screams as bodies hit the floor.

My adrenaline kicks in, can't breathe, can't move. I look to Noah, and we're both frozen, looking at one another helplessly.

"I said get down!"

Both Noah and I cautiously crouch to our knees.

I count out six of them—six masked men parading around as adorably frightening piglets. Two of them jump over the counter and hustle the tellers into the safe, while two others come around to the woman quivering next to me and—well, *me*.

"Take off the jewelry," one of them shouts, shoving a bag my way.

A breath hitches in my throat as I do my best to invert that giant rock on my finger with my thumb. There is no way I'm going to give this lunatic Everett's mother's ring. Both Everett and his mother might be moved to kill me.

"I said *now!*" He tips his head to the side, and his mask dislodges just enough for me to see something tattooed along the side of his neck, a diamond pattern of some sort. His skin looks pink around the edges. He jabs the butt of his gun to my shoulder.

"Lottie!" Noah barks and I glance over to find a gunman trained right over him—and wisely so. Noah is packing heat himself, but they don't know that. They just figure he's the strongest person in the room.

A spray of starlight bursts into the vicinity as a magnificent tiger I've grown to love jumps in through the glass window. Beastie.

Beastie is an enormous white and gray striped exotic Bengal tiger with menacing blue eyes. Okay, so he's menacing in general, but he is equally majestic.

"Lottie, don't move," Beastie growls it out as he steps around the goon with a gun bent on butting it against my shoulder. "He's a killer. I can smell it on him."

A tiny squeal of terror comes from me.

Two masked men hop back over the counter with a couple of

canvas totes, and my stomach churns. The masked man in front of me bolts toward the door, and I breathe a sigh of relief.

The ghost of Nell appears, then the ghost of Maximillian Finmore. Max was here a few months back. He's a handsome college man who was murdered by way of manure. That's about as tragic and stinky as it gets.

"I'll do my best to stop them!" Nell shouts as she chases them to the door.

I want to scream *no*. For heaven's sake, I want them out of my face with their hostile weaponry and terrifying commands.

Maximillian crouches down low.

"Incoming," he pants just as another masked man descends upon me.

"Dang!" the masked man grunts.

This little piggy yanks my left hand forward and slips off my ring so easily you'd think that it voluntarily fled my finger.

Max does his best to snatch it back, but the masked man catches it midair.

He runs to the door with the rest of his crew. "You missed some serious ice, dude." He smacks the first piglet that held me at gunpoint on the back of the head.

And then just as quickly as they came, they're gone.

Nell shouts a salty tirade as she glides right through the door as if she was on their tail.

Noah bounces to his feet and takes off after them.

"*Noah!*" I cry out, but it's too late. He's out the door and on the chase.

I help the woman next to me up as the tellers come around and make sure everyone is safe.

Maximillian places a hand over my shoulder. "I'm sorry, Lottie. I'm sorry there wasn't anything we could do to stop them."

"Max." I pull him in, quickly trying to play it off as if I were straightening my clothes. "Why are you all here if you can't be of any help? No offense, but I'm guessing paradise is—well, paradise."

"You got that right." Max has a boyish innocence about him, something about that rounded jaw and those full cheeks that give him an affable appeal. "But you're wrong about us not being able to help you. We might not have been able to interfere with the homicide investigations, but that's not what we're here for."

"What are you here for?"

"To make sure you stop these thugs before they hit the Canadian border. Let's just say you're the only hope some people have. If you stop them, Lottie—you will save many, many lives. These men have killed before. They're not afraid to do it again. And they will. We're here to avert a great tragedy."

A chill runs through me.

"How am I going to stop them if I don't know who they are or where they'll strike next?" I whisper before glancing around at the women huddled together just as a flurry of deputies burst through the door.

Max steps in close as his ghostly frame slowly begins to dissipate. "We're going to help you figure out exactly who they are. We won't let you miss a thing, Lottie," he says as he evaporates to nothing.

I won't miss a thing. And that's exactly what I'm afraid of.

Noah rushes back inside and takes me in his arms.

"Are you okay? Did he hurt you?" he pants the words out quick and heated.

"I'm fine." My arms wrap themselves around his body, and Noah and I hold onto one another so very tight with no sign of letting go.

The dead are here to avert a great tragedy. A novel concept, considering it's never worked that way before.

I just hope they can help me stop this tour de force of evil before it's too late.

It already feels just that—too late.

CHAPTER 7

$\mathcal{O}$nce Noah and I are thoroughly interviewed by the sheriff's department, we indeed pick up that pizza from Mangias—to go, of course. But we don't get any farther than the bakery.

Once inside, we're accosted by Keelie, Lily, Meg, Lainey, Cormack, Britney, my mother, Chrissy Nash, Carlotta, and Mayor Nash.

It's utter melee while we both assure everyone we're more than fine. And both my mother and Mayor Nash look as if they can use a cup of coffee or twelve.

Noah runs through the entire story for a fourth time, trying to answer the barrage of questions as they come, just as Everett dashes through the front door.

I'm locked in his arms faster than I can process what's happening and he lands a tender kiss right to my lips before pulling me in aggressively once again.

"Lemon," he whispers hard into my ear. "I left Ashford as soon as I got Lily's text. I'm sorry I couldn't be here sooner. Are you okay? Did they hurt you? Did they touch you?" There's a fire in his eyes that I haven't seen before, not even in his most ornery state back in his courtroom.

"I'm more than fine." Tears come to the party, and I try to blink them away. "I, um…" I hold up my left hand, unable to say another word.

Cormack must sense the matrimonial implications of it all because she pops up like an unwanted apparition.

"They took the ring!" she belts it out like a tragic country song. "Tell me it was a replica, Essex. I couldn't stand the thought of that precious baby floating around in some criminal's hot hands." She looks my way. "Eliza is simply going to kill you. And to think she actually approved of you marrying her son." She clicks her tongue. "Don't worry, Linda. The replica odds are in your favor." She rushes back to Noah's side as he finishes answering yet another question about the robbery.

"Do not worry about the ring." Everett's jaw tenses. "I'm going to find whoever put you through this, and I'm going to kill them myself."

"Trust me, they're not worth the time behind bars." I glance around before leaning in. "Max Finmore told me it's a band of thieves on their way to Canada. For whatever reason, they're hanging out in the area."

He nods as if it makes sense. "Getting what they can before they presumably clean up their act when they get to the other side. They're probably running from something big."

"Max said they've killed before." I shudder as I say it. "And I bet they're the same gang that was responsible for all the robberies the night of the murder."

"I wouldn't doubt it."

"Anyway, he said the dead that have returned are going to help me capture them."

Noah pops up. "No way." Both his brows and his lips are drawn into a line, and he looks decidedly unhappy with the news.

"I agree." Everett shakes his head. "They are armed and

dangerous, and you mentioned they've killed before. I can't stand by and let you put yourself in harm's way like that."

"Absolutely not," Noah echoes.

Cormack trots back as she wraps her arms around Noah from behind. "Sorry, Luanna. I just asked Eliza if that ring was a replica and she said no. But don't worry, I didn't hint at all that you lost it—she guessed that herself."

I can't help but glower at her. "I didn't lose it. It was yanked off my finger." Okay, so they didn't have to yank all that hard, but that's beside the point. "And I'm going to get it back."

"No, you're not." Noah doesn't mind contradicting me.

Everett takes a breath. "The Ashford Sheriff's Department will get it back." He offers Noah a stern look. "Got that?"

Mom and my sisters come up and offer me a group hug.

Lainey wipes a tear from her eye. "I have to get back to the library. Try not to get yourself killed, would you?" She hikes up and whispers, "And you might want to see someone about warding off all that bad luck. I'm genuinely worried about you!" She takes off and Meg steps up.

"I have to get back to my girls. I told them to keep up the deep lunges until my break was over." She says *break* in air quotes. "They should have thighs the size of tree trunks by now. See you Thursday night." She takes off, and both Noah and Everett exchange a glance.

Noah tips his head to the side. "What's Thursday night?"

Mom bats her lashes at me as if wondering the same thing. Shoot. She would have been a convenient excuse had she not been here.

"Sisters' night out." I shrug. "Girls only. Meg is going to make sure we have a rough and rowdy night out on the town. Both Lainey and I need a breather." Not that Lainey will want to be anywhere near me.

"And me!" Keelie shouts as she jumps on my back with a strangulating hug. "I'm never letting you out of my sight again."

"Count me in." Cormack fans herself with her fingers. "After losing Amanda, I thought I'd lose my mind with all the wedding details to tend to. Thank goodness her sister stepped in and saved the day. She's taken over all of Amanda's event planning duties. She even mentioned she's going to get her real estate license and take over Amanda's position at Redwood Realty if they'll have her."

Mom coos as if it were an adorable gesture. Personally, I find it odd, bordering on creepy. If Meg died, I wouldn't be barking at the girls at Red Satin to do a rep of deep lunges, nor would I be gunning for Lainey's position at the library. But then, I've got my own bustling career and I guess Hazel doesn't.

Mom glances at her phone. "I'll text Hook down at Redwood Realty and let him know asap. There's nothing sweeter than a girl trying to fill her big sister's shoes." She looks my way. "You keep out of trouble, missy. Oh, and before I forget, the funeral is set for next Monday. If you provide the baked goods, I'll foot the bill. That girl was a blessing to your sister." She sniffs hard as she pulls me in for a quick embrace. "I'd better get back to Pastor Gaines. I was helping with funeral arrangements. Now that Amanda is gone he'll need to hire an event staff himself. I'll see if I can get her sister to help out with that." She dashes out the door with a wave.

Cormack pulls Keelie to the side, and they dive deep into all things wedding-related.

"It seems Cormack is wedding obsessed," I say to Noah and Everett just above a whisper. "But since she's got a close connection to Hazel, I suggest we keep it that way."

Everett wraps an arm around me. "I'm in complete agreement with you."

Noah averts his eyes. "Fine, but once this case is solved, the farce is over. The last thing I want is an ambush wedding." His lips flicker my way. "Unless, of course, you're the bride. In that event, ambush away."

Everett takes a deep breath as if he were completely relaxed. "She will be a bride. You just won't be the groom."

"Pizza anyone?" I ask as I stagger over to a table and fall into a seat.

Noah, Everett, and I each grab a slice as we lose ourselves in mozzarella heaven.

"No matter what the problem, Mangias' pizza always seems to be the answer," I point out.

Noah's chest bounces. "I wish it was that easy. Did you get a read on any of those idiots? Is there anything at all you think would be able to help me out?"

I frown when he says the word *me*. I don't like being locked out of the fun. Not that capturing killers and thieves alike is fun, but a part of me thirsts to do just that.

"There was a diamond pattern on the neck of one of the men. His skin looked pink just under his ear."

Noah freezes and looks straight ahead for a few seconds before swallowing. He snaps up a stack of napkins.

"I think I'll take my slice to go." He gets up and lands a kiss to my cheek. "Everett, if you can, maybe hang out with Lottie for a while. My nerves are rattled, and I know hers are, too."

"Where are you going?" I ask frantically as he edges to the door.

"To the office. I'll call you in a bit." He takes off, and I sigh as I look to Everett.

"You don't need to babysit me. I'm closing tonight."

"Then I don't mind closing with you. And, for the record, I'm not babysitting. I'm spending quality time with the girl I love."

"In that case, why don't we head to the kitchen and I'll teach you how to use the Hobart mixer?"

Cormack plops down in Noah's empty seat, and Everett looks more than a little relieved.

"What's up, lovebirds?" She gives a cheeky wink. "I bet you're right back to planning your wedding." She elongates the last word. "Hey? I was going to surprise Noah this Saturday night and take him to hear the wedding singer Amanda introduced me to"—her voice quiets down a notch—"the night she died. He's performing at a wedding in Leeds, and the bride and groom have already given me the go-ahead to attend after the dinner portion of the reception. Why don't the two of you come along? Amanda assured me that Christopher Castaneda was the one and only wedding singer we would ever want."

"Chrissy?" I perk up as I look to Everett. "Are you free Saturday night?"

"For you? Always."

Cormack squeals with delight. "Then it's a date." She claps as if it were a victory on her part. "How I love our double dates. Oh, Essex, did you ever think we'd be like family someday? And now that Noah and you have patched things up, we're going to be exactly that. Hey? I know. How about the two of you get married next June, too? Oh, wait"—her cherry red nails strum against her cheek—"Noah and I are scheduled to get hitched first weekend of June, and I'm planning a honeymoon to end all honeymoons." It comes out throaty and seductive, and suddenly I have the urge to shove Cormack's face into the pizza box. "Maybe you should shoot for the first weekend in July?"

Everett cocks his head as if he were amused. "Why not the Fourth of July?"

Cormack gasps while dramatically clutching at her chest. "And that way not only will you have the easiest anniversary on record to remember, but the entire world will be celebrating with you."

"It's just the U.S. that will be celebrating," I'm quick to point out before frowning at Everett for going along with her delusions. Now I'll have to watch my back next Fourth of July in the event Cormack decides to throw us an impromptu wedding, and I'm pretty sure she'd do it. She seems to be our biggest cheerleader.

Cormack hops to her feet. "I'd better secure Hazel for all your wedding needs. Her calendar is bound to fill up just as quickly as her sister's. See you Saturday night!"

Lily zips over. "Where are we headed Saturday night?" She shrugs. "I'm desperate for another date with Alex."

"A wedding out in Leeds. Don't outshine the bride."

"I wouldn't dream of it." Her eyes are wide and vacant looking as if she's dreaming of exactly that right now.

Lily takes off, and I lean in toward Everett.

"The Fourth of July?"

"What? A good time will be had by all."

I bite down on my lower lip. "I miss our good times." My cheeks flood with color.

"Good," Everett says it sober, as those serious cobalt eyes pierce through mine. "I like you missing me. It gives me hope."

My chest pinches as he says it.

"My heart isn't going anywhere, Everett."

I'm afraid we both know it. Like it or not, my heart is very much tethered to two different people. My splintered heart doesn't seem to be going anywhere indeed.

But I, however, am going somewhere this Thursday night whether Noah or Everett approves or not.

I may not be getting lucky with Everett tonight, but I'll be getting lucky in just a few short days.

I'm coming for you, Connie Canelli.

And I hope whatever you're about to tell me will make me shout *bingo*.

CHAPTER 8

"*B*ingo!" Cormack shouts and I yank her back just as she tosses her arms up.

"I'm pretty sure that's not how it works," I say as we step into the cavernous basement beneath a restaurant called the Trattoria. Meg led the way, but once we arrived, she had an emergency down at Red Satin she needed to tend to. Something about a slippery runway and strippers down.

But Keelie and Cormack are with me. Lainey kindly declined my invite for a sisters' night out, which I completely understand. Poor Lainey probably thinks she needs to start wearing a helmet and a Kevlar vest just to be in my presence, and she's probably right.

The Trattoria is an upscale Italian restaurant—or at least as upscale as you can get in Leeds—complete with a back entry that has a set of stairs that lead to this alphanumeric nirvana.

Dozens of plastic round tables are set out with matching plastic chairs, and each one of those is nearly filled with a body hunched studiously over at least a half dozen cards each. At the front of the room there's a large round cage that a pretty brunette spins into oblivion and periodically plucks a number out of.

I scan the crowd for signs of Connie, but there's an entire sea of dark hair tilted down toward the tables. I'll never find her like this.

And then, just as if He knew I needed a sign, a spasm of light explodes above a table near the front as Owlbert Einstein shimmers to life—or death as it were.

"This way, ladies." I lead us straight to Connie's table, and sure enough there she is in a hot pink tracksuit, her matching pink lips twisted as she studies the plethora of game boards scattered around her. She's chewing a piece of gum frenetically as if her life depended on that tiny pink ball of slime, and her hair is teased up over her head as if she were paying homage to the eighties. A couple of girls are seated on either side of her, but, for the most part, the rest of the table is open.

"Take a seat, ladies," she barks our way as if we were disrupting her concentration, and I'm sure we are. "Next round starts in two minutes." She lifts a hand in the air and snaps her fingers, prompting a couple of girls to come around, and we purchase about six game boards apiece.

Cormack sets down her enormous green tote bag. She let us know on the way over that she chose the size and the color because both were omens for good luck. I'm sure her large green trust fund is a magnificent source of good luck, too.

"Hi, Connie." Cormack falls in the seat next to mine and gets to arranging her cards. My mouth falls open with deep regret for ever mentioning Connie's name on the way over. Wait a minute. I didn't.

"Hey, Mack." Connie doesn't even bother to look up.

"You two know each other?" I make crazy eyes at Keelie. Of course, I let Keelie in on who I would be investigating.

"Bingo!" Connie launches out of her seat like a bottle rocket, and a deep groan emits from around us.

Cormack waves me off. "Sure, we know each other." She gets

up and blows air kisses at the chipper brunette. "We do naked yoga together down at the gym."

Good Lord.

"I think she cheats, Lottie." Owlbert's voice whirs like a motor and echoes as it rings out across the room. "I don't know how, but I'm almost positive of it. And according to the rumors that have been swirling here tonight, others feel the same."

I make a face at the revelation. She is a Canelli. They're all cheats as far as I'm concerned. The entire family is comprised of criminal masterminds. What can you expect?

"Connie Canelli." She nods over at Keelie and me as her lips expand with a winner's grin. "Welcome to my world." She frowns over at me as she takes her seat once again. "Haven't we met before?"

"At my engagement party." And how I hate to frame it that way.

Cormack shoves her hand toward Connie. "My engagement party. Lita was an add-on item. Buy one engagement party, get one free." She cackles up a storm while Connie inspects the hardware on her finger.

Keelie leans in. "Don't worry, Lot. When you really get engaged, I'm going to throw you the world's biggest party."

"And I'm doing the same for you." I give a sly wink.

"No way." Her eyes grow wide. "Bear and I are low-key, remember?"

"No, you're not. There's nothing low-key about you, Keelie. And if Bear thinks so, allow me to introduce the two of you sometime."

Connie groans as if Cormack just shot her. "You've got a good man there, Mack Mack. Any man who picks out a rock like that is in l-o-v-e."

"Oh yes, he is," Keelie adds, kicking me from under the table because she knows that Noah picked that ring out for me.

Cormack draws her hand back. "It's a replica, of course. I

would never be foolish enough to run around with the real deal, considering all of the many unfortunate events that can befall a person and their jewelry these days." She shoots me the side-eye.

Great. Of all the people to judge me, I've got Mack Mack—the exact person I'd like to smack smack.

Connie's face brightens as she looks my way. Her features are well-defined. She's wearing enough rouge for the entire table, but the peachy shade makes her look like a Kewpie doll, and that might, in fact, be the look she was going for.

"How's Essex?" She gives a cheeky wink my way, and every muscle in my body freezes. Connie Canelli? *Really*, Everett? Have you no bounds? "Kidding!" She claps her hands together and laughs violently to the point of wheezing. "I know all about that rough and dirty bad boy, right down to the verbal privileges he doles out to women. He used to date a good friend of mine. Maybe you know her? Fiona Dagmeyer?"

I suck in a quick breath. I guess on the surface it makes sense. Fiona is a defense lawyer—and a family like the Canellis more or less needs an entire entourage of defense lawyers in their back pocket.

"Yes, I do know her." I try to act casual while arranging my game boards. "She's a good attorney."

Connie lifts her empty glass, and immediately a girl is there to replace it with a fresh glass of something dangerously fruity and most likely toxic.

"You know what they say"—Connie leans my way—"a good lawyer knows the law. A great lawyer knows the judge."

The entire table breaks out into cackles as if everyone were in on the joke.

Yes, I get it. In fact, I've heard it before.

And she's right. After all, Fiona has most certainly earned the right to call Everett by his proper moniker.

The next game gets underway before I have a chance to ask

another question. It's concentration central. Who knew keeping an eye on multiple cards at a time would prove challenging?

I glance over to Connie who seems to have colored in half her cards by now.

"It's a shame about Amanda," I say and she doesn't lift a brow. I'm about to give it another go when I spot a glowing figure stepping in behind her, and that glowing figure looks exactly like someone I love.

"Judge Baxter!" I call out as I jump out of my seat. Judge *Edward* Baxter to be exact.

"It's *bingo*, Lola. Get it straight." Cormack doesn't sound amused as she gets right back to work.

"I'll watch your cards," Keelie calls out.

Owlbert flies in low. "And I'll watch Connie. She's inexplicitly close to winning again. That would make three times in a row. You know what they say, third time's a crime."

"Sounds good," I say before motioning to the handsome poltergeist before me. "Come here," I practically mouth the words as I navigate him to a corner. "It's so good to see you, Judge Baxter!" I stop myself from lunging my arms around him. Honestly, I don't know him all that well, and there are enough eyes here to catch me trying to hug a ghost. It's the exact reason I'm facing the wall as I carry out this spirited dalliance. Spirited in the literal sense, of course. "Swing by my place later, and I'll invite Everett over."

He frowns, and in the process looks so much like his son it's eerie. Save for some gray peppered in around his ears, he's all the same.

"I can't." He offers a simple shrug. "It's not up to me when I appear and where. I can move within the vicinity once I arrive, but this time around it's a bit more orchestrated where I end up." He points skywards.

"I see." I scowl over at Cormack as if this were somehow her fault. "Well, then I'll have to invite Everett to join us. But believe me when I say he won't be thrilled to be here. Technically, it's me he doesn't want to be here." I pull the phone out of my pocket.

Guess who I ran into tonight in Leeds? Your father! Come join the fun!

I send Everett the address, give him directions, and ask him to text once he gets here.

He texts back. **Be right there.**

I flash the phone his father's way. "Everett will be here in no time." I glance back to Connie, and a knot tightens in the pit of my stomach. "On second thought, I'd better ask him to meet up with us in the parking lot." And I do just that. "So, how is eternity treating you? Are you thrilled to be back on this spinning rock to help put away the bad guys?"

He takes a breath he clearly doesn't need. "Eternity couldn't be better. Believe me when I say, dead is where it's at. It almost makes this planet and everything that happens on it feel as if you're watching a film in black and white, in slow motion, and backwards all at once."

"Wow. That says a lot. I bet my father is having a great time."

A warm smile graces his familiar face, and it makes me automatically return the favor.

"I've met your father, Lottie. He is indeed having a great time. We golf."

"You golf?" Every last bone in my body tingles at the thought. "That's wonderful! Have you met Noah's father, too?"

He glowers at the mention of him.

"Never mind. I'm going to get back to the table, and as soon as Everett gets—"

"Lemon," a familiar deep voice rumbles from behind. If his voice hadn't given him away, the heady scent of his cologne would have.

My body goes rigid.

I spin slowly on my heels, only to face the hottest judge this side of the living.

"How did you get here so quickly?"

"I was down the street."

My mouth falls open. "At a nudie bar?" I poke him in the gut with the accusation.

"No." He winces. "Yes. But I was with Noah. It's for the investigation."

"With Noah? Are you and Noah cheating on my investigation with each other?" Wait. That is not what I meant to say.

His brows hood low. "And what are you doing here? Why are Keelie and Cormack sitting at a table with Connie Canelli?"

Edward chortles at the thought. "Tell him to go easy on you. This is your calling."

I pick up Everett's hand. "Say hi to your daddy. He says to go easy on me, by the way. This is my calling."

Everett looks to where I nod, and his eyes grow wide. "Dad? Is it really you?"

"It is, son. I'm back, and I couldn't be happier that you're finally able to hear me say this. I love you, and I'm proud of you. You're a wonderful man, and you have a wonderful woman by your side."

Everett's eyes water on cue, and he takes a quick breath as if trying to stave off his emotions.

"Thank you," he whispers. "Thank you from the bottom of my heart. I'm going to cherish those words for as long as I live."

"Good." The older version straightens with a smile. "Because once you stop living, I'll be there to greet you, and I'll say it all over again."

"Aw." All this gushing of emotion is turning me into a puddle. There's nothing sweeter than some good old-fashioned family lovin'. "So, what about those thugs that are terrorizing Honey Hollow? Max mentioned you were sent to assist me."

"Oh, we are," he muses. "Nell followed them as they left the bank. They were in an old blue cargo van with mud covering the plates. She traced them right to Leeds, and then she vanished."

"Great," I say. "It sounds as if whoever is in charge of your appearances has a sense of humor."

Everett looks questioningly to his father. "Dad, who are these thugs? You must know something."

"I do." His ghostly frame leans in as if someone might hear. It never fails to amuse me how much the dead act and feel as if they're still alive. "I want you and Noah to do a search of recent burglaries, starting from the base of the country and work your way up. Look for a pattern. I think you'll find a few ominous clues as you do. I'm afraid that's all I know for now. I'll speak to you both when I can." He nods to our left as he dissipates, and we look over to see Connie Canelli grinning wildly at Everett as she sashays her way over.

"*Essex.*" She shakes her hips as she wraps her arms around him. "I just had drinks with Fiona last night." She chews her gum quickly as she speaks, and it really does look like an impossible feat she's pulling off. "She told me some pretty wild stories about you and that courthouse. *Eh?*" She jabs his arm with her fist. "You're a real freak, you know that?"

He straightens with a sense of pride. "I've been called worse."

"Amanda thought so, too," I add without any regard to how Connie might take that. And to be honest, she can take it any way she wants so long as she spills what she knows about Amanda Wellington.

"Mandy?" she gasps as she leans back to get a better look at him. "You must have been a pre-billionaire boyfriend. Don't get me wrong, money is nice, but a body like yours, that face—I'd rather live in a box with you than a mansion with that, if you know what I mean."

Everett's chest rumbles with the idea of a laugh. "I'm a hair above living in boxes, but I like where you're going."

"You and Mandy, huh? Go figure." She shakes her head. "Hey? You don't think Mark got wind of it, do you? I heard whoever bumped her did it with poison." Her dark eyes slit my way. "And they used those turnovers as a conduit. You're not still selling those rat traps, are you?"

By the vat, I want to say but wisely decide against it.

Everett shakes his head. "She had nothing to do with it. But I want to get to the bottom of this and know who did." He gives my hand a squeeze. "I'll be honest, I had a beef with Mandy."

She blinks back with surprise before waving him off. "Who the hell didn't? Did she rip you off, too? I had her do a baby shower for my cousin a couple weeks back and she forgot the balloons. I could have shot her on sight—I like to take care of things like that myself." Her affect falls flat as if the latex malfeasance truly did call for bullets in retribution.

I lean in. "Do you know if she owed anyone money?"

"Why would Mandy owe anyone money? She knows better than to borrow from anyone but my brothers." She blinks up at Everett as if suddenly feigning innocence. "They're loan officers at a totally legit operation. Let's leave it at that, big boy, got it?" And she's right back to flirting.

"Hey?" A thought comes to me. "Did she borrow money from your brothers?"

"How do you think we met? But before you get any funny ideas, my brothers don't go around poisoning their clients."

"Of course," I say, at least hoping that it's true.

Everett takes a breath. "If you were to guess who killed her, who would it be?"

Connie tips her head back, her tongue still kneading that pink wad of gum in her mouth. "Okay." She tucks her chin to her chest, her eyes set directly to mine. "I'm going to say it, but only because we're all thinking it. Mark Russo needs to be thoroughly investigated for these so-called offshore accounts where he stashes his fortune from the government. But is he a killer? I don't think so. Yeah, the guy is shady. Yeah, he's unfaithful—but let's be honest. Mandy wasn't tying herself to the dock because this guy was an upstanding moral character. She liked designer shoes just as much as the next girl."

"Then who?" I elongate the word, and Owlbert flies over as if it were a calling card.

"Janelle Hastings." Connie lifts a penciled in brow. "About yea tall"— she holds her hand to her forehead—"brassy blonde, enough plastic parts to qualify for a stamp that reads *Manufactured by Mattel*? She had a real beef with the girl."

"Janelle Hastings?" I shake my head as I try to place the name, and sure enough an image of her standing next to Amanda that night flashes through my mind. "But Amanda introduced her as her best friend."

Any trace of a smile glides right off her face. "Exactly."

"Bingo!" someone shouts, and we look over to find Cormack waving a card in her hand.

Connie takes a quick breath. "That witch." She takes off, and it's just Everett and me.

"I wasn't investigating her." I shrug up at him. "*We* were."

He wraps his arms around my waist. "I love the we part."

"And why exactly is there a we when it comes to Noah and you?" I wrap my arms around his neck, and he frowns at the mention of his old stepbrother's name.

"Because there are some things that we can agree on. *We* like you alive and in one piece."

"Every piece of me misses every piece of you." I bat my lashes up at him.

"Then let me reintroduce myself."

Everett lands a soul-melting kiss over my lips that makes me forget everything about poor Amanda, about her so-called best friend, Janelle Hastings, and about where I am and who I am.

Everett's kiss reminds me of just one thing—exactly how very much he cares for me.

The Moose Lodge is the setting for this down-home reception, which looks to be hosting about five hundred of the newly minted Mr. and Mrs. Bradley Frisky's closest friends.

It's Saturday night, and, due to a previously scheduled engagement, my linear investigative trajectory, which included Janelle Hastings as my next target, was momentarily derailed. Okay, so it wasn't derailed just because this wedding was cropping up on the horizon. I can't seem to figure out where to locate the girl, and Hazel hasn't returned any of my calls ever since I rejected the six thousand legal tender motivators to help nab her sister's killer.

Lily and Alex are adorably matching tonight. Her red dress is the very same shade as his tie—and terrifyingly enough, it matches the rage in Naomi Turner's eyes. Yes, she's followed us here like a well-seasoned sleuth. It turns out, Lily left on the location services on her phone, and she was easier to hunt down than a mall Santa at Christmastime.

Both Noah and Everett look arrestingly handsome. I myself

have donned a simple black dress and heels because I don't like to stand out when it's another woman's day to shine.

I glance into the entry of the Moose Lodge and frown as I spot a sea of little black dresses already bopping to the music. Owlbert is already here, his feathery plumage spinning to the music high above the dance floor. He's adorable, and I wish I could keep him around long after this fiasco winds down.

The guy up on stage is killing a cover of some old rock song, and I recognize his dark curly hair and prominent chin as the guy I met the night of Noah's—*my* engagement party. The lodge itself is a little bit scary with taxidermy busts of every living creature known to man lining the walls of the cavernous room the reception is held in. A group of teenagers angles for a selfie with a ferocious looking bear dripping with fingerlike fangs.

"Mr. and Mrs. Frisky," Naomi muses as she pulls Noah's doppelgänger brother in by his long red tie. "I think I like where they're going with that fancy name of theirs." She giggles as she pulls him in close. She's donned a white silk gown that clings to her skin like wet paper. That's two fashion strikes as far as wedding etiquette is concerned.

Full disclosure: I tried to invite Keelie to our impromptu wedding crashing soiree, but she made up every lame excuse in the book to evade the matrimonial scene. I'm starting to wonder if she and Bear are actually engaged. The Keelie I know and love would never eschew an open bar.

"Mr. and Mrs. Frisky!" Cormack hops into Noah's arms, and he grunts as he catches her unexpectedly. Cormack has pulled out the big guns tonight, and I mean big literally. She's dressed in a powder blue number that has some sort of plume built in around the collar that jets out a foot over her head. Lily called her "a peacock in heat" on the way over from the parking lot, and she's not too far off base with that one. Cormack looks as if she belongs in some sort of a pornographic Valentine's Day card with her gown that shows off more than it does cover anything up.

Everett leans in. "I think they're going to get frisky."

Cormack does some body gliding maneuver as she shimmies down Noah as if he were a stripper pole.

"They're already frisky," I counter.

Cormack hops up as she takes Noah by the hand. "Come on, everybody. Let's get inside! Noah, let's pretend this is our wedding night."

"You do that." Everett blinks a dry smile Noah's way. "Lemon and I will do the same." His lids hood low as he looks my way, and it suddenly feels as if all of that *I think we should take a break* business is off the table.

Lily snatches Alex from Naomi and whisks him off to the dance floor without missing a beat. Of course, Naomi is dancing right there with them, and oddly enough they blend right into the hip swinging crowd.

We head in on their heels, and soon Cormack hijacks Noah once again as she hoists herself up and around his body like a seasoned gymnast.

I'm about to let a smart-aleck remark fly when my eyes gravitate to the impossible.

"Holy stars up above Honey Hollow!" I say, making a beeline to what could only be described as the wedding cake as it hangs from the *ceiling*.

A wooden platform adorned with white roses braided throughout the outer rim plays host to a three-tiered plain white cake with incandescent glowing blue butterflies floating up and down every surface.

"Oh my word," I say breathlessly.

Owlbert flies overhead, and his tiny body shimmers as if a thousand fireflies were trapped inside him.

"Stunning, isn't it?" he says as he flies around the periphery of the display. "Now let's get back to finding the killer. Chop-chop." He takes off back to the dance floor and whirls and twirls with the best of them. Something tells me he's enjoying this tiny bit of respite.

"Look at that." Everett points to the corner of the wooden base where it reads *A Cake Above Bakery* and I gasp.

A Cake Above is owned and run by my personal nemesis— okay, so she may not be aware of the fact she's my nemesis, but it's completely true in my mind.

"That's Crystal Mandrakes' place," I hiss her name out like a curse. "She's the one that beat me out of winning that refrigerated van last fall."

"That's because you let your pies burn in order to catch the killer we were after."

I turn and wrap my arms around this sweet, ornery, very good at getting frisky judge. "And you bought me a refrigerated van anyway."

"That's because you risked it all to clear my name."

"It must be love." I shrug up at him playfully.

"It is, Lemon." He comes in for the kill, and a body slices between us.

Noah offers a devilish grin. "I believe they're playing our song." He wraps his arms around me and begins to sway to the rhythm of the slow song Chrissy is currently warbling out.

"We don't have a song, Detective Fox."

"We do now."

I glance back, and Cormack has wrapped herself around Everett like a python with its afternoon snack. He shrugs over at me, so I go with it.

"Noah, you do realize had that disaster last winter with Britney never occurred this could have been our wedding. I've always envisioned myself as a fall bride. There's just something magical about this time of year. Plus, it's a great excuse to have a pumpkin spice wedding cake and it wouldn't be weird at all."

He moans as if it sounded delicious. I'm sure everything I just said sounded delicious to Noah.

His dimples dig in deep as a look of regret sweeps across his face. "I would do anything for this to have been our wedding, Lottie." He sways us closer to the dance floor. "How about we pretend this is our first dance as husband and wife?" There's a soulfulness in his voice, the underpinnings of agony just beneath that.

"I would love that." I close my eyes as I land my head over his chest, and I can feel his heartbeat reverberating against my cheek. My husband's heartbeat. The father of my future children.

Noah and I sway steadily as our bodies warm one another with desire. An entire montage plays out in my mind. Noah and I enjoying our own wedding cake in a far more intimate setting. Noah and I ducking out early, eager to start our first night as a married couple. Noah and I alone in some rose petal strewn love nest. I can feel his kisses. I can feel the warmth of his body pressed to mine just the way it is now. Noah would love me ferociously. He already does. He would love our children just the same. Of course, I'd make him buy a safe for that gun of his.

Come to think of it, he is in an awfully dangerous line of work. He could leave me widowed and my children fatherless at any given time. My eyes spring wide open as I have a mild panic attack over a family that's yet to exist.

"Liking what you see?" He drops a heated kiss over the top of my head.

"Would you consider turning in your gun and taking up a desk job?"

Before he can answer, Cormack chops her arm right through us as if we were a couple of seventh graders caught making out under the bleachers.

"Music finished five minutes ago." Her blonde locks fall haphazardly over her eyes as if Everett just gave her a good shakedown. "I believe Essex is looking for you." She scowls over at me a moment, and I do believe it's the first time Cormack has ever looked threatened by me.

I pull back, and spot Everett chatting it up with none other than Chrissy himself.

"Would you look at that? He sure does move fast," I muse.

"I'll say," Cormack purrs as she straightens her gown.

I choose to ignore her as I glide right over to the front where Everett and Chrissy are yucking it up as if they were old buddies.

"Lemon." Everett pulls me in, and his arm warms my shoulders. "I'd like you to meet Christopher Castaneda."

The dark-haired gentleman has a squiggly smile bouncing over his lips. "Judge Baxter sentenced me to three months of community service about four years ago. He didn't remember me, but I sure as heck remember this guy. Turned my whole life around. My community service was doing cleanup by the oil refinery up north. I ended up making nice with the grounds manager, and now many moons later, I'm a manager myself."

"Wow," I say, genuinely impressed. "You really did turn your life around."

"Judge Baxter has that effect on people." Chrissy slaps him on the shoulder. "He's a good guy. You're a lucky woman, Mrs. Baxter—or the future Mrs. Baxter. I happened to be at your engagement party."

Mrs. Baxter.

It does have a nice ring to it.

Everett leans in. "It's a shame what happened to the wedding planner. Any idea what went on that night?"

Chrissy glances to the ceiling before casting his gaze to the ground and scratching the back of his neck. "I don't know." His voice is threadbare. "Amanda was a beautiful woman. Full of life. She had everything going for her, and it kills me that someone saw fit to snuff the life out of her." He looks up with a fire in his eyes. "If I find out who did this, there might just be another murder to contend with."

"You really cared about her, didn't you?" I ask as I wrap my arms around Everett.

"I did. And I don't get it. She didn't have an enemy in the world."

"What about her friends? Connie? Janelle?" It's that second name I'm hoping will trigger something in him. Connie seemed determined to hand-feed her to us.

"Janelle is a cool girl. But Connie? She and Amanda were oil and water. That relationship was all about saving face."

"What?" I stumble forward. I don't want to miss a word. "But I thought she and Connie got along great." At least Connie made it seem that way.

"They did." He pauses as he looks from Everett to me. "That is, until Amanda snatched Mark Russo right from under Connie's nose."

I suck in a sharp breath and give Everett's waist the death squeeze in the process. Connie is a Canelli, and everyone in their right mind who knows anything about the Canellis knows they shouldn't do anything at all to enrage a single member of that crooked clan, Connie included.

"That's shocking." I try to play it off as if maybe it wasn't.

"It sure is," Everett adds. "Especially knowing that the Canellis are generally feared around these parts."

He shakes his head. "Amanda didn't have the common sense to fear them. She started seeing Mark on the heels of a hot and heavy relationship with Jimmy Canelli."

I happen to know that Jimmy is one of the aforementioned Canelli brothers.

My mouth falls open. "You mean to tell me that Amanda had the cookies to dump Jimmy and steal Connie's boyfriend? That doesn't sound like the Amanda I knew." Not that I knew her all that well, but still.

Chrissy's brows hike up into his forehead. "That doesn't sound like the Amanda I knew, but she did it."

Everett nods. "How did you know her?"

"Met her on a dating app. She dumped me right after I introduced her to Jimmy. Jimmy and I grew up together."

The band starts up, and he glances back at the stage and signals for them to wait.

"I'd better get up there. It's nice seeing you both again. And congratulations on the upcoming wedding. I'll do your gig for free!" He hops on stage and doesn't miss a note of the song already playing.

"Hear that, Lemon? We've already booked a wedding singer."

"Next July is starting to shape up nicely," I tease. "What do you think of that stuff about Amanda?"

Everett takes a breath, and his chest expands the size of a door. "I hate to say it, but he painted her to be something akin to a social climber."

I nod in agreement. "And she didn't seem to mind that the rung she was stepping on was set over a Canelli landmine. Why do you think Connie omitted that little tidbit about Amanda stealing her man?"

"Saving face?"

"Or deflecting us from the fact she put a hit on her?"

Everett wraps his arms around me, and we sway slowly to the music.

"I don't know, Lemon. The Canellis aren't known for poisoning women. This would be a first."

"It's almost something that a woman might do," I say, locking eyes with his. "A woman who was scorned and likes to take care of things herself." I don't mind quoting Connie one bit.

"Do you think Connie is our killer?"

"I don't know, but it's sure not looking good for her. Monday is the funeral. I'll try to feel out Connie again. Maybe invite Fiona? She really likes her, and she might loosen her up a bit. I'll try to speak with Janelle Hastings as well."

"Working at a funeral. There really is no rest for the weary."

"There's no rest for the wicked," I counter. "Amanda Wellington's killer had better watch their back."

Everett's chest rumbles with a dull laugh as he spins me, and my line of vision falls to Noah and Cormack dancing just the way we are a mere three feet away. Cormack has her eyes closed, her cheek pressed right up against Noah's heart, and I can't help but wonder if she's envisioning what it would be like to be his wife.

I'd give anything for our lives not to be so complicated.

But then, maybe we're both in the arms of the ones we belong with.

I turn my head, and my gaze snags on Chrissy. He gives a quick wink my way, and I wonder how much of what he said was the truth and how much was a lie.

The song ends, and the bride and groom are ushered to that floating cake in the proverbial sky as the guests all gather around en mass awaiting a bite of its sugary goodness.

A drumroll starts up and the cake is slowly lowered, smoothly at first then in odd, uneven spurts, causing the cake to slide to one end. The crowd gasps in horror, and I clap my hand over my eyes to watch through my fingers. I may not care for Crystal, but what's unfolding is every baker's nightmare. And at a wedding no less.

The groom grabs a chair and jumps up in time to straighten the wood panel before it dumps a bucketful of buttercream over the guests below.

"I got it!" he calls out as the crowd erupts in cheers.

The ropes that hold it to the ceiling snap like rubber bands, and the platform, the entire cake comes crashing down. Chrissy swipes the bride from danger as the cake falls to her feet with a splat.

Owlbert flies overhead who-whoing away, and it sounds as if he's laughing.

"There is something to be said for doing things the old-fashioned way, Lottie."

"Amen to that," I whisper under my breath.

Now that the debate as to if cake installations are better than a traditional setting has been answered, I've got a far more pressing question I need answered.

Who killed Amanda Wellington?

And why?

CHAPTER 10

*M*onday morning brings crisp winds as autumn is ushered into our world with a rich abundance of color. All of Vermont has made the transformation, taking off its verdant green coat in exchange for rich ambers, golden yellows, and fiery reds.

Every maple that lines Main Street is alive with citrine brilliance, and slowly pumpkins begin to dot the storefronts and residences alike. It's my favorite time of year to cozy up by the fire with a stack of good books, a hot cup of cider, and my cats on either side of me. I wouldn't mind Noah and Everett being there as well, but that could prove to be disastrous—the three of us. What an awful coital conundrum I've gotten myself into. What a horrible situation when your heart simply cannot choose.

It's the afternoon of Amanda Wellington's funeral, and the skies are thick with dark clouds with navy underbellies. It seems our whole world is full of ominous signs as of late. After that bank heist, every resident in Honey Hollow has been on edge. The Ashford Sheriff's Department has stepped up patrol up and down the streets of our cozy small town and, in truth, it feels as if we're under siege.

Honey Hollow Covenant Church is packed tightly with all of Amanda's nearest and dearest friends. Her sister and her brother are huddled up front. I'm not sure what the story with her parents is, but I don't see anyone sitting in a prominent position who might qualify.

Noah and Ivy are seated in the back, per their usual funeral stakeout. Noah likes to keep it all business at events like this even though he is firm on paying his respects and offering the family his condolences. Everett and I are seated together, his strong, warm hand holding mine, and it feels right like this with him, safe.

Pastor Gaines conducts a brief yet beautiful service, that creepy smile never leaving his face. I'm not sure why it irks me so, but it does.

There is no casket, no body, just an oversized picture of Amanda's face. It's the same picture she used at Redwood Realty, and if you look closely, the tagline *Selling Honey Hollow* is still prominent on the border to the left.

Connie Canelli is seated next to Hazel. And Chrissy and Mark flank Amanda's brother on the other side. I don't see Janelle, but maybe she's running late? Or perhaps she opted to sit outside of the glaring funeral spotlight and is somewhere in the back with Noah. I couldn't blame her.

And as much as there isn't a dry eye in the house, it's easy to deduce that the one being that appears the most distraught over Amanda's passing is Owlbert Einstein himself. He sits perched over the enormous framed picture, letting off his low raspy hoots two at a time, but sometimes six in a row. And oddly enough, Dutch, the ghost of the Golden Retriever I met last December, is seated below her picture dutifully as well, with his burning fiery eyes staring sullenly out at the crowd.

But that's not the only oddity here. Beastie, the grand white Bengal tiger, has been traipsing up and down the aisle with little Lea on his back. Lea has her long hair pulled down over her face

—I'm guessing that's the way she likes it. And despite her incessant giggling as Beastie bobs up and down, she's wielding that hatchet in her hand as if she means business.

It's all a bit unnerving to say the least.

Once the funeral is over, we're all quickly ushered into the reception area, a hall that's attached to the church. Lily helped me haul over enough cookies and brownies to feed all of Honey Hollow. Of course, out of respect for Amanda, there's nary a single apple turnover in the bunch.

The hall is brightly lit, and there are bodies swirling in every direction, accompanied by chatter and bouts of laughter as if it were a joyous occasion.

Everett leans in. "Who's on your radar, Lemon?"

"Connie and Janelle." I frown into the crowd when I spot Lainey and Forest huddled together. "And Lainey, but I doubt this is the time to try to convince her I'm not a walking broken mirror." I shoot Everett a look. "I might be, but that's not the point."

His cheek flickers with devilish delight before his attention is snagged away. "Fiona is here. I'll go talk to her and let her know we want to get Connie to open up to us."

"Do you think you can get her to cooperate with us? I mean, she is friends with Connie, too."

"I can get Fiona to do anything I like." His lids hood low, and my stomach bisects with heat in response. No sooner does Everett take off than Carlotta clip-clops her way over in a pair of sky-high heels.

"What's with the stilts?" I can't help but ask. I've never seen Carlotta in anything but boots or sneakers. She's been known to dress for comfort and not for style. "Looking to impress the dead?"

"Oh hush." She plucks off her left shoe and sighs as soon as her foot hits the cool comfort of the floor. "I'm looking to impress Harry. He's been sneaking off with your mother behind my back again."

I cringe at the thought. "Maybe you should try to steal Pastor Gaines from her?" I giggle at the thought. "And just to clarify, I'm teasing. Do not intermesh yourself with my mother's love life more than you already have."

"I'm not going anywhere near Pastor Gaines." She shoves her finger in her mouth and pretends to vomit.

"Oh, come on. He's not so bad. He always has a smile on his face, so that has to count for something."

Carlotta squirms as she steps back into her shoe. "And that's the exact reason I plan on staying away. Mama Nell always said 'never trust a man who doesn't know when to stop smiling.'"

"I'm with her on that." I spot Pastor Gaines, and a shiver rides up my spine. "I wish my mother would realize that. Hey? You don't think he's dangerous, do you?"

She makes a face while staring him down. My mother is by his side and so are Mayor Nash and his ex-wife, Chrissy. An odd crowd if ever there was one.

"I don't know," she says. "But personally, I plan on staying very far away. Now if you'll excuse me, I promised Lea I'd eat a cookie or twelve for her."

She takes off just as I spot Everett speaking with Fiona and—oh! Connie Canelli pops up behind her and covers Fiona's eyes with her hands before they both break into cackles like a couple of sorority girls. I hustle on over, and Owlbert beats me to it, landing his white fuzzy talons on Everett's left shoulder. I can tell by the way Everett is jerking his shoulder slightly that he feels a presence there.

I'm quick to take up Everett's hand. "Connie, Fiona, so nice to see you both. How I wish it was under better circumstances."

Connie's dark hair is curled and sprayed into crunchy submission, she's chewing her gum at a million miles an hour, and I'm beginning to think it's a nervous habit. She's donned a black skirt, a matching blazer, and there's a pop of pink coming from her tank top underneath. As far as I can tell, the perky hue is her calling card.

Connie leans in. "What are you gonna do? You can't bring the dead back."

"Yoo hoo!" a warbling voice calls to me from the left, and I spot Nell waving my way.

We may not be able to bring back the dead, but sometimes they pop back all on their own. I give a quick wave back and then motion for her to stay put. Carlotta makes a beeline for her, and it offers me a sense of security. Carlotta has been known to yap her mother's ear off, so hopefully I won't miss a minute with Nell because of this investigation.

Fiona huffs, "My ex-husband died years ago, and I don't mind one bit that he's trapped on the other side."

"I didn't know that about you," I say just as it occurs to me it may not be entirely true. Everett did say he would fill her in on the fact we're trying to pump Connie for information.

Connie gasps, "I didn't know that either." She smacks her lips like she might be sick. "What did the louse do to end up on the outs with you?"

"Cheated." Fiona shoots me the side-eye, and I sincerely hope it's to tip me off that she's trying to shake Connie down for details, and not because she thinks I'm cheating on Everett. I would never do that to him.

Noah bounces through my mind, and I bounce him right back out.

Connie's eyes flare with rage. "I hate cheats."

Fiona nods. "To make things worse, he cheated with my very best friend."

Connie gasps, and the veins in her neck pop as her agitation grows. "I hate best friend boyfriend stealers even more." She gives a quick glance around. "There is no greater betrayal in my book. I've had to handle one or two of those myself."

Handle? Why do I get the feeling *handle* can easily translate into kill?

Fiona grunts, "When you're up for it, tell me how to handle it. She's still hanging around trying to annoy me."

Connie's face smooths out. "Tell me her name, and I'll take care of the rest." Someone whistles our way and she waves. "I'd better mingle."

"Mingle." Owlbert shudders. "She did it, Lottie. She poisoned poor Amanda. I demand you arrest her immediately."

"It doesn't work that way," I say it lower than a whisper.

Mingle?

Everett and I exchange a glance.

Fiona steps in. "What do you think?"

"What do you think?" Everett throws it right back at her.

"Listen, Essex"—her heavily drawn in eyes look up at him —"I've come to be very good friends with Connie. And I certainly don't need to tell you how dangerous her family can be. Let's just say if Connie wanted Amanda out of the picture, we would most certainly be standing here today." She glances my way with a look of disdain on her face. "But that doesn't mean she did it. Everyone deserves due process. Now, if you'll excuse me, I see my favorite chunky peanut butter bars waiting for me."

She takes off and leaves us with a trail of her lavender-scented perfume.

"Everett." I pull him in close by the hand. "She sounds terribly guilty."

"She is!" Owlbert screeches right into Everett's ear and causes poor Everett to groan as if he were shot.

"Not officially." Everett gives his shoulder a dirty look before reverting to me. "Let's make use of the venue. Where's her friend? The one Connie implicated?"

"I haven't seen Janelle." I do another scan of the vicinity. "I can't imagine why she wouldn't be here today. Maybe it's too hard? Maybe she's not feeling well?"

I spot Hazel in the corner having what looks to be a heated conversation with her brother.

"Do you see that?"

"Yes. But I also see something else. Follow me." He leads us through the crowd, and soon enough we come upon two men, Chrissy Castaneda and Mark Russo, the billionaire who dumped Connie for Amanda. Talk about brass cookies. He's lucky *he's* alive.

"Chrissy," I say, perhaps a little too perky. "You were great the other night. It's nice to see you again. I'm sorry this isn't under better circumstances."

He's wearing a crisp black suit and black undershirt to match. He looks perfectly somber. Gone is the affable smile he shed so easily the other night.

"I wish that more than you know." He nods to his friend. "This is Mark, Amanda's fiancé."

Both Everett and I extend our sincerest condolences.

"How did you and Amanda meet?" Yes, I went there. I don't see why not. It's innocent enough on the surface.

Mark looks to be in his mid-thirties, dark hair, dark eyes, clean-shaven, has an air of superiority about him, and yet he seems simultaneously down-to-earth. But his suit looks expensive and his cologne holds a rich scent that I'm sure was strained through hundred dollar bills.

"Mandy and I met through a friend." He glances just past Chrissy, and I follow his gaze to Connie. Some friend. "I knew she was the one for me the minute I laid eyes on her. I was in another relationship, but I quickly got out of it. I would never entertain two hearts. It's not who I am. It's most certainly not how I was raised."

A horrible sinking feeling presses over me, and I suddenly feel like a girl guilty of entertaining two hearts—one of which is holding my hand at the moment.

"That's commendable," Everett offers. "But it couldn't have been easy. I've been on the receiving end of a breakup before."

I give his hand a quick squeeze because I'm fairly certain he hasn't—and then Cormack pops up between us and I gasp.

Of course, it was her. It's always her.

"Mark, I'm so sorry." She's wearing a black feathered number with a low-cut décolleté and a full skirt that looks as if it were better suited for the red carpets than a Honey Hollow funeral. "Have they caught the killer? Any idea who could have done this?"

Mark ticks his head to the side as if he were stymied. "There were motives, but we'll have to let the sheriff's department do their job."

"Motives?"

He nods my way. "There are lots of speculations about Connie's connection. She knows it."

Owlbert screams as if someone just yanked off a wing. "The other two—*who-who* are they?"

Everett grunts—I'm guessing due to all the screaming in his ear. "What are the other two motives?"

Mark looks to Chrissy, and a huff of a laugh bounces through his chest. "Greed. The answer is right there. And, of course"—he turns to his right, and his gaze sharpens hard over someone —"secrets."

I follow his gaze, but there's no one to see but my mother standing with Carlotta, Mayor Nash, and Pastor Gaines.

"If you'll excuse me." Mark takes off into the crowd.

"That was ominous," I say to Chrissy.

He does a quick sweep of the vicinity before stepping in. "Mark has his theories, but he doesn't want to share. Soon as word gets out, he's afraid it'll spook whoever did this."

"Do you know what he meant by greed and secrets?" I'm hoping he does.

He shakes his head. "He won't spill it, and I've stopped asking. I have full confidence in the Ashford Sheriff's Department."

"As do I," I echo. "You know, I haven't seen Janelle, and I was hoping to. Have you seen her?"

His lips crimp as he scans the crowd. "She wouldn't be here."

"Why not?" I hold my breath, frozen solid in anticipation.

"You'll have to ask her yourself."

A moment of silence bounces by.

Everett clears his throat. "Where can we find her?"

Chrissy looks my way. "The Egyptian Room. She's a teacher. If you see her, tell her to call me sometime. I miss her." He takes off in a rush, and Owlbert follows along with him.

"There's that," I say.

Everett begins navigating us through the crowd. "Noah is by the door. It looks as if he's leaving."

No sooner do we get there than Noah and Ivy are already moving through the parking lot.

"Noah!" I call out, running into the brisk air to catch up with him. "Not even a goodbye?" I'm only partially teasing.

His dimples press in, no smile as he looks past me to Everett. "I'm headed down to Ashford. I'll let you know the details as they arise. Something's come up."

"Wait," I say, glancing back to Everett, confused. "What details? What's this about?" I gasp as I look to Noah. "This is about the thieves, isn't it? Noah, please—I want to be a part of this. The dead said they would help me."

The muscles in Noah's jaw pop with tension. "Lottie, this isn't for you. I don't care what the dead say. I've got this handled, and I'm imploring you to stay out of my investigation."

"Again with this?" I'm stunned at the words that just came from his mouth. "This is my investigation, too."

"No, Lottie, it's not. This is *my* investigation. You need to back down and let the professionals handle this because it's not a game. People are in a lot of danger. You cannot put yourself in the middle of it."

A breath hitches in my throat. "Noah, I have never treated an investigation like a game. I can do this. I can help you track them down. I'm the best there is." I cringe internally at how horrific that sounded. I've never been one to toot my own horn.

Noah glances back at Everett. "Forget it, Lottie. You are too important to me, and I will not be a willing participant in anything that might put you in harm's way. Everett"—he glowers at him a moment before taking off—"I'll talk to you later."

"Talk to who? Everett?" I turn his way, panting and angry. "You're in agreement with him, aren't you? Neither of you wants me to be a part of this."

Noah's truck cruises by with Ivy in the passenger's seat. He slows a moment to roll down his window.

"I'm sorry, Lottie. I just want to keep you safe. Stay away from this. I mean it."

I suck in a breath. "You stay away from my investigation, Noah," I growl at him. "Both Amanda and the thieves belong to me. I'm going to bring justice to both of those cases, and you'll be sorry you ever shunned me."

I glance back to Everett. "You, too."

I take off for my car.

How dare they team up against me.

How dare they underestimate me.

Amanda's killer is going down. And as soon as I talk to the dead, the thieves' days are numbered.

I don't need Noah or Everett.

I head home feeling so very alone.

CHAPTER 11

*T*he next morning, as I step into the Cutie Pie Bakery and Cakery ready and willing to bake up enough apple turnovers to feed the free world, I'm met with one of the sweetest ghosts on the planet—and I suspect the nethersphere, too.

"Nell Sawyer!" I pull her into a tight embrace. "You are a sight for sore eyes." I take her in with her silver glowing hair, her wrinkles, her wide grin and knowing eyes. "How I've missed you!"

"Tell me everything. Start with the juicy bits, would you? What about those men?"

"Noah basically told me to stay out of the investigation—specifically with those thieves who were responsible for the bank heist. Then I told him to stay out of *my* investigation, and that I was the best and didn't really need him. It got pretty ugly."

"Oh dear. Then what?"

"Then I pretty much turned on Everett, too, and I left. Everett texted as soon as I got home with just one word, *Lemon*. But strangely enough, I could feel the emotion behind it. And, of course, Noah texted, too, asking if we could get together today and have coffee."

"Did you answer? It would be immature of you not to have done so," she scolds me sweetly, and I can't help but smile.

"I did. I said no. Then he asked if later this week would work better, and that's the text I didn't respond to. I never claimed to be mature."

"Oh heavens." She rolls her eyes. "Go on. Get your day going. I'm not here to slow you down. In fact, let me help you."

Nell dons an apron, and sure enough we crank out my morning inventory in half the time and all the while chatting up a storm about anything and everything.

"It's almost time to open the doors." I give her a wry smile. "Spill it, Nell. Tell me who those men are."

"Have you looked into the clue that Max gave you?"

"About the string of robberies spanning from the bottom of the country on up? It seems like a daunting task."

"It won't be. Noah has already done it, and he's figured out exactly who they are." She lifts a glowing brow. "With a little elbow grease, you could easily catch up with Noah. Are you going to let him best you?"

I gasp at the thought. "Certainly not." I glance to the clock. "It's time to open up shop, but I can assure you, this day doesn't end without me diving into the deep end of that mystery."

The morning rush never lets up. In fact, it morphs right into the afternoon rush with Britney's Swift Cycle castoffs—she sends her clients my way to gain back their calories, and I don't mind one bit. Of course, this usually sends Britney herself and Cormack, her forever sidekick.

They come this way swinging their matching blonde pony-tails, Britney's left eye safely hidden from the world by a loose lock of hair.

"Did you hear the news?" Britney chortles as she says it.

Lily scuttles over. "News? What news?" Lily is a gossip in training, so I understand her need to know.

Britney looks to Cormack. "Go ahead and spill it, Mac and Cheese."

I can't help but feel a little vindicated when Britney gifts her the silly nickname. Neither of them has ever gotten my name right.

Cormack sniffs with pride. "It's official. Noah and I have entered into couple's counseling. After much research, Noah has decided on the exact counselor he and Britney saw to oversee the dissolution of their marriage."

Britney grunts, "That wasn't the point. But it will be for you."

Cormack waves her away. "Don't listen to her, girls"—she leans in—"*bitter* grapes. Noah and I have begun our journey to the altar. Everyone knows the church recommends a series of counseling sessions before you tie the knot. And next June will be here before you know it."

I'm not sure how much more of this delusional soon-to-be jilted June bride I can take.

Carlotta and my aunt Becca all head in at once, and Nell zooms forward.

"Here are the girls I long to see," Nell sings dreamily at the sight of them.

Lily takes Britney and Cormack's orders while I wave them over.

Becca taps into her phone. "I've just texted Keelie." She wrinkles her nose. Becca is Keelie and Naomi's mother. She has amazing creamy blonde hair with crimson highlights and high cheekbones that would make any supermodel envious.

No sooner does she say those words than my best friend appears and wraps an arm around my shoulder.

"What's going on, ladies?"

Nell purrs with delight. "What's going on indeed?"

Keelie gasps as she looks around, "I could have sworn I just heard Grammy Nell!"

Both Nell and I exchange a horrifying glance, and she's quick to make a zipping motion across her lips as if she were sealing them up. In all fairness, Keelie is touching me so that makes anything Nell says fair game.

Becca looks up at Carlotta from under her lashes. "That would be a bit serendipitous. And knowing our spunky mother, she would indeed be here if she could. We've got news on the will. My brother's court date is next Thursday. We're all invited to the Ashford Courthouse to see what the judge will decide."

My body breaks out into a sweat all at once. When Nell passed away last January, she stipulated in her will that I get the lion's share of her real estate empire. Of course, she gave each of her children enough to live comfortably on, but that wasn't nearly enough for my new uncle William. A part of me can't blame him. Nobody even knew I was related until that very moment.

"I guess I'd better be there."

Carlotta gets a glazed look in her eyes. "We're all going to be there, Lottie, and we're all going to cheer when my greedy brother eats crow."

I sigh. "Please don't let this drive a wedge between you. Even if the judge doesn't dismantle the will, I'll certainly give everything I gain right back to the three of you."

"Don't you dare!" both Carlotta and Nell shout in unison.

Keelie wraps her arms around her body and shudders.

"Fine," I say. We'll cross that burned bridge when we come to it.

Mom, Carlotta, and Becca put in an order and take a seat.

Keelie is about to take off, and I catch her by the elbow.

"What are you doing tonight?" I ask, hopeful that her calendar is clear.

A devilish gleam comes to her eyes as she swoops in close. "You tell me, Lottie Lemon. I hope there's a good time involved because I've been itching to cut loose."

"You bet there is. I'll pick you up at seven."

"Great!" she sings as she takes off.

"Don't you want to know where we're going?"

"I don't care! As long as I'm with you, I know we're in for a good time!"

It will be a time, all right.

I glance back to find Nell seated at the table with her daughters and my mother. If I didn't know better, it looks as if she's still among the living.

The crowd has settled, so I ask Lily to man the fort for a moment. I head to the back and steal a moment to huddle in my office as I run a search on my phone, looking for a chain of robberies, thefts, or home invasions all over the country. And what I find is staggering similarities to the events in Honey Hollow regarding the home robberies and the bank heist. Similar events happened in Florida just eight weeks ago, South Carolina seven weeks ago, Virginia six weeks ago, Pennsylvania four weeks ago, and New York three weeks ago. The bank robbery consisted of six gunmen, each in masks. The masks are always different—clowns, monsters, *animals*.

Son of a gun.

Six sons of guns.

Nell was right. With a little elbow grease, I could easily catch up with Noah.

And catch up I did.

According to Nell, they're still in town. That means there's still time to catch them. I wonder where they'll strike next?

I wonder...

THE EGYPTIAN ROOM is on the border of Leeds and Ashford, and since I'm not crazy about the dicey proximity to the aforementioned sleazy town, I've asked Meg to tag along. She didn't spend the last few years on the Las Vegas wrestling circuit without a few moves to show for it. She can headlock with the best of them. Besides, I'm down one Glock at the moment. Boy, how I miss Ethel. And here she didn't even have a name while she was with me.

The Egyptian Room is a restaurant up front and a belly dancing studio in the rear.

Meg shakes her head as we're led toward our belly dancing nirvana by a woman in silk pink and gold pajamas.

"Business in the front, party in the back." My sister shoots me a sly eye. "Do your boyfriends know you're on the loose tonight?"

Keelie snickers. "Please, Lottie's on their radar. Not only that, but Noah told her he's got a tracking device on her car. I wouldn't be surprised if we bumped into them to—"

She stops mid-sentence, and every part of me freezes when I see it myself.

"Noah?" I step off the beaten path and stagger into the dining room to find him seated with Cormack enjoying what looks to be delicious Egyptian cuisine.

"Lottie." His lids fly up like roller shades. "I can explain."

Cormack swats him with her linen napkin, and personally I'm cheering her on in that department.

"We just came from our very first couple's counseling session." She giggles like a schoolgirl. Cormack looks exquisite tonight in a bright red dress, her hair glossy in perfect gold ringlets running down her back. "And guess what? He's signed us up for a couple's belly dancing lesson! Isn't that perfectly romantic?"

Meg laughs under her breath. "Perfectly."

"So that's what this is about," I mutter. "I can't be a part of your schemes because you already have a partner—your *fiancé*." I turn Meg back around and we join Keelie and the waitress kind enough to navigate us to the bowels of this establishment. "Onward and forward." I'm getting to Janelle first.

The studio in the back is spacious and airy. The floors are

comprised of dark stained wood, and there's an oversized mirror that takes up the entire wall in front of us.

A smattering of women and couples are already here, and I spot Janelle herself right up front. I don't waste any time as I speed over.

"Janelle Hastings?" I say in that exaggerated tone people utilize for the classmates of yesteryear. "Is that you?"

Of course, it's her. That blonde hair of hers is swept up into a bun, and she looks just as perky and delightful as she was the night I met her. Her nose is turned up a hair, and her lips are naturally pouty. She has an air of likability about her and an—owl over her shoulder.

"*Boo!*" Owlbert chortles and hoots as he floats above her. "She's the one, isn't she, Lottie? That's why you're here. That's why *I'm* here!"

I twist my lips at him before reverting my attention to her. "Amanda introduced us that horrible night. I'm so sorry for your loss."

"Oh my goodness, yes!" Her whole affect brightens. "What in the world are you doing here?"

Meg pops up next to me. "It's her bachelorette party. We're hoping you can teach her all the tips and tricks to keep her man happy at home."

A guttural laugh emits from her. "You betcha. Hey? When's the wedding?"

"July," I say without thinking and cringe on cue once I realize the proximity of my bachelorette party to the main event.

"Wow, you're really starting early, but I commend you." She winces. "Amanda wasn't your wedding planner, was she?"

"She sure was."

"Well, don't worry. I hear Hazel has absorbed all of her clients." She rolls her eyes. "Hazel has spent her whole life living in Amanda's shadow. I guess you could say she's really stepping into her own these days—her own sister's life."

I sort of came to that conclusion myself.

"Come on. It's time to get started!" She claps the class to attention, and we're all positioned to stand in rows.

Noah and Cormack sneak in the back just as the music gets going. It's twangy and sultry, and every now and then it sounds as if someone is clanging pots and pans.

Noah scoots in close to me.

"Lottie." His dimples dig in deep, and he has that look on his face as if imploring me to understand.

"Don't you *Lottie* me."

"Lottie?" Janelle waves from the front. "Since you're the bride-to-be, let's have you come up and demonstrate."

Noah's brows arch. "Bride-to-be?"

"That's right, Detective Fox. Two can play at that game. And who knows? I may not be playing."

I make my way up front, and Janelle teaches me how to sway and swivel my hips with the best of them.

"All right!" Janelle cries out over the music as Owlbert floats in our midst, observing the masses while purring like a feline. He's a boy that way. He's probably enjoying this immensely. They often do.

"Lottie, your husband is really going to thank you once he sees his big surprise!" Janelle doesn't mind throwing it out there, and I look to make sure Noah is receiving it. Sure enough, he looks as if he's about to be sick. "Now let's get a couple down here."

Cormack hops up and barks like a seal until Janelle waves them down front, and I'm quick to reprise my spot between Keelie and Meg.

"All right, mister," Janelle belts it out to Noah. "Hold her by the hips and really feel her move." Cormack does her best to swivel as if her relationship hinged on every move those hips were capable of. "See this, Lottie? This is how you'll encourage your partner to participate. There is nothing more sensual than having the love of your life share this delicate dance with you."

Or with Cormack.

Cormack shakes a little too hard, her hips a little too eager to grind their way over to Noah's, and Janelle shakes her head at the maneuver.

"No, no." Janelle plucks Cormack out of Noah's arms. "Lottie, why don't you come down here and show Cormack how you move and glide? It needs to be loose and fluid. Lottie, you really are a natural."

Meg shoves me forward. "Go on Lot. Show 'em what you got."

I growl at both her and Janelle—and mostly Noah.

Owlbert buzzes from above. "This is amazing, Lottie! It seems at every turn you and Noah are forced into one another's arms. It must be fate."

"Or very bad timing," I mutter as I step up, and Janelle lands Noah's hot hands over my hips. I can still feel the heat from Cormack's body on his sticky fingers, and it makes my blood boil.

Janelle moves my hips and away I go.

"Very good!" She offers me a spontaneous applause. "Keep it up until the music stops." She takes off to bark out orders at the rest of the class while I wiggle for Noah, and Cormack huffs at our side.

"She's right." Noah's dimples look as if they're mocking me. "You're a natural, Lottie." His eyes glaze over with lust, and soon enough he's bedroom eyeing me. "Come over tonight," he whispers it low—lest his fiancée hear the salacious offer.

"I can't. I have to show off my moves to Everett."

He frowns. "Word on the street is you're giving him the cold shoulder, too."

"Word on the street is that I don't like that word on the street that the two of you are sharing words behind my back." I don't even care if that made one iota of sense. I'm sick and tired of

Noah trying to protect me by way of leaving me in the dark. "And guess what? I found a pattern of break-ins and bank heists that fit the pattern of those imbeciles who held us up. It stems from Florida to South Carolina"—I watch as his eyes enlarge as I go on —"Virginia to Pennsylvania to—"

"New York to Vermont." He closes his eyes a moment as I swivel in close.

"You know?"

"Of course, I know," he smothers the words with ego.

"What else do you know?"

He looks perturbed by the conversation. "That's for me to know and for you not to find out. Lottie, please."

"Cormack?" I slip out of his grasp and pull her in my place. "Dance for your fiancé. It really is such an aphrodisiac."

The class wraps up, and I sic both Meg and Keelie on Noah. Under no circumstances are they to let him out of their sight.

I head over to Janelle as she's packing up her things.

"Wonderful class. Expect a basket of muffins sent over by my fiancé. Baked by me, of course." I belt out a laugh as Owlbert lands heavy on my shoulder. *Geez*! He weighs as much as a toddler. "So, what do you think happened to Amanda? I mean, she told me all about that drama between her and Connie before she passed. You don't think Connie did her in, did you?"

Too much? I can't tell, but I thought it was best to get it out there.

Her blue eyes jet out like hardboiled eggs. "She told you that? I thought she'd go to the grave denying it. You know, to hear Mark tell it, he's the innocent one in all this. He's just trying to save face by going around telling anyone who'll listen that he broke up with Connie first like a real gentleman blah, blah, blah." She makes a face. "The truth is, he was two-timing Connie for months."

"With Amanda?"

She nods. "Amanda had the perfect cover. She told Connie

that she and Mark had real estate to look at, and it was true in the beginning. Soon enough, they were doing it in every empty house in Honey Hollow." Lainey's new house comes to mind and I cringe. "Her brothers got wind of it. That's when the relationship hit the fan and he really broke it off with Connie."

"How did Connie react?"

"She didn't." She slips a backpack over her shoulder, indicating she's ready to leave. "That's the strange part, don't you think?"

"Are you're implying Connie did this?"

"I don't know. There are so many other things that were going wrong for poor Amanda. That whole drama with her parents dying. Slater wasn't happy at all."

"What drama was that? Who's Slater?"

"Her brother. Apparently, there was some glitch in the will—or with some bank account? I'm not really up on the details, but Amanda thought she'd better lawyer up and Connie was going to set her up with her gal."

I bet that's Fiona.

"How about Hazel? Was she upset?"

"I don't know. Amanda only ever complained about Slater. They weren't too close at the end."

"But he was there the night of my engagement party." That still feels strange to say.

She nods. "He's good friends with Chrissy. And, of course, Chrissy and Mark are inseparable."

"So maybe Slater did this? Although, I can't imagine a sibling being responsible for such a grisly death."

"This is true. Something was definitely going on with her, though. Just a couple days before her death, she made mention of going to the police. Something to do with people getting ripped off. I don't know. And I could never tell if she was afraid of her brother. It sure seemed that way at times."

"Huh." The picture seems to be filling in, but too bad it's still fuzzy. "Is there anyone else she talked to? Another friend she might have confided in the last few days?"

She shakes her head as she looks to the ceiling. "Outside of Connie and me, I can't think of—" She snaps her fingers. "There was that guy, the cute pastor? She said they were great friends. She spent a ton of time at that church up in Honey Hollow. You know, weddings and funerals every weekend. She said he was a great ear to bend. He might know something."

"Pastor Gaines?" This flummoxes me.

"That's the guy!" She claps her hands in my face for getting it right. "But you might be wasting your time speaking with him. You know, that whole confidentially thing those guys have. Anyway, whoever killed Amanda that night wasn't thinking, if you ask me. Why kill her in a crowd when you could have done it in private?"

"The more suspects, I suppose?"

"I guess. But none of this makes sense. Despite her flaws, Amanda was well-liked. I used to tease her that even the people she hurt the most still *liked* her." She shrugs.

"You mean Connie?"

"And me." Her face turns an instant shade of crimson. "Make it Happen was my baby until Amanda thought she could make a few improvements. And before you know it, she was running the show. I stepped aside and eventually sold it to her for a couple hundred dollars. I guess I wasn't cut out for that line of work." Her lips press white. "But then, she's not cut out for it now, is she?" She scoops up her boombox. "Excuse me." She takes off, and a cold chill runs through me.

Owlbert flies right through my chest, but that doesn't explain the icy shivers running up my spine.

Noah comes up along with my sister and Keelie.

"What did you glean, Lottie?" he asks, burying those evergreen eyes into mine.

"Nothing. And everything," I say hypnotically. "Let's get out of here."

All the way home I think about what Janelle revealed.

Connie seems far too nice and forgiving. Not even mentioning a betrayal that big? Of course, she didn't. She knew revenge was coming. And Slater? A will or a bank account? I smell greed. I know all about that drama intimately. And then, there's Janelle herself. She could be deflecting me with all that talk about why the killer chose the engagement party as a venue for death. But that revelation toward the end?

Janelle Hastings had her company stolen right from underneath her.

It seems Amanda Wellington was well-versed in stealing boyfriends and companies.

And ultimately, it drove someone to steal the most precious thing of all—her life.

CHAPTER 12

$\mathcal{T}$he next day, I decide to progress my investigation by asking my mother and her questionable boyfriend out to dinner.

I knew there was trouble in paradise when she asked which one. But, of course, I insisted she bring Pastor Gaines. No offense to Mayor Nash, but he won't do me any good as far as moving this case along. And since I've dubbed this a double date, I had to go about the business of eating crow.

Since Noah crawled up on my already rattled nerves last night and burrowed on in, I quickly scratched his name off the list of potential prospects. I texted Everett the invite and he agreed to meet me for dinner, but only if I'd agree to a nightcap at his place later. My mouth watered just thinking about heading to Everett's place in just a few short hours.

How I miss those wild kisses, those wild nights we spent lighting his entire house on fire with our desire. And, of course, I feel like a ninny for even thinking about any of that because Noah and I are supposed to either find closure or each other. I can't help it, though. I'm weak.

Mom and I settled on the Honey Pot Diner. For as much as I

walk in and out of that establishment all week, I hardly ever dine there, so it's a perfect excuse to partake in whatever feasts the master chefs have on special.

It's well into the evening. The sun set hours ago, and the crisp autumn breeze whistles outside the window we're seated by as the moon illuminates the maples a magical shade of yellow.

Inside the Honey Pot, the large resin oak tree is aglow with twinkle lights. Nearly every table is filled to capacity—a few townies, but mostly tourists. A group of young men laugh boisterously nearby, and I happen to glance over just as a young man with red hair, a pushed-in nose, and wide-set eyes does a double take my way and glowers as if I was admonishing them. That's not true. I couldn't care less how loud they were as long as they paid their bill and tipped Keelie twice what she was due.

I scoot my seat closer to Everett and decide not to look past this table for the rest of the night.

Both my mother and I decide on the lemon chicken, and both Everett and Pastor Gaines have decided on the surf and turf special.

Everett looks dangerously handsome tonight in his jet-black suit with gray pinstripes, and his tie gleams as if it were filled with stars. There's something supernatural about Everett's comely looks regardless of his glowing tie. He's a man's man through and through, and I can't help but become hypnotized by him.

He and Pastor Gaines are busy carrying on a conversation about some law that Pastor Gaines inquired about, but I'm too love-struck to keep up with it.

"*Psst.*" My mother gives my arm a quick tap and snaps me out of my Everett-induced trance. Her hair is lightened more than usual, giving it a buttercream appeal, and her lips are swathed a glossy cherry red. Miranda Lemon truly is a stunning woman. "You're looking at him just the way I used to look at your father."

She touches her chest as if the idea melted her. "It must be true love, Lottie."

I glance to Everett, and every cell in my body heats up for him.

It is love. That I can never deny.

Our food comes, and Pastor Gaines says a quick blessing. No sooner do I open my eyes than I spot Owlbert on the table doing his best to peck away at Pastor Gaines' sirloin.

"Please, Lottie, do something about this inability to digest. You can't expect us to show up at a meal this tempting and not steal a bite or two."

I do feel guilty about that. But since there's nothing I can do about his present digestive wishes, I can at least get right to the chase—or *case* as it were.

"Pastor Gaines"—I start, picking up my fork—"Hazel tells me she's filling in her sister's shoes. How's she working out for you?"

His eyes flit to the ceiling a moment. "Hazel is no Amanda, but she's learning the ropes. She booked a live band for a funeral and had a eulogy set out for a wedding I did last week."

We all share a warm laugh on her behalf, and I casually pick up Everett's hand in the event Owlbert feels the need to squawk his mind.

Owlbert hops my way, landing smack in the middle of Everett's side of mashed potatoes. "Good work. You've warmed him up. Now go in for the kill."

I glance to Everett and smile before reverting my attention to Pastor Gaines. "Hazel seems like a sweet girl. But Amanda was a powerhouse."

Mom chortles when I say *powerhouse*. My mother is a powerhouse in and of herself, so I'm guessing she likes the camaraderie.

"That she was." He lifts a brow. "Amanda could do spectacular things that Hazel can never do."

Mom clicks her tongue at him. "Now don't say that. I'm sure Hazel will rise to the occasion."

Why would Pastor Gaines close off to Hazel like that? A thought occurs to me.

"Amanda once told me you were very close friends." She didn't, but that's beside the point.

His eyes widen, and for once that creepy smile glides off his face as he glances to my mother.

"We were. She was a sweet soul. Lost her parents earlier this year and was in need of counseling. Of course, I stepped onto the scene just a few months ago myself, but I lent her an ear whenever she needed it."

Mom breaks apart her dinner roll in anguish. "The poor girl. Losing one parent is bad enough, but *both* of them? Do you know what happened?"

"Helicopter crash." He nods. "They were touring a volcano in South America and it went down."

"That's terrible." I shudder as I think about it. "And how terrible for Amanda and her siblings. She has a brother, too, right?"

"Slater." The creepy smile bounces back to his lips. "Amanda didn't care much for him. He felt slighted by her—something to do with a joint bank account that belonged to their parents. Perhaps a will?" He shakes his head as if he were unclear on that.

Note to self: Speak to Slater.

"Well, I certainly understand how things can go south quickly whenever there's a will involved."

Mom lifts her glass as if she were toasting me. "But, Lottie has a court date set for next Thursday concerning the will she's involved in, and we're confident she will come out the victor."

Everett gives my hand a light squeeze, his lips curling at the tips. "It sounds as if you'll be in my neck of the woods. Please feel free to stop by my chambers if you get a chance."

"That sounds like an exciting date." My entire body sizzles from head to toe as I recall our last dalliance in his coital chambers. I do believe my motion to speak was denied and a good time was had by all.

Everett's chest thunders with a barely-there laugh because I have a feeling we're sharing the same memory.

"Speaking of exciting dates"—Mom starts in, and I'm terrified we're getting too far off the subject of Amanda—"I ran your idea of having Keelie and Bear's surprise engagement party at the Apple Festival by Becca and she's simply in love."

"Great. I'll hire Hazel." I look to Pastor Gaines. "It's something Amanda would have jumped on. Speaking of Amanda again, has her fiancé come by for counseling?"

His lips pull into a line as if the mention of her fiancé makes him sick.

"No, he hasn't. But why would he? He and Amanda were on the rocks right before she perished."

Owlbert squawks as if it were news to him.

"They were?" It's the first I'm hearing of this. "They seemed so happy at the engagement dinner."

He nods through a bite. "They remained good friends. Mark Russo likes to remain on good terms with those he's parting ways with. He was eyeing other women, but Amanda had her sights set elsewhere, too."

"Really?" I can't focus on anything but extracting all I can from him. I certainly can't focus on my food.

"Oh yes. She was a lover and not a fighter." He gives a sly wink my way, and I'm not sure I'm loving the implication.

"Amanda was spirited," Everett adds, his eyes pinned directly on Pastor Gaines because I can tell he wants more. "I guess you could say she was passionate."

He nods vigorously as he takes a sip of his water. "As passionate as they come."

Wait a minute… Was Amanda having an affair with Pastor Gaines? Or did my mind just jump over a horny hurdle that wasn't there to begin with?

Mom's lips twitch, and I can tell she suspects something, too. Well, this is certainly a bombshell I had no intention to unleash.

Dinner drags on with Mom trying her best to keep the conversation alive.

We each order a slice of my apple pie for dinner. The Cutie Pie provides all the sweet treats for the Honey Pot Diner, and I wouldn't want it any other way.

And all the while Everett's leg is pressing over mine, my leg wrapping around his with glee. His hand warms mine, and I'm about to faint with desire if he takes it a single step further.

We wrap it up and say goodnight. Mom and Pastor Gaines take off, and we watch them as Everett warms me in the chilly night air.

Owlbert circles the sky above before diving down low. "Something is not right, Lottie. There is just something odd about that man. I can't put my finger on it."

I look up at Everett. "I agree."

He gives a slight nod. "We'll figure it out." His hand dips down and warms my lower back, and we move as if we're slow dancing in the breeze.

A breath hitches in my throat. "I think we're about to figure something else out, too."

"How about we head back to my place and continue this slow dance?"

Everett speeds us back to Country Cottage Road, and we speed our way right into his living room.

We figure it all out and complicate things a heck of a lot more in the process.

Everett knows he's my weakness, and he certainly isn't playing fair.

CHAPTER 13

*J*t took a google search—which yielded nothing, and a quick conversation with Hazel to learn that Slater works as a bartender at a place called the Devil's Punchbowl, an upscale bar in Fallbrook.

I didn't come right out and ask Hazel anything about her brother. I had to skirt the issue by way of hiring her to help with Keelie's surprise engagement party. It turns out, Hazel's price points are a bit steeper than her sister's were, but she did say she would give me a significant discount if I brought her sister's killer to justice. Of course, I assured her I would do my best to make this happen. And I plan to.

As soon as we hung up, I called the smarmy so-called upscale establishment to confirm whether or not Slater was on the schedule tonight, and thankfully he is.

And since I have no intention on showing up to a place called the Devil's Punchbowl all by my lonesome, I rustled up my posse, which includes Lily, Naomi, and Alex—a threesome that is destined for heartbreak and maybe a broken nose or two—I should know, I'm still playing that horrific game—Cormack and Noah, Everett and myself. To be fair, Noah and Cormack are coming off a counseling session in the area. And honestly, she's harder to ditch than a bad habit.

The entire lot of us congregates outside of the establishment and takes a moment to observe the neon pitchforks set at either side of the entry. A pair of elongated horns that gives the illusion they're on fire sits above the threshold to the entry, pointing up at a flashing neon sign bearing its wicked moniker. A smaller neon sign boasts the fact that every night is karaoke night.

"Wonderful," I say as I look to Everett. "I don't suppose you're up for doing a little crooning."

"Not if my legal seat depended on it."

"I'm in." Cormack snaps her fingers as if she were already on stage.

"Me too," Naomi coos into Alex's ear.

Noah's doppelgänger fights the goofy grin doing its best to erupt over his face. "I'm in, too."

"Really?" Lily and I say in unison. You can bet I'll be snagging a front row seat to hear Noah's brother belt out a tune.

"Yes, really. Our mother had both Noah and me in choir for as long as I can remember. We're both perfectly capable of carrying a tune."

Both Naomi and Lily swoon hard.

Okay, so I'm silently swooning myself. There is nothing sexier than a hot detective that can carry a note.

"You'll have to delight us, Detective Fox." I try to keep it formal since Cormack is pawing all over him. He's tried to casually deflect her, but she nearly fell over the last time and he ended up scooping her into his arms instead. I don't doubt for a minute that Cormack knows what she's doing.

Alex and his harem head inside.

Everett threads his arm through mine before looking to Noah. "Come on, choir boy. It's showtime."

Cormack giggles up a storm as we head on in, and instantly I'm both floored and offended by the atmosphere. Red lights glare down at us from above, giving the room a smoky hellish appeal, and I suppose that's the point. Booths are strewn about with oversized cushioned leather backrests, and there are riding crops hanging from each one as if ready to use at the patron's discretion. The counter of the bar is lined with handcuffs encased under a glass surface, and a bevy of ropes and other toys of sexual destruction hang in various places around the establishment.

The karaoke is going strong. And whoever that woman is up on stage, she's killing it with a cover of a song I must have belted out myself a thousand times when I was in high school. But I can't see her. The stage is far deeper inside the club, and I've already spotted Slater serving up drinks right here at the bar.

Noah leans in. His heady cologne holds the scent of every one of our carnal memories, and it makes me feel bad for indulging in that heavy-duty make-out session with Everett the other night. But, then again, Noah is fresh off his counseling session with his newly minted fiancée.

Naomi grabs ahold of Alex. "Let's get in line for the karaoke. I'm thinking a duet. Something slow and romantic." She glances to Lily. "Maybe you and that scary bartender can dance to it?"

Lily growls as they take off and head for the dance floor instead. No one is ever going to accuse Lily of being shy.

Cormack pulls Noah toward the dance floor. "Come on, Boss. Let's show 'em what we're made of."

Everett's chest bucks with a silent laugh. "Sing us a song while you're at it."

Noah rambles out twelve different excuses all at once just as the woman on stage hits a high note destined to shatter glass and eardrums alike.

Everett's brows peak as he cranes his neck, trying to get a better look at the stage.

"I'll be right back, Lemon."

He takes off and Cormack gloms onto his arm, begging him for just one spin on the dance floor.

"And then there were two," I flatline as I look to Noah.

He motions toward a couple of seats at the bar and we take them. "How was your day?"

"It's ending in Hades, so if that's any indication..." I can't help the downer routine. I'll admit, there's a part of me that's very much envious of Cormack Featherby. Why is she always with Noah? I get that he's trying to break off their non-relationship gently—in fact, I was the one who encouraged him to do so, but in the end—as greedy as it sounds, I'm afraid of losing Noah again. Of course, he's no longer mine to lose. After I lost him abruptly last winter, it sort of traumatized my heart. I guess you can say that Cormack has been a trigger in that sense.

I press my shoulder playfully to his. "How was counseling? Are you and the missus on the road to happily ever after?"

His dimples flirt shamelessly with me. Come to think of it, so is he. "Tonight was the first real session. I pulled the counselor aside before we began and let her know that I was trying to break it off with Cormack. I explained the situation to her, and she said this sounded like a classic obsessive compulsive relationship disorder."

"Who has the disorder? You or her?" I couldn't help it. He walked into that one.

"Very funny." He presses his shoulder gently to mine. "I also told her about you."

My cheeks flush with heat. "*Me?*" This takes me aback. "I'm surprised you remembered who I was." I'm teasing again but also still stunned.

"Lottie," my name presses from him, low and guttural, just the way it used to in our most intimate moments. "You are unforgettable. I've tattooed you over my heart, my mind—and when I close my eyes at night, your beautiful face is right there staring back at me. I breathe you, Lottie. I remember who we are, and I'm hoping that I'm right about who we'll be."

My heart detonates one raucous explosion at a time as I look deeply into his lime-green eyes.

"What can I get for you?" a chipper male voice calls from across the counter, and I clear my throat as I look to none other than Slater Wellington himself. His hair was red to begin with, so in this garish light it makes it look as if it's aflame. His smile is warm, and if I squint, I can see Amanda hiding there in his features.

I open my mouth as if to say something, then scoot back in my seat a notch. "It's you," I say enthusiastically. Works every time—I hope. "I recognize you from my engagement party."

He blinks over at Noah and me. "That's right. But weren't the two of you engaged to different people?" He holds out a hand. "Never mind. You're in a safe place. I'm not saying a word. What can I get for you lovebirds tonight?"

"Oh"—I look to Noah, unsure of how we got to this awkward place—"just a tonic water for me."

"Beer." Noah waits until Slater disappears to work on our orders to say anything. "I think I like where he's going with this. Your hotel room or mine?"

A familiar cologne engulfs us. "I heard that."

We turn to find not just Everett, but his sister, Meghan, as well.

Her dark hair is slightly mussed, and she's red-faced as if she ran a mile around the dance floor. "Well, if it isn't Lucky Lottie and my *favorite* brother." She winks at Noah. "Don't tell the others." She pulls us into an impromptu rather sweaty embrace. "Group hug!" The scent of vodka plumes from her as she says it.

Everett frowns as he helps her into the seat next to me. "Meghan is here with friends. Male friends." He scowls back at the dance floor.

261

"Did you hear me singing?" she practically roars the words out at Noah and me.

"That was you?" This floors me. "You were fantastic!"

"Essex's got a set of pipes, too," she laments. "Rumor has it, he only uses them in the bedroom."

He does, but it's strictly in the capacity of barking out orders. Everett likes to be in charge of the carnal production, and I've never minded one bit.

She dips her chin my way. "But you know all about that, don't you? My brother has always been a hot commodity. I've often wondered if he'd ever settle down. I didn't think it would happen, but I'm glad it's with someone like you, Lucky. Hey? You don't mind if I call you Lucky, do you?"

"I don't see why not." *Join the club*, I want to say. Not many women seem to care for my proper moniker anyway.

Noah flinches as if he thought it was funny. "Or you can call her Lemon. Your least favorite brother can't seem to get her name right either."

"Oh?" her voice squeals as if Noah just let a juicy morsel fly. "Do I sense a little dissension among family?"

Slater comes back with our drinks. "Hey, hot stuff." He holds out his fist, and Meghan gives him a knuckle bump. "You were great out there."

"Yeah, but then this killjoy showed up and hauled me off stage." She hitches her thumb at Everett.

"You had a line six deep waiting their turn," Everett is quick to defend himself. "And you needed to hydrate yourself." He looks over at Slater. "Coffee, black, and a beer for me."

Meghan groans, "There he goes again. Look out, Lucky. Once you hitch yourself to my brother, all the fun goes out the window. There's no one more by the book than this guy." She glances to Noah. "Except maybe that guy."

I'm starting to think I have a type.

Slater takes off again, and I frown. I'll have to catch him once he comes back. But in the meantime...

"So you know Slater?" I say, leaning in toward Meghan, then quickly regret it as the scent of vodka nearly knocks me out of my chair.

"We go way back. I'm a regular here. I've been drinking the devil's trash can punch for years now." She swings in toward my ear. "I may have slept with the guy a time or two."

"*Geez.*" Everett nearly has a heart attack on the spot.

Noah chuckles. "Don't worry, Essex. She's just taking a cue from you."

Meghan cackles if it were the funniest thing in the world and slaps Noah five right over my shoulder.

"Are the rumors true?" She nods his way. "Are the two of you sharing Lucky here? Is this one lucky lady or what?"

"*No,*" they both grunt in unison.

She laughs so hard she's wheezing. "Me thinks they protest too much. So let's hear it, Lucky. Who's better in the sack? Keep the details fuzzy. I'm still clocking in as a sibling."

"Right." I give a nervous glance back at Noah.

"It's Noah?" She slaps the counter as she explodes with laughter once again.

"I never said it was Noah." I shake my head vigorously at Everett.

"So it's this guy." She rolls her eyes. "I guess the rumors are true. There used to be a line outside of his college apartment. But that's back when he was honing his chops." She shoots Noah with her fingers. "I lost touch with this guy for a while. You married what's her face. And now you're getting hitched again to what's her other face. You do realize you're setting yourself up for a lifetime of Chanel bags and couture runs to Paris. I never figured you for that kind of a guy. You seem far more down-to-earth. Like you should be marrying a baker, too. You know—come to think of it, if you and Essex were smashed into one person, you'd make a hell of a guy."

I've often thought the same thing.

"But this way there's plenty of you to go around. And no offense, and I will totally deny this once I'm sober"—she leans in —"but Essex is getting the better end of the deal. You should ditch the Featherhead while you can and find yourself a girl like Lucky."

Noah's eyes flit to mine. "That's exactly what I was thinking."

Cormack jumps onto his back, and a part of me is terrified that gun strapped to his hip will go off in the process.

"It's a hoot out there! Come on, Boss. You owe me a spin."

He shakes his head, then stops midway. "I think that's Alex singing. Excuse me, but I've got to see this."

"Whoohoo!" Cormack whoops it up, bopping him all the way to the dance floor as Noah navigates his way through it.

Slater comes back with the coffee and the beer. "Made it fresh for the freshest woman in the club, and I mean that." He nods to Everett. "The girl likes to get lucky."

Everett is back to growling before turning to his sister. "Do I need to keep you on a leash?"

Slater flips a towel over his shoulder. "Funny you should ask. She likes that, too."

"*Enough.*" Everett all but threatens to cut the poor guy.

"How are you doing?" I ask, pulling Slater's attention away from the sexual intervention Everett seems to be having with his sister.

Slater comes over and mops up the bar between us. "Not well, but thank you for asking. Mandy and I might not have been as close as I would have liked in the end, but I still miss her fiercely." His lips turn down hard. "Life changes on a dime. You have to really appreciate those around you, because you never know when they might be gone."

"I feel those words right down to my weary bones," I say,

curling my glass in my hand. "My dad died way back when, and that grief still lives with me today. I'd do anything to have another day with him."

He glances to the wall as if he were looking right through it. "I get it. The thing with Mandy is, it wasn't her time. Someone did this to her."

"Do you have any idea who would want to do something like this?"

"Me," he says it flatly, and I startle to attention. The conversation—or argument—to my right between Everett and Meghan stilts for a moment as well. "It's true." He pulls a bottle out and starts flipping it before putting it back. "I had enough rage in me —I said I could have done it, but I didn't mean it. It's the kind of thing you say when you're a kid with no real malice behind it. Yes, I was angry, but I wouldn't have killed my sister." His voice cracks. "My parents hadn't made up a formal will yet. They were in the middle of it. Who could blame them? They were young. But they did put Mandy's name on their bank accounts. In the event anything happened, we could access their funds. Mandy was the oldest, and in their eyes the most responsible. Hazel and I were just kids at the time, so it made sense. And even though Mandy claimed to love both Hazel and me, she decided she knew how to spend their money best. She didn't see the need to share. She said she'd invest in something for the three of us."

"What did she invest in?"

"Herself. That company she swiped from Janelle. But then, that's how Mandy got ahead in every aspect of life—taking what wasn't hers."

So I've heard.

"Did Amanda have any enemies that you're aware of?"

"You mean, did she have any friends that I'm aware of?" He cocks his head thoughtfully to the side. "You know, come to think of it, she did mention some preacher she was getting close to. We were hit-and-miss with conversations these last few months, but she'd ring me up and we'd chat a bit. She wasn't going to budge on the money, but she wanted to maintain ties. Mandy always did want to have her cake and eat it, too."

Meghan moans to life. "I never did get that expression. Everyone who has a cake wants to eat it. What the heck is wrong with someone who has a cake and doesn't want to eat it? It's a common courtesy to the cake." Another angry groan comes from her. "Speaking of which, what does a girl have to do to get a little cake around here?" She pounds the bar three times fast.

"All right, cake girl." Everett plucks her out of her seat. "Lemon, I'm going to have to take her home. There's no way I can leave her here in this state."

"Please, don't worry about me. I'm sure Noah and Cormack will give me a ride back."

"Okay." He comes over and lands a searing kiss to my cheek. "Don't stay out too late. The freaks come out at night as evidenced." He points hard to his sister, and she swats him as he navigates her out of the bar.

Slater clicks his tongue at her. "She's a good one. Doesn't know her limit, though. She reminds me a lot of Mandy. She had it good with that billionaire. But, rumor has it, she gave him the boot."

"What? I mean, she mentioned to me they were on the rocks. I had no idea about the boot thing." Okay, so she didn't tell me directly. Pastor Gaines mentioned they were on the rocks.

He frowns at the ceiling. "Maybe she didn't give him the boot quite yet, but she mentioned something about trouble with a man she was with and that she was going to take care of him. Something about turning evidence over to the police."

That's the second time I'm hearing this. Janelle said the very same thing.

Someone calls him from the other end of the bar and he excuses himself politely.

I head deeper into the establishment just in time to hear Alex making all the women in the room swoon as he belts out a love song while Cormack rocks her body against Noah's side.

Noah glances my way before doing a double take and heading over, sans the barnacle doing her best to adhere to him.

"May I have this dance?"

"Does it come with six counseling sessions and a blonde?"

His brows dip as he swallows a laugh. "Come here." He takes me in his arms, and our bodies move to the soothing rhythm of his brother's voice.

"Did you get anywhere with Slater?"

"No."

"You will. Who's next on the list?"

"I think I'll revisit Pastor Gaines."

"Perfect. I'll go with you. We'll ask him to marry us."

A laugh bubbles from my throat.

Mrs. Noah Fox. Just last year I thought it was doable. I wanted it. Okay, I more than wanted it. And here we are, all these months later, and it feels like a pipe dream.

"Something tells me Cormack doesn't like to share her toys." I glance her way as she tosses what looks to be granny panties up at Alex.

"I don't think Everett does either."

Noah drives us home, with me in the back seat and Cormack up front as his official plus one. In his defense, Cormack called shotgun.

I have a feeling she'll be doing just that forever.

Thank God I have more than I need to distract me. A killer. Thieves. A house full of ghosts. And an ornery judge who likes to lay down the law in the bedroom.

For Noah and me, the road to reconciliation feels as if it grows wider and wider by the moment.

CHAPTER 14

*T*he next afternoon the Cutie Pie Bakery and Cakery is bustling and hustling at the seams.

Not only has my mother offloaded her Haunted Honey Hollow tourists my way—and, oh my stars, she's selling *shirts* now—but Holland called from the orchard and put in an enormous order for my apple turnovers with their infamous caramel dipping sauce. In between impossible amounts of bodies clamoring for turnovers, I've been trying to place orders for more supplies in keeping up with the demand.

Once the chaos dies down, both Lily and I sigh in unison.

"Geez, Lottie. I never thought working here would be akin to a marathon. You do realize I have a tracking device on my wrist, and each day I surpass the ten thousand steps I'm allotted to have."

"You're allotted to have as many as you like—and good thing, too, because I'm positive we just did twenty."

She checks her Fit Watch. "You're right. We're about to break a record." A wicked grin plays on her lips. "You know what else I broke a record doing?"

"Eating all the batter out of the side of the mixer once I pulled the cookie dough? Honestly, I've never seen it so clean. Good work, Lily."

"No." She leans in, her eyes sparkling with devilish delight. "Beating Naomi to the mattress punch with Alex Fox."

"*What?*" I swat her arm with the kitchen towel in my hand as if she were on fire. And she will be once Naomi catches her. "Are you kidding me?"

"Nope. Naomi may have sung a decent duet with him last night, but we made our own music once he took me to my place. Naomi was the first drop-off of the night, so I made my move by inviting him in for a drink."

"That's a lure that Everett uses often with me, and it's usually enough to cinch the deal." True confession.

"Whose playbook do you think I ripped it out of?"

"Oh. *Eww.*" I wrinkle my nose at the implication, even though I'm well aware of Everett's history with Lily. And just about everyone else.

Keelie comes in with her cheeks flushed, panting as if she just ran all the way over from New York.

"Did you hear the news?" Her eyes flash like lightning.

"You slept with Alex, too?" I'm teasing both Keelie and Lily at the very same time, and I don't mind a bit.

Lily takes the kitchen towel and swats me right back.

"No." Keelie takes a moment to giggle at Lily. "And congrats, by the way."

Lily nods. "Nobody gets the pleasure of telling Naomi but me."

"Done." Keelie crosses her heart in haste. "Three different shops were broken into last night, right here on Main Street."

"*What?*" I grab ahold of her and pull her in. "Which ones? Did they catch the thieves?"

"The Busy Bee Crafts Shop, the Wicked Wok, and the Woodhouse Grill."

"Oh my gosh." Lily clasps her hands to her chest. "Lottie, we need to step up security around here."

Keelie shudders. "And to think, you're here at ungodly hours all by yourself!"

Lily wraps her arms around her body. "I don't like it."

Keelie nods. "*I* don't like it."

"Neither do I," a deep voice strums from behind, and the three of us jump as we look across the counter to see a handsome devil who just so happens to be packing some heat.

"*Noah*," I pant through my next breath. "You scared me. What are you up to today?"

"I was wondering if you were up for a drive. I hear there's a preacher you'd like to talk to."

"Sounds like a date," I say, taking off my apron and tossing it to Lily.

Lily catches it midair. "While you're there, reserve the church for Alex and me. I'm hearing wedding bells!"

Keelie belts out a laugh. "And Bear and me! I can't wait to get me some wedding bells!"

"Wedding bells," I mutter under my breath as Noah and I take off into the icy arms of autumn.

Something tells me the last thing we'll be discussing is marriage.

ALL OF VERMONT is bathed in orange and gold. Autumn has hit hard, turning our green belt of a state into a virtual playground for every citrine color. The lush fields and pines remain true to their verdant color, but every leaf has transformed into a thing of beauty as it masters the art of dying.

Noah and I park just outside the offices of Honey Hollow Covenant Church and head on in where it's toasty and warm.

The office is light and bright—and surprisingly, it's Hazel Wellington here to greet us. She's sitting behind a desk, her red hair in a ponytail as she smiles up at us as we head her way. She's donned a cranberry sweater and a matching scarf, and she looks like fall personified.

"Hello, you two. Can you believe how chilly it is out there?" Her expression dims a notch. "Are you here because you have news on my sister's killer?"

"No." I wince because I can only assume the torture she's going through while she waits.

"Oh." Her shoulders droop with disappointment. "Then what can we do for you? I'm covering for the secretary."

Noah wraps an arm around my shoulder. "We're here to get married."

We share a warm laugh. "Yes, a quickie wedding without a stitch of friends or family to witness the event." I avert my eyes at the thought. Although, the more I think about it, the more romantic it sounds.

"All right." She thumbs around the desk until she procures a clipboard. "Sign here and here and Pastor Gaines will see you soon enough."

About ten minutes go by before a couple exits his office and we're ushered inside in their place.

"A marriage, Hazel tells me," he teases with those smiling eyes.

"Yes," I say equally sarcastically. "And a few questions if you don't mind."

"Not one bit. I always suspected it would be the two of you in the end. You have what they call chemistry. A wedding was bound to happen." He hands me a basket of dried flowers no bigger than a paperback. "It never hurts to give it a go."

A shy smile comes to me as I look to Noah. "I suppose not."

His dimples press in as he links his arm with mine. "I couldn't think of a soul I'd rather do this with."

"Sure wish I had Amanda here for the big day." I shoot the words right to Pastor Gaines to see if he's biting.

That perma-smile contorts into something shy of agony. "How I wish dear sweet Amanda were with us as well. Any luck with the killer? Your mother says you're the best, Lottie."

"None." Great. No wonder his defenses are up. He knows we're investigating. I'll have to play up the wedding angle. I'm about to do just that when a swirl of stars spray up above and Owlbert Einstein materializes in his ghostly form.

"Well, I'm anxious to marry this big strong man," I say to Pastor Gaines, but I'm looking right into Noah's deep green eyes.

Owlbert squawks, "What did I miss? Oh, a wedding! A wedding? I'll have to call the others, Lottie. Oh, they'll never forgive me."

Noah threads his fingers through mine and kisses the back of my hand. "Our wedding will be the happiest day of my life, Lottie."

A breath hitches in my throat, my stomach bisects with heat, and my insides explode with butterflies all at once. This, right here, is the very best feeling. A part of me wants to believe this is all real.

I clear my throat. It's a struggle to break my gaze from Noah's. "Pastor Gaines? Did Amanda ever confide in you about her life? You mentioned her relationship with Mark Russo was rocky. Do you think her fiancé would hurt her?"

"Heavens." His eerie smile expands. "I'm afraid I can't answer that, but a man with that much money should be severely scrutinized in my opinion."

"I suppose it would hurt his ego if Amanda left him. But a man with money is never short on women."

Noah lifts a brow. "That's true, but maybe Amanda had something on him." He looks to Pastor Gaines. "Or on someone else?"

The smile depletes from him momentarily, and he's nearly

unrecognizable. "Perhaps. A man like Mark Russo must have a secret or two. I suppose a man with money could make arrangements for that secret not to get out."

I glance to Noah. Both Janelle and Slater mentioned that she was threatening to go the police over something.

"Strange, though." I shrug over at Pastor Gaines. "You wouldn't think a man like that would resort to poisoning someone. It's such a horrible way to die."

"It was quick." His lids widen a notch. "I had just spoken to her, and no sooner did a few minutes go by than you had discovered the body. The thought of the poor girl suffering pains me so." His lips quiver as if this were truly the case.

"She didn't suffer long," Noah offers. "The coroner confirmed she went quickly. Most likely passed out before she ever figured out what was happening. Her airways were constricting, and that might be why she went outside."

Unless the killer lured her out there, but I keep that tidbit to myself.

Pastor Gaines tips his head to the side. "Come to think of it, I did see the man who was with her fiancé that night head out the door shortly after she left."

"Chrissy?" I look to Noah. Could Chrissy be hiding under our radar this entire time?

Pastor Gaines picks up a small black Bible off his desk and opens it by way of a thin crimson ribbon.

"I've done more weddings than funerals, and for that I'm thankful. Shall we proceed?"

"Please," I say as I turn to look at Noah. This is all in fun, all in the name of the investigation, but a tiny part of my heart wants this to be real.

Pastor Gaines produces that infamous smile of his as he looks to the two of us. "Lottie, Detective Fox, you are about to embark on the most wonderful journey of your lives."

Noah gives my hand a squeeze. He's so painfully handsome, I really could buy the fact he cleaned up just for our wedding day. His gaze penetrates mine so deeply that it feels as if he's touching my very soul.

"Noah, do you take Lottie to be your wedded wife? To care for in sickness and in health, to comfort and honor her, forsaking all others so long as you both shall live?"

Noah's eyes grow glassy as if his emotions were getting the better of him. "I do."

Pastor Gaines takes a breath. "And, Lottie, do you promise to love this man as your wedded husband and forsake all others through the good times and the bad?"

My throat is so dry it burns. "Of course, I do." I love Noah. This is easy. It almost feels as if this is what we were destined to do all along.

"Do you have a ring for the bride?" He looks to Noah.

"Actually." Noah pats his pocket and frowns as if he meant it. "I think figurative rings will have to suffice for now."

Pastor Gaines chuckles. "That is not a problem. Let these figurative rings act as a token to represent this union between the two of you for as long as you both shall live. I now pronounce you Mr. and Mrs. Noah Fox. Detective, you may kiss your bride."

Noah leans in hesitantly, pausing as his lips curve with joy. Noah bows down and kisses me, slowly at first, then with something just this side of all-out passion.

The sound of riotous applause breaks out, and my mouth falls open as I see all of the dead surrounding the two of us: the orange tabby, the quivering squirrel, Everett's father, Dutch, the ornery bear up on its hind legs—its head nearly touching the ceiling—the sweet herd of paperwhite Chihuahuas, Macon, Greer, Winslow, and little Lea sitting on Beastie's back, Max, Cookie, Owlbert, and, of course, Nell.

Nell offers a heartfelt smile. "Congratulations, Lottie. I love you so."

And just like that, they're gone. It's just Pastor Gaines and that smile that never ceases.

We thank him and show ourselves out.

"Oh, I forgot to give back the flowers." I make a face as the door clicks shut.

"I'll take them," a small female voice calls out from the desk, and it looks as if the secretary is back. A woman in a red cardigan and yellow scarf waves us over. She has a heart-shaped face and short curly hair that clings to her scalp.

There's no sign of Hazel around.

Noah warms my back with his hand. "We were just visiting. It's a shame what happened to Amanda. I hear she was a staple around here."

She averts her eyes. "That she was." She takes the flowers from me and plops them on her desk as if they weren't just a part of one of the most special days of my life. "She would come in, and they'd lock themselves in there for hours on end doing God knows what." She shudders before her eyes spring wide as she looks to us. "Counseling, of course. Pastor Gaines is a great counselor." Her lips harden. "Especially with the women," she says that last bit under her breath.

My mouth falls open at the implication. "My mother is seeing him," I utter without meaning to, and Noah mercifully navigates us out. We make our way into the chilled air, the sun quickly setting. "Noah, she implied—"

Noah touches my lips softly with his finger. "I know what she implied." There's a pained look in his eyes as he presses his gaze to mine. "I just want to take a moment to enjoy looking at my beautiful wife."

Every last part of me melts. "That was kind of fun, wasn't it?"

"It was the best." Noah swallows hard. "How about a kiss for the road?"

I bite down hard over my lower lip and nod.

Noah blesses me with a kiss that says *I love you today, tomor-*

275

row, and forever. Noah kisses me in the exact way that I've always dreamed my husband would.

That little wedding of ours might not have been real, but it sure felt official right down to my bones.

Maybe Noah and I aren't destined to have closure. Maybe we're destined to have a future?

CHAPTER 15

*T*hursday shows up like an eager groom at the altar—okay, so an eager bride as well.

I still can't believe Noah and I exchanged I dos. Of course, it was all in fun—even though I meant every last word—but I didn't dare mention it to Everett last night at dinner. And I've been artfully avoiding Noah—lest he lay another one of those red-hot kisses on me and it leads to an all-out wedding night.

I'm supposed to be exploring my heart, not his body. Although, in all fairness, I explored Everett in a moment of weakness a few weeks back. But who in their right mind could blame me? Technically, we're still together, I think. Oh, never mind. I have no clue where I stand with anyone but my cats these days.

The Ashford County Courthouse stands proud, wrapped in creamy glory with its stately stone exterior and stunningly tall columns. Inside, its polished floors and dark paneled halls lead us straight to the proper courtroom we're due to arrive in. My mother is here with me, as well as Carlotta, Lainey, Meg, Becca, Keelie, and Naomi.

Everett strides up, looking dangerous in his sharp navy suit, and stops my heart cold with those stormy blue eyes.

"Hello, beautiful." He lands a soft kiss to my lips, and it feels completely easy and natural, and yet a twinge horrific because I happened to have kissed Noah with these same lips and I feel terrible about it. "You ready to do this?"

"Yes. Are you coming in?"

"I cleared my schedule. I wouldn't miss it."

Everett escorts us inside where we find Will and his attorney already whispering amongst themselves and stealing a moment to glower at us.

Will looks just like Becca, same reddish-blonde hair, same seemingly serene disposition. His three daughters are seated behind him, looking weirdly identical with their strawberry-blonde hair, their noncommittal smiles. They're all a touch younger than me. They seem sweet, but you never know. My family has surprised me before.

Becca urges me to take a seat beside our attorney, and it feels terrifying. The last time I was in front of a judge it was Everett who was taking the stand, and it was a menacing sight. Wait, that's not right. The very last time I was in a courtroom Everett was presiding over someone else's case, and I dropped a box of cookies as if it were a piñata. Which led Everett to bring me right back to his chambers and teach me one delicious lesson. A spiral of warmth rides through me just thinking about it.

The judge finally takes the stand, a woman who happens to look at Everett with a genuine surprise. She wears her hair in a medium-length bob, each strand a stunning silver streak. Her eyes are bright and light, and there's a general radiance about her.

She quickly goes over the facts and sighs heavily, taking a moment to contemplate them.

A swirl of incandescent light fills the space to my right and slowly Nell forms before me. She offers an affable smile. The look of knowing is sharp in her eyes.

"How is the bride?" she muses playfully, and I shoot her a look that says *not funny*—but my cheeks are blushing because I rather like the idea. "I take it I haven't missed much. Will still looks reasonably happy." Her own expression sours at the thought of it.

The judge clears her throat, and you could hear a pin drop. "It's matters like these I wish would never reach my courtroom." Her crimson lips pull down hard. "I've seen this scenario play out many times. I have dismantled estates against the deceased's wishes. I've seen family homes forced to go to market—despite the fact the widow still resides there—just to please a disenfranchised child. However, I do have a heart for disenfranchised children." She glowers over at Will a moment. "Ms. Lemon." Her head snaps my way. "You were newly grafted into the family, I see. I understand that's why Mr. Sawyer saw fit to fight you on the terms of his mother's will." She peruses the papers before her once again. "Mr. Sawyer, it seems your mother left you and your siblings, your children and theirs, a sizable amount that would allow you to live very comfortably." Her lips twist as she scans the document further. "And to you, Carlotta Kenzie Lemon, she has left the Honey Pot Diner, the land under the Cutie Pie Bakery and Cakery, and all of her remaining real estate holdings, which include her primary residence in Honey Hollow, her summer home in Nantucket, as well as her beloved cat, Waffles."

Nell's entire person brightens like a star at the mention of that wily Himalayan.

"I have Waffles," I say it low, and the judge glances my way, clearly unimpressed with the questionable outburst.

"Good," she muses. "Because I'm awarding you the rest of the things your grandmother desired to give you. Motion to dissolve the will, denied." She slams her gavel over the granite, and my uncle Will jumps up in protest.

"This can't be the end," he cries after her as she rises from her seat.

"I assure you it is," she says as she disappears down the stairs and out the door on the side of the room.

The attorney next to me offers a handshake, and soon we're all on our feet and everyone is showering me in congratulations.

Carlotta smacks me on the arm. "Now that Nell's house is free and clear, you're going to let me live in it, right?"

My mother waves her off. "Don't you dare, Lottie." She winks my way. "Carlotta is a treasure at the B&B."

Becca shakes her head. "I trust you'll listen to wise counsel. If I were you, I wouldn't make a move in any direction for at least a year." That's exactly the advice Everett gave me. "And we should all discuss this together."

Keelie scoffs at her own mother. "Lottie doesn't have to run a thing by anybody. She's a businesswoman. She has a level head. It's not like she's going to up and sell the Honey Pot. Right, Lottie? *Right?*" She sharpens her eyes over me, and I shudder.

"No, heavens no." I look to Nell, and she nods my way before disappearing in a sparkle of miniature stars.

Will bounds over, his three sulking daughters flanking him from behind.

"Becca, Carlotta, I hope you're happy." Judging by his tight lips and that pomegranate hue taking over his face, he's certainly not. "I'll have you know our father and mother worked very hard for every nickel they had, and you've up and turned it over to a virtual stranger."

Everett steps in. "They didn't turn it over to her. Nell did." His voice is low and curt and has every female's undivided attention. "And she's not a virtual stranger. She's blood. But even if she were a stranger, your mother would have retained the right to do so. If I were you, I would be very pleased with the outcome, because your mother could have legally given it all away to virtual strangers if she pleased."

Will stiffens before charging to the exit, and his girls follow along in a fury like three angry ducks.

Becca sniffs. "There's that. How about lunch, ladies?"

We give a wild cheer as my mother and Carlotta lead the way out of the room.

Naomi leans my way. "Don't think this is going to change how I feel about you."

"I should hope not," I say as she takes off to catch up with the rest of them.

"I'll be right there." It's just Everett, the bailiff, and me left in this dark cavernous room.

"Congratulations, Lemon." He wraps his arms around me and warms me with his body.

"Come to lunch with us," I say, locking my wrists behind his neck. "And just so you know, I will be relying heavily on your sound counsel to get me through this real estate bonanza I seemed to have acquired."

"I will give you whatever counsel you desire, but I can't do lunch. I've got a case in just a bit. Rain check?"

"You bet."

"How about I come over tonight? I'll bring champagne."

"*Ooh*! I'll bring apple turnovers." I shrug up at him. "I have a serious surplus."

"Sounds delicious." He leans in and steals a kiss from my lips. "Just like you."

Everett pulls me in one more time and holds me like that. His eyes bearing hard into mine, speaking to me far deeper than words could ever venture, intimately sharing his affection for me. Those magical eyes make me forget everything that just happened, everything that's still happening. But Noah lingers in the back of my mind like a ghost.

THAT NIGHT not only does Everett come bearing champagne—an exquisitely expensive one at that, but Noah comes by and so do Keelie and Bear.

"To Lottie!" Keelie lifts her champagne flute, and we follow suit.

I cringe at the thought of toasting myself. "To justice, I think." I wrinkle my nose at Everett and laugh as we drink up.

Bear is the first to hit the bottom of his glass. "Whew, that was the good stuff. You deserve it, Lot. And if you think having two men vying for your heart is tough, just wait until you have them lining up out the door. Now that you're loaded, people are going to take notice."

Keelie grunts, "The wrong people. All of the people who love you won't mind one bit—we'll just expect better Christmas presents."

We share a warm laugh.

Noah lands his champagne flute onto the counter. "I have an announcement. I'm looking into purchasing a piece of real estate myself—a lodge up in Hollyhock."

"What? That's great," I beam, proud of him.

Everett leans in from behind, his chest warming my shoulders. "Hear that, Lemon? He's trying to one-up you."

Noah laughs. "If that were the case, I've got a long way to go."

"Noah, I'm so happy for you. Let us know when escrow closes and we'll celebrate."

"I haven't quite got that far. I'm still weighing the investment potential. And I'd like to take you up there sometime to see what you think."

"Noah, I'd love that."

Keelie shudders. "Any news on those thieves? Or how about that killer?"

Noah shakes his head. "We should go over the investigation," he says my way.

Everett grunts, "You know how to a kill a party, don't you?"

"No, I don't mind," I say. "It's the perfect time. Let's go over the suspects for Amanda's case first. There's Hazel. She sure stepped into Amanda's shoes without missing a beat. But I'm not entirely sure about a motive."

"The money her parents left," Everett reminds me. "Money is a strong motivator even among family. We witnessed that today."

"Amen to that." I take a quivering breath at the memory of how angry my uncle was when he stormed out of that courtroom. "Okay, so she has a motive. There's Connie Canelli. Her motive is far more pronounced."

Bear groans as if he might be sick. "You have a Canelli involved? I'm afraid to even listen to this."

Keelie dusts his face with her hair. "Hush, you coward," she teases before rewarding him with a kiss.

I shake my head. "Connie's motive is pretty strong. Amanda swiped her billionaire boyfriend from under her. And then she carried on as if it never happened. I would have been worried if I were Amanda."

Everett takes a breath. "What about Janelle?"

"She mentioned that Amanda pulled her business from under her. It turns out, Make it Happen was Janelle's baby, and Amanda came in and basically took over. Buying her out for a few measly hundred dollars."

Noah folds his arms. "There's Chrissy, the wedding singer. He seemed nice, for the most part."

I hold up a finger. "But Pastor Gaines did say he saw Chrissy head out the door just after Amanda on the night she died." I think on it for a moment. "Mark Russo, her fiancé. He basically implicated both Connie and Pastor Gaines."

Both Keelie and Bear balk at that one.

"Pastor Gaines?" Keelie shakes her curls as if she were restyling her hair. "Come on."

"No, I mean it. He's on the suspect list. I think he might have been having an affair with Amanda. And he was the one that mentioned Amanda and Mark were on the rocks. I didn't get that feeling from Mark, though."

Noah's chest expands with his next breath. "Mark might have been saving face, and Amanda did go to Pastor Gaines for counseling."

Everett gives my shoulders an impromptu rubdown, and it's all I can do to keep from moaning.

"What about the brother?" he whispers it into my ear like a secret.

"Slater." I straighten as he continues to melt the tension off my body. "Yes, he said he loved his sister, but he also said he could have killed her."

Keelie raises a hand. "I know the feeling."

"So do I," both Everett and I say in unison, and I glance back and offer a guilty twitch of the lips. "Slater could have done it. Their parents left everything to Amanda, hoping she would do the right thing—which I assume is parceling it out evenly, but she kept it all. Hazel never really voiced that as a concern, but Slater admitted to it. She said she would be a very good steward of their money for the entire family's sake."

Keelie gurgles out a laugh. "That sounds like you, Lottie."

"Very funny. I'm not laughing."

Bear pulls Keelie in. "So who did it? Who killed Amanda Wellington?"

I shake my head at Noah and Everett. "I don't know. I'm completely stumped. Any updates on that den of thieves?"

Noah glances to Everett, and they both clam up.

"Oh, I see. There are updates. They're just not for me."

We call it a night, and I walk everyone to the door.

I pick up Pancake and Waffles and hold them tightly as I watch both Everett and Noah leave for their respective homes.

Noah and Everett are keeping things from me—and I am not amused.

CHAPTER 16

 $\mathcal{I}$ t is a rare occasion that I toss and turn at night. I've often dubbed myself the Queen of Sleep. In fact, I've honed the unique ability to fall asleep on cue, time and place permitting. I can sleep on planes, on trains and buses, but last night I couldn't fall asleep to save my life.

Instead, I went through Amanda Wellington's social media profiles. I looked through pictures upon pictures of her smiling face—of the beautiful venues she was in charge of procuring for her clients. Lainey's wedding was in her portfolio, and I had a chance to relive that day all over again. One particular picture stood out to me, the one that she took of Pastor Gaines. He was smiling for her, as one would assume, especially since he never ceases to do so—but it wasn't his usual smile. It was a wicked grin that I've seen on Everett just before he pulled me into a dark closet to have his way with me. Suffice it to say, it gave me the willies. So, of course, that segued into an extensive internet search on Pastor Gaines, which didn't yield much at all. I tried to remember what state he said he came from, but it all felt a little fuzzy at that ungodly hour—details and my sanity were fleeting.

Once I was in my car, on the way to the bakery, my sanity

really took a back seat. Instead of making the right on Main Street, I turn left and end up at the Honey Hollow Covenant Church.

It's still pretty dark out. The sun has just kissed the horizon, and a tangerine glow casts its glory over our small corner of the world.

I park and get out, trying the front door that leads to the office, but it's locked. I'm not sure why I expected anything different. I make my way around back, nearly tripping over a bucket, and look into the window of Pastor Gaines' office using the flashlight feature on my phone.

Nothing of importance sticks out. That dried flower arrangement that I held as my bouquet while Noah and I pretended to get married brings a weak smile to my face.

Out of sheer morbid curiosity, I try to wiggle the window open and to my horror it not only moves, but the upper portion slips right into my hands.

"Oh my God—oh my God, oh my God!" I land it carefully onto the ground below and jimmy the lower half out of its socket as well. It's still too tall for me to hop on in, and just as I'm about to look around for something to give me a step up, a shimmer of light explodes from inside.

"GAH!" I sink down a notch, only to find a luminescent being —Owlbert, leaning over the ledge.

"Need a boost?"

"Yes, I need a boost!" I try my hardest to scale the wall, but it's no use.

"There's a bucket around the corner, left out by the janitor."

"A bucket? You're a genius!"

"They don't call me Owlbert Einstein for nothing."

Great, I've got a wise guy on my hands. Hey? Owls *are* wise. I'm totally correct in my assumption.

I spot the bright orange bin, and before Owlbert can say another word, I've all but pole-vaulted my way into the office.

My feet carry me deeper inside, despite the fact my brain is screaming *get out*. I prattle my way around spastically, mining through the trash—nothing but wadded-up tissues and candy bar wrappers, the desk—pencil city. I check every drawer and nook and cranny I can find, but there's nothing here of any use to me.

"This way." Owlbert leads me to the secretary's desk. "Try that contraption," he says, floating to the oversized monitor.

"It's probably locked," I can hardly maintain my breathing as I sit behind the behemoth desk, and the monitor brightens in an instant. "It's on," I marvel, pulling the keyboard forward, and the screen lights up with multiple files sitting right on the desktop. "And it's not locked."

"This is a church, Lottie, not a prison."

"Yeah, but you never know when a common criminal will waltz right in."

"Or a baker."

I pause a moment to shoot him a look. "I'd kill you, but the Grim Reaper beat me to it," I tease.

He chortles with a laugh. "A little gallows humor. I do appreciate the morbidity of it all."

"Look at this," I say, opening a file and quickly perusing it. "It's employee records. This is perfect. And here's Pastor Gaines'." I click it, reading over it quickly. "It's just your basic application. Name, social security number, a few odd facts, the previous church he worked at." I pull out my phone and take pictures of it from top to bottom. "I think that should do it. Help me get out of here."

Owlbert illuminates my path as I make my way back out that window. "Unfortunately, it's not going to be put back together, and terrifyingly enough, it has my fingerprints all over it." I look up at the ethereal being flying just above my head. "Well, genius? What now?"

"The janitorial closet is still ajar. Might I suggest a little window washing?"

And window wash I do. I spray liquid detergent over the front and back of both pieces of glass and run the hose nearby over it before hopping into my car and making a squeaky clean getaway —emphasis on the *clean*.

∼

THE SUN HAS RISEN JUST a notch. It's usually at this point in the new day that I have my ovens filled with croissants with the dough I made up the night before. I park out back like I usually do and note the door ajar.

"Did I leave the door open last night?" I'm about to get out of the car when a seam of light flashes underneath the door, and every muscle in my body tenses.

I throw the car into reverse and turn the heck around with my heart pounding a mile a minute. I pull in just shy of the cleaners down the street and call Noah. Thankfully, he picks up on the first ring.

"Mrs. Fox? How can I help you?"

"I just passed by the bakery. I think I'm being robbed."

"Don't move!" he roars, and from there it's just a blur.

A giant blue cargo van comes barreling down the street, and I seize.

"It's the van!" I shout. "The one that Nell saw. They just took off past me. I can follow them," I say, starting up my engine once again.

"Don't you dare!" he riots in my ear. "Just tell me which way they're headed."

"West," I say, pulling my car forward, but it's too late. They're already gone. I park in front of the bakery and wait for Noah.

He shows up in seconds, followed by a bevy of squad cars.

"Lottie!" he thunders as I get out of the car and he lunges for me.

Noah holds me tightly as if he almost lost me. "You could have been killed." He runs a breathy kiss over the top of my head before pulling back. "You're usually inside at this point."

"I was running a little late." I wince up at him as if it wasn't true.

"Thank God. I'd hate to think what would have happened if they found you in there alone."

"I'm safe," I say in an effort to comfort him, but at the same time it feels as if I'm trying to comfort myself.

We head on in and not much is out of place, just a few cooking utensils knocked to the floor. The office looks like a whirlwind blew through it, but they couldn't open my ground safe.

"I guess they didn't get away with much." I shudder. "But just knowing they were in here gives me the heebie-jeebies."

"I'm not leaving, Lot. You don't have anything to worry about."

A sheriff's deputy approaches us. "There's a call about a break-in at the church. I think we're going to head over."

Every muscle in my body freezes.

"Good call, I'll take it from here." Noah waves them off. He looks my way and opens his mouth as if he's about to say something, then pauses abruptly. "Lottie? Why do you have an extremely guilty look on your face?"

"Oh? I—I'm not guilty." I shake my head a little too vigorously.

"*Lottie?*" His tone is suddenly curt, and very official, which sponsors a bout of giggles to strike.

"You're actually going to find this a little funny."

"What am I going to find funny?" Noah doesn't look humored in the least.

"Okay, fine. I was at the church."

"What?" He takes a full step back. "Lottie, you were the one who broke into the church? Were you digging for info on Pastor Gaines?"

"Yes." I bat my hands in an effort to keep his voice down. "I found this." I quickly produce the pictures on my phone. "It's his application. I've got his social security number and his last place of employment."

"Lottie, I am not looking to hire Pastor Gaines." He gently braces me by the shoulders. "Do you know what I'm going to do? I'm going to casually tell those deputies not to worry about fingerprints because I don't want you to be incriminated."

"Good thinking," I pant at the thought of going to prison for simply looking up Pastor Gaines' employment history, never mind the breaking and entering. "But I've already wiped my prints from the window that I may have accidentally broken."

"What about the computer where you swiped this information? Did you wipe down your prints there, too?"

"*Gah!*" I do a little odd tap-dance fueled by my fear of orange jumpsuits. "Make a few calls, Noah. I've got an owl to yell at."

After the kitchen is cleared and I've sterilized it to the hilt, I get right to baking up a bazillion apple turnovers for the Apple Festival tomorrow. And in addition to that, I bake a beautiful three-tiered cake with white roses cascading up and down the front for my bestie and the beast she's looking forward to sharing her life with—Bear. I can't believe Keelie is going to be Mrs. Otis "Bear" Fisher one day. It has a nice ring to it.

Sort of like Mrs. Noah Corbin Fox.

Or Mrs. Essex Everett Baxter.

I just hope when I do get married someday there won't be a bride with two grooms as a topper on my wedding cake.

And as horrible as it sounds, a part of me doesn't think it would be all that bad.

The Grand family owns the apple orchard, and it sits nestled high above Honey Hollow with its behemoth barn that pulls double duty as a souvenir shop. The hilly terrain is beautiful this time of year, and everywhere you look there seems to be miles and miles of orchards filled with every variety of apple you can imagine. In fact, it's the Grands' own Golden Delicious apples that I use to make all of my apple desserts. The Golden Delicious is buttery in flavor, soft, and melts in your mouth like a sugar-laden dream.

Once Noah, Everett, and I arrive, the festivities are already well underway. The entire orchard is decorated with banners and balloons. It's almost evening, and twinkle lights are strung out like stars over an expansive area that acts as a midway.

It's body to body out here. The throngs have turned out for tonight's festivities. Crates of apples lie everywhere you look. There are hayrides and booths serving hot apple cider, an area with a press in which you can make your own apple beverage, pony rides for the younger sect, and craft booths where you can make your own fall wreaths out of fresh fallen leaves. And there are even appletinis being served for the adults.

Noah and Everett have essentially been my bodyguards ever since the day of the break-in at the bakery. Noah kindly asked me to confess my sins to Everett about my own break-in, and let's just say my boyfriend, the judge, did not appreciate the fact I'm fostering the criminal facet of my talents.

Noah gets a call and drifts off.

"Lemon." Everett wraps his arms around me. "How's it going with—" He ticks his head toward Noah. "Any luck in finding closure?"

I make a face when he says it. "Not really. I've been too busy getting held at gunpoint and trying to hunt down killers and thieves." I'm just about to tell him about my mock marriage when my mock groom bounds over.

"Interesting news." He does a quick sweep of the vicinity. "I just got some information on Pastor Gaines."

"Did you run that information I gave you?"

"Yes." Noah's breathing ticks up a notch, a clear indicator he's onto something big. "A few of the references he put down never heard of him. Two of them turned out to be bogus, maybe friends that vouched for him. But that's not the interesting part. I ran his social security number, and the name didn't add up. If the number does belong to him, then his name isn't Stephen Gaines. It's Stephen Heartwood."

"Stephen Heartwood?" I glance to Everett. "Then Stephen Gaines is a phony, right? I bet Amanda knew this. I bet this is why she wanted to call the sheriff's department. What else do you know?"

"I'm still working on a few things." Noah stares pensively off in the distance. "Everett, don't let Lottie out of your sight. I'll be right back."

I gasp as I look up at Everett. "I bet we've got our killer. I need to tell my mother. I need to make sure he doesn't kill my mother next!"

"He's not killing your mother." Everett nods down the hill. "I see her. She's with Meg. Maybe ask Meg not to leave her side tonight. We'll leave the rest to Noah."

"You're right." I quickly pull out my phone and do just that. "Meg said no problem."

"Come on. Let's get the rest of these apple turnovers out of your van."

Everett and I do just that. It takes a million trips, but we cover all of the refreshment tables with my apple turnover caramel sauce dippers, and I've got Keelie's cake in there, too, just waiting for eight o'clock when all of our friends and family are going to gather around and shout *surprise*!

It's not anything too fancy, but I know that Keelie and Bear would prefer it this way. Becca has sent out the invitations, and we've routed any and all gifts to the B&B so Keelie didn't stand a chance of running into them. And, I paid Hazel a handsome fee to oversee the decorations and those special details I can't even think about right now. It's a relief to know everything is going to turn out perfectly.

Everett and I finish up our final run and take a breather while watching the hayrides go by.

A woman with dark hair whipping back and forth screams like a banshee as she holds up a drink.

"I'm going to take my top off!" she howls.

I shake my head as the tractor hauling a flatbed stacked with hay cruises on by.

"Some people can't hold their liquor. I knew selling appletinis would amount to no good."

Everett groans hard. "I think that person in particular shares my genetic makeup." A blouse goes flying, and Everett shouts for the hayride to stop as he speeds in that direction.

"Great. A drunk sister. That's exactly what this night needed."

I make my way over to the booth selling hot apple cider, and just as I'm about to get in line, I spot a couple of men laughing. The tall one with the ruddy complexion has something red tucked under his arm, and it looks like he's concealing a—purse?

I suck in a quick breath.

"Hey!" I call out, but not a soul seems to notice. I thread my way through the crowd and come up behind the purse thief, and then I see it.

"Oh my God," I whisper. Tracking along the back of his neck is a diamond-patterned snake. The exact pattern that was on the gunman that day in the bank.

I pull out my phone just as a group of girls glides by, and it falls right out of my hand.

"No!" I panic as I try to look for it, but a mob streams by. I glance back at the men, and they're nearly to the parking lot. "God, help me," I pant as I quickly search for my phone, but I can't see it anywhere.

I jog up a few yards and watch as the men head toward the tourist buses. Probably hoping to get more loot.

Noah went in that direction. I bet he's nearby.

Without thinking, I jog on over, and as I do a series of lights explode from the sky. And one by one they arrive: the tabby, the squirrel, Judge Baxter Senior, my sweet dog Dutch, the crankiest bear on the planet, the miniature angelic Chihuahuas, Greer, Macon, Max, Beastie, Cookie, and Owlbert.

"Nell?" I look around, unsure why she didn't join the rest of the apparition brigade.

Greer waves from the front of the buses. "They're not alone, Lottie! Go get Noah!"

Beastie jumps right through them before circling around to me. "They're armed. Turn back, Lottie."

"Why are you stopping me? I thought you were here to help *me* stop *them?*"

The ruddy one turns around. The shorter one looks back, and he's got a familiar face, red hair, pushed-in nose, and wide-set eyes. It's him, the young man from the Honey Pot who glared at me that night I was at dinner with Everett, my mother, and Pastor Gaines.

Max zooms forward. "They see you, Lottie. Turn around."

"Okay," I whisper under my breath.

But it's too late. The young men turn my way fully, and soon enough they're headed in this direction.

Dutch barks at me incessantly, and I do my best to maintain my composure.

"Excuse me?" the shorter one says, and soon they're upon me. "We're from New York. Do you know where we can find a map of this beautiful town?" He points to the bus. "Our driver must have taken off for the festivities."

The one with the snake tattoo leans in.

"Yeah." He nods to no one in particular. "She's onto us."

And just like that, I'm in his arms, his hand clamped over my mouth as he moves me between the buses.

Greer comes in close. "Now you've done it." And honestly, I'm not sure if she's speaking to them or me.

Beastie roars as ferocious as thunder, jumps on top of the man with the pushed-in nose, and sends him flying abruptly into the wheel well. And then slowly Beastie's light begins to dim.

No!

He's helped too much. He has to go back. I'm not sure why, but too much assistance in the natural world is a one-way ticket back to paradise, and I bet that's exactly where that magnificent beast is headed.

"What the hell?" the one holding me hostage shouts to his disoriented buddy. "Watch where you're going!"

That oversized bear ambles up and growls at the man with his arms secured over me.

I can feel his muscles shudder as he holds me tightly. He stops a moment and looks around.

"What the heck was that?"

I bite down over his hand so hard I think I taste blood.

He howls and pulls back just as Max pins him down. "Run, Lottie! I won't be able to hold him for long!"

I take off and glance back in time to see Max fading to nothing.

His friend growls out a series of salty words as he struggles to get up off the ground and takes off after me.

I bolt to my right and slam into a body—and all too familiar detective-like, *husband*-like body.

"Lottie?"

"Noah!" I'm about to say something—anything, pull him along with me when his eyes round out.

"Hold it right there," a voice calls out from behind, and judging by the way Noah's hands are rising, I'm willing to bet they brought a gun to the party.

I turn slowly, and sure enough I spot a tiny Glock with *26 Gen4* printed on the side.

"That's Ethel," I hiss.

"Who's Ethel?" Noah asks from the side of his mouth.

"Never mind."

"Both of you, in the bus." The thug points wildly with the working end of that gun—*my* gun.

"You did it, didn't you?" I say to him as Noah and I slowly back up. "You're both a part of that gang. You were at the bank that day."

"Good eye," the snake tattoo man pipes up as he pulls out a gun of his own. Perfect. Two idiots with a gun apiece—and I thought a drunk sister was the last thing this night needed. "It's nice to be recognized by a pretty lady. I bet it'd feel even better to be kissed."

"Not happening," Noah whispers for my ears only.

"Darn tootin'!" Greer shouts as she dives over the redhead and knocks him to the ground.

"Crap!" he calls out, and his friend jumps to his feet as Max begins to dissipate.

The tiny Chihuahuas attack, latching onto the gunman, making him stumble, and that ornery bear knocks him to the ground and takes a seat right over his lap.

A string of expletives roars from him as his friend heads over to help him up. That gun is still pointed sloppily in our direction, and my adrenaline hikes to unsafe levels.

"Noah, we only have a few seconds."

"Both of you freeze!" Noah shouts so loud I'm sure everyone at the festival has just solidified in their tracks.

Greer heads over to the redhead and kicks the guns loose out of his hands. And then, just like that, her light begins to dim.

"Greer!" I shout just as she dissolves to nothing. "No, not Greer," I whimper.

The squirrel takes over, picking up the weapon and bringing it my way. He gets just past the two men before evaporating into a plume of celestial dust.

The man with the pushed-in nose picks it right up again and aims it at us just as Dutch, the ever-faithful Golden Retriever, bounds onto him and wrangles it loose with his mouth.

"What the hell keeps happening?" the man shouts as his buddy crawls his way over. Dutch begins to fade, and a horrid sound emits from my vocal cords.

"Dutch! *No!*"

He turns my way with those burning coals for eyes and pants. I would bet anything he was smiling at me.

"Goodbye, Lottie. I love you." It sounds so precious coming from his deep, husky voice. I want to memorize it and drink it down straight to my bones. I'd give anything to have Dutch with me forever.

Macon the Macaw appears. "Oh, Ms. Lemon," he bemoans. "There are no talons stronger than those I possess." He plucks the gun right out of the man's hand and lands it in mine before he lets out an egregiously loud squawk.

The men roll on the ground, their hands fly in the air, but there's still one gun unaccounted for, mine.

Cookie bounds up in all his dark, fluffy glory, translucent as he might be.

The man with the snake tattoo pats the ground under the bus.

"Cookie, get it!" I howl, but the man comes up victorious.

He points the gun our way, and an explosive sound detonates into the night. Both Noah and I exchange a glance. Cookie deflects his arm, and the shot shoots straight to heaven—and in a ball of brilliant light, so does Macon.

Cookie jumps up and goes for the jugular. He clamps his mouth over that tattooed snake, and the gun drops right out of the man's hand.

I'm about to lunge that way, and Noah pulls me back. "We don't need a hostage situation, Lottie."

"He's right," a gentle, all too familiar voice bleats from behind, and I turn to find Nell walking forward.

"No," I cry out. "I don't want to lose you again."

"Oh, Lottie. You'll never truly lose me." She walks right through me, right through the man on the ground, and picks up the gun from under the tire before walking over and laying it in my hand, where it rightfully belongs.

"*Ethel.*" My chest bucks as I laugh and cry at the very same time. I wrap my arms around Nell and sob as she dissolves with my tears.

"Did you see that?" the man with the snake tattoo shouts. "That gun—it just flew!"

Ivy runs up from behind with her weapon drawn, and soon the deputies are here to take them in.

"What about the others?" I ask as Noah holds me tightly.

"I don't know. I'll try to make them sing. Get back down there, Lottie. I'll take care of this and be back as soon as I can."

Everett runs up and pulls me in hard, and we watch as Noah takes off.

That was one heck of a way to start off the night.

Let's just hope this night doesn't hold any more surprises—other than the one I have planned for Keelie and Bear, of course.

But something tells me it will.

CHAPTER 18

*T*he Apple Festival is well underway.

The sun has set, the sky is glittering with stars, and the twinkle lights strewn about the Grands' orchard give the grounds a haunted romantic appeal. Although, I suppose it's not nearly as haunted as it was a few minutes ago. All of those beasts of days gone by have up and disappeared—and each and every one has taken a piece of my heart with them.

I am pretty thrilled to be reunited with Ethel, though. I've already stuffed her into my purse for safekeeping—after I made sure there were no rounds chambered. I swing Everett's hand between us as I bat my lashes up at him.

"I hope with everything in me they find your mother's ring. You have no idea how bad I feel about that."

"Don't give it a second thought." He pulls me in and carefully brushes the hair from my forehead. "Are you sure you're okay? I can take you down to the emergency room and have them give you a once-over. I don't mind one bit."

"Not on your life. Or mine. There's no place I'd rather be than at the Apple Festival. I love fall, and I love that Honey Hollow gives it the kickoff it deserves. Besides, Keelie's surprise engagement party is starting soon. There's no way I can miss that."

"I completely understand. But if you change your mind, I'm your man."

"You're always my man." I hug him hard just as a woman moans out his name—his proper name.

"Essex," she calls out again, and we turn to find Meghan sprawled out on a bale of hay so we head over.

"Feeling better?" Everett helps her sit upright. Meghan's dark hair is strewn every which way with stray pieces of hay spiking up out of it. Her sweater is on backward and she's missing a shoe.

Meghan looks up at me. "I'm doing just fine. Could either of you please get the planet to stop spinning?"

Everett and I chuckle at the thought.

"Stay put for a little while longer." Everett takes up my hand again. "Lottie and I will get you some hot cider."

"And a handful of my mini apple turnovers," I volunteer.

"Two handfuls, please," she moans as she plops back down on the hay. "Don't mind me. I'll just be taking a short nap."

She's snoring before we get five feet in the opposite direction.

"I'm sorry you have to see this side of my sister." Everett takes a breath, and a white plume expels from his mouth as if he were a fire-breathing dragon. Everett would make one sexy beast, and he does.

"Please, she's just having a good time."

"Too good of a time."

We step up to the hot apple cider booth, and the line is discouragingly long. A couple walks by, giggling from behind the booth as they head into an orchard marked *Jonagold.*

"Hey, look at that," I say, pointing over to that familiar dark-haired duo ditching into the thicket of dimly lit trees.

Everett straightens. "Was that Connie?"

"Yes. Connie Canelli and Chrissy Castaneda. I think they were holding hands."

"It sounds as if they're having a good time, too. You think they hit the appletinis?"

I make a face. "I don't know, but we're about to find out." I pull Everett along until we get to the mouth of the entry, and sure enough we spot them kissing like a couple of teenagers.

Huh.

Everett walks us back a few feet out of their line of vision, and far enough away where they won't hear a thing we're saying.

"Looks like Connie has a new man. Good for her. Chrissy seems like a nice guy."

"Everett." I glance around as a thousand thoughts click together in my mind at once, but before I can expound on any of them, Everett's phone rings.

"It's Noah," he says, picking up and putting it on speaker

"Everett—is Lottie with you? She's not picking up."

"Yes." Everett holds the phone out my way.

"Lottie. Are you okay?" Noah's voice is tight and anxious. "I just had to check in."

"I'm fine. I lost my phone. I'm here with Everett. Did you catch the rest of the thieves? Did you find out anything else on Pastor Gaines?"

Noah gives a hard sigh from the other end of the line. "It looks like we're about to close in on the rest of those idiots responsible for the bank heist. These two are singing in hopes for a good deal. As for Pastor Gaines, I don't know much. All I could figure out is that the pastoral committee that hires for the church didn't do much digging. They got a few false references and a feel-good interview from the guy. There are a lot of legitimate reasons someone might want to change their name, but considering his line of work—I'm a bit stymied by this one. I wouldn't worry about it tonight."

"Sounds good." I shrug up at Everett as we say a quick goodbye to Noah. "I don't want that man anywhere near my mother—at least not dating her or God knows what else. And I'm afraid I know exactly what else."

The sound of caustic voices erupts from behind, and Everett and I glance toward the orchard.

Everett leans in. "Lover's spat?"

"I don't know, but curiosity killed the cat, and I'm pretty sure I'm next. Don't you think it's interesting that Connie and Chrissy are together? This must be new. I didn't get the idea they were together before." Their voices pick up as their argument grows more heated. "I have to know what they're saying, Everett."

"I'm not going to be able to stop you, am I, Lemon?"

"Nope."

I hustle us back down into the orchard as the sound of their voices carries to the sky.

"You're not going anywhere," Connie grunts.

"We made a deal," Chrissy snaps back in haste. "I took care of Mark, remember?"

"You didn't take care of Mark," she tosses it back at him in a mocking tone. "You took care of Amanda." Connie laughs as she says her name.

My mouth falls open as I look to Everett.

Oh my God. We have our killer.

A sparkle of light shimmers up above as Owlbert floats down our way.

"I heard everything, Lottie," he purrs as his wings flap wildly in the night. "Arrest them."

I shake my head at him. If only it were that simple.

Everett nods back toward the cider booth, and I shake my head as I pull him in close. We hold our breath, stealing a moment to listen once more.

"I took care of Amanda?" Chrissy laughs as if he were taking umbrage with the thought. "You took care of Amanda. I was supposed to find the body."

"First, I didn't kill her. Second, you didn't find the body—that hot baker you've been lusting after stumbled upon her first."

Everett lifts a brow my way.

Chrissy chokes on his response. "I'm not lusting after anyone but you, Connie. It's always been you!"

"Then you should have set Mark up better! Why the heck hasn't that hot detective rummaged through his glove compartment yet?"

My jaw roots to the ground as I give Everett's hand a hard tug.

Owlbert flails and hoots. "What am I hearing? Are they guilty or not?"

I nod up at him, and he zooms their way.

"Ouch," Connie yelps. "Something just pegged the top of my head. Never mind, let's get out of here. Tomorrow you'll take the rest of that rat poison—and I don't care if you have to litter his front lawn with it, you make him look guilty. I can't sleep at night knowing the sheriff's department is still fishing around."

They step out from the cover of the overgrown apple trees and come face to face with Everett and me.

"Oh, for freak's sake," Connie tips her head back and groans.

"Connie—Chrissy?" I swallow hard. "We were just headed off for some privacy." I wrap my arms around Everett and nearly climb him in the process. "You know, just two lovebirds who can't keep their hands off one another. This big boy's got a gavel and he knows how to wield it, if you know what I mean." It comes out throaty and undeniably silly because I would never in my right mind say that to anyone, let alone Connie and Chrissy.

Connie exhales hard and pushes out a white fog from her lips. "She heard."

"No, no, I didn't hear." I bat my lashes up at Everett. "Did you hear? We didn't hear."

"They heard, Chrissy!" she barks at him as Owlbert's wings expand four feet before he lands back on top of her head. "Fix this right now," she growls, grabbing a fruit picker off the ground as if she were arming herself.

Chrissy shoots us a nervous glance. "I'm not fixing this, Connie. He's a freaking judge."

Her eyes narrow in on Everett's. "He'll be a dead judge."

Everett grabs me by the waist and attempts to pull me past the trees to our right, but Chrissy reaches around his back and produces a pistol pointed at the two of us.

"Drop her. Step forward or this gets messy fast," Chrissy says it with a touch of boredom in his voice, but I'd like to think it's his unwillingness to play along.

"*Hey.*" Everett holds a hand up, the other still securely wrapped around my waist. "We're not sure what's going on. I don't know who said what. I just want a little alone time with my girlfriend. It looks like you two hit the liquor hard, and I can't blame you. So why don't you go that way, and we'll go this way and forget all about this little altercation?"

Chrissy glances to Connie, and she cuts her hand through the air as if rejecting the offer.

Owlbert swoops down and clamps his talons right over Chrissy's hand, and the gun starts to slip between his fingers.

In one svelte maneuver, Everett kicks the gun out of Chrissy's grasp and it plummets to the ground. Everett lunges for it, but Connie swings that fruit picker at his head and strikes him over the temple, creating a horrible thumping sound.

"*Connie,*" Chrissy thunders it out like a reprimand—either that or he's cheering her on.

Everett staggers back a moment before falling to the ground, a seam of blood erupting just over his cheek.

"Everett?" I fall to his side and shake him until he gives a hard moan, his eyes fluttering open.

"*Geez,*" he groans.

"Geez is right," I growl up at Connie. "You could have killed him!"

"Then I'm off to a good start," she pants, wielding that gun my way. "Why don't you get on top of him one last time? I like an easy target."

Owlbert hoots four times fast. "What do I do, Lottie? I've never intervened in a homicide about to happen. Tell me what to do and I'll do it."

And how I hate the thought that Everett and I are the homicide about to happen.

"Go for the eyes," I say breathlessly, as he does just that, and I hop over the two of them just as Connie fires the gun into the air, screaming her head off as if she were being eaten alive. I latch onto Connie as we struggle for the weapon.

Chrissy does his best to pluck me off, but I prove tenacious as I dig my fingers into Connie's hair.

"*Freeze!*" a female voice calls out from behind, but I can't stop until I get that gun away from Connie.

A hand clamps down over it just as a shot is fired, and the entire lot of us finally gets around to freezing.

"Got it." Everett pulls me back and holds the gun up victoriously, a trickle of blood running down the side of his quickly swelling face. Everett pushes Chrissy against the ground, and Connie decides to make a break for it.

Without thinking, I extend my foot, and she goes sailing to the ground with a thud.

Owlbert chuckles as his illumination grows dim. "Good work, Lottie. Good work indeed. Until we meet again... I'm afraid they're calling me home. Oh, look! There's my Amanda. And what an angel she is, Lottie. If you could only see her now."

My chest bucks with emotion as Detective Ivy Fairbanks tosses Everett a pair of cuffs, and she subdues Connie while he handles Chrissy.

Soon they're back on their feet. Both Connie and Chrissy are a little dirtier than they were before, but no worse for wear.

"They tried to set up Mark Russo," I pant as Everett navigates

Chrissy over to Ivy. "If you look in his glove compartment, you'll find the pills they used to poison Amanda."

Connie glares over at me. "I didn't poison anyone. You can't pin this on me and you won't. Do you know who my brothers are?"

A chill rides through me at the mention of her family. The Canellis are a notorious crime family that everyone in their right mind knows to steer clear of. I'd be a liar if I didn't say the threat didn't bother me.

In a moment, we're surrounded by sheriff's deputies that Ivy called over, and both Chrissy and Connie are led off the premises.

Ivy looks to the two of us, her lips twisted as if she were contemplating something.

"You're a good team." She lifts her chin to Everett. "Get that cut checked out. I'll need to speak to the both of you in a bit."

We nod as we make our way back to the festivities. The laughter of the crowd, the screams of delight from the people on those hayrides, the hustle and bustle of a beautiful fall night, it's all unfazed, untouched by the horror of what just happened.

Everett pulls me in under a silver moon as a sprinkling of stars shimmers above us. "She's right, Lemon. We do make a good team."

"I've always suspected as much." I lean up on my tiptoes and offer him a kiss on the cheek. "Oh! The party."

"Go. I'll be fine."

"No. I'm getting you checked out. There's a nurse's station just outside the barn. Let's get your sister before she wanders off again and sheds another article of clothing."

We do just that. We collect Meghan and head straight to the nurse who gives Everett a questionable bill of good health. She cautions me to watch him through the night and gives him an ice pack and a bandage. If anything looks amiss, she instructs us to go straight to the emergency room.

But, upon Everett's insistence, we head into the barn instead. The inside of this home to all things hay and horses looks amazing with a plethora of white balloons, a huge sign that reads *Congratulations, Keelie and Bear,* and Mason jars filled with tiny twinkle lights strewn about the refreshment tables. Dozens of crystal chandeliers hang from above that Hazel had installed for just this occasion. Each one illuminates the cavernous space with stunning brilliance. It's perfectly magical for a perfectly magical couple.

I text Lainey and Forest, and they're kind enough to bring out the cake, a three-tiered whitewash of roses that looks impeccably delicious, impossibly elegant. And after all the guests are amassed under the canopy of twinkle lights and crystal chandeliers, Meg ushers in the guests of honor.

The entire lot of us shouts *SURPRISE* at the top of our lungs and watch as my best friend bursts into tears—happy tears.

I wrap my arms around her, and then pull Bear in close. "You two deserve the very best in life, and I'm going to do everything I can to make sure you get it."

A live band starts up, and soon everyone is dancing to the music.

Naomi wrangles Alex to the dance floor, and Lily looks as if she's after blood. But she joins them anyway.

I spot Meghan shaking her body along with Holland himself.

"Look at that," I say as I pull Everett close. "I think she's right back to having a good time."

"How about you?" Everett wraps his arms around me as the music slows to something more our speed. "Are you having a good time?" He sways our bodies to the rhythm and looks deep into my eyes with a look of adoration that I could definitely get used to.

"I am. And thanks to you, it just keeps getting better and better."

"Good." He presses out a rare smile. "Because it only goes up from here, Lemon."

"Life gets better?"

"We get better."

He pulls me close, and we dance the night away.

Everything feels better already.

CHAPTER 19

Seasons change. Time waits for no one.
It's a saying my father used to recite often. On the surface, those very words used to frighten me, and in a strange way, they now bring me comfort.

Every last one of those thugs has been apprehended. Noah and Ivy have been hailed as the town heroes. Noah tried to correct the press and include me in on the fun, but honestly, I want nothing more to do with any of it. Most of the money and all of the jewelry were recovered—including Everett's family ring. He tried to give it back to me, but I couldn't take it. The responsibility alone was far too much. I asked him to return it to his mother and he agreed, but not before he promised he'd land another one on my finger one day. My heart melted in a puddle over that one.

Connie never did admit to poisoning Amanda Wellington, but they found the Conium capsules in the glove compartment of one of Mark's sports cars, just the way she and Chrissy discussed. They found a bottle of the toxin in Chrissy's house and traces of it on the dress Connie wore to the party that night. I guess that right there is a good argument for getting your laundry done in a timely manner.

Everett says they'll both be going to trial.

As for Pastor Gaines, Noah, Everett, and I are still keeping an eye on him. Noah is doing some digging, so am I, but neither of us has availed much. However, my mother and Pastor Whoever He Is are on the rocks, and nothing pleases me more.

It's a chilly Saturday at the tail end of September, and Everett stopped by the bakery after running a few errands, so I grab a platter of apple turnovers and a couple of cups of coffee and join him in the café.

"What's next on the agenda?" I ask as I set the goodies down.

"Dinner with you tonight, if you're up for it?"

"I'm always up for dinner with you."

The bell on the door chimes, and we turn to find Mom, Carlotta, and Mayor Nash heading in.

"Lottie!" Mom makes a beeline my way. "I just talked Mayor Nash into declaring all of October Haunted Honey Hollow month, and I managed to work both of our tours into the extravaganza. In fact, I'll be having a haunted open house every weekend, and it's going to be spectacular. I've already hired Hazel Wellington to oversee the festivities, and she's determined that this will put Honey Hollow on the map. All of Main Street is about to get a haunted makeover. The tourists are going to eat it all up, I tell you. The big kickoff is next weekend. Why don't you bake up a treat and we can give them to the passersby? It will be a great way to drum up business. I just know Mayor Nash will be fine with the expense."

"That sounds great. How about cupcakes? They're easy enough to pass out, and they're irresistibly delicious, if I do say so myself."

Everett reaches over and picks up my hand. "And I agree."

Mom links arms with Mayor Nash as the two of them head

for the counter where Lily is ready to greet them, but Carlotta lingers.

She frowns at the two of them. "Would you look at that? She's making an open play for my man."

"Carlotta, the two of you have been bouncing Mayor Nash around like a ping pong ball."

She takes a breath and fluffs her caramel waves. "Nobody said it wasn't fun." She gives a sly wink. "May the best *ghoul* win." She starts to trot off, then backtracks. "Speaking of ghouls, Greer wanted me to let you know she's back and none the worse for wear."

"Oh, thank goodness." For whatever reason, once the dead finish their task, they're whisked away to paradise. But Greer has remained right here in Honey Hollow, happily haunting my mother's B&B. "And just in time. It sounds like we're going to need all haunted hands on deck to get through this next month."

"October has always been my favorite." She wrinkles her nose at Everett. "I was arrested once in October, and I had a heck of a good time with my defense lawyer. You legal eagles are pretty eager to please. He's a keeper, Lot."

Noah strides in just as Carlotta finishes singing Everett's praises. "He's a keeper, too. Do me a favor. Once you make a decision, chuck your leftovers my way." She leans in toward the two of them. "I bet you boys can teach me a thing or two about crime and punishment."

"Hello, Noah," I say, choosing to ignore Carlotta as she scuttles to the counter to load up on treats right alongside my mother. "What brings you this way?"

He flexes a quick smile. "Just wondering if you were up for heading to Hollyhock to check out that lodge I'm hoping to purchase."

My mouth opens, eager to say yes, just as Keelie and my sisters walk in.

"There she is." Keelie points an accusing finger my way. "The best friend a girl could ever ask for."

I flash a smile up at them. "What are you three up to?"

Keelie shrugs. "I just wrapped up lunch with Bear, and I'm back to finish my shift."

Lainey raises a hand. "I thought I'd get an early jump on Christmas presents and dragged Meg out with me." She frowns over at me. "Are you ever going to have a Saturday off?"

"No. And I hope you got me something good." I give a sly wink before cringing. "You're not still afraid of me, are you?"

She twists her lips as she shuffles my way, and I rise as she hugs me.

"You're my baby sister, Lottie. I want to protect you, but I can't."

Meg belts out a laugh. "She's got two beefy boyfriends who can't protect her. Join the club, Lainey."

"Sit down and I'll get everyone something hot to drink."

"I'll help," Keelie offers.

We're just about to take a step in that direction when Hazel Wellington strides in with a smile on her face. Her red hair is heaped on top of her head in a bun, and she's wearing a cozy red sweater and long suede boots that are to die for. She looks so much like her sister, it sends a pang of grief over my heart.

"Here you are!" She waves a large white envelope my way. "I bet you've been waiting for this. Or not." She shrugs as she hands it to me. "I guess the actual marriage is a lot more exciting than staring at a piece of paper. But you're all legal now. I guess you could frame it or put it in a safe."

"What is it?" I say as I pull it out, and my mouth falls open.

"It's your marriage license. It came to the rectory, and I said I'd hand-deliver it to you. I'm the town clerk, so when you and Noah signed the paperwork, I took it in to be filed and certified. I called the bakery to get the other information I needed, and Keelie gave it to me."

313

A bustle of words gets locked in my throat. "But we didn't get —I didn't think..."

Everett hops to my side, as does Noah, and Everett takes the paper and examines it.

His blue eyes flit to mine. "Lemon, this is legal."

Meg breaks out into a cackle. "I guess it's *Fox*, then, isn't it?"

"What?" I look up at Everett. "Wait, there were no witnesses. We were investigating Pastor Gaines," I practically whisper that last part.

Everett takes a breath, his chest expanding for miles. "You don't need a witness in Vermont. I'm sorry to break it to you, but this marriage is legally binding."

I gasp as I look to Noah, and his dimples press in. That disbelieving look on his face quickly dissipates as he quickly acquiesces to the idea.

"Legally binding?" I say absentmindedly. "That must mean..."

Noah nods. "You're my wife."

NEW YORK TIMES BESTSELLER
ADDISON MOORE

MURDER
IN THE MIX

Killer
Cupcakes

Table of Contents

BOOK DESCRIPTION

My name is Lottie Lemon, and I see dead people. Okay, so rarely do I see dead people, mostly I see furry creatures of the dearly departed variety, who have come back from the other side to warn me of their previous owner's impending doom.

It's October and the entire town has come out to celebrate the Haunted Honey Hollow Festival. In between doling out cupcakes and partaking in the festivities myself, I happen to stumble upon a body. Not just any body—one that has far too many skeletons in the closet for me to ever sift through. Add to it my already complicated love life, the ghost of a black cat named Thirteen, and a surprise that I never see coming and you'll have the most frightening Halloween Honey Hollow has ever seen.

Lottie Lemon has a brand new bakery to tend to, a budding romance with perhaps one too many suitors, and she has the supernatural ability to see the dead—which are always harbingers for ominous things to come. Throw in the occasional ghost of the human variety, a string of murders, and her insatiable thirst for justice, and you'll have more chaos than you know what to do with.

Living in the small town of Honey Hollow can be murder.

CHAPTER 1

I see dead people. Mostly I see furry creatures who have crossed the rainbow bridge, but on the rare occasion I do see a dearly departed of the human variety. But right now, all I can see, hear, or think about is accomplishing the task at hand.

"Get it in, Lemon," Everett grunts. "I don't know how much longer I can hold on."

"I'm trying," I grunt right back. "It doesn't seem to fit." I can hardly get the words out as I struggle and squirm.

"*Lottie?*" Noah's voice floats from somewhere down below. "My God, you're going to kill her," he howls and I'm guessing that last part was meant for Everett.

I'm currently standing on Everett's shoulder, partially that is. In truth, I'm leaning hard against the awning just outside my shop, the Cutie Pie Bakery and Cakery, as I struggle to attach a sign to a metal hook that the city uses to hang garland on at Christmastime.

A body pops up next to me and I look over to see Noah's deep green eyes and his dimples digging in deep as he manages to hitch the sign right where it needs to be.

"Thank you," I say as Everett helps bounce me down into his waiting arms and dots my lips with a kiss.

Judge Essex Everett Baxter is my current plus one—or he was.

Initially, I dated Noah, and we were hot and heavy until that wife he was hiding from me breezed into Honey Hollow and decided she wanted him back. Of course, once I learned of the matrimonial blunder, I went straight into his old stepbrother's— Everett's—arms.

Noah's divorce finally came through and Everett suggested I try to gain some real closure with Noah before we moved in a matrimonial direction of our own. But then, a few days ago the unthinkable happened. And, as it stands, it looks as if I'm legally married to Noah. It's a long story. In fact, once the festivities here come to a close today, Noah and I are off on our first official date as a married couple.

Noah gets down from the ladder and quickly folds it back up. "Looks like I saved the day." He offers a sly grin to Everett.

Everett and Noah were related briefly in high school and got along great up until Noah saw fit to steal Everett's girlfriend— Coconut Featherhead—but we'll get to her in a minute. Suffice it to say, they haven't gotten along ever since. And once I came into the picture, it only seemed to compound their hatred for one another.

They've been getting along in a hobbling sort of way for the last month or so but, let's call a spade a spade, they're still tottering on the edge of oblivion.

It's the first Saturday in October, the day of the first official Haunted Honey Hollow month-long festival in which our little spooktacular corner of Vermont embraces the fact things are darn right horrifying in our neck of the twisted woods.

It's true. We've had thirteen murders in thirteen months and, as strange as it sounds, I've had the displeasure of finding each and every corpse thus far. To make things worse, each and every corpse happened to be either holding, attempting to swallow, or in very close proximity to one of my tasty treats. And because of that grizzly fact, Noah and Everett teamed up and bought me an adorable yet deadly Glock. I try to keep it in my purse wherever I go. And when I'm at the bakery, I usually put it in the ground safe in my office if I bring it at all. And that's where *Ethel*, the aforementioned Glock, is at the moment—tucked away in my ground safe.

I glance up at the sky.

It's a little past noon, but you wouldn't know it, what with all the dark storm clouds looming overhead. It looks more like evening than it does the afternoon, but that sure didn't stop the throngs of people who have clustered right here on Main Street as they converge to join the festivities. Every business in town is offering up their wares and scares to the tourists and townies alike.

My bakery is giving away free cupcakes this afternoon in honor of the scary shenanigans that are bound to ensue. I've set out three tables laden with the frosted little confections, and I've just put a sign up top that reads *Come and get your FREE cupcakes!*

The cupcakes are adorably scary, all frosted like the Halloween spectacles they are in orange, purple, green, and black. I've placed gummy worms and gummy fingers over the tops of them, tiny pumpkins and candy corn, too. And there are a few with candy skulls and colorful monster faces. It's a feast for the eyes as much as it will be for the palate.

The festival features just about everything you could think of. There are haunted carriage rides, games with questionable prizes, face painting, and enthusiastic artists who are willing to sketch out a spooky version of whoever is brave enough to pay for a sitting. There's even a pumpkin carving station down the street. And, of course, Mayor Nash is dressed up like a werewolf, taking pictures with the masses as he makes his way down Main Street.

A few months back, I learned that Mayor Nash was my

biological father. I was adopted as an infant by Joseph and Miranda Lemon and happily raised with two wonderful sisters. But last January, my biological mother, Carlotta Sawyer, barreled back onto the scene, and then months later she rather indelicately revealed who her baby daddy was, and now I have more parents than I know what to do with.

That's not entirely true. My real daddy, the aforementioned Joseph Lemon, passed away over a decade ago. But between my mother, Carlotta my bio mom, and Mayor Nash, I'm usually ducking for parental cover. I might be twenty-seven, but that doesn't stop the three of them from freely tossing their opinions my way.

Everett wraps an arm around my shoulders, and I look up at him and sigh. Everett is a god among men with his jet-black hair and ocean blue eyes. He's serious and pensive and getting a smile out of him is rather hard-won. He's heart-stoppingly sexy, and every woman in all of Vermont seems to have him on her radar. His first name is actually Essex, but he much prefers for the masses to call him Everett. However, for some reason, the women he's done some serious mattress moves with have garnered the honor to call him by his proper moniker—his mother and sister withstanding, of course, because that's the only name they've ever called him by.

Noah is a heartthrob himself, with his dark hair that turns red at the tips in the sun, evergreen eyes, and deep-welled dimples that have the power to melt me to a puddle at the sight of them. He's a homicide detective down in Ashford County, and I'm pretty sure women at every stage and age of life wouldn't mind him doing a very thorough pat-down of their person.

Here's the kicker. I'm in love with them both. It's not fair that I've accidentally given my heart away to two handsome men, but, as it stands, I happen to be legally bound to one of them at the moment.

Everett blows out a breath as he takes in the burgeoning crowd quickly taking over Main Street.

"What else can we do to help out?" He lands a sweet kiss to the top of my head.

"Nothing. You've done far too much today already," I say. "The kitchen staff is helping give away the goodies, and Lily is manning the register. I'll float in and out, making sure everything is running smoothly."

"Perfect." Noah's dimples invert. "Then maybe in a little bit you and I can catch one of those haunted carriage rides. I hear it's the ride of a lifetime—the last ride of your lifetime."

Everett grunts, "I'd be careful if I were you, Lemon. He's been prone to pull a fast one on you before. I'd ask for a clear-cut definition of what exactly he's asking you to ride."

I swat Everett on his rock-hard stomach for teasing me. As far back as I can remember, Everett almost exclusively calls me by my surname, and I don't mind one bit.

The *fast one* he's referring to is the accidental marriage Noah and I found ourselves in. But that wasn't at all Noah's fault—at least not his alone. We both walked into that one. And the funny thing is, we meant every word we exchanged in that questionable ceremony. It was beautiful and, frighteningly enough, it was real, too.

"Noah, that sounds lovely. A haunted carriage ride might be exactly what I need to tone down my anxiety over this entire event. A month-long celebration of the spookiest time of year sounded brilliant when my mother birthed the idea, but the thought of putting the entire town on display for thirty days straight is already panning out to be a bit more taxing than I bargained for."

A pair of hands covers Noah's eyes, and judging by that all too familiar engagement ring glittering in my face, I know exactly who's playing peek-a-boo with my new husband—and it's not me.

Cormack jumps into our midst, laughing up a storm as if she hit the brewery on the corner good and hard.

"*Boo!*" She smacks Noah with a kiss right on the lips.

Cormack is the aforementioned Coconut Featherhead. She happens to be delusional enough to believe that she and Noah are engaged. Last month, she went as far as throwing a surprise engagement party for her and Noah—and oddly enough, she threw one for Everett and me as well.

Cormack is an impossibly thin blonde with celadon green eyes and bony features. She comes from old money and has a penchant for flashy clothes, cars, and purses.

Before Noah can respond to the assault, my sisters, Meg and Lainey, pop up.

Meg has long since dyed her blonde locks raven's wing black, and it looks stunning juxtaposed against her ice blue eyes. Lainey shares my caramel-colored hair and hazel eyes—so much so that when we were little, I had hoped my parents had the details of my adoption wrong.

Meg slaps Cormack on the back. "How'd you take the news, Mac Nut?" She turns my way. "I can't believe Noah *wifed* with you a bouquet of dried flowers."

It's true. I held a bouquet of dried flowers for the ceremony and I felt like the luckiest bride in the world. Even though we tied what we thought was the faux knot in Pastor Gaines' office with zero pomp and circumstance, that rugged little ceremony will forever hold a special place in my heart.

I shake my head at my sister, silently begging her not to speak another word. I know for a fact that Noah has a very distinct and intricate plan on how to make things clear to Cormack once and for all regarding where they stand. He's tried alerting her to the fact that they are *not* a couple in the past, and somehow it always seems to bring them closer to the altar rather than farther from it.

Everett leans in. "Let Meg take over, Lemon. This might be the most entertaining part of the day."

"Or the scariest."

Noah lifts a finger as if ready to interject, but Meg hops right in front of Cormack.

"I'm talking about the wedding that took place," my sister snarks.

Cormack is quick to bat Meg away like a giant gnat just as a rush of tourists comes and attacks my cupcake stand.

"What are you talking about? What wedding?" Cormack takes up Noah's hand and looks as if she's about to bolt off with him in an effort to escape my intimidating sister.

Truthfully, who could blame her? Meg has always had an intimidating air about her. In fact, she spent a good portion of the last few years on the female wrestling circuit in Las Vegas.

Mom ambles up. Her hair looks wild and her face is pinched red. She has a look of fire in her eyes and she's clearly worked up over something.

"You don't get to talk to me that way," she growls at the poor soul behind her. "You have no idea how outraged I am right now. I'm fit to be tied. I'm fit to *kill!*" She stomps on up. "Lottie, what can I do to help?"

I glance past her and spot a pasty-faced Pastor Gaines trailing her. He's got on a rather loud purple and green striped sweater, and I can't help but think it looks as if he's dressed appropriately for the haunted lunacy that's about to ensue.

Oh my goodness, she was telling off her boy toy.

Pastor Gaines and my mother have dated for the last few months, but I don't trust Pastor Gaines as far as I can throw him. In fact, just last month, Noah and I discovered that his real name is Stephen *Heartwood*. What kind of pastor has the need to change his identity?

Everett thought maybe he had a good reason for it. But I think there's something sinister afoot. So I gave my mother the heads-up and made her promise not to say a word while Noah and I investigated it further, but it looks as if it's all coming to a head for her.

"Go inside," I tell her. "Lily will gladly give you something to do."

She nods before glancing his way. "And don't follow me. I'm at a breaking point today." She ducks into the bakery, and he glares my way a moment.

Stephen Gaines—*Heartwood*, whoever he is, always has a smile plastered to his obnoxious face, and this moment is no different. It's tight and manufactured, but nonetheless it never leaves his face.

"Lottie." His dark eyes linger over mine as he heads in after her.

Some men simply don't know the value of following orders.

Everett leans in again. "You want me to go after him?"

"Not yet," I say as Cormack struggles to leave our intimate circle with Noah stapled to her hand, but now it's Lainey jumping in front of her.

"Let go of that man!" Lainey does a karate chop move that renders Cormack Noah-less. I'd laugh because it's a touch comical, but I'm terrified this will turn ugly fast.

Personally, I don't want to be around once Cormack is given the news. Her delusional relationship with Noah has been spurring her along for the last few months. There's no telling what might unravel once the truth comes out.

Meg wraps an arm around Lainey's shoulders.

"That's right." Meg flashes a short-lived smile. "Noah Fox is a married man, and he's not married to you, missy, so take a haunted hike. Or better yet, step out in front of the next haunted chariot. Trust me, no one is going to stop you. Least of all this poor man you've been terrorizing."

"Meg!" I try to pull her back, but she's proving immovable.

"Enough is enough, Lot," Meg riots. "You have to be tough

with some people or they won't accept the truth." She turns back to Cormack. "Noah married Lottie a few days ago. They've already hopped on the baby train, too. So get out of their way or I'll forcibly remove you."

"Oh God," I groan as Everett holds me back.

Cormack's lips contort into all sorts of scary shapes as she turns to Noah.

"What is she rambling about?" She swats both Lainey and Meg with her pricey purse until they offer her decent clearance in which to leave our circle.

"It's true." Noah looks my way. "Lottie and I were married just a few days ago."

"What?" Cormack squawks as she trots in front of him. "What do you mean you married Luella?"

Dear Lord. I groan at the malfeasance she keeps perpetuating when it comes to my rightful moniker. For reasons unbeknownst to me, both Cormack and Noah's ex-wife, Britney, cannot get my name right to save their lives.

Speaking of which, the blonde bombshell herself struts up in a body-hugging cat suit, her hourglass figure on full display—and she's earned it. Britney is a franchisee of the Swift Cycle gyms. She's planted one across the street and has an entire slew of them all around the great state of Vermont. She's a real-life blonde version of Jessica Rabbit, a sultry vixen that doles out the sass and doesn't take flack from anyone.

"What did I miss?" she pants to Everett as a loose strand of hair covers her left eye. I'm not entirely sure Britney has two eyes. In fact, I don't think she does. I've yet to see that sultry hairstyle dislodge itself to prove me wrong.

My half-brother, Finn, is standing by her side and offers me a friendly wave. He's Mayor Nash's son and my newfound brother. He shares my caramel-colored hair and hazel eyes and looks like the adorable boy next door. He runs the Sugar Bowl Resort up north, but he's been spending a lot of time in Honey Hollow with his new sweetie, Britney.

"You didn't miss a thing," I say to Britney just as something soft and furry brushes against my right arm, and I look over to find that a black cat has jumped onto my cupcake table. It's about a foot tall, seated, and its glowing green eyes are pointed straight at Cormack as if it were settling in to watch the show.

I'm about to shoo it away when Cormack groans as if she were just hit with a bullet.

"Noah Corbin Fox!" Her voice booms over the expanse, and I'd swear there was a silent lull for a solid two seconds on Main Street in her honor. "What is this about?" A breath hitches in her throat as she freezes solid a moment. "Oh, I get it." Her head tips back as she lets out a frightening laugh.

Everett leans in. "That's the cackle of a madwoman."

"You're not wrong," I whisper back.

Cormack brays like a dolphin. "Noah, say you're teasing. With all these people around you're bound to start rumors. Think of poor Essex. He and Lolly are practically married themselves."

"I wish," Everett whispers the word hot into my ear, and a shiver rides through me.

Noah rubs his eyes a moment as if trying to wake from a very bad dream. "It's not a joke, Cormack. In fact"— he takes a few bold steps in my direction, and suddenly I'm fearing for both our necks—"Lottie, I spoke with my counselor and she suggests you join me for the session."

Cormack balks, "You want her to join *us*? Noah, we're not bringing her to our couple's counseling. Lolita, you can just march yourself right back into your little bakery and take your fiancé along with you. You don't have to attend a single counseling session with my beloved and me."

Meg steps in. "Nutcase!" she riots in Cormack's face. "The dude is off the market."

Cormack remains unfazed as she lifts her ring finger and shows off the glittering rock, albeit a replica of the real deal.

"Darn tootin', missy." Cormack flaunts her faux engagement ring enthusiastically as if she were sharing a far more colorful finger with us. "The man is off the market, and he's mine!"

Lainey tosses her hands in the air. "All right, let me at her. Listen here and listen good, Featherby. Noah purchased that ring on your finger for my sister. He didn't give it to you. You pried it out of his closet!"

It's true. Cormack found the ring that was intended for me and quickly popped it on without giving Noah a chance to explain.

The growing crowd around us gasps. A robust band of tourists has amassed along with the fine yet eager-to-know-the-truth people of Honey Hollow.

Oh dear. This is turning into a certifiable nightmare.

"Noah?" His name comes from Cormack, low and throaty and dare I say a tad bit threatening. "Is this true?"

"It's true." His dimples invert, no smile, and the collective crowd seems to stop breathing.

It *is* true. In fact, the ring on her finger is a replica that Cormack herself had made of the original—and thankfully so. Her farce was heartbreaking enough to witness without the thought of her wearing the treasure Noah bought with me in mind.

A high-pitched scream knifes its way out of Cormack's throat, and if I didn't know better, I'd think it served as some sort of tribal communication system between her and her old sorority sisters.

Cormack reaches back and snaps a cupcake off the table and jams the frosting in Noah's face. And before I know it, she's picked up another one and another as she pelts him a mile a minute.

The black cat lets out a deafening roar as it jumps on all fours, its hair standing on end giving it an electrocuted appeal.

I'm about to reach for the poor thing and pull it to safety when it turns around and jumps through the glass and into my shop, sending my heart right up my throat.

That wasn't just any black cat. That was a supernatural specter who comes bearing bad news for its previous owner. And by bad news, I mean death.

Meg holds her hands to her mouth like a megaphone. "FOOD FIGHT!"

And soon enough, it's raining cupcakes in every direction.

Everett catches one midflight and gently dots my lips with it before kissing off the frosting.

Meg laughs as she spots us. "Looks like fun."

I hook my gaze to Everett as the melee ensues. "And in a bit, it's going to look like murder."

His eyes widen as if to ask the question and I nod.

"It's happening again," I say. "Death has come to Honey Hollow."

Everett exhales deeply. "And someone will die today."

CHAPTER 2

*C*haos.

Complete and utter chaos.

Everett pulls me out of the madness as we ditch into the bakery and watch Noah try his best to subdue a cupcake wielding Cormack.

Lily runs up. "Oh, Lottie!" Lily Swanson is a brunette stunner who has worked for me since the bakery opened a year ago. She happens to be best friends with Naomi Turner, my best friend's—Keelie Turner's—twin. But Lily and Naomi have since had a falling-out over Noah's younger brother, Alex. He's a muscular ex-Marine turned investment banker who strolled into town a few months back and stole a few hearts and destroyed a few friendships along the way. Lily and Naomi were his first casualties. "Lottie"—Lily drops her face in her hands a moment—"we worked all morning to get those cupcakes out there for the public to enjoy."

"Don't I know it. I just wish I could fix this mess."

She makes a face. "Speaking of which, you need to remember to fix the ground safe. The lid won't lock, and you've still got last night's deposit in there."

"I'm one step ahead of you. I already have a locksmith scheduled to come out tomorrow. I just wish I was one step ahead of
this food fight."

A cupcake hits the window with a splat, leaving a bright
orange stain in its wake.

Meg and Lainey head inside, laughing hysterically as
frosting drips from their hair, and my mother and Pastor
Gaines run out from the back to see what the commotion is
about.

My mother's hair looks like a hurricane just blew through it.
Her blouse is buttoned in all the wrong places, and her pants look
as if she's hiked them up in haste. I'm betting she has. It looks as
if she went from furious with the sneaky shepherd to passionate
in a single coital bound.

"Mother, where were you?" I ask, exasperated at the thought
of what might have been happening between the two of them.

A guttural laugh emits from her as she wiggles her shoulders.

"Mom! A minute ago, you were threatening to kill him. And,
seeing that things clearly went sideways for you in that department, I volunteer to do the deed myself!" Before I can lunge onto
the demon, the entire bakery floods with the frosting covered
masses.

Noah threads his way through the crowd as he makes his way
over. His hair is slicked with black frosting and it's a good, not to
mention delicious, look on him.

"Cormack took off." He pauses a moment to shoot my sisters
a wry look. "She's threatening to do all kinds of things. I think I'd
better find her—maybe talk to her in private."

Everett's chest bucks with a silent laugh. "Something you
should have done months ago." He looks my way. "Have you
noticed he has a pattern of omitting pertinent information from
women?"

Meg jumps forward. "And don't forget stringing them along
in false relationships."

Noah groans, "I'll catch up with you tonight, Lottie. Everett, try not to stir the pot while I'm gone."

He takes off just as the floodgates open, and soon enough both the bakery and the Honey Pot Diner are filled with patrons.

The Honey Pot Diner is connected to the bakery by way of a walk-through built into our conjoining wall. Both places once belonged to my grandmother, Nell Sawyer, who left every piece of real estate she owned to yours truly.

Nell died last January, but the will was contested by my uncle who sorely lost his legal battle last month and now, indeed, I own what feels like every bit of real estate under the sun. Everett promised he'd go over it all with me and help me get organized. I've never been a land baron before, and I have no idea what to do next.

The Honey Pot is where I worked for years, alongside Keelie, right up until Nell helped me open this place. In the center of the Honey Pot's adorable dining room there's a large resin oak tree with its center hollowed out. A honey pot sits inside, dripping its golden goodness, surrounded by resin bees. The branches of that oak stretch across the ceiling and right into my bakery. And each of those branches is covered in twinkle lights. It adds a magical appeal to both establishments, especially on a dark cloudy day like today.

Mom looks to my sisters. "I'll try to reserve us all a table at the Honey Pot."

"It's no use." Keelie comes over, her blonde curls bouncing over her shoulders. "We've got a two-hour wait as it stands. No offense, but this Haunted Honey Hollow thing might be working a little too good."

"Agree," I say as I spot my spooky kooky bio mom seemingly talking to herself in the corner. But, alas, she's chatting up a storm with that fluffy black no-doubt-about-it supernatural cat.

"Would you please excuse us?" I pull Everett along with me.

Only Everett and Noah are apprised of my transmundane

status, further classified as supersensual. At first, when I started seeing long deceased pets—and on occasion the rare dead human —it served as a rather harmless bad omen for their loved ones. And that usually translated into nothing more than a sprained ankle at best, but now it almost certainly means death. And slowly over the last solid year my supersensual powers have begun to grow. About a few months ago, the dead garnered the ability to move things within the material world—whenever they wished. And as of recently, I can hear the dead—and fortunately for me, these ghostly pets and people love to jabber.

I give Everett's hand a squeeze. For some reason, I discovered that I act as a conduit. And if someone touches me, they can then hear what the dead have to say as well.

That gorgeous ebony fur ball sits fanning his long plume of a tail over his back as it regales Carlotta with a story. Its fur shimmers as if a spray of stars is trapped inside its fur and it looks perfectly magical.

"Lottie! Judge Sexy!" Carlotta pats the spot next to her. "Take a seat and join the party. Thirteen here was just about to tell me about the scariest Halloween Eve he's ever seen."

"A boy, huh?" I give him a quick scratch behind the ears and he shivers as he leans against my fingers hard. It never fails to amuse me the way the dead can feel as solid as they please just before they dissolve to nothing. "What's this Thirteen business?"

The cat growls, "That's my name." His neon green eyes shine like beacons.

"Thirteen?" Everett tips his ear this way as if he didn't hear right.

"That is correct." His tiny pink nose turns toward Carlotta. "Thirteen is the name my master gave me."

I lean in hard, a breath hitching in my throat. "What's your master's name?"

"I would love to tell you." His voice grows faint as he dissipates to nothing.

Carlotta bounces out of her seat, looking every bit like an older version of me. "Now look what you did. Didn't your mother ever teach you not to be nosy?"

I can't help but roll my eyes.

Mayor Nash pops up from behind holding out a cupcake toward Carlotta.

"Lottie, Judge Baxter." He tips his head forward, and his were-wolf-inspired ears nearly fall off. He's covered with fur from head to toe, and he's got long, claw-like contraptions over his hands. "Quite a mess out there, but I managed to salvage what I could." He pats his belly as he laughs.

"Well, thank you," I say, glancing out the window at the cupcake-covered street. "I have a feeling I can use all the help I can get."

A stream of tourists bustles out the front door, and I spot Pastor Gaines wiggling his way inside like a salmon swimming upstream. He's donned a black leather jacket and a baby blue button-down shirt underneath and looks as if he's dressed to impress my mother. I bet someone pelted him good with my cupcakes for it to sponsor a wardrobe change. Although, I don't see why he'd wear that malfeasance of a sweater to begin with. Being pelted with cupcakes or not, the sweater deserved the incinerator.

I head on over and block his path. "You have a lot of nerve, you know that?"

His smile widens, but his brows dip as if he were confused by my comment.

"What may I help you with, dear?"

"Oh, please. You've done enough. And since my mother didn't kill you, I might just have to do it myself!"

A hush falls over the café for a solid second before the conversations roar back to life.

"Excuse me." He nods his way past me as he heads into the Honey Pot.

Everett comes over and blows out a deep breath. "Why don't we lock ourselves in your office and forget about all the chaos out here?" His thumb glides over my lips like a dark promise.

"Believe you me, I'd take you up on it if I didn't know my mother and Pastor Gaines defiled it." My fingers slap over my lips a moment. "Oh my goodness, Everett. I'm a married woman! And I happen to be married to someone else entirely." A hard groan comes from me. "I can't sleep with you anymore."

"*Noah*," he growls his name out like a threat—and I'm convinced it's a real one.

And as if on cue, Noah himself burrows through the crowd.

"Where is she?" His eyes are wild, and he looks disheveled and frustrated. The front of his shirt is covered with purple fingerprints—I'm guessing Cormack's.

"I don't know." I hike up on my tiptoes and crane my neck as I look around. "How did you possibly lose her?" Believe me, he's tried, and it's proved impossible for months.

Everett grunts, "He didn't lose her. He escaped."

"That makes more sense," I say just as Everett gives Noah a hard shove to the chest.

"And I finally caught onto your matrimonial shenanigans," Everett roars. "You did this because you knew she wouldn't sleep with me as long as she was legally bolted to your side."

Noah's dimples press in. "I don't know what the hell you're talking—" He pauses midflight as his mouth rounds out into a perfect O and he looks my way. "So now she's cut *you* off? The tables have turned, huh, buddy?" An easy grin glides across his face.

It's true. Everett cut me off a few weeks back so that I could gain some closure once and for all with Noah. I'm pretty sure our jaunt to the proverbial altar was a turn in the wrong direction as far as closure goes.

"Don't you smile at her like that!" The sound of a screaming female, extricating the words like a war cry, comes from behind, and I turn to find Cormack storming her way over as she makes her way through the kitchen.

"What are you doing back there?" I holler as I head that way myself and note the entire kitchen island is brimming with unfrosted cupcakes.

My God, what am I thinking?

I have a bakery to run. I certainly don't have time for Cormack Featherhead's shenanigans.

"Cormack, get out there and make sure Everett and Noah don't kill each other." I think on it for a moment. "They're fighting over *you*." That stroke to her ego should assure she interjects herself between them for a good long hour.

She sucks in a quick breath. "I knew it. Essex wants me back, too. Of course, he does. That boy has always loved me. But don't you worry, Loki. The Big Boss and I are just going through a rough patch. Cold feet is a very real thing."

Big Boss. I shudder at the nickname Cormack has for Noah. I've never understood it since bossing her around is the last thing Noah wants to do. In fact, he doesn't want anything to do with her at all. Cormack is basically a stalker, and I think I've just sicced her on poor Everett, too.

"Cold feet? You keep believing that," I mutter as I put on an apron, pick up a piping bag, and get straight to work. She takes off in a furor, her high heels leaving a muddy trail in their wake, and I groan. "No, no." The last thing I need is someone from the health department shutting me down on the busiest day of the year. "Lily?" I call out, but she's too swamped with customers to hear me. The rest of the kitchen staff has migrated right back where they belong—to the Honey Pot Diner—and left me to my own devices.

I land the piping bag where I found it and head to the back for a mop, but it's not in the janitorial supply closet. It's still outside drying off from its initial use this morning. I head out to the alley behind the shop and steal a moment to take in the crisp autumn breeze. There's an old sweetgum tree across the way, and tucked in its branches I spot that spectral black cat, Thirteen, glowing as if it had an entire constellation of stars trapped in its fur.

A smile comes to me.

That's the way the dead always look, and I do love their ethereal glow. I traipse across the way to have a private chat with the cute little beast, only to trip over something solid, yet rather soft at the very same time. I land on all fours and find myself nearly eye to eye with an all too familiar face—Pastor Gaines.

But this time he's not offering that eerie smile. Instead, his mouth is smeared with orange frosting, and one of my cupcakes is still clutched in his hand.

My mother won't have to worry about him bothering her anymore.

Pastor Gaines is dead.

CHAPTER 3

A violent scream evicts from me, sharp and biting as it claws its way from my throat.

Noah and Everett come racing out the back door shouting expletives at one another and at the horrid situation, but I can't pull my eyes off Pastor Gaines as he stares blankly at the sky. His leather jacket lies open, and a crimson stain has drenched the front of his dress shirt.

"Lottie!" Noah lifts me to my feet and wraps his arms around me before sending me sailing into Everett. Noah crouches down and checks for a pulse, shaking his head up at us before confirming the worst.

Everett warms my arms with his hands. "What happened, Lemon? What did you see?"

"I didn't see anything. I was headed to the tree, and I didn't even see the body." My hand clamps over my mouth. "Oh my God, Pastor Gaines is the body," I hiss as if the truth just hit me. "This is terrible! The entire town is going to mourn his loss. My mother is going to lose her mind with grief." Or relief—it's a toss-up right about now.

Everett inches back. "If I remember correctly, she was threatening to kill him just over an hour ago. And so were you."

"Oh dear." I bury my face in Everett's chest for a moment. "Wait." I glance back toward the tree as Noah taps into his phone. I'm sure he's notifying his partner, Detective Ivy Fairbanks, a leggy redhead who doesn't think much of me, but I don't think much of her so we're good. "I did see something. I saw that cat in the tree. That's why I came all the way out here. And now it's up and disappeared."

Everett glances to the tree himself. "You saw the cat again?"

"What?" Noah steps over, incensed. "You knew she saw another one of those ghostly visitors and you let her out of your sight?" His voice hikes up an octave as he stiffens with rage. "This is exactly why she should be with me. You are irresponsible with her."

"He's not irresponsible with me." I'd swat him, but he's a good two feet away. "I'm not a child, Noah. Nobody needs to be responsible for me but *me*."

"No, he's right." Everett exhales deeply as if acquiescing to defeat. "I shouldn't have left your side."

"FYI, I left *your* side. And now you're both sounding equally condescending. Is that what you want, Everett? To be on equal footing with him?"

Before he can answer, the entire area floods with sheriff's deputies, along with Detective Ivy Fairbanks herself.

Ivy tosses her long red hair effortlessly as she struts our way in a pair of four-inch stilettos. She has cheekbones that could reach the moon and a scowl that could burn a hole right through any human soul.

"Lottie, Everett." She lifts a brow at him as if to ask an obvious question—one I'm certain that has to do with me. "Noah, fill me in."

"Lottie was just coming out here to…uh, look at the tree."

"Get a mop," I add. "Cormack trailed dirt into the kitchen and

I needed to clean it before the health department came out. I mean, not that I was expecting them. But anyway, I came out and it was so nice, I thought I'd look at the tree." I shrug up at Noah.

Ivy squints my way. "Back up for a moment. What was Cormack doing in your kitchen? Does she work for you?"

"No."

"Did you invite her back there for a tour?"

"We're not friends." I'm quick to make that clear. "I wouldn't offer her a tour of my—"

Noah lifts a hand. "We get the picture. Cormack was probably looking for me."

Ivy's penciled in brows arch high into her forehead giving her that villain appeal that comes so effortlessly to her. "In the alley? Because Lottie said her feet were muddy. And look." She points over where Pastor Gaines still lies with his body sprawled out for all to see. "There's mud to the right of him. It's the first thing I noticed when I came out here. A girl in heels notices these things."

I suck in a quick breath at the implication.

"Look"—I say with a twinge of regret for what's about to come out of my mouth—"Cormack is a lot of things, but she's not a killer. I don't even think she had a connection to Pastor Gaines."

Ivy sniffs the air between us. "Let's leave that to the professionals to determine." She takes off toward the chaos surrounding Pastor Gaines just as the deputies roll out the caution tape.

"CORMACK COULDN'T HAVE DONE THIS." I shake my head at Noah as if it were my sole duty to defend her.

"I don't think so either." He cranes his neck toward the entry. "But if she was out here, she might have seen something. I'd better go speak with her. And I'll have all the security cameras that line the front examined to see if they can offer any clues. We've got one back here, but it looks as if that tree grew right over it."

Everett ticks his head toward the bakery. "Come on, Lemon. Let's get back in there and leave this mess to the pros." His brows bounce as if he found the comment comical himself.

We head back in through the back door, and both Keelie and Lily are there to greet us.

"Is it true?" Keelie's big blue eyes bulge. "Did you find another body?"

Lily jumps in close. "What were they eating? My God, Lottie, spill it so I can get to ordering more ingredients, stat!"

I groan. It's true. My mother happens to own and run a happily haunted bed and breakfast. And being the savvy businesswoman she is, she's set up tours of the haunted facility. Once she's through bilking tourists for her pricey poltergeist show-and-tell session, she ships them all my way for what she's dubbed The Last Thing They Ate Tour. In the last year alone, whatever the poor deceased was found noshing on at the time of their demise has become an instant morbid sensation.

Lily snaps her fingers. "It was a cupcake, wasn't it?"

My mouth opens, but before I can confirm it, Lily gives a victorious cry as she heads for the office.

"Geez, Lottie," she balks as she pokes her head inside. "You really need to keep this place a little more organized."

"Keelie, have you seen Cormack?" I ask as we plow past her on our way to the front of the bakery.

Keelie catches up quickly. "Yes, she's out front sitting in Alex's lap, mumbling something about making Noah insane with jealousy."

"Dear God," I moan as we head to the café, and, sure enough, there she is planted in Alex's lap and the poor guy looks as if he has no idea how to evict her.

"Cormack"—Noah is the first to call her name—"can I have a word with you?"

An impish grin floats on her lips as she gives Alex's cheek a quick pinch.

"Works like a charm." She bounces to her feet. "All right, Big Boss. I forgive you for a momentary indiscretion. Essex"—she points his way—"I want this marital mess mopped up by a top-notch family practice lawyer. See to it that Lydia here doesn't get one red cent of my future husband's estate." She sighs deeply as she takes Noah by the hand. "Let's go to your place. It's time to kiss and make up."

"Hardly," I say. "Cormack, you tracked mud through my kitchen. What were you doing in the alley behind the bakery?"

If Noah won't get down to brass tacks, I will.

Cormack's brows pinch together. "If you must know, I was seeking sage counsel from a man of the cloth."

I shoot a look to Noah. "That's Pastor Gaines she's talking about."

Everett leans in. "Who else was out there with the two of you?"

Cormack's lids hood low as she glowers my way. "Her mother."

"What?" The breath gets knocked out of me as efficiently as a sucker punch.

Mom and Carlotta head this way, both with concerned looks on their faces.

"Lottie"—Mom accosts me first—"what in heaven's name are all these deputies doing crawling all over?"

I bite down on my lower lip and Mom gasps.

"No," she says it sharp and demanding. "Lottie Kenzie Lemon, do not tell me you found another one."

My mouth opens, but only a croaking sound emits from my throat.

Noah leans in. "I'm sorry, Miranda. Can I speak with you

outside for a moment? I'm afraid I have some news to share and I'll have to ask you a few questions."

Mom is quick to follow him, and Cormack raises her hand as she trots along.

"What about me?" Cormack cries. "Does this have anything to do with the fact I tracked mud through Lonnie's kitchen?"

Everett and I head outside with them, and I wrap an arm around my mother as she shivers in the breeze.

"What is it, Detective Fox?" Mom's voice trembles. "Don't keep me in suspense. I don't think I can take it."

"It's Pastor Gaines"—Noah nods as if she might be able to fill in the blanks herself—"I'm sorry, Miranda, but he's no longer with us."

Mom gives a few quick blinks. "You mean he went back to Nevada?"

"No, Mom." I pull her in close. "Not Nevada—somewhere a little farther than that. He's gone—as in, he passed away."

Noah nods, affirming this grim fact. "Someone shot him in the alley behind the bakery. I'm sorry I'm going to have to ask you this, but do you have access to any firearms?"

"What?" Her face bleaches white, as does Cormack's. "No, I don't."

Cormack begins to hyperventilate. "There's been a murder!" she shrieks. "I was in that alley right along with him. Oh dear God, I could have been *killed*! It would have been the end of me. Oh, Noah, I feel faint." She falls limp over his chest and he struggles to hold her upright.

Alex comes out and jogs over. "What's going on? People are starting to talk."

"There's been a murder." Everett is quick to fill in his old step-brother. "In fact, if you don't mind, could you take Cormack home? I think Noah has his work cut out for him for the night."

Noah sighs. "I was about to ask the same thing." He's quick to tilt Cormack his way, and soon enough Alex has muscled her into his arms as she does her best impression of a corpse.

She tilts her head up. "I'll be at your place, Big Boss. I'll warm the bed for you."

Noah shoots his brother a look and shakes his head. But I have a feeling not even Alex and his blow-up muscles will be able to stop Cormack from getting what she wants.

My sisters, Lainey and Meg, head on out.

"Lottie!" Lainey's stern tone lets me know she's about to let into me. Suffice it to say, Lainey is not amused by the body count I've amassed these last few months. "I don't even need to ask, do I?"

Mom shakes her head. "I'm afraid not."

Meg belts out a laugh with little regard for the dead. "Who'd you off this time, Lot? The butcher? The candlestick maker? I have a feeling the baker is pretty safe."

"Not funny," Mom says as she pulls a wad of tissues out of her purse and the butt of a small black gun stares back at us.

"Mother," I say as I pull her purse forward and pluck it out just enough to reveal it's an all too familiar gun—mine. "What are you doing with Ethel?"

"Don't touch it," Noah pants as he takes the purse from me. "Miranda, I'm going to have to ask you to come down to the sheriff's department for questioning."

And just like that, Miranda Lemon is at the top of the suspect list.

CHAPTER 4

*A*rrested.

Okay, so my mother wasn't arrested, but she might as well have been what with all the crying and screaming and histrionics—and that was just me.

Meg and Lainey drove down to Ashford to be with my mother. And Everett drove me down as well. But after a few hours, my mother demanded that Everett take me home so that I could get some sleep before opening the bakery this morning.

But believe you me, not a wink of shut-eye was experienced last night. Instead, I ruminated over the scant facts in this case, tossing and turning until my alarm mercifully went off.

Everett offered to stay the night. He said he had a surefire way of getting me to sleep—and now that I've been wandering around the bakery like a zombie all morning, it's clear I should have taken him up on the lusty offer.

And really? Who am I to shut down Everett?

I'm not really married to Noah, am I? I mean, I am in the eyes of the law—and boy, I meant every word I said to him that day. But I'm pretty sure whatever could have happened between

Everett and me last night would have been far more medicinal than it ever would of the philandering nature.

I wonder how many cheats have armed themselves with the exact same defense?

"That's a lot of cupcakes, Lottie," Lily says as I head over to fill up the refrigerated shelves in front.

"Friendly ghost cupcakes," I muse as I carefully place the delicate goodies in one by one. The cupcakes themselves are devil's food. I took the tops and dipped them into a chocolate glaze to give it a nice glossy sheen, then piped a three-inch white ghost made entirely of frosting up top, complete with miniature chocolate chip eyes.

Lily swipes one for herself. "So, how did things turn out with your mother?"

"I don't know. I mean, I stayed as late as I could, but I ended up coming home before they let her go. Lainey texted at about one in the morning saying they had just got back. So I'm guessing everyone had a pretty rotten night's sleep."

"Well, I didn't have a wink of sleep either." Her voice is low and throaty, and I stand upright and close the refrigerated shelf in the event Lily is about to spill some juicy tidbits on exactly why she didn't catch a wink. "Alex came over to tuck me in and made sure all of my dreams came true last night."

"*What?*" a female voice screeches from behind and we turn to find both Keelie and her sister, Naomi, with their mouths open wide. Keelie and Naomi are twins, both my age, but Keelie has decided to keep her blonde curly locks natural as opposed to Naomi's harshly dyed black tresses. Naomi's hair is long and glossy, and the raven's wing black hue looks magical on her, enhancing her already shocking beauty.

I'm guessing the screeching came from Naomi since both she and Lily have been warring over Alex. Lily has already slept with Alex as far back as last month, but no one has dared to breathe this information in Naomi's direction, so I'm guessing this is the first she's hearing about it.

Naomi digs her fingers into Lily's shoulder and yanks her to the side.

"Take it back!" she shouts so loud that what little customers I have in the bakery scuttle on out.

"Oh no, you don't!" I bark as I pull Lily to the side, and Keelie does her best to subdue her sister. "Not in my bakery, ladies. If you want to duke it out over that shirt full of muscles, you can take it to the alley."

Naomi huffs my way, "Wouldn't you just love to stick me out there with a killer running loose. Not on your life, Lottie Lemon."

Naomi and I might have a touch of bad blood between us, but it's entirely on her side. Way back in high school, she wanted to date my boyfriend, Otis *Bear* Fisher, while we were still locked in a relationship and has never forgiven me for the fact she couldn't get him to cheat. The irony being that he cheated on me with just about everyone else. However, Bear has since cleaned up his cheating ways and is currently engaged to Keelie.

Naomi leans in toward Lily as far as Keelie will allow. "And you are dead to me. Don't bother coming to the Monsters Ball." She looks my way. "It's a formal event, costumes required, taking place Halloween night at the Evergreen Manor. Lottie, the Evergreen would like for you to cater the sweet treats. I'll leave the details up to you." She sneers at her once upon a best friend. "All the who's who of Honey Hollow will be there. And since you've been banished, I guess Alex will be my date that evening—just like he will tonight."

Lily's mouth falls open. "Where are you going tonight?"

"Wouldn't you like to know." She winks over at her before taking off.

"That was brutal." I shudder in their heated wake.

Lily flits a hostile stare to both Keelie and me. "If either of you finds out where they're headed tonight, I want the heads-up. There's no way I'm letting her run off with my man. I'm raising my spear and heading into battle."

Keelie shrugs. "They're headed to Mangias tonight with Bear and me."

I smile at the thought of Keelie and Bear Fisher making it work. As of last month, they officially became engaged.

"Any word on the wedding details yet?" I scuttle forward. "Have you got a date? A season?"

Keelie sighs dreamily as she looks out the window. "I don't know. Every season feels like the right season to marry Bear. I guess it depends on how fancy I want the event to be. Naomi already said I could have it at the Evergreen."

"And I'm baking all the treats, including the cake," I offer.

Keelie's cheeks pinch pink. "Thank you, Lot. That means everything to me. I'll try to figure it all out and get back to you. Speaking of weddings, how's it feel to be the new Mrs. Fox?"

Lily makes a face. "I heard Essex is livid. Personally, I think you had it backward. If you were to marry anyone accidentally, it should have been him."

"Believe me, that would have been easier. Everett and I have maintained our hot and heavy status, but I just can't get my head around being with him physically now that Noah and I are hitched."

Lily gives a husky laugh. "It's not your head you need to wrap around him. It's your other body parts." She takes off for the register as a cluster of customers wanders in.

Keelie leans my way. "This sounds like the perfect time to give Noah a trial run just the way Everett demanded. Isn't he the one who said you should look for closure with Noah? Now that you're Mrs. Fox, I say feel out the lay of the land. See if the glass slipper fits."

"You mean really dive into the deep end of matrimony?"

ADDISON MOORE

"Yup. What better way to know if the two of you are destined to spend your lives together."

"Huh." I think about it for a minute. "Maybe I will."

∼

A LITTLE PAST NOON, once the lunch rush dies down—and believe it or not, the bakery does have one, I decide to hightail it to my mother's bed and breakfast armed with enough delicious ghostly cupcakes to entice the dead back to life.

I can just imagine how upset she must be. Not only is she grieving the man she spent quite a bit of intimate time with these last few months, but she's a suspect in an active homicide investigation.

The B&B was my mother's big purchase with the life insurance money once my father passed. Of course, she had enough stashed away to put my sisters and me through college, but the rest went to polishing up this place.

The autumn air is crisp as I come upon the enormous structure. The B&B is an oversized white mansion with innumerous bedrooms and bathrooms. And as far as places to stay in Honey Hollow go, both it and the Evergreen Manor are the only shows in town.

Much like Disney's famed Haunted Mansion, this one too is full of disembodied spirits. It used to be that my mother was getting the overflow from the Evergreen, but as of late it's the other way around. You might say that my mother is the hostess with the *ghostess* when it comes to giving her customers what they want. And apparently, what they want is to have the socks scared right off of them.

I head on in with my big box of cupcakes and take in the dark mahogany wood lining the walls and the thick emerald carpet that offers this place a cozy appeal. The B&B might be cozy in theory, but it's mammoth inside, with a formal grand room, a main dining room that serves dinner nightly, and recently my mother had a colossal conservatory attached that has played host to many events. During the day it serves as a café, and that's exactly where I'm headed to land these spooky sweet treats. The entire room is constructed of glass and steel, and it makes you feel as if you're having a picnic in the middle of the woods.

I head straight for the conservatory and spot Carlotta seated with the ghost of Greer Giles, a girl about my age who was shot to death last winter, and ensconced between them is that unlucky cat, Thirteen. His fur is thick and glossy and tiny sparks emit from around his ears as he twitches his head. And both Greer and Carlotta look to be rapt at attention to whatever it is he's regaling them with.

I set the cupcakes down on the refreshment counter and quickly take a seat at their table.

"Hello all," I say as I lean over and give Thirteen a quick pat over the head. "You belonged to Pastor Gaines, didn't you?"

The tiny beast jerks his head my way. "Pastor who?"

"That's right," I say, looking to Carlotta and Greer. "His name wasn't Stephen Gaines at all. It was Stephen *Heartwood*."

They both suck in a quick breath.

Greer leans in. Her dark hair is long and glossy and looks as if she just had a fresh blowout. "Carlotta says your mother is a suspect." Greer is beautiful, with high-cut cheekbones, dark hook-like eyebrows that lend her a villain appeal, and plump pink lips that always look ready to pucker.

I make a face. "Not only is she a suspect, but she's the prime suspect. Noah doesn't have anything else to go on at the moment." I bite down on my lip. "That's not entirely true. Cormack was the last to speak to him."

Carlotta waves it off. "We both know that dimwit would have shot herself in the foot if she were holding a loaded gun in her hand."

"I don't know," I muse. "She did pass a gun safety course with me a few months back."

Greer bats her unearthly long lashes at me. "Word on the street is that it was *your* gun that did him in."

Now it's me sucking in a quick breath. "Have they made it official?" My heart wallops against my chest. "I can't believe my mother or anyone else would take my gun and do that. But then, Cormack was in my kitchen. She could have found a way to open the safe, plucked the gun out, shot im-*pastor* Gaines, and planted Ethel in my mother's purse." A thought comes to me as I remember that conversation Lily and I had about fixing the ground safe. The lock wasn't working. My mother didn't have to break in—and neither did Cormack.

"Who's Ethel?" Greer looks genuinely concerned.

"Her gun." Carlotta takes a breath.

Thirteen twitches his whiskers and he looks so very adorable. Something about his sweetness reminds me of my own two cats, Pancake and Waffles. They're fluffy cream-colored Himalayans with rust-tipped tails, but they share that same aloof adorableness that all felines seem to possess.

The tiny cat lifts his pink nose my way. "You really have it in for this Cormack person, don't you?"

"*Ha!*" Carlotta honks. "I'll say. Lottie has been ticked for months that the blonde bimbo attached herself to her ex-boyfriend's side." She narrows her wicked peepers at me. "But then, he's not your ex-anything anymore, is he, *Mrs. Fox?*"

Greer gasps, "You finally made a decision between the two? You dumped *Essex?*"

No, I didn't dump Essex. And no, Greer and Everett never did get around to doing the deed. She bit the big one before she could pin him to a mattress, but she takes liberties with his name regardless, so Essex it is.

"I haven't dumped anyone," I'm quick to correct, and Carlotta rolls her eyes.

"That's the beauty of being Lottie."

Greer lifts a glass as if she was toasting. "Hear, hear."

"More like see, see," I say, taking the glass from her in the event a seemingly innocent guest should see the paranormal phenomenon and pass out. A glass that is seemingly floating all by its lonesome is sure to draw its fair share of supernatural attention.

"Oh my God!" a woman shrieks from behind and we turn to find Cormack white as a proverbial ghost. "That glass!" She hightails it over and sits right onto Greer's lap. "It just floated in midair!" Her eyes bulge as she looks to me. "It's true then what Britney says."

I can't help but roll my eyes at the mention of Noah's ex-wife. "Lay it on me."

"You're a witch!"

Greer bubbles with laughter, and it sends Cormack bouncing up and down as if she were about to morph into a human jackhammer. Just the sight of the spectacle has Thirteen tossing back his furry head with laughter. Honestly, there is no sweeter sight.

A sharp yelp comes from Cormack as she hops right out of her seat.

"Don't you hurt me!" She lifts her arms in the air as if surrendering. "You think you can intimidate me into staying away from Noah, but I'll tell you right now. That is never going to happen. You might have dark powers at your fingertips. You might have the ability to turn me into a frog, but one thing you lack. You will never pry me away from my one true love, Noah Corbin Fox." She takes off, and a sigh of exasperation expels from me.

Just as I'm about to tear my gaze from the exit, a young girl—a six-year-old girl to be exact—heads this way with her long brown hair covering her face. She's wearing an old dingy pinafore and a pair of scuffed Mary Jane slippers. She's wielding a bloody knife in her hand and growling like a monster ready for its next kill.

Poor Thirteen hops to all fours at the sight of her and his back arches dramatically as his hair stands on end.

"Azalea Marie!" Greer scolds.

"Marie? Is that her middle name?" I marvel. Little Lea—I don't dare call her Azalea because she doesn't care for it—was adopted by Greer and her two-hundred-year-old boyfriend, Winslow Decker. Winslow died right here in Honey Hollow in his prime and has yet to leave the area. Same is true for little Lea. It turns out, her family was hacked to pieces on the land the B&B was built on and she's stayed on to procure her vengeance.

Greer combs back the little ghoul's hair with her fingers until the tiny tot's adorable upturned nose peeks through. Lea is a beautiful little girl despite her gruesome scare tactics.

"I want the cat," Lea spits it out as she snatches Thirteen off the table and skips off with him.

"So?" Greer sparkles back to life as she taps her garnet red nails over the table. "Have you and Detective Fox consummated the union? Or is the big night still on the horny horizon?"

"Stop." I quickly look to Carlotta. "And don't you get started either. Noah and I are taking things slow—think glacial. In fact, last night, after the haunted festivities, we were going to go on our first official date as a married couple. But, as you can see, fate threw a body in the way."

Carlotta grunts, "Death and marital destruction seems to be a theme with you and the dicey detective. What happens when you spend some time with the judge?"

Greer belts out a deep-throated chuckle. "She sees stars, Carlotta. And don't try to deny it, Lottie. They're right there in your eyes."

"Yes, well, Noah had me seeing stars, too, right up until his wife showed up in town. But Britney is old news." I hold out my bare finger. "And Noah and I are new again."

"Take him for a spin, Lot." Carlotta kicks me from under the table.

"I'm not taking him for a spin." Keelie's battle cry comes to mind from earlier this morning and I'm sensing a theme.

Greer purrs like a kitten. "I'd take him for a spin. That man is one delicious hunk of beefcake. I don't see what's stopping you. It's perfectly legal with both the earthen and the heavenly laws."

I'm about to toss out a sassy comeback when I spot an all too familiar face in the rear of the B&B, laughing it up with friends while carving holes in the tops of pumpkins and filling them with gorgeous sunflowers.

"Is that my mother out there?" I balk at the sight of her strange behavior.

"Yuppers." Carlotta is quick to snap me back to reality.

"Excuse me." I head out through the back door. And sure as the stars are in the sky, my mother stands nestled with a cluster of her best friends—Chrissy Nash, the Mayor's ex-wife, and Becca Turner, Keelie's mother, and some women I've never seen before.

"Lottie!" My mother waves a pair of pruning shears my way. "Come join the fun! The horticulture club is making centerpieces for all the autumn festivities happening in Honey Hollow this month." She taps her finger to the pumpkin in front of her. "This one is going to the bank, and that one is going to the mayor's office." She gives me a sly wink because Mayor Nash is the reason I'm witnessing this lunacy being that he's my bio daddy. "And, of course, the B&B and the Evergreen will get the bulk of them. But don't you worry. I'll send a choice few to the bakery as well."

"Mother"—I quickly pull her to the side where I can rage at her in private—"you're the prime suspect in a murder investigation. Don't you think you should spend at least one day mourning the deceased? I mean, Pastor Gaines was your boyfriend."

She makes a face as she steals a moment to crane her neck back at her horticulture cohorts.

"The truth is, I don't miss him, Lottie." Her features harden as she looks me in the eye. "And I don't know who killed him, but a part of me wonders if he didn't deserve it."

She stalks off and resumes her position at the table with her friends.

My mouth falls open as I look to my sweet mother and wonder how on earth her heart grew so cold.

CHAPTER 5

*T*here is nothing more majestic than an October evening right here in Honey Hollow. The sky is just as scarlet as the leaves, and the wind holds an icy bite to it as if reprimanding you for being outside in the first place. Pumpkins have dotted every porch and storefront, and there are scarecrows cropping up on every front lawn, including the town square at the end of Main Street.

Noah sent a group text to Everett and me earlier, asking if we'd be up for dinner at Mangias to discuss the case. Of course, we said yes. Everett has always been up for whatever sleuthing adventure I tossed his way. I don't think I could have solved half the cases I did without him.

Everett and I drive out to Mangias together. It was only a little over an hour ago I closed the bakery, but that afforded me enough time to freshen up and feed Pancake and Waffles their Fancy Beast dinners.

We get out of Everett's expensive car and head up to the front door of our favorite Italian restaurant located right here on Main Street across from the bakery.

Everett looks devastatingly handsome tonight, and I might just have to tell him one more time for good measure.

"Have I mentioned how gorgeous you look tonight?" I ask just as he swings open the door to the establishment and a blast of mouthwatering scents hit us at the very same time—a perfect marriage of garlic bread and thick, sweet marinara sauce. I'm not sure how it came to be, but I'm pretty sure I'm addicted to the pizza they serve here.

"Only ten times, Lemon. And yes, I'm counting. It sounds to me you're having a bout of buyer's remorse."

"What?" I force a laugh from my throat. "I do not have buyer's remorse. Partially because I had no idea I was shopping at the time." It's true. It was sort of an ambush wedding—no fault of Noah's, of course. We were simply going undercover, investigating Pastor Gaines of all people during yet another homicide case.

"Good," Everett flatlines as he nods to a table with Noah and two women, Cormack and—Naomi? "Then you won't mind what's about to unfold."

We head over and exchange polite hellos. I shoot a disparaging look to Noah for his inability to rid himself of what I think I should dub as the Featherby Disaster.

Naomi's face lights up as soon as she sees Everett. "There you are!" She pulls him down next to her and plants a wet one on his cheek.

My jaw unhinges at the sight.

Everett's lips curl in my direction. "I have a date."

"A what?" I don't mind at all the curt inflection in my voice.

But before he could say a word, Alex stalks over from a table next to us where I find Lily, Keelie, and Bear offering a meager wave in this direction. Bear is the sandy-haired blond who cheated on me in high school and now owns his own construction company.

"What's this?" Alex and his bombastically large muscles look more than mildly perturbed by Everett and Naomi, and suddenly the picture is growing a little clearer. I think. "I thought you and I were having a dinner date?"

Naomi flashes those icy blue eyes. "We were, right up until you informed me that Lily would be joining us. So I did the only thing I could think of. I found a date of my own." She pulls Everett in close. "One that I don't have to share with anyone."

Noah groans, "Lottie, why don't you come sit by me in the safe zone?"

"Yes, Lou Lou." Cormack pats the spot next to her, and farthest from Noah, but I choose to rebel against her wishes and sit on the other side of him instead.

"And how is my husband this evening?" I couldn't help it. If Everett gets a dinner date, I get mad and get myself a spouse. It only seems fair.

"Better now that my beautiful wife is here." Noah leans over and dots a kiss to my cheek and my insides bisect with heat with the simple action.

Cormack clears her throat as she looks at Noah. "Okay. I can see you're still upset about that little stunt I pulled yesterday."

My lips twist as I examine her. "If you're about to confess to a murder, be aware of the fact this table is full of witnesses."

She glances to the other end of the table where Naomi and Alex continue to bicker. Everett looks as if he's trapped between a rock and a hardened Naomi. I'd feel sorry for him, but since he decided it would be fun to blindside me, I decide he's receiving his due.

"I'm not confessing to anything." Cormack leans in. "Besides, Lucinda, Noah is all but poised to throw the book at your mother. I can see why you're so full of vim and vinegar. It's part of the reason the Big Boss here is going along with your little charade. Noah explained it all to me."

My brows hike a notch his way. "Care to explain it to me?"

His mouth opens, and I hold up my hand.

"On second thought, let's save some fun for later."

Naomi gives Everett's cheek a pinch. "I agree," she says, jumping out of her seat. "I've decided to share a quick bite at the next table." She leans in close to Everett once again. "Save a good-night kiss for me, big boy."

Alex growls at Everett, and suddenly I'm fearing for those pearly white teeth.

Everett wastes no time scooting in toward me. "Let's talk about the case."

"Yes," I'm quick to agree. "Did you see anything on the security footage that could lead to the killer?"

"Nothing out of the ordinary. But I'm still reviewing it. And the body is still unclaimed at the morgue. We have no clue how to get in contact with his family or if he's got any." Noah takes a breath. "Did you find out the name of that woman?"

Everett pulls out his phone. "Thought you'd never ask."

"What name?" I ask, but no one seems to notice. "Hey?" I'm more than amused by this criminal based camaraderie. "Can I just say how much I love the way you're working together? And why exactly are you working together?"

Noah quickly peruses his menu. "He's got a guy."

"You've got a guy?" I ask Everett as he presses those baby blues my way.

"I've got a guy."

Cormack snaps her fingers at the nearest waiter. "And I've got an appetite."

We put in an order for a large "everything" pizza, breadsticks, and a round of drinks before Everett gets right back to looking at his phone.

"So who's this guy?" I'm suddenly intrigued by this new investigative side of Judge Baxter.

"It's an old acquaintance that I run into every now and again down at the courthouse."

My eyes enlarge. "Run into him? As a *defendant*?"

"Details." His cheek flickers with a smile of its own before he turns to Noah. "Her name is Madeline Underwood."

"Who's Madeline Underwood?" I look from Everett to Noah, but they seem to be having a nonverbal conversation of their own.

Cormack scoffs. "I know Maddie." She averts her eyes and all breathing stops at the table.

Noah perks to attention, offering his stalker her due. "You know this woman?"

"If she's the same Madeline Underwood that belongs to my parents' country club, I do. I went to school with her daughter, Melody." She rolls her eyes and wiggles her body as she says her name. "She's such a pest. She had a propensity to follow me around wherever I went. She was harder to get rid of than head lice."

Noah and I exchange a glance.

Cormack is worse than head lice. She's essentially scabies because she gets under your skin.

Everett raps his knuckles against the table. "We need to talk to her. Can you help us do that?"

She grunts as she looks to the ceiling. "The Denim and Diamonds Charity Event is in two days. She won't miss it. She's on the board. The board has to show for every major event. It's mandatory."

"Is that at the country club, too?" I ask as I do my best to type the information into my phone.

"Nope. It's at my mother's house. She hosts every year. There's champagne and canapés and a huge silent auction, so if you plan on going be prepared to bid your wallets away."

"Done," Noah says as he looks to Everett and me, and we nod in agreement. He turns to Cormack. "So what do you know about her?"

Our food arrives, but not one of us blinks as we wait for Cormack to spill the dirty details.

"Wealthy woman, beautiful. A widow."

I look to Noah. "Wait a minute—what did you know about her that had you digging for her name? Spill it, Fox, if you know what side your matrimonial bread is buttered on."

Noah shoots Everett a wry look. "I asked him to find out the name of Stephen Heartwood's wife and that's what he came up with."

I gasp so hard I nearly inhale every olive right off that pizza. "He was married?"

Noah shrugs. "According to legal documents, this woman is still actively listed as his spouse."

Cormack moans through a mouthful of pizza. "She married again. That's right. I don't know to whom, though. She was on her fifth or sixth husband."

"Wow. I can't fathom being with that many men." And just like that, my man mathematics gets going and soon I'm itemizing—Bear, Curtis, Noah, Everett. "Okay, never mind."

Everett's chest rumbles with a laugh. "Don't worry, Lemon. I have ways of making you forget other men exist."

Cormack nearly chokes. "It's true." She nods emphatically my way.

I'm well aware, but I don't dare affirm this fact with my husband seated next to me. I can't help but shoot a sly grin his way and Noah is quick to frown.

Noah's chest expands as he glances at the faces around him. "Everett, Cormack. I know that what happened between Lottie and me was in no way intentional." He picks up my hand and offers a gentle smile my way. "But I meant every word of my vows, Lottie."

My mouth falls open and a croaking sound emits from me as I look to Cormack in horror. Everett knows which end is up, but Cormack doesn't even understand how the gravitational pull in the situation works. She's so far out in orbit she might as well be in another solar system. She still thinks Noah is her official plus one.

Cormack takes a quick sip of her drink before lifting her finger. "Excuse me while I dash off to the ladies' room." She trots off seemingly emotionally intact, but you never know what's lurking under that blonde mop of hers.

"Noah," I whisper. "You're going to send her into cardiac arrest. You do realize she's wrapped you around her heart."

Noah glances in the direction she took off in. "I don't know. We had a counseling session this afternoon and I laid it all out there. But I think her takeaway was that it's a phony marriage."

Everett's shoulders sag. "It's time to lay something else out, too—any lingering feelings the two of you might have. Lemon, I was sincere in asking the two of you to winnow out your feelings for one another. But it seems to me, you're both slow to press the gas." He bears his electric blue eyes into mine. "Don't hesitate because of me. I genuinely want you to be happy." He growls at Noah. "And for God's sake, don't hesitate period. If you wanted something with Cormack, you could have easily had that by now. Your divorce is final. I've backed off with Lemon as far as I'm comfortable. I've looked into this little union you've found yourself in and discussed it with a family practice lawyer I work with. He suggested an annulment. He's willing to take you both on and give you the good guy discount. I've overseen a small number of annulments in my courtroom and I will handle this for you as well. But"—he offers Noah a hardened glance—"it will be a few weeks before we can file the paperwork and then about two to six months after that before you appear in my courtroom."

A very real part of me wants to gasp out loud, but out of respect for Noah I don't dare. And two to six months? How am I going to go that long without Everett and his special goodnight kisses? Who is going to frost my cookies?

I turn to Noah and his lids hood low as if he heard. Noah has frosted my cookies in the past, and I know for a fact he's perfectly capable.

"Slow down," Everett barks over at him as if he were reading his mind. "Maybe—just maybe, Lemon, try this matrimony on for size. In a strange way, I think this might be a blessing in disguise. Once this is said and done, you should have the clarity you're looking for. You don't have to guess what it'll be like being married to Noah. You'll know firsthand."

Cormack bounces back, looking bright-eyed and bushy-tailed as she goes on and on about the Denim and Diamonds Charity Event we'll be forced to endure at her parents' estate.

It's funny how for so long we were waiting for Noah's marriage to Britney to dissolve so we could figure out where we stood, and now we have our own marriage set before us like a hurdle.

I might be married to Noah for months.

Everett wants me to get behind it, and yet I can't even wrap my head around it.

I'm officially married to Noah.

I'm Mrs. Noah Fox.

A sharp cry emits from the next table over and I look up in time to see Keelie and Bear jumping from their seats. Naomi pulls her hand back and launches a cheesy slice of pizza, pegging Lily right over the forehead with it.

Lily groans so loud the entire restaurant falls silent in honor of her rage.

"You little witch!" Lily slings a meatball at her newfound nemesis, but Naomi ducks and it pegs me right between the eyes instead.

Cormack laughs up a storm while snapping pictures of me with her phone.

"Great," I say as I wipe away the saucy debris. And meanwhile, a full-on food fight has broken out at the next table, sending salad and breadsticks alike into the air like wayward Tomahawk cruise missiles.

Noah and Everett join Alex in an effort to break it up, but Naomi and Lily prove tenacious in their spaghetti slinging ways. And then, just like that, the entire lot of us is kicked out on our ears.

We all head for home with our hearts just as confused as they are torn apart—with the exception of Keelie and Bear, of course, and probably Noah.

Who would have thought that Keelie and Bear would be the pillars of normalcy when it comes to relationships?

And why not? There's not a third component to their equation.

One plus one could never equal three. It seems like both Alex and I need to figure out these strange mathematics, which in the end should be pretty simple.

The problem is that the choices are too tempting to simply take one away.

One plus one equals three.

And that, my friend, is the new math.

CHAPTER 6

"*J*'m married to Noah," I say to both Pancake and Waffles once we get back from dinner at Mangias.

I've been pacing in front of the fireplace for close to a half hour, hesitating on whether or not I want to build a fire or go to bed or—I don't know what else.

"I mean, I knew I was married to Noah. I've known this for days but, boy, Everett really took it home tonight." I place my balled up fists over my hips as I look to Pancake. "We might be married for months! We could be married until next spring. That's technically three whole seasons away." I can hardly catch my breath at the thought.

Waffles hops up onto the back of the sofa as if to get a better view of the ball of anxiety I've become. Both Pancake and Waffles are covered with thick cream-colored fur and have identical rust-tipped tails, but I've never had a problem telling them apart. Pancake's nose is a bit more elongated and Waffles is a touch more smooshed. Their fur is equally as thick and fuzzy and they both can double as a pillow in a pinch.

"What do you think I should do?" I stare intently at the two of them as if expecting a response. Pancake lets out a hearty meow and Waffles seems to agree with him by way of a nod. "A lot of help you are. No offense, but I don't speak Himalayanese. However, I do know of a talking cat whom I've yet to spend any quality alone time with and his name is Thirteen." A thought comes to me. "Hey? Maybe I should spend some quality time with Noah?"

I speed to the kitchen and raid the tiny wine cooler built into the cabinetry. Since I'm not a big wine drinker, it's stocked mostly with water bottles and a few odd bottles of sparkling cider. So I go with it. I grab a festive looking bottle of cider, fluff my hair in the foyer mirror, and head across the street.

I'll admit, I wish I had the power to become invisible at times like these. I'd feel awful if Everett saw me sauntering over, all perky and cute, with what looks like a bottle of bubbly. Okay, so maybe I'm not all perky and cute, but there is a bottle of bubbly involved even if it doesn't have the power to go straight to my head. But, then, I can pin this little nighttime jaunt right on his legal eagle shoulders if I wanted to. I'm more or less following his orders.

Noah, Everett, and I all happen to live on an adorable little street called Country Cottage Road. Last fall, while I was still dating Noah, a rental came available across the street from his cabin, and since I was in serious need of housing, I took it. And since Everett came to inspect the property with me, he noted the house next door to my rental was available and so he purchased it for himself. And that's exactly how we all came to be within prying distance of one another. For the most part it's worked out. I can spy on both Noah and Everett right from the comfort of my living room, so it's a win-win for me.

Noah's house is lit up like a peach and my adrenaline kicks in as I step onto the porch.

"Everett's fault. Everett's fault," I keep repeating as I make my way to the entry.

I can't be held responsible for what happens tonight. I give a quick knock on the door and Noah opens up while my hand is still in motion.

There he is, tall, dark, and impossibly handsome, those glowing green eyes bearing hard into mine. His dimples dip in deep with approval at the sight of me and he holds up a bottle of champagne, dripping with condensation from the chill emanating off it.

He tips his head to the side. "Jinx?"

My entire body relaxes as I laugh. "Maybe we should start our union with a word that doesn't represent bad luck."

Toby barks and whimpers as he makes his way over and I pull him into a hug. Toby is Noah's gorgeous strawberry blonde Golden Retriever that he still shares with his ex-wife. And he's just as adorable as he is sweet.

"You are so handsome," I say, giving him a scratch under the chin. "And smart. You are such a smart boy!"

"Thank you, Lot. You always know how to make me feel better," Noah teases as he ushers me in and takes the bottle from me. He lands them both on the table as I close the door behind me.

Noah is quick to wrap his arms around me, those hooded lids of his hanging dangerously low.

"Lottie Lemon." My name comes out in a hoarse whisper, his breath scented with something minty.

"Really?" A tiny giggle vibrates in my chest. "Because I thought it was Lottie *Fox*."

He moans hard as if he just took a bite of the most delicious meal. "I definitely like where this is going."

"Oh, we've landed. *Surprise*."

We share a warm laugh, but Noah's features sober up quickly.

"What do you want to do?" His voice is low and husky, and I don't think I need to ask him the same question. That look he's giving me says it all.

I shrug up at him. "Maybe toast to *us*?"

"To us." His head inches back as if it were a victory.

Noah whisks me into the kitchen and has the champagne poured into two fluted glasses all the way to the brim before I can take my next breath.

"If I didn't know better, I'd say you were trying to get me a little tipsy."

"If I were trying to get you tipsy, I would have poured it into a pilsner glass, but feel free to have seconds." He gives a sly wink as he lifts his glass high and I do the same. "To my beautiful wife. May we find exactly what we're looking for in each other and never regret a moment of our union all the days of our life."

"Hear, hear. *Salute.*" Surprisingly, I knock back half the glass and Noah is quick to refill it. "You are a devil."

"Let it be known I'm a celebratory one. Come on. I'll build a fire."

Noah gets the fire roaring, and soon we're snug on his sofa watching Toby curled up in a ball on his oversized dog bed. Noah lands an arm around me and pulls me in against his rock-hard body. The warm scent of his familiar cologne makes me feel right at home.

"Lottie—" Noah starts and I press a finger to his soft, cushioned lips.

"If you don't mind, I want to go first."

He gives a sober nod before playfully biting down on my finger and landing a kiss to the tip.

"Noah, when I found out you were married to Britney last winter, it sent me into a complete and utter tailspin. At first, I wanted to do exactly what Cormack is doing—disassociate and pretend it wasn't happening. But then, my anger got the best of me and I flipped out. I ran into Everett's arms for cover, which I confess was far too easy to do. He already had feelings for me." I shake my head as the memories flood me. "But Noah, I never got over you. I couldn't. I was ready to say yes if you asked me to marry you last February. And then, as quick as a blink, I tried to cut you out of my life. Of course, that didn't work. But my point is, we went from zero to hero with nothing in between. I loved you and yet I hated what had happened to us. It's an impossible feeling trying to process those emotions at the very same time." I give his chest a light scratch over his shirt. "And now we're caught in another extreme."

He winces as he wraps his other arm around me. "And that's exactly why I think we should see my counselor."

"The one you've already worn down with both Britney and Cormack?"

A laugh bounces in his chest. "Yes. And, in the event you were wondering, she is dying to meet you."

"*She*, huh?" I hike a brow at him. "Fine. I acquiesce." Noah has been after me to do this for a while and I think it's time. "If not now, when?"

"If not now, when." His gaze drops to my lips. "I've missed you, Lot."

"I've missed you, too, Noah."

He clears his throat and straightens just enough as he struggles to settle his gaze on the fire.

"So, do you want to talk about the case?"

I'd laugh at the idea, but I can't seem to initiate the action.

Instead, I shake my head and run my fingers through the sexy stubble peppering his cheek.

"I'd much rather do this." I pull Noah down to me, his eyes never leaving mine. I can see the questions brewing in his eyes, the uncertainty of how I might truly feel, and I give a little nod.

No words.

Tonight is about actions.

Noah gently lands a kiss over my lips—a kiss from my husband's mouth to mine. Noah sighs into the kiss as if it were hard-won, a long time coming, something he's waited for his entire life. This kiss says *I love you*, *I'm sorry*, and *I will never put you through that again.* And I drink down his apology right to my weary bones.

It's as if these heated kisses have the ability to rewind time, to return us to the very place I believed we were at all those months ago.

Noah pulls me onto his lap, his mouth never breaking from mine.

The crackle of the fire and the beat of our hearts drumming wildly are the only sounds we hear.

Noah and I are lost in our affection for one another and it is pure bliss.

A part of me had always suspected Noah and I could get back to where we once were. What I wasn't expecting was to surpass it by a mile.

Noah and I don't have to worry about playing house. Like so many other things, this marriage was thrust upon us when we least expected it. And now here we are, exactly where I once wanted so desperately to be.

Do I still want this with Noah?

Something tells me, I'm about to find out within the next few months.

CHAPTER 7

Since October is a month known to host all the thrills and chills that any good horror movie can provide, my mother has increased the Haunted Honey Hollow tours of her B&B from once a week to once a day.

Yes, she is making money hand over fist. And, as an added perk, she's sending the tour buses my way right after, as she's prone to do. But, in truth, I wish she wouldn't. The excursion to my bakery that she's dubbed as The Last Thing They Ate Tour is essentially a free add-on that her customers get as a perk—and the one who really benefits financially is me. But, as it stands, I can't keep up with the demand.

"Lottie"—Lily moans as we watch the last of the tourists leave the register—"we have every oven fired up and baking up a new batch of cupcakes, and it's been like that nonstop all day. You do realize we sell other treats, right?"

"I realize it, and you realize it, but our customers don't seem to realize it. I have a surplus of everything else and not a cupcake left on the shelves."

"True." She slings a dishtowel over her shoulder as we look out at the bakery. The walls are painted a butter yellow and the furniture is a mish-mosh of mix and match pieces, each painted a different shade of pastel. With the twinkle lights glowing over the ceiling it's a perfectly dreamy scene.

Lily shrugs. "How did last night go? It looked pretty tense at your table."

Keelie saunters over. "Don't start without me!"

I swear, either she has remarkable hearing and she's being horrifically underutilized as a national spy or she's got some sexual homing beacon built in that alerts her to all racy conversations in a ten-mile radius.

I balk at Lily, "Tense at my table? My table wasn't sharing their food by way of aeronautics. And thanks for that unexpected bite of your spicy meatball. I hadn't had it before. It was quite delicious—even if I did have to pick it out of my blouse. How did things end with Alex?"

She shrugs as if she were indifferent. "He came over and helped me shower. And then he made me breakfast this morning before he left, scrambled eggs and bacon." She wrinkles her nose with delight. "Just FYI, he looks awfully good wearing nothing else but bacon."

Keelie groans, "This cannot end well."

"I agree with Keelie. It's a shocker Naomi lets you live," I say just as the door chimes and both my sisters, Lainey and Meg, walk in along with our mother.

"Oh, Lottie!" Mom trots over in her kitten heels. She's wrapped in a gorgeous cranberry-colored sweater and matching scarf. And both my sisters look extra cozy in pea coats, orange for Lainey and navy for Meg. If there's one thing about fall, it's that it brings out the fashion best in just about anyone. "It's terrible." Mom practically collapses on the counter. "People really do believe I was involved with Pastor Gaines' murder."

"Well, you did have the murder weapon on you. Not that it's been confirmed that Ethel dealt the lethal blow. And you threatened to kill him."

Keelie nudges me in the ribs. "Who's Ethel?"

"My gun. Mom found it in the ground safe in my office and used it to off her boyfriend."

Mom gasps, "You are insufferable." She looks to Lily. "Coffee, please, strong and black. I'll need an IV drip just to make it through this day."

Meg smacks her lips into a smile. "So how's it feel to be Mrs. Noah Fox?"

"It feels perfectly romantic. Noah and I had a nice time last night after the food fight at Mangias. There was champagne involved."

Lainey sucks in a quick breath. "Did you do the deed?"

"Yeah, Lot." Meg leans in. "Did you consummate the union?"

My cheeks fill with heat as I give Mom a sideways glance.

"No," I all but whisper. "But we came close."

Lainey waves me off. "I don't see what you're waiting for. You were with Everett willy-nilly whenever the mood struck. Don't make me remind you of that ballroom fiasco. Everyone else was dancing, and the two of you found a closet to do the vertical mambo."

Meg smears a smile over her face. "That's my big sister. Keeping it classy."

Keelie leans in. "More like trashy." She's quick to offer me a congratulatory slap on the back. "What's stopping you from diving in with Noah? I mean, you are married."

"Yes, technically. But now Everett's involved."

Lily grunts, "If you're that into technicalities, wasn't Noah involved when you were hot and heavy with Essex?"

"Would you stop calling him that?"

She blinks a greedy grin my way. "No can do. I've earned the right."

"Whatever. I don't want to talk about my love life anymore. If Noah and I do decide to take the next step in our marriage, the last place I'll be announcing it is right here in the bakery."

"Good thinking," Mom bounces back, cup in hand. "Let's talk about the case."

"Noah and Everett tracked down a woman by the name of Madeline Underwood. She's going to be at a charity function tomorrow night put on by the Fallbrook Country Club. It's a western themed event called Denim and Diamonds, and it's being held at the Featherby estate."

"*Ooh.*" Mom does a little shimmy. "A fancy event like that is bound to bring out all the well-behaved country club boys. Do you mind if your sweet mother tags along?"

"Only if she promises not to amass a testosterone-laden harem."

Lainey raises a hand. "I'm in, too."

Keelie does the same. "You couldn't keep me away. I love me an overpriced gift basket."

Lily holds up her phone. "Alex just confirmed he'd be my date."

"That means Naomi isn't allowed." I glance to Keelie. "I can't get kicked out of this one."

"I'll be there." Meg shrugs. "I already know most of the women."

"Are you still teaching yoga at the country club?" Of course! Why didn't I think of Meg?

"Twice a week. But that name doesn't ring a bell. She probably doesn't go by Madeline, though. They're all Muffy or Buffy or Puffy."

"Okay, you can all come, but remember it's a western theme and we really want to fit in."

"Fit in." My mother salutes me. "And if I play my cards right, I just might find me a new stud to ride."

My sisters and I groan hard on cue.

Words you never want to hear coming from your mother's mouth.

I'm already regretting this.

CHAPTER 8

*A*s it turns out, the Featherby estate is so sprawling it could easily be compared to England—as in the entire British Isles. The monolithic stone structure is nestled on acres of verdant rolling hills, complete with an Olympic-sized swimming pool, Cyprus hedge maze, six different rose gardens, and a museum with bona fide Picassos and Monets peppering its walls.

Of course, I garnered all that information from one of the informational pamphlets at the gate.

Once Noah and I turn his truck over to the valet and mosey on toward the back as the sign suggests, it becomes clear they won't actually be letting me nose around their extravagant palace.

Noah takes a moment to steal a kiss. I'll admit, it felt next level driving out here with him, like a tried-and-true married couple. Everett said he'd meet us at the event because he wanted to have a drink with his sister after he got off work. Both Everett's sister and mother live out here in Fallbrook. But I think it was an excuse to have me spend more time with Noah. He's been a saint that way.

"You look amazing," Noah muses for the umpteen time as his

eyes do that broken elevator thing up and down my body. "You should consider looking into a rhinestone apron for the bakery. It's a good look on you."

"Funny," I say. I'm head to toe in bedazzled denim. I hopped over to the Scarlet Sage Boutique after work and she set me up with the best western duds she could drum up.

My jeans are a notch too tight and my shirt feels stiff, but every stitch of denim I've donned is encrusted and bejeweled with every color crystal under the sun. I've split my hair in pigtails and tied a pink ribbon in each one to complete the country bumpkin look.

Noah, however, didn't dress the part. He's wearing his jeans and a twill jacket with a baby blue dress shirt underneath and has his holster and gun on him as he does at all times. I'll admit, I feel miles safer when he's around, whether or not he's packing heat.

We crest the side of the monstrous structure Cormack once affectionately called home and we're each handed a glass of champagne by a rather dapper looking waiter, complete in a tuxedo.

I scan the crowd, and to my horror I note every last person here is looking rather dapper. The men are either in suits or dressed much like Noah, and the women are wearing floor-length gowns in solid colors, primarily red and black, and their hair is swept up elegantly and there isn't a pigtail in sight.

"Oh my God, Noah!" I give his arm a quick yank. "I look like a spectacle. How could you let me leave the house like this?"

His dimples press in deep. "You look beautiful, Lot." He takes a moment to smolder at me and my insides pinch with heat. "Besides, nothing says denim and diamonds quite like you tonight."

"Way to make me feel better. Hold this"—I shove my champagne glass his way—"I'm losing the pigtails."

"Not on your life. I can work with those," a deep voice booms from behind and I turn around to see Everett striding up in his dark inky suit, his lips curving their way to a dangerous smile just before he winces. "Ooh, sorry. I forgot we're taking a break." He pulls me in for a quick embrace. "And anytime you need a break from this clown, you know where to find me."

"Funny." Noah nods his way. "So where's your date? Or are you traveling solo these days?"

"Lemon is my date." His brows edge in like birds in flight. "But she happens to be slumming with you."

"Funny," I say as I steal a moment to get my bearings and look out at the event. A trio of violinists plays in the distance and the air is perfumed with the scent of the rose gardens surrounding us. The grounds are covered in elongated tables covered in elegant white linen tablecloths, and every inch is brimming with baskets and gadgets and gift cards, and a few thick, homey quilts wrapped with ribbon. It's all set on a lush green lawn, and it's a feast for the eyes that goes on for miles. The tall space heaters sprinkled about are silver, slender beasts, and even they look far more elegant than me. There's a refreshment bar to the right and strewn up above the area are twinkle lights already brightening the quickly dimming light.

I spot a few familiar faces by one of the auction tables.

Meg has a denim jacket thrown over a simple black dress, and I can't help but make a face. By design I should have more fashion sense than Meg. She wears gold lame and spandex on the regular for Pete's sake.

Hook Redwood, her official plus one, is dutifully by her side looking the requisite amount of dapper. And I spot Lainey and Forest just past them. Lainey has her hair up in a chignon and she's donned a blush pink dress that looks suspiciously like one of the bridesmaids' dresses from her wedding. Lainey fell so in love with them I wouldn't put it past her to have purchased one for herself. Her husband, Forest, looks decent, too.

Great. I'm the only clown around. And just when I'm about to make this known, I spot my mother in a ten-gallon hat encrusted with gold glitter and jewels, and I cringe at the crystal cata-strophe I've inadvertently caused. Her denim shirt is knotted up under her chest and thankfully she'd donned a T-shirt under-neath. I'm betting my mother's belly button, much like my own, isn't ready for primetime. She's donned a pair of white pedal pushers with what looks to be a brown fringe of some sort running down the side seams.

She spots me and waves us over.

"Lottie!" Mom lunges at me with a hug and her hat collides with my pigtails. "I can't thank you enough for the invite. Who knew this was just what I needed to get my mind off things?" She primps her hair with her hand. "Do I have lipstick on my teeth?" She bears an eerie crimson grin my way.

"No, you're fine. And if by 'things' you're referring to the homicide investigation you're starring in, then you should prob-ably tone down your enthusiasm, and maybe your hat."

"Now, now. No need to bring up past grievances like dead ex-boyfriends. You look adorable, by the way." She pats me on the arm before waving to Noah and Everett who are already exam-ining the plethora of items up for bid. "Have you and the mister had a little alone time?" Her shoulders do that annoying shimmy.

"*Mother.*" I pull her farther from Noah and Everett. "No, not yet." I glance back at Noah and note the fact he's looking like the tall glass of detective he is. I've always had a wild attraction to him. I don't know what I'm waiting for.

"Well, thank you, Lottie, for expanding my horizons. I'm going to get out there and mingle. I've never seen a sea of gray-headed gents with more sophistication and style in one place. *Ooh,* I should call Chrissy and Becca and tell them to don their cowboy boots and scoot down to Dodge. Honestly, there are three men for every woman here, and that's a rare treat in and of itself."

She quickly dissolves into the crowd just as an ethereal black cat saunters this way.

"Looking lovely, Lottie," he purrs through the alliteration. "I see you've chosen something subtle as not to detract from catching a killer. You do realize dressing like a homing beacon will repel those who prefer to lay low—say someone on the suspect list?"

"Am I really getting this from you right now?"

"I can always dole it out later." His ebony fur sparkles in the night like a sea of black stars. "Who are we here to see?"

"A woman by the name of Madeline Underwood."

"Excuse me?" an older woman calls from behind and I jump as I spin her way. "Did I hear someone call my name?"

She's tall, blue-eyed, with medium-length curly blonde hair, cherry-stained lips, and has a black and white floral slip dress on. If I had to guess, I'd say she was about my mother's age, but she has nary a wrinkle to uphold my theory. It's safe to say her face has been ironed out with the best of them.

"Oh yes!" She shakes her head at me before I can answer. "You must be a part of the entourage we hired—Wild Bill's harem. All entertainers are to remain in the back until the show begins. We won't start that portion of the evening until everyone has been ushered under the big tent that houses the champagne and appetizers. There is to be no commingling with the guests." She grabs me by the elbow and does her best to navigate me through the crowd, but I dig the heels of these rhinestone-laden cowboy boots I've donned into the ground and I'm not moving an inch.

"I'm afraid you've mistaken me for someone else. I'm a guest of Cormack Featherby's."

"Mackie?"

I knew she had some preppy nickname rattling around in her bourgeois closet.

"Yes, *Mackie*. In fact, I was hoping to speak with you. Madeline is it?"

"*Mitzi*, please. Any friend of Mackie's is a friend of mine. I do hold the Featherbys in the highest regard. Now, what can I do for you?"

I glance back and find Noah being accosted by Tacky Mackie, and I can't help but scowl at her.

Everett gives me a three-finger wave before pointing at the woman before me and I give a slight nod.

"Mitzi, I have some shocking news for you. I don't know if you've heard, but Stephen Heartwood was murdered."

Her penciled in brows jump a notch.

"Has he?" She averts her gaze. "Would it be terribly crass of me to say this doesn't surprise me?"

My mouth falls open. "No, actually." I decide to go low. "It tells me you've met him before."

She belts out a laugh, and just like that, I've broken the ice in the most indelicate fashion.

Thirteen lets out something just shy of a growl. "You should have met him in his younger years. He was quite the stick of dynamite. It's a wonder he didn't detonate sooner." He laughs and it sounds like a yodel.

I'd join him, but I've got a live one myself.

Mitzi leans in close. "What happened to the fool? Let me guess. He married one widow too many and the last one caught onto his scheme?"

"His scheme?" I don't bother taking my next breath. I can't afford to miss a word.

"You know, marry the *merry* widow." She says *merry* in air quotes. "Suck them dry for what they're worth, then move right along. It turns out, I was wife number five."

"*Five?*" I balk at the audacity that man had to even be in the same airspace as my mother. Or as I bet as he liked to call her —number *six*.

"Oh yes. But I didn't know it at the time. We were married only a few short months. Then one morning he must have grown tired of the situation. He took what we had in our joint checking account and the cash I had hidden in the wall safe at home—enough to buy a small home—and I never heard from him again. I was so embarrassed, I didn't dare tell a soul. But, now that he's received his comeuppance, I'm feeling a bit justified."

"When was the last time you saw him?"

"Late spring." She nods. "I don't know where he went after that. Wait a minute... did you say Stephen Heartbright?"

"*Heartwood.*"

"Oh no, that's a different man."

I doubt it.

I whip out my phone and pull out a picture of him with my mother.

"Does he look familiar?"

"Oh yes, that's him." She huffs a quick breath at the picture. "And that floozy by his side looks exactly like someone gullible enough to fall for his deviousness."

"You might be right." I'll be the last to contest the idea. "But she's free of him now. You all are." I look over at this older woman who Pastor Gaines ripped off. I don't care what his name is. That's the pseudonym I'm sticking to for now. "I'd like to speak to someone else about him. Do you have any idea of who I might contact?" This is the first murder investigation without any significant leads. It's as if whoever did this pulled off the perfect murder.

"Let's see..." She tips her head back to the sky. "Ah, yes. I actually met one of his ex-wives. I ran into her at a charity function not unlike this one. It was in Burlington. Her name is Elaine Gilmore." Her expression sours.

"Is there something specific you remember about her?" Judging by the fact she looks as if she's about to be sick, I'd say yes.

"Let's just say they were a match made in—well, it wouldn't be heaven, now would it?" She gives a sly wink and takes off.

"Ha!" I look down at Thirteen. "She was a treasure trove."

"She looks familiar to me. Did she look familiar to you?"

"No. I can't imagine why she would." I traipse back to Noah and Everett, choosing to ignore the fact Cormack is attempting to climb my husband like a jungle gym.

Everett wraps an arm around me and pulls me in.

"What did you glean, Lemon?"

Noah leans in, nearly sending Cormack flying into a basket filled with cheeses from around the world.

I spill everything I know like a rash of bullets from a machine gun.

Thirteen taps my leg with his paw. "I just figured out why she looked so familiar."

A breath hitches in my throat. "Why did she look so familiar?"

Cormack waves me off. "She was at the Haunted Honey Hollow kickoff. She was right there for the food fight. But once the cupcakes started flying, I didn't get a chance to say hello."

Thirteen lets out an adorable roar. "That's exactly why."

Noah gives a wistful shake of the head. "That places her at ground zero the day of the murder."

"Oh, Mitzi"—I whisper as I crane my neck into the crowd—"if you were hiding that, what else were you hiding from me?"

Noah extricates me from Everett's arms much to Cormack's dismay.

"I don't know," he whispers directly into my ear like a warm secret, and it makes my insides quiver with delight. "But we will find out together."

One might say that Haunted Honey Hollow month started off with a spine-chilling bang considering it was kicked off with a murder, but that little homicidal detail hasn't stopped the tourists from pouring into our sweet town by the droves.

My mother's B&B is filled to capacity, and according to Naomi so is the Evergreen Manor. She dropped by the bakery this afternoon to grab a cup of coffee with Keelie, and both Lily and I can't stop ogling the two of them.

The bakery is bustling, but there's currently a lull at the register. I've been baking pumpkin spiced cupcakes all morning just to switch things up, and I've gone as far as pulling out my sensory secret weapon—pumpkin spiced cinnamon rolls. Nothing pulls the people right off of Main Street faster than the heady scent of luscious sweet cinnamon rolls baking in the oven. There is nothing quite like it.

Lily bumps her shoulder to mine. "What do you think she wants?"

"What does Naomi ever want? *Blood*. I'd say she was looking for her next virgin sacrifice, but don't worry. It's too late for you."

Lily scoffs. "It's too late for you, too. And oddly enough, even though we're safe, I'm not feeling so secure. I wouldn't let her into the kitchen if I were you. She might just reenact the food fight that started it all."

"The one in front of the bakery? It didn't start a thing. This is all Alex's fault as far as I can tell. Why don't the two of you draw straws to see which one gets to keep him and get back to the business of being best friends?"

"That's not how it works, Lottie, and you know it."

"In the least, get ahold of yourselves."

"You're talking to the wrong party."

Keelie and Naomi get up at once and head over.

Naomi blinks her china blue eyes at Lily. "Afternoon." She turns my way. "Grandma Nell's things are officially out of probate and we have the key to her house. Our mother has agreed to let Carlotta live there if it's all right with you."

Lily chuckles. "That's right. You have to ask permission from Lottie because she owns everything now."

It's true. Last January my grandmother Nell, whom I didn't have a clue I was related to at the time, left me the lion's share of her estate. She left her three children each more than enough to live off and she even left a good chunk of change to her grandchildren, too, but she left all the real estate—and most of Honey Hollow was included in that deal—to me.

"I'm totally fine with Carlotta living there. And I don't have plans to sell or make any moves with anything I've inherited whatsoever. Everett told me to sit on everything for at least a year before making any big moves. That way I'll have a moment to process all this."

Naomi sneers at her sister. "Hear that, Keels? She's putting it all up on the market in one year's time and cashing out. You can kiss the Honey Pot goodbye."

I shake my head at Keelie. "The Honey Pot isn't going anywhere. Nothing is going anywhere."

Keelie makes a face at her sister. "I wouldn't be too sure about that. Naomi is on her way to raid Grandma Nell's house. I'm sure she'll have it picked clean by midnight."

Naomi waves her off. "Only of the good things. I'll tell Carlotta the news." She takes off and Lily sighs.

"It's as if I wasn't even visible."

Keelie shrugs. "Don't worry."

Lily takes a breath. "You think she'll get over it?"

"No," Keelie flatlines. "She'll get even. I'd watch my back if I were you." Keelie takes off just as an entire swarm of women in spandex prattle on over to the counter looking ravenous and focused on carbs.

Lily tightens her apron. "Get the cupcakes ready, Lottie. We don't want this mob to turn on us."

Britney and Cormack saunter in holding up the rear, and I groan at the sight of Cormack. They have matching blonde pony-tails—save for Britney's stray lock that protects her left eye as if it were the holy grail.

Cormack rolls her eyes at the sight of me. I'd feel terrible for her, but no matter what seems to happen, she just doesn't get that she and Noah aren't a thing anymore.

Britney steps up first. "Pumpkin spiced latte, hot, no whip."

Cormack lifts a finger. "Ditto for me."

Britney is the one responsible for the sweaty Bettys that just strolled in. Her Swift Cycle gym down the street just let out and she's notorious for ushering them my way to replenish what few calories they lost.

I quickly make up their drinks and slide them over.

"Brit, one day, these ladies are going to catch on to the fact that the needle on the scale is traveling in the wrong direction no thanks to your devious practices."

A throaty laugh bubbles from her. "Not true, Lucia. I tell them often that muscle weighs more than fat—and they're more than glad to see the progress they're making." She toasts me with the latte Lily just slid her way.

Cormack leans in. "So what's new with the case? Has the Big Boss made an arrest? I hear that mother of yours is as guilty as sin."

My lids lower a notch as I glare her way. "I can assure you of her innocence. Besides, she doesn't even know how to *hold* a gun let alone fire one."

"Well, it was your gun that killed him." Her eyes grow wild. "Maybe you did it, Luella. Maybe you pulled the trigger thinking it was me!"

I blink back as if she just pulled a trigger herself.

"Cormack, why would I want you dead?" Aside from the obvious.

She tips her head back, her nostrils flaring at me. "Come now, drop the false pretenses. We both know you've been gunning to have both Noah *and* Essex as your suitors. It's not only unfair to them, but it's not fair to me. I can handle so much, but let it be known that I have a line and you've crossed it." She looks to Britney. "I'll be at the table by the window." She takes off and I exhale hard in her wake.

Britney nods. "She's delusional. I realize this." Her eye sharpens over mine. "But you do realize that sometimes those are the most dangerous people." She takes off and I glance to Cormack who's shooting me with daggers at the moment.

Cormack is delusional, yes. But dangerous? Doubtful.

The bell chimes and in comes my mother along with Chrissy Nash and Becca. Each one has her arms filled with a pumpkin centerpiece as they set them down on the counter.

"Oh, these are gorgeous!" I say as I take in their stunning beauty. Each large orange pumpkin is hollowed out at the top and filled with sunflowers, gerbera daisies, yarrow, and chrysanthemums in every shade of gold and russet. "Thank you so much!"

"You're welcome!" Mom sings. "They should last about a week or so and then we'll be by again to refresh them."

Becca nods. "Pumpkins and all." My aunt Becca is Keelie and Naomi's mother and she shares the same wide gorgeous eyes. But, as opposed to Keelie's blonde locks and Naomi's onyx tresses, Becca dyes her hair a perfect shade of pumpkin both in and out of this fabulous season.

"Yup." Chrissy lands hers right on the counter next to the register and it looks perfect there. I've always felt bad for Chrissy since Mayor Nash, my unexpected father, never made a secret out of cheating on her. And even though I've known Chrissy forever, my half-siblings spent a majority of their time in boarding school, so I never really knew them growing up. "This little pet project is going to keep our horticulture club busy right up until Thanksgiving." She sniffs the air. "Is that a cinnamon roll I smell? Oh, Lottie. You just sold half a dozen."

"They're pumpkin spiced cinnamon rolls. And I'll be glad to get you a fresh box."

Lily waves. "I'm on it, Lottie."

I look to my mother. "How did you like the Denim and Diamonds Charity Event the other night?"

She makes a face. "I didn't have any luck with the men."

Chrissy practically gags on her next words. "What are you talking about? You were just telling us all about Topper. If he's not a catch, I don't know who is."

My mother's cheeks turn rosy as she takes a deep breath. "All right, I may not have been totally forthcoming with information. I did meet a very nice and handsome man named Topper Blakley. But that phone call he promised wasn't what I expected. Instead of asking me out on a date, he asked if we could host a mixer for local seniors at the B&B. It turns out, he operates a dating app for silver foxes and gray panthers—his words, not mine." Her lips crimp because obviously she found the proposition upsetting. "And here I envisioned him stealing me away for a fall picnic on

Honey Lake. In my mind, I was already the next Mrs. Topper Blakley." She frowns as she says it. "He's high society in Fallbrook."

Chrissy hugs her good friend. "I happened to research his investment company and he's worth millions."

"My mother doesn't care about money," I'm quick to point out. "It's all about finding the right person to spend her golden years with."

Mom waves me off. "A little padding in the bank never hurts, Lottie. It doesn't mean I'm a gold digger. It simply means the difference between having pizza at Mangias down the street or in Italy on the Spanish Steps."

My poor mother. "You'll find the right person at the right time."

"Oh, I know I will," she's quick to agree. "I've agreed to host the senior fall mixer in the conservatory next Saturday. Please put some platters together for me. I'm having the Honey Pot cater the appetizers. If Topper doesn't want me for himself, then I'll simply move along and see who's next. Who knows? I might even meet someone at the mixer."

I wince at the thought. "Maybe you should cool your heels," I whisper. "You are under investigation for Pastor Gaines' death."

She looks to Becca and averts her eyes as if the thought were ridiculous.

"Pastor Gaines wasn't even Pastor Gaines. Rumor has it, that man was trying to swindle me out of my money!"

I decide to zip my lips on the matter lest I really make her blood boil.

The three of them scoot down the counter and put in their orders with Lily.

I'm about to head to the back when a handsome dark-haired devil strolls through the door and makes his way over. Noah's dimples press in deep before he ever smiles.

"You look a lot like my husband." I bite down on my lower lip playfully.

Noah steps in close, his gaze penetrating mine and it feels intimate, special.

"And you look a lot like my gorgeous wife. Do you think I can steal you away from this place for an hour or two?"

"It depends if we can outrun your fiancée."

Cormack bounces up and wraps her arms around him, planting a kiss right over his lips.

"Where we off to, Big Boss?"

He looks my way as he carefully extricates her from his person.

"I'm sorry, Cormack, but I've got official duty I need to take care of. I need to take someone downtown for questioning."

She scoffs. "By all means, give 'em all you got."

"That's exactly what I intend to do. Lottie, you're coming with me."

I ask Lily to watch the shop as I grab my purse and follow Noah outside into the crisp autumn air. I glance back and spot Cormack glaring at me from the window.

"I think we made our escape," I say as Noah takes up my hand. "Too bad you had to shed a white lie to do it."

"I didn't shed a white lie. I am taking you downtown for questioning. Downtown Fallbrook. We've got a counseling session in twenty minutes."

"Counseling? Not exactly the date I envisioned."

"How about afterwards we do something you envision?"

"Fair enough. Be warned. I've got quite the vivid imagination."

"I'm counting on it."

CHAPTER 10

*F*allbrook.

Dr. Frankie Allen's office is in an unassuming white square of a building that sits nestled next to a Pilates studio and a Tex-Mex restaurant. Inside it's clean and spacious, and the office itself is small and cozy with a sofa in the back and two navy tufted chairs for Noah and me to sit on. Her desk is a sprawl of mahogany, and the walls are lined with a plethora of degrees staggered apart just so, creating a stairstep effect as they creep along the wall.

The door opens and in walks a tall redhead with her hair in a bun, pretty, a touch older than myself, and this surprises me on many levels. She wears red-framed glasses and has matching painted lips, and bears one big toothy smile as she comes at me with an extended hand.

I rise to meet her. "So nice to finally put a face with the name," I say. That's not entirely true. I can't think of once where Noah has uttered her name, but it's the kind of thing you say at odd intervals of life such as this.

"Please," she growls it out throaty. "The pleasure is all mine. I've heard so much about you, I feel as if we're old friends about to catch up." She wrinkles her nose as she looks to Noah. "And you look as handsome as ever. You ready to get this show on the road? Because I am anxious to get to the heart of the matter."

She hops behind her desk and I steal a moment to glance to Noah. In no way has he prepared me for what I'm up against, but in his defense, I didn't even think to ask. Is she young? Is she pretty? Exactly how intimately does she know me?

"So"—she folds her hands over her desk and her lips expand clear across her face—"Lottie, as I'm sure you realize, Noah has been here with both Britney and Cormack."

"And now he's brought me to complete his frequent flyer mileage. I think he's trying to secure a trip to warmer climates."

We share a quick laugh on Noah's behalf and he bounces his brows my way, pleasantly amused.

Dr. Allen leans in. "Noah, may I?"

He nods. "I feel more than comfortable with anything you would like to disclose to Lottie. I have no secrets from her."

"Anymore," I say, taking up his hand.

Dr. Allen takes a breath. "Yes, anymore." She offers a slight nod at the quasi-dig, and now I feel bad for inadvertently dishing it out. "Noah initially came to see me with his wife, Britney. Their marriage had dissolved not long after it began, and together we were able to untangle that knot. And privately, Noah shared with me his longing to reunite with you, Lottie. There was no confusion as to where his heart stood." She sighs dreamily at Noah. "And then came Cormack." Her lips pull down just shy of a grimace. Believe you me, lady, I feel the same. "I think that's one knot we're still trying to loosen. As we all know, some knots prove more difficult than others."

A dull laugh bounces in my chest. "And some require a restraining order." I give Noah's hand a squeeze and we all share a laugh on Cormack's behalf.

"That they do," Dr. Allen muses. "And yet again, Noah approached me privately once Cormack was no longer in the room and let me know that he was having great difficulty removing her from his life. And again, that you held the spotlight of his affection." She pulls a pencil from a mug and jabs it into her bun. "Sorry. Whenever I feel it loosening, I put a pin in it so to speak. Much like Noah, I like to take action before things get out of control." She winks his way.

"Just for the record"—I lean forward—"Cormack is out of control. The wheels are off and she's barreling down the mountainside ready to crash and burn. It won't be pretty."

"I agree." She tosses her hands in the air. "But we can't control Cormack, or anyone else's reactions to your relationship." She nods knowingly. "And there's someone else you're trying to protect, isn't there, Lottie?"

A breath hitches in my throat and I can't seem to formulate his name on my lips.

"My old stepbrother," Noah offers. "After Lottie gave me space to clean up my marital mess, she dated him. And now that my divorce is final, he's offered us the space we needed to find our way back together or find closure to what we had." He sighs heavily as if it were the last thing he wanted and I know it is.

"And then about a week or so ago, Noah and I found out we had accidentally gotten married. It's one hundred percent legally binding, but seeing that we weren't totally aware of it at the time we're in the process of getting it annulled."

"Another marriage," she says, brimming with surprise. "That's fascinating, Noah. You seem to have more relationship tricks in your bag than Houdini." She belts out a hearty laugh. I'd be laughing too if I thought it was funny. "So that's where you are." She shakes her head at the two of us. "Certainly not a textbook case, but I dare say you're ahead of the curve."

"We are?" She lost me at Houdini. Wasn't he an escape artist? Noah can't seem to escape psychotic relationships. First Britney, now Cormack—and, ironically, he can't seem to pin me down— and I mean that in just about every sense.

"Oh yes," she's quick to assure me. "Noah expressed how deeply in love the two of you were before Britney came onto the scene. Would you agree with that?"

"Yes," I say emphatically. "I actually thought Noah was about to pop the question. I would have married him in a heartbeat. Noah was and is everything to me." I look his way as I say it.

"But?" Dr. Allen postures herself as she prods deeper.

"But Everett—his stepbrother—and I have exchanged I love yous. We've been intimate." My cheeks heat just saying that out loud.

"Yes"—her shoulders hike as she considers this—"but this new relationship came with a considerable amount of baggage. Would you agree that you had Noah between the two of you the entire time?"

"Yes," I moan it out in utter exasperation. "God yes. It's like you know me." I turn to Noah. "Wow, she really is good."

Dr. Allen chortles softly. "I am. And that's why I want you to give a considerable amount of weight to what I'm about to suggest. I'd like for the two of you to embrace your marriage."

"This again?" I look to Noah with surprise.

Dr. Allen's lips expand politely. "You've heard this before?"

"Oh yes," I begin. "Everett, my boyfriend"—I wince at Noah as I say it—"he suggested the same thing. And so did my best friend Keelie and my sisters—wow, my sister Lainey is really advocating for this." I shake my head at Noah as if it were a pity.

Dr. Allen strums her scarlet nail over her desk. "And what do you think, Lottie?"

"I'm perfectly fine with it. In fact, Noah and I have already agreed to it."

"Good." Her lips stretch like a rubber band before she grows somber. "I'm going to give you some delineation so the idea isn't so vague. Noah, are you comfortable embracing Lottie as your wife until the annulment is complete? Are you comfortable with caring for her emotionally and once again being intimate with Lottie if that's something she decides on?"

"I am." Noah doesn't need a moment to answer. He's such a boy.

I can't help but bite down on a smile as I look his way.

"And you, Lottie? Would you be able to put Noah above all others and tend to his emotional needs?"

"Done." I shrug like a champ.

"And what about intimacy? Do you think you're ready to take things with Noah to the next level, or would you rather wait until you're more certain?" Her eyes needle into mine, and I can't help but feel as if one wrong answer will cause this whole thing to blow up in my face. This is terrifying. It feels downright dangerous.

"Lottie"—Noah gives my hand a squeeze and looks lovingly in my eyes, and I feel safe all over again—"you don't need to answer that. I think we made good progress today. We can leave."

"No." I shake my head. "Everett, Keelie, and my sisters are right. Noah, we're married. This is what I wanted just a few short months ago. And I think the only way to know for sure if this is the direction we should head in is to step fully into those shoes. Noah, I love you. That has never changed. I loved you right through my relationship with Everett. Even he knows that." I take a deep breath. "I'm ready. I'm ready to be your wife in every capacity, and at any time if I feel different I will bow out grace-fully—and I want you to do the same. But right now"—tears blur my vision, and I'm quick to blink them away—"I am more than ready to be your bride." A tingle rides up my spine as every cell in my body exhales with approval.

Noah's dimples dig in deep, and his eyes remain unblinking as if I just stunned him into submission and I believe I have.

Dr. Allen clears her throat. "Just one thing. I'll need the two of you to commit to the annulment. That way there is no lingering pressure that this might roll over. What you need is a trial, and that's exactly what you've accidentally afforded yourself. If I were you, I'd take full advantage. And when it's through, Lottie, I think both you and Noah will be elevated to the place you were last winter, or further."

And what about Everett?

A soft laugh bounces through her. "And I bet you're wondering about Everett. Not to worry. I plan on untangling that knot as well. In fact, the next time you come in, I'm going to ask you to invite him in as well."

And just like that, I feel better.

The session wraps up, and Noah and I head out into the brisk autumn air.

"So what should we do next?" I wrap my arms around him and bite down on a smile. Noah looks alarmingly handsome as he stands against a stormy sky. "Hey, I know. We should do something that perfectly normal married people do, like go to the grocery store and then go home and cook dinner."

Noah's dimples invert fully as he takes a deep breath. "That sounds like heaven. Your place or mine?"

All of those heated nights I've spent with Everett at my place flash through my mind.

"Definitely your place. In fact, I think we should dub your place *our* place. My place can be our place, too, but I sort of—um —it's a bit tricky because…"

He shakes his head. "I get it." He dots my lips with a kiss. "Let's get to the grocery store so we can start cooking."

Noah and I head back to Honey Hollow and stop off at the market, picking up shrimp and pasta, the fixings for a salad, and some oven hot bread that has this baker's stamp of approval.

We stop off and feed Pancake and Waffles before heading over to his place to cook up a storm. Noah makes a fire and we feed one another, laugh, and curl up on the sofa, catching up on life as if we had been doing exactly this for years.

I pull Noah back into the kitchen, and while he washes the

dishes, I whip up a batch of chocolate chip cookies and the entire cabin smells like brown sugar and vanilla heaven. Even Toby looks delighted to wait for one of those delectable treats. Lucky for him, I made one without sugar or chocolate.

The cookies are hardly cool, and I pull Noah into my arms and feed him a bite. Noah closes his eyes and moans through a mouthful. He goes in for some more, but I pull the cookie back and shake my head, a naughty grin blooming on my lips.

"What's this? Withholding cookies from me?"

"That's right, detective. Can you figure out why?" My adrenaline kicks in, and my heart wallops against my chest as if the house were on fire.

Noah's lids hood dangerously low. "It's because you're about to give me a bite of something sweeter?"

I nod as I put the cookie down and wrap my arms around this gorgeous man, my husband.

Noah lands a kiss to my lips to end every other kiss. He makes my mouth his own until I'm dizzy with desire, and soon enough he makes the rest of me his, too. It feels natural and right, and explosively satisfying—far more so than I remember.

Noah has brought his A game tonight—and so have I. And we bring it over the kitchen table, the sofa, in front of the fireplace, and in that cozy comfy bed of his where I cozy up in his safe, strong arms.

Noah and I are right back where we were last winter.

Sort of.

Noah reaches over and pulls something out of his nightstand and holds it between us.

I sit up a notch to get a better look at what it can be and gasp.

"*Noah.*" His name presses out of me as my heart ratchets up again.

Pinched between his fingers is the ring he purchased for me last summer. The original he picked out just for me.

His evergreen eyes bear into mine. "Lottie Kenzie Lemon, will you do me the honor of being my wife?"

"I'm one step ahead of you. I already am."

Noah glides the ring onto my finger, an emerald cut diamond surrounded by smaller diamonds, and it's a perfect fit.

"I love you, Lottie."

"I love you, too, Noah."

And just like that, this is truly a night to remember.

CHAPTER 11

"There's just something different about you," Thirteen muses, his ebony-colored fur glowing like a constellation of black stars.

"There's nothing different," I say as I frost a dozen more friendly ghost cupcakes as quickly as I can.

Of course there's something different about me. I'm tense, I'm ecstatic, I'm on edge, and I'm floating on air. It's perfectly psychotic, and Lord knows if a deceased cat has got my number, how much more will the human population be able to tell that I'm wearing that post coital glow like a slutty calling card?

Lily pops in. "Are you hiding in here?"

"I'm working." I hold up the piping bag as proof.

"It's well past noon and you haven't been up front once."

"That's because there are a lot of cupcakes that need to be frosted." It's true. I've frosted vanilla cupcakes with purple frosting and given them candied eyes so that they look like adorable little monsters. I've fashioned black frosting in the shape of witches' hats. I've frosted an entire slew of cupcakes in bright green, orange, and electric blue, and to add a festive spooktacular appeal, I've sprinkled them with miniature eyes.

Keelie heads in. "Hey, Lot. The Honey Pot needs a few pies. I'm thinking apple and pumpkin. You'll really have to amp up your production of both from here on out straight through the holidays."

"I'm on it."

Lily scoffs. "Please don't give her another thing to do. For reasons unknown, she's sequestering herself in the kitchen."

"What's this?" Keelie's BFF radar goes up. "Don't tell me you're having a good old-fashioned bake-a-thon, are you?"

"I'm a baker, Keelie. My entire life is a bake-a-thon." I cringe because I know where this is going. When we were growing up, and I had one of these so-called bake-a-thons, it was always due to trouble—boy trouble to be exact.

Keelie sucks in a quick breath. "You did it! You slept with Noah and you feel guilty because half of you still belongs to Everett."

Aw, crap. I can't keep a single secret from Keelie. The tragedy is, I don't even need to verbalize it anymore.

"Ah-ha!" Thirteen hops onto the marble island and plants his furry tushie in a tray of cupcakes. Thankfully, he's not choosing to smash them at the moment. "This explains the unearthly glow. Noah must be quite special to invoke that aura of bliss around you."

Lily gasps twice as hard. "You cheated on Essex?"

I spin her way, accidentally dropping a metal mixing bowl to the floor and it sounds as if the world just shattered.

"I didn't cheat on Essex." My stomach churns because I just so happened to use a moniker I'm not all that familiar with—but have earned the right to use. "Everett encouraged me to fully explore my relationship with Noah."

Keelie moves in with the speed of any seasoned poltergeist. "How was it?"

"It was amazing. Noah was always amazing." I bite down hard on my lower lip before I exhale, giving in to the situation fully.

"He's my husband. We're taking your—*everyone's* advice and embracing the situation. It felt strangely normal, sort of like coming home."

Lily scoffs. "She's just trying him on for size, Keelie. The problem is once you have a taste of Essex, it's nearly impossible to want a normal life. Lottie, you're in a bigger quagmire than you realize. The best you can do is ride this marriage out like you plan on doing, but mark my words, you'll be ten times more confused than you were before once this Noah disaster is over."

"It's not a disaster."

Thirteen lets out a simple mewl. "Might I suggest getting your mind off of things for a while and focusing in on the murder at hand? I do believe your mother has received some bad press this morning."

"What?" I pull out my phone, and sure enough both Lainey and Meg have texted me with links to articles in our local paper. "Keelie, they're calling my mother the Black Widow, the Merry Widow. They're all but accusing her of killing Pastor Gaines."

"Oh, I know. But don't worry. My mother said it was great for business, especially this time of year. You have no idea how many people are willing to spend the night at the B&B just so they can say they slept with a serial killer."

"A *serial* killer?" I balk at this new horrific nickname—and my mother seems to be collecting them by the dozens.

"They're still linking her to the death of that one guy she dated. The one who liked to boss her around? There are entire women's groups who hail her as a hero for that one. Not so much for killing Pastor Gaines. We'll have to put a good spin on it. Any dirt on him you think we can use?"

"Plenty. I just don't want to rock the already rocky investigation. Don't worry. I'll handle this. Today." I take off my apron and quickly text Noah to see if his afternoon is free. He texts right back, letting me know he's swamped but will be home by six and is bringing us dinner. That's so sweet and it feels so right, I want to cry.

I didn't dare tell him what my intentions were with him this afternoon because Noah wouldn't approve of me going off on my own.

I look to Keelie. "Can you get a few hours off?"

"Are you kidding? Margo and Mannford are in New York taking some fancy cooking class, as if they needed it. I don't even have time to stand here and chat with you." Margo and Mannford are the five-star chefs who run the kitchen of the Honey Pot Diner.

Keelie scoops up an armful of pies. "Don't do anything crazy. And don't go investigating alone. Take someone with you!" she shouts as she heads on out.

"You'll take me." Thirteen bounds his way over, and I give his head a quick pat.

"I'm taking you for sure."

My phone bleats in my hand, and I jump when I see who it is. Everett.

Lemon, my afternoon just cleared up in a moment. I'm sensing a supernatural disturbance. Are you up for a late lunch?

I text right back. **Sounds perfect. I hear Burlington has great Chinese food.**

My phone pings again. **Burlington it is.**

CHAPTER 12

*E*verett parks in the alley behind the bakery, and I head out to meet him. He must sense something is off because he gets out of his car and wraps his arms around me tightly.

"Lemon? What's going on?"

Noah and everything that's happened between us flits through my mind and tears burn my eyes because Everett remains buried in my heart and now what.

But I don't have any words I'd like to share. Instead, I hold on for dear life as he drops a heated kiss over the top of my head.

"It's okay," he whispers. "I'm still here. I'm not going anywhere."

We hop into the car and start off down to Burlington, and suddenly it's as if everything is normal between us. Everett tells me about his morning at work, his cases, and the judgments he's passed down recently. And I tell him all about my morning with Thirteen and the millions of cupcakes which seem to be repopulating all on their own at the bakery.

Soon enough, there's a large wooden sign off the highway welcoming us to Burlington and I groan.

ADDISON MOORE

"It just occurred to me I don't know where we're going and if Elaine Gilmore lives here. For all I know, Mitzi Underwood could have been spinning a tale. Oh, Everett, I'm so sorry. I don't know where my head is these days."

"I've got this. As soon as you said Burlington, I knew we were looking for Elaine. I talked to my guy. And in two right turns and a left we should be face to face with her."

"Your guy?" I practically moan with delight over this. "I'm a little bit in love with your guy. He really knows a thing or two."

"Watch it," he teases. "He'll have to stand in line behind me."

"There's no line. And if there were, you'd be at the head." My stomach churns because I don't want to tell him that Noah is standing right beside him. A big, beautiful body of water pops up on the right. "Oh, I just love Lake Champlain—and look at all the maples surrounding the shoreline!" A burst of fiery citrine hues erupts as far as the eye can see, and it looks stunning when juxtaposed against the deep blue of the lake.

"Lucky for you that's where we're headed. It turns out, Elaine Gilmore runs a B&B right on the water."

"No kidding?" I'd be amused if I wasn't so creeped out. "Wow, Pastor Gaines is starting to look more and more like a predator by the minute."

Burlington is a charming city with an old-world appeal that has always made it feel homey. We take a few private roads down evergreen-lined paths, and then in a burst of glory the lake seems to be at our feet. A small sign to the right reads *Breakfast at the Lake*.

Everett leans in and squints at it. "This is it."

We take a turn in the road, and a beautiful Victorian building comes up on our right. It's large, about the same size as my mother's B&B, and there are dozens of bright orange pumpkins dotting the entrance.

"Everett, this is adorable," I say as we head on out.

There's a sign to the right that reads *Shoreline Café*. The grounds are immaculate with trimmed emerald lawns and sweet-gums in an array of fall colors lining the property.

Everett takes up my hand. "Let's head inside. If I'm right, she should be there to greet us."

We head on up the monstrously large porch, and inside it's cozy with paneled walls stained in walnut and matching wood floors. There's a fireplace in the center of the grand room and people milling around. It looks comfortable and inviting and just the perfect place to curl up with a book. To the right there's a stairwell with an elevator just to the left. Now that's something you don't see every day, but a modern necessity for some guests. My mother is still looking into getting one installed.

We make our way to the reception area, a long wooden counter adorned with a pumpkin hollowed out and filled with flowers much like the ones my mother and her horticulture club are churning out these days.

"Just a minute!" a voice calls from around the corner, and no sooner do we look that way than an older blonde bounces her way over and I gasp.

As I live and breathe.

I shake my head at the woman because I can't believe what my eyes are telling me. Standing before me is an exact representation of my mother. Same medium-length hair with loose vanilla curls, same bright blue eyes, same mischievous smile.

"Elaine Gilmore, how can I help you?" She looks breathlessly from Everett to me. "My, I have never seen such a stunning couple before. Let me guess, *honeymoon?*"

Everett pulls me in. "Close. We're actually exploring local places for just that. Your inn looks perfect."

"Yes." I nod wildly at Everett's genius. "Maybe you could give us a tour?"

"Oh, heavens yes. In fact, I'll do you one better. Once we're through, we'll head out to the café and I'll give you both compli-mentary mimosas. There is nothing like young love." She wiggles her shoulders, and it's Miranda Lemon all over again. She makes her way around the counter, and I'm astounded to see her mannerisms are so much like my mother's. She's donned a red and purple tweed jacket and matching pencil skirt. Her feet are pressed into an adorable pair of kitten heels, and if I didn't know better, I'd think she raided my mother's closet.

She quickly shows us the grand room, the reading room in the back, and we poke our head into the dining room and the glass-encased courtyard that eerily resembles my mother's conservatory.

"So when's the big day?" Her voice trills à la Miranda Lemon, and I shudder because suddenly it feels as if we've crossed over into some other dimension laden with doppelgängers.

"July fourth," Everett offers and a soft chuckle bounces from me. That's a Cormack-inspired date if ever there was one. In fact, not long ago, she helped Everett and me whittle it down. She said we couldn't have June because she was marrying Noah that month. And if Noah doesn't watch his back, that is exactly what will happen.

"Oh, it'll be here before you know it." She points to the stair-well. "I have a honeymoon suite that looks over the lake. It's twice the size of our other suites and boasts a hot tub the size of a swimming pool. She gives a little wink. But, unfortunately, all the rooms are currently booked. The café, however, is calling our name. Come, come." She beckons us to follow along with her finger, and we head out the back onto a sprawling indoor-outdoor café brimming with guests and visitors alike.

The scent of something mouthwatering emanates from the direction of the kitchen, and there's a friendly waitstaff circulating around the dining area.

She motions for a waitress and shouts for two mimosas before turning our way. "Lunch is on me. I've got the perfect table for you." She walks us out to a table closest to the expansive view of the lake, and it suddenly feels as if we've been transported to a sunny seaside villa.

"This is amazing!" I say as we take our seats and soon two champagne flutes appear, clouded with a touch of orange juice.

Elaine bubbles with laughter herself. "If you think this is amazing, wait until you see the sunrise from the honeymoon suite. It's stunning—especially at that time of year. Is there anything else I can help you with?"

"Um"—I look to Everett for help—"how about some marital advice?" I shrug up at her, hoping this will somehow segue to the fact she offed Pastor Gaines. But she's so lovely, she reminds me so much of my mother, and her B&B is simply adorable—oh heck, if she confessed to the crime, point-blank, I might just toast her with my mimosa and call it a day.

A sharp laugh bellows from her. "Do you have all day?"

"We actually do." Everett pulls a chair forth. "And we would appreciate any words of wisdom you have to offer."

She averts her eyes in the same way my mother is prone to do before falling in the seat across from us, and just like that, Thirteen appears seated on the table. I take up Everett's hand and offer up a squeeze.

"I don't know about words of wisdom." A throaty laugh brews from her.

"Perhaps words of caution?" Thirteen muses, his green eyes glowing supernaturally and it's a stunning sight. "Considering she might be the killer, I'd take her thoughts on the sacred union and toss them into that body of water. Fire away, Lottie. Here's your chance."

"How long have you been married?" I ask, and with each passing moment I feel just as comfortable with this woman as I do my own mother. Honestly, I think they might be long-lost sisters.

"I'm not married now. However, I've been married twice. First to my true love, a man by the name of Kenneth Gilmore who gave me three beautiful daughters."

I'm right back to gasping. Three daughters? Just like Mom!

"That's incredible," I say and Everett shakes his head ever so slightly at me. "I mean, that's wonderful."

"Oh, it is. Children are a great blessing. The two of you should have an entire gaggle. You both have such striking features. I'm sure they'll be beautiful."

Everett pulls my hand to his lips and presses a kiss over it. "We can't wait to get started on our family."

Our family? *Aww*! Everett is killing me today. First a wedding on the Fourth of July and now children? I'm toast.

"And how about with your second husband?" I shrug over at her. "Any children with him?"

"Heavens no. We just married a little over three years ago." She glances to the table as her demeanor shifts on a dime, from jovial to somber. "I'm embarrassed to say he was more of a cautionary tale. When my first husband passed away, I took the insurance money and bought this place." Gah! Just like my mother! "I put the girls through school, of course, and then spent time getting my business up and running. I had only begun to date just recently. Just before I met Stephen, in fact." She scowls at the lake when she says his name, and I can't blame her. "He said he was from Nevada. He came into Burlington and swept me off my proverbial feet. He was a pastor at the local church. And seeing that he was a man of God, I never questioned anything about him."

Everett takes a breath. "Did he give you reasons to question him?"

"Not until he was gone." She makes a face at the lake again. "One morning I woke up and he had disappeared, just like that. Our joint checking account had been cleared out. It was just after I sold the house my first husband and I shared, the one my girls grew up in. He took it all, left me with nothing. It was his idea to sell the house. I had kept it and rented it out. I thought maybe one of the girls would want to live in it one day, but he convinced me we could travel with the money—see the world." She sighs heavily.

"I'm so sorry," I say, clutching my chest. If Pastor Gaines were still around, I'd wring his neck myself. "Did you suspect anything at all? Did anything seem off about him? What about his family?"

"Ha! He never talked about them. He mentioned his parents were dead."

Thirteen twitches his whiskers. "That they are."

"And I think he mentioned a brother and sister once—Jack and Joyce? But for all I know they could have been manufactured."

Thirteen lets out a sweet meow my way. "It's the truth."

Jack and Joyce. I make a mental note of it.

Elaine shrugs as she glances to the water once again as if that's where she buried all these truths so long ago.

"My middle daughter, Rachel, was forever trying to warn me about him. 'There's just something about him, Mom,' she'd say." She shakes her head wistfully as if scolding herself for not listening. "Anyway, it turns out, she was right. Once he left, it was Rachel who presented me with all sorts of information about him. She had the goods all along, but I wouldn't listen."

Everett tips his head, looking innocently inquisitive.

"What kind of information?" I ask.

"Oh, I don't know. I turned a deaf ear to it afterwards, too. I was in shock to say the least. I had turned into a swindled old woman—something I never thought I'd be. But I've had my guard up ever since. And I'll never entertain the notion of marriage ever again."

I clear my throat. "So you never saw him again after that day? Ever?"

She glances to her watch and back toward the kitchen. "Would you look at that? It's almost time for the dinner rush. If you'll excuse me, I need to move along." She jumps out of her seat and offers a sweet smile. "If you decide on the inn for your honeymoon, ask to speak to me directly. I would just love for the two of you to begin your journey in life right here on the lake. You won't be sorry." She takes off like a wildfire, and Everett and I lock eyes.

"She never answered my question. Maybe she did see him again? Maybe she is the killer?"

"You never know." He glances back in the direction she took off in. "That level of agitation in my courtroom is always indicative of guilt."

"Ugh. I don't want to believe it. I say we leave and let this poor woman enjoy her peaceful existence at the lake. She sure did have a good reason to off him."

"Maybe she didn't. Maybe her daughter did?"

I take a quick breath just as Everett's phone bleats on the table.

He glances at the screen and frowns.

"Come here, Lemon. Let's toast to life." He pulls me in close, and Everett snaps a picture of the two of us holding up our bubbling mimosas with a gorgeous view of the lake behind us.

Everett fidgets with his phone a moment as he shoots off a text.

"That was Noah asking if I had a minute. I told him we were busy."

"Everett!" A laugh bounces from me. "You are so very bad."

"I do believe the words *you are so very good* came from your lips not that long ago."

"Touché." My cheeks heat ten degrees. "How do we go about speaking with Elaine's daughter?"

He glances at the growing crowd in the café as a waitress comes our way.

"I have an idea," he whispers.

A young blonde comes up with a notepad and a pen.

"Have you had time to peruse the menu?" She blinks at the two of us.

"Actually, we have to run off," Everett says, pulling a rather large bill out of his wallet and landing it onto the table. "For you." The girl's eyes grow as big as that lake. "You know, I went to school with Rachel Gilmore. Whatever happened to her?"

"Rachel? Oh, she's living in Ashford now. She's Rachel Kane. I think she works in PR or something like that."

"That's right." Everett nods. "I heard the same thing."

Everett and I make our way back to the car, and this time it's my phone that bleats.

"It's a text from Noah."

I read it quickly and groan.

"Oh, Everett. We need to get to the B&B right away. Something is terribly wrong."

CHAPTER 13

$\mathcal{T}$hankfully, Everett and I manage to beat Noah to my mother's B&B.

We head on in and the ghost of Greer Giles is the first to greet us.

"Oh, we've got trouble." She gives a cheeky wink. And just as I'm about to pick up Everett's hand so he can listen in, I realize he's already holding my hand and my heart warms despite the impending doom Greer is spelling out.

"What kind of trouble?" Everett asks as we slow down for a brief moment.

"Miranda has herself a hottie," Greer trills with glee. "A bona fide silver fox with a real tan and all of his original teeth right where they're supposed to be!"

"That's the trouble?" I ask, glancing around, unsure of what direction to head in next.

"Oh yes." Greer fans herself with her fingers. "It's the exact kind of trouble your mama likes. Let's be honest, me too!" She gives a ghostly chortle that vibrates straight to my bones. Props to Greer for finally getting this haunting gig down pat.

"Where is the lucky lady?" I ask. "I've got news for her. Miranda Lemon's luck is about to run out."

I turn to head toward the conservatory, but Greer blocks me off at the pass—not that I can't walk straight through her but choose to respect her hostage-like wishes.

"What is it, Greer?" I snip. "Noah is on his way to make an arrest, and I need to shake my mother silly until she comes up with a decent alibi." Did I just say alibi? I look to Everett as if I just asked the question out loud and he shrugs.

"It works," he grunts as he looks at the dead space before me. Just because he can hear Greer doesn't mean he can see her. "Where's Miranda? I'd like a moment to give her some advice before the homicide detective exerts his prowess."

The thought of Noah exerting his prowess makes my entire body heat with the memory of his touch.

Greer moans, "She's in the pantry. But before either of you pass judgment, you should probably know she hasn't been this excited about anyone in months."

"The pantry?" The words extricate from my throat with a certain heft only an exasperated daughter can provide.

I glide through Greer on my way to the kitchen, and Everett is right there with me when I fling the pantry door open with a lurch—promptly and wisely squeezing my eyes shut when I see the fleshy sight.

"*Geez!*" Everett barks, and I hear the pantry door slam shut and a string of salty expletives coming from the other side—all delivered by my salty and all too saucy mother.

Everett pulls me to the side. "I think I might have sustained an injury to the rods and cones."

"I'm sorry," I say, blinking back to life just as my mother and an older gentleman come tumbling out of the poor innocent pantry, struggling to adjust their clothes.

If the health department knew about my mother's sexual

shenanigans, they'd nail the doors and windows shut before sprinkling the property with gasoline.

My own sexual shenanigans at the bakery rush to the fore-front of my mind, and I shoot a guilty look to Everett—the prop-agator of those sexual shenanigans.

"Lottie?" Mom staggers over, and it makes me question whether she successfully pulled her pantyhose back where they belong. "What in the world? Do you need to borrow some sugar?"

I take a moment to scowl at her gentleman caller. He's tall, relatively decent looking with a full head of thick silver hair. Okay, I'll admit, he's an impressive specimen considering he's had a considerable number of go-rounds on this spinning blue rock.

"Topper Blakley." He offers his hand my way accompanied by a toothy grin. "Delighted to meet you."

I glance down at his hand disapprovingly. "I'd say the same, but that was my mother you were conducting a full body search of."

He cringes as he looks to Everett. "Are you the son?" Suddenly, there's a note of terror in his voice.

"I'm her daughter's boyfriend."

No sooner does he get the words out than Noah bursts into the room.

"Hey, Lottie," he says breathless with a smile as he plants a sweet kiss to my lips.

"And who is this?" the silver fox sounds off—more as a passing thought he said out loud than a judgment.

Noah wraps an arm around me. "I'm Lottie's husband."

Topper gags as he struggles to express himself.

"Oh, you're one to judge," I say as I pull my mother in. "Noah, would you mind if I have a few words alone with my mother?"

"Sure," he says while inspecting the mismatched buttons on Topper's shirt.

I yank my mother straight out of the kitchen and into the hall.

"Are you insane?" I balk as her fingers dance over the buttons on her own blouse in haste. "Don't answer that. I'll answer it for you. You are certifiable! And in the pantry? *Really*, Mother?"

She swats me before carrying on with her endeavor. "Oh hush, you. When you're my age, you'll be thankful for a visit to the pantry or two." She fluffs her hair with her fingers before settling those sparkling blue eyes on me. "Now what can I do for you?"

"Noah is here to arrest you."

"What?" she squawks so loud a group of tourists nearly tumble down the stairs in fright.

"Yes," I say as I pull her deeper into a darkened corridor. "He says your fingerprints were all over my gun the day of the murder."

"Well, of course, they were. How else was I supposed to do what I needed to do?"

"What?" Now it's me squawking like a chicken about to have its mother hen hauled off to Ashford. "Explain yourself quickly. You have less than two minutes before Noah sniffs you out like a bloodhound."

She scoffs. "Lottie, please, you're getting yourself all worked up over nothing." She makes a face while craning her neck past my shoulder. "Fine." She pulls me in close. "The afternoon of the Haunted Honey Hollow Festival kickoff, I—*we* set out to have a little fun. He was raving about your devil's food cupcakes, and I told him I knew where he could get a fresh one." Her left brow rises with the double entendre.

"Very funny. And let me guess, you were that fresh one."

"Only after we had our fill of your cupcakes. Oh, Lottie, they really are to die for." She plucks at her blouse as if trying to cool herself off.

"Go on. Get to the homicidal details."

"Oh, I didn't kill him, and you know it. We were in your

office, and it's so darn tight in there we could hardly get around one another. Anyway, the back of my heel hooked onto something and the lid to your ground safe popped open. You really should have a professional look at that."

"Perfect. I know just what to say to the repairman. Not only does my mother find my office a tad too cloistered to get coital in, but the broken ground safe has placed her as a prime suspect in a murder investigation."

She waves me off once again. "I didn't even know what it was until Stephen pointed out it was a safe. He tried fixing the do-hickey up top to close it. That's when I spotted the gun. And that's when I said, 'Lookie here, Lottie has a toy gun in her safe' and I reached in and picked it up and pretended to shoot him. Of course, he didn't think it was funny and made me put it back. He said the last thing he wanted to happen that day was to get shot and killed." She sobs instantly into her hands.

"Talk about a horrific prophecy." I pull her into my arms. "Don't worry. I believe you're innocent. We'll get this all figured out. Let's explain this to Noah."

"I can't do that." She wiggles out of my grasp like a toddler being faced with a needle.

"Yes, you can. Noah doesn't bite." Technically, he does, and in all the right places. In fact, every cell in my body was sounding off the hallelujah choir.

"Lottie?" Noah's voice echoes from our left, and it sounds as if he means business.

"Come on." I take her by the hand, with a death grip in the event she gets any wily ideas, and we meet up with Noah by the reception desk.

"Mrs. Lemon." He exhales hard, his eyes compressed with a twinge of grief. "I'm sorry, but I need to look around, maybe have access to your personal computer? And I'd like to take a peek at your private quarters."

Her mouth falls open. "Don't you need a search warrant,

Detective Fox? Where's my attorney?" She cranes her neck past him. "*Everett?*"

Noah's dimples press in, no smile. He's all business, and I'd be lying if I didn't find it incredibly sexy.

He sighs deeply. "Everett stayed behind to distract Mr. Blakley. We wanted to spare you any unnecessary embarrassment. And the reason I didn't go ahead with the search warrant is because you're my mother-in-law. I didn't want you to have to shut down the B&B while a bunch of deputies pillage the place." He offers an affable smile. "I thought there was a chance you might give me access to things so I can have a quick look and then I'll be on my way."

A choking sound gets locked in my throat. "But aren't you going to arrest her?"

"Lottie!" My mother gives my hand a hard yank. "My kind son-in-law has no intention whatsoever of arresting the best mother-in-law he will ever have, now do you?" She gives a sly wink. And if I didn't know better, I'd say Miranda Lemon was flirting.

"That's right." Noah bows her way. "Unless, of course, there's criminal evidence. We'll start with a quick look around your bedroom, and then I'll open up your laptop and we'll be all done."

She scowls and grumbles as she digs out a ring full of keys from her pocket and hands them to me. "The gold key is to my suite." She glowers at Noah. "My laptop is on my desk. If you two don't mind, I'm going to offer those gentlemen in the kitchen some hot apple cider. I'll be lucky if Topper ever speaks to me again."

She huffs off, and I lead Noah up the stairs and down the darkened hall on the way to my mother's private chambers.

The upstairs walls are covered in wood paneling, but there are enough wall sconces to provide a trivial amount of light for the guests.

Noah picks up my hand and kisses the back of it just as a tiny hatchet-wielding poltergeist drops down before us and roars like a lion on fire.

"*Geez!*" Noah howls as he wraps his arms around me and lands us up against the wall, caging me in with his body. "What the hell was that?" he pants, quickly inspecting the vicinity.

"It was a six-year-old girl." I glance past his shoulder and wave at the little ghoul. "Hi, Lea!"

A sparkle of light erupts at her feet, and soon enough Thirteen is here in all his glittering glory.

"Lottie, Detective Fox." Thirteen hacks and chokes until a glowing orb emits from his throat. "Excuse the celestial hairball."

I wrinkle my nose up at Noah. "That's Thirteen, Pastor Gaines' once upon a cat."

Lea falls over him. "Oh, I love him, Lottie. Don't you dare take him away. He's mine. I've claimed him. It's bad enough you took Beastie and Cookie. If you take Thirteen away from me, you'll regret it." Her voice echoes out that last sentiment, demonically low, as she dissipates to nothing.

"She's gone," I whisper to Noah.

He glances to the left without the benefit of moving his head. "Will you think less of me if I say I'm glad?"

A tiny giggle gets trapped in my chest.

I hook my gaze to his. "I'm so glad you know my secret."

"I'm glad, too." He lands a sweet kiss to my lips and lingers. Noah kisses me long and strong, pouring all of his love into me until I'm delirious and dizzy.

A shrill meow erupts from somewhere by our feet. "Can we get on with things, detective? I've a little girl to charm. If I play my unlucky cards right, I'll be around to witness more than a couple errant kisses."

Noah hitches his head toward my mother's room. "Let's do it."

I take him on in, and Thirteen bristles right past us and hops up on my mother's four-poster bed. I flip on the lights, and my mother's cozy peach walls greet us with a warm visual embrace.

There's a wedding ring quilt that my grandmother made covering her bed and a stack of white ruffled pillows piled high by the white tufted headboard. On either side there's a bone white nightstand—of which I will not delve into lest I cast my eyes upon objects that a daughter should never see.

Noah walks right over and opens the nightstand drawer before slamming it shut with finality.

"*Geez.*" He blinks hard. "Okay, let me do a quick sweep." Noah looks in the closet, does a quick search of her drawers, looks under the bed, and glides his hand along the top of her bookshelf before sitting at the desk and opening her laptop. "There's no password to get in. I'll just do a quick search of her history," he says, tapping into the keyboard. Noah freezes as he stops breathing for a moment. "Lottie," he says it low and filled with disappointment.

"What is it?" I lean in over his shoulder and take a look at the screen. An entire history of all her recent searches is laid out for the two us to see, and I let out a hard groan.

Noah shakes his head. "I'm sorry, Lottie, but this casts a significant level of doubt regarding her innocence."

"There must be some mistake. *How to kill a person? How to get away with the perfect murder? Ways to commit the perfect crime? To poison or not to poison?* Oh, Noah, I don't know how she's going to tap-dance out of this one."

"Let's give her a chance."

"And if she can't?"

"She'll have to get a very good lawyer."

Noah and I head downstairs and find my mother in the conservatory with Everett.

"Mother"—I close my eyes as I land before her—"please tell me you didn't kill Pastor Gaines."

She gasps as if she had just been caught. "What did you find?"

Noah twists his lips. "I looked at your search history, on your laptop."

She looks to Everett with a genuine fear in her eyes. "What's a search history?"

Everett leans in and whispers into her ear as if he were indeed her lawyer and Mom straightens like a pin.

"Noah Corbin Fox!" she snips at him. "How dare you invade my privacy."

"*Mother*, you looked up different ways to kill a person."

Everett's eyes widen with alarm. "As your legal counsel, I advise you to not say a word, Miranda."

Her nostrils flare his way. "Nobody shushes me, Judge Baxter." She sets her wild gaze to Noah. "Of course, I looked up those things. It was all a part of my plan."

A hard groan comes from me. "I think this is a good time to listen to Judge Baxter."

She waves me away. "Detective Fox, if you must know, I looked up those things purely for research. And it was all Stephen's fault. He's the one that encouraged me to do so."

Noah tips his head to the side, looking more confused than ever. "Why did he have you research those things?"

"To write a book. Why else?" She tosses her hands in the air with exasperation. "Stephen saw how involved I was with the book club and how much I enjoyed reading. He thought it would be a natural progression for me. He helped me brainstorm a murder mystery and gave me assignments each night, a different thing to research, and I would write down my ideas. Oh, Lottie, you're going to love it. The story revolves around a woman who can see the dead!" Her enthusiasm returns full force. "The *dead*. Can you imagine?"

"I can try," I say, pressing my lips shut tight as I look to Noah and Everett.

Noah decides to let my mother be for now, and the three of us take off and congregate outside the B&B.

"Thoughts?" I say to either of them.

Noah shakes his head. "It is odd."

Everett tips his head back. "It's highly coincidental."

"I agree," Noah says, casting his gaze out into the woods. "And I don't believe in coincidences."

"Do you think Pastor Gaines was setting my mother up in his own murder? It doesn't make sense."

Noah shifts his gaze to the B&B. "No, it doesn't."

CHAPTER 14

"*And* then what happened?" Keelie's eyes are the size of coasters.

"And then Noah went back to the sheriff's department trying to figure out how to defuse this bomb."

Lainey leans forward from the back seat. "And how exactly is it that we're on our way to Ashford ourselves?"

It's the very next night, and Everett gave me a hot tip about Rachel Kane. He didn't tell me exactly where we'd find her but asked us to meet him down at the courthouse.

Correction, he asked me to meet him down at the courthouse, but Keelie and Lainey were there when I closed the bakery and neither of them wanted me to drive down to Ashford alone. And —they also hinted that they were itching for a little adventure. The only instruction Everett gave me was to dress warm. I texted Mom and asked if she would stop by my house and feed Pancake and Waffles for me and she kindly agreed so I don't have to worry about rushing back home.

I turn to Lainey. "We're on our way to investigate a woman by the name of Rachel Kane. She's Elaine Gilmore's daughter, the one I told you about yesterday." Oh yes, I did. I called both Meg

422

and Lainey and told them all about Mom's doppelgänger—then I was obligated to tell them about her pantry session with Topper Blakley—silver fox pervert extraordinaire—and then that segued into the murderous evidence Noah and I found on her laptop and the fact Pastor Gaines was coaching her to write a murder mystery.

I shudder just thinking about it.

Meg said that if Pastor Gaines weren't already dead she'd hunt him down and kill him. She's working late tonight at Red Satin Gentlemen's Club where she teaches strippers their hip swaying moves or she would have joined us on our endeavor.

Lainey takes a breath. "You know what I don't get? Is how the church hired him in the first place."

"Last month, when we discovered he had a different identity, Noah suggested he might have easily explained it away. And the church is so trusting. Apparently, he had bona fide referrals. Elaine mentioned he was a pastor up in Burlington, too."

Keelie warms herself with her hands. "Creepy. It's almost like you can never really know somebody. I mean, you thought you knew Noah—heck, you were about to marry him up until you discovered he had a wife hiding out in another state."

My stomach churns just thinking about it. "True, but that was just an anomaly. I mean, Everett doesn't have any skeletons hiding in his closet. He already told me all about the woman who was killed while carrying his baby—and we all know how that turned out. Bear for sure doesn't have any skeletons in his closet—neither does Forest." I glance to Lainey in the rearview mirror. "But I'm just going to take a wild stab in the dark and say that Topper Blakley most certainly does."

Lainey chuckles. "Mom sure knows how to pick 'em."

"She used to." I sigh as I think of my father. Joseph Lemon was a saint. If only he could see the way we all turned out. I'm not sure what he'd think of my love life. Married to one man, in love with two. It's not a love story by a long shot. It's a tragedy.

Speaking of Noah, he had to work so late last night, he was just coming home as I was leaving for the bakery this morning. I guess that's the reality of his job. If I were married to Everett, there might be a little more stability, but then he's around his fair share of nutcases. I suppose both jobs have an element of danger.

I pull into the Ashford County Courthouse parking lot and spot Everett seated in his car. He gets out and slips his hands into his pockets. He's still wearing his suit and looks like he could be on a billboard in Times Square. He's so heart-wrenchingly gorgeous, he makes my stomach squeeze tight.

"Geez, Lottie"—Lainey chirps—"are you sure you want to break up with that big bad wolf?"

"Technically, I didn't break up with him. We're still together in a twisted sort of way."

Keelie scoffs while shaking her head in disbelief. "You really are something, Lot. I wish I could fast forward time and see how this whole thing works out for you."

"Works out?" I muse as I kill the engine and the headlights. "Newsflash, I don't think this works out for anyone."

We hop out of the car and I run over and offer Everett a firm embrace, and he lands a sweet kiss to my cheek, leaving both Keelie and Lainey fanning themselves.

"What's the big secret?" I ask, looking around at the desolate parking lot. "Where are we off to?"

"Hop into the car, girls." Everett's lips curve with the slightest hint of a smile. "We're headed to a second location."

Everett drives us two blocks south, and we gasp as he slows down just shy of a huge silver sign that reads *Ashford County Cemetery*.

"Oh no"—Lainey squirms—"you can just turn this car around. I don't do graveyards."

Keelie whimpers, "Neither do I, but something tells me we will tonight."

Lainey yelps as Everett pulls the car into a brimming parking lot. "Teaches us a lesson for following Lottie anywhere. I'm texting Forest to pick us up."

"Don't do that," I say as Everett parks and we get out of the car. "The fun is just about to begin," I say, pointing over to a large crowd congregating through the enormous wrought iron gates. There's a small sign staked into the ground that reads *graveyard tours six p.m. to midnight, twenty-five dollars apiece, adults only.*

"Twenty-five dollars?" Lainey balks. "I'm a librarian by trade, not a lady of the night. I'm not exactly working for tips in the stacks."

"Ooh"—Keelie butts her shoulder to my sister's—"working for tips in the stacks sounds steamy. Maybe you should write a book about it? I bet your mother and Naomi would feature it in their book clubs."

I shrug over at her. "I'd buy a copy."

Everett wraps an arm around my waist. "Lemon, with me, you could live it."

Both Keelie and Lainey sigh in unison.

We head over to the gargantuan line, and once we're up at bat, Everett graciously purchases all of our tickets. Of course, he's met with much protest, but he has a way of tuning that out.

The cemetery itself is laden with ground fog as eerie music blasts from the speakers overhead, filled with the sound of creaking doors, peppered with screams and howls. The air holds the scent of something sugary and sweet, and just past the ticket booth I spot a stand selling hot fresh churros.

My phone bleats, and I suck in a quick breath. "It's Noah."

Hey, Lot, almost done. You mind if I pick up a pizza from Mangias?

I moan at the sight. "He's not going to be happy that we're investigating."

Lainey averts her eyes. "Has he met you?"

"Funny," I say, trying to figure out how to respond to his text. I look up at Everett. "What do I say?"

"Tell him to absolutely pick up the pizza and to go ahead and start without you. Tell him you're on a hot date with a hot judge and you won't have time for cold pizza."

The peanut gallery titters away.

"You're a comedian," I say as I start typing away.

In Ashford with Lainey and Keelie and we happened to bump into Everett. All is well! Be home soon. XOXO

Everett ushers us into the next line, and we wait in a relatively short queue before a stagecoach pulls up. A burly man in an old tattered suit dusted with cobwebs is holding the reins, and the horses leading the helm look every bit as tired.

Everett heads up to the driver.

"We're looking to hitch a ride with our friend Rachel Kane?"

The driver hitches his thumb back. "Two coaches away." He looks right at us. "Have a frighteningly good evening." He doesn't crack a smile as the crowd before us hops into his stagecoach and away they go.

The next stagecoach fills up, and soon there's just us and an old couple huddled under a blanket.

I glance to my phone. "Noah is being uncharacteristically quiet. I wonder what happened?"

"Lottie!" a male voice shouts from behind and we find Noah paying for a ticket and running this way. He wraps his arms around me and lands a steamy kiss to my lips. My hand bumps against the gun concealed under this tweed blazer without meaning to.

"How in the world did you find me?" I marvel as I pull back, my heart racing as I see a sly grin on my husband's face.

"I'm a detective. It's my job to figure things out."

Everett groans, "Lemon, he uses the location services on your phone as a homing beacon. Face it, you have a certifiable stalker on your hands."

"I'm not sure I disapprove."

The sound of hooves clip-clopping our way manifests into an

adorable pair of dappled horses. A woman with her face painted gray, large dark circles under her eyes, and her hair colored in a shock of silver motions us into the glorified wagon. And next to her is a gorgeous glowing cat with ebony fur and matching ebony sparks that seem to swirl within his ghostly frame. It's my favorite long-deceased black cat, Thirteen.

The woman motions us aboard once again. "Hop on if you dare. Hold onto your hats and souls—of course, I can always arrange for you to lose both." She breaks out into a maniacal cackle.

The carriage itself is open air, and there are hay bales set on either side of the tractor-trailer for us to sit on. Noah sits to my right and Everett to my left, and both Keelie and Lainey sit on the other side of us. The old couple huddled under their blanket takes their seats near the back.

Thirteen lets out a horrific roar before turning his head completely around unnaturally, and it's an unnerving sight. "I like this one, Lottie. She's dead on with her humor." He chortles away, and I join him.

The woman turns around and looks at me with those dead eyes of hers. She really is a great actress.

"Laugh while you can," she muses. "Soon you'll have reason to scream."

I pull back and whisper to Noah and Everett, "I guess the PR gig was pretty much a dead-end job."

We share a quiet laugh as the chariot begins to move out slowly. Rachel regales us with enough tales from the dead to set a crypt keeper's hair on end.

We watch as the fog rolls by in long fingerlike protrusions and the gravestones peek through its misty talons. The oaks and the maples that surround us are already bare and their skeletal arms glow white under the pale three-quarter moon. The sky is pregnant with dark clouds but rich with hues of navy and electric blue. It's an enchanting night, a perfect night for a carriage ride through a cemetery—although I have no idea how we're going to cage Rachel into giving us info on Pastor Gaines.

I glance back to check on the older couple and gasp.

"They're gone!" I cry out, pointing to the back. Both Keelie and Lainey glance that way, and in no time flat the two of them are shrieking. I join right in on the fun, forcing Rachel and those poor ponies carting us around to stop cold.

Rachel spins in her seat. "What the heck is going on back there? We haven't even gotten to the scary part yet."

Thirteen leaps right through her and lands his sparkling self right onto the empty bale of hay that once held the seemingly happy couple.

"There was this old man and woman"—Lainey's voice wavers—"and they were sitting right there. And now they're gone!"

Noah jumps ship. "They must have fallen off."

Everett bolts out the back, and soon Keelie and Lainey follow suit.

"Great fun." Thirteen arches his back as he stretches out. "Why don't you let the men tire themselves out looking for those poor souls and drill our friend Rachel instead?"

"Good thinking." Keelie helps me jump down, and I make my way over to Rachel who's busy typing into her phone.

"We've got a couple of runners." She shakes her head. "Happens at least once a night."

"That sweet old couple? They could hardly hobble onto the proverbial bus. There's no way they hopped off while we were in flight."

She shrugs as she finishes up her text. "You'd be surprised. Some people are obsessed with crawling around this place after dark."

Rachel is a tall woman, strong jawline, bright eyes. Her gray tattered dress sweeps the ground and is noticeably dirty around the hemline, but I suppose it just adds to the wicked charm of it all.

"Sure is a creepy night," I say and she finally looks my way.

"This is usually when I say it's a good night to die, but it's almost quitting time and things like this tend to pull me out of character."

"I get it. My mother's fiancé was murdered last weekend and that pulled me right out of character, too."

"Murdered?" She perks up as if it were her favorite topic.

"Oh yes. Someone shot him in the alley behind my bakery. His name was Pastor Stephen Gaines. He just persuaded my mother to put all of her money into his checking account, and now there's a whole legal nightmare with trying to get it back. They were just about to turn it into a joint account." My God, I pray that didn't happen. But I needed something that would ring familiar to her and jar her into disclosing something personal to me.

"Wow, your mother sure sounds gullible."

I can't help but frown up at her. "She is." Fine. I'll call a spade a spade. "Are you saying your mother would never fall for anything so foolish?"

"Ha!" she squawks so loud an owl flies out of a nearby ever-green, expanding its pale plumage overhead. "My mother wrote the book on cheated widows. She married some freak—a pastor just like your guy…" she stops cold, her pale eyes glowing in this strange light. "Oh my God. Did you say he was a pastor?"

"Yes."

"And his name was Stephen?"

"Yup."

"Stephen Gailmen?"

"Stephen *Gaines*." It's nice to know he kept his initials intact this time.

Her eyes flit around as if she half-expected him to pop up from behind an overgrown gravestone.

"You're not going to believe this, but I think this man and the nutcase my mother married are one and the same." She closes her eyes a moment. "So he's finally dead. I can't tell you how much joy you've just brought upon me. I actually took a hit out on him once—but that was ages ago."

"Really?" This morbidly fascinates me. And in a strange way, I admire her for it.

"Yup. I went down to Leeds, to some seedy strip club, found myself a mob boss, and gave him cold hard cash."

"What happened?" Obviously not death.

"I don't know. His henchmen took my money and said they'd take care of it. But I never heard a thing."

Hey? Maybe this was it? Talk about a delayed reaction.

A tense knot builds in my stomach. If Rachel's hit on Pastor Gaines worked, sadly I don't think I want to push this further. Hasn't her poor mother been through enough? And was that swindler really worth the trouble a trial would bring?

Thirteen hops before me. "Now, Lottie. I know what you're thinking. But I've come to garner justice for the dead. You must focus on justice."

I quickly glance away from his glowing green eyes.

For once, justice is the last thing on my mind.

"So how long ago did you put out that hit?"

"Like I said, ages. It must have been over a year ago." She shrugs it off. "It wasn't me. I can honestly say I'm glad to have been ripped off by the mob."

"You should be counting your lucky stars. Was there anything odd about him? Anything you'd want someone to know?'"

"Not now that he's dead. But our mothers weren't his first victims. In fact, he married another woman after my mother. A woman by the name of Julia Wright. She lives in Newport."

"Newport? That's not far away."

"Nope. He kept his gig local. I didn't have the heart to tell my mother he turned up again. I figured he already spent the money and was better off dead. That's when I put the hit on him. But, in hindsight, I should have gone for the legal jugular. And I was about to, but by the time I arrived to speak with his new wife, he had already bolted from her as well. She, like my mother, was too embarrassed to contact the authorities."

"And that's why he was able to propagate the same shtick in Honey Hollow—with *my* mother as his next victim. I wonder if I spoke to Julia if I'd glean anything new about him?"

"Who cares. We should be at the nearest bar celebrating—chasing down shots, not chasing his ghost. It's not like either of us would turn in the killer. Heck, they're practically the hero in this equation."

"I totally agree," I say it low in hopes Thirteen won't hear, but judging by the scoffing coming from him, he heard plenty.

Noah and Everett come back, panting and breathless.

"We looked everywhere." Noah places his hands on his knees as he pants violently.

"They took off." Everett hops back into the wagon and helps Keelie and Lainey onboard. Noah and I jump in, and Rachel takes the reins once again.

Soon enough, we arrive right back where we started, and as the carriage comes to a halt, I glance back and scream at the sight before me.

Seated right back in their proper positions are the old man and woman, the blanket still pulled over the tops of their heads.

Both Keelie and Lainey let out a howling scream, and I swear I feel both Noah and Everett tense on either side of me.

The old man lowers the blanket and offers a smile that shows far too many teeth, his face a tad too bony to be comfortable to look at.

His wife looks equally emaciated. Her hair is styled in stiff, white bristles at least three inches over her head, catching the light like a silver halo.

"Have a nice night, all." The old man helps his wife down before he turns to look my way. "Nice cat you have there." He gives a little wink as they hobble off and are quickly swallowed whole by the fog.

Rachel chokes as she observes the scene. "What cat?"

Thirteen hops right down off the haunted chariot and prances on by.

"It's nice to have friends in dead places." He belts out an obligatory meow before sauntering off into the haunted night.

Ha! Thirteen knew I'd need some one-on-one time with Rachel. Who says the dead are useless?

Both Keelie and Lainey cry—literal tears—begging to go home and swearing off any future adventures with me that don't involve half-dressed men. Okay, so Keelie threw in that last part.

We head to the parking lot, and Keelie and Lainey practically jump for cover in my car and I tell them to head on home. I then turn to Noah and Everett and spill everything Rachel told me.

Everett shakes his head as he looks back at the ticket booth where she's talking with a fellow coworker. "She doesn't realize she could have just incriminated herself."

Noah stares pensively in that direction as well. "I'll keep it in mind, Lottie. And I'll check out Julia Wright, see what I come up with. This sure is turning out to be a strange case."

"I agree." I shudder as the wind whistles past us, moaning like a ghost in a graveyard and I'm sure it is. "Maybe this is one case we should just let die right along with Pastor Gaines."

A crackle of lightning goes off in the sky, followed by a ferocious growl of thunder.

Everett takes a breath. "We'd better get back before the storm hits." He pulls me in quickly and offers a kiss to the top of my head. "Goodnight, Lemon. Night, Noah." He takes off, and Noah and I do the same.

The rain starts in heavy and thick, coming down over the windshield in sheets that make it almost impossible to see.

"I'm going to pull off the road for a moment." Noah pulls into the woods to the right of the turnout and kills the engine.

"I agree. Better safe than sorry. I wouldn't want to spend my future haunting the Ashford Cemetery or any other cemetery for that matter. I bet it'll clear up in just a few minutes. How ever will we pass the time?" I bat my lashes at him innocently, and soon enough his mouth is covering mine.

Noah and I fog up the windows in record time. The rain eventually lets up, and Noah races us back to Honey Hollow, right to his place so we can finish what we started.

Noah does his best to shield me from the rain with his jacket, and I laugh all the way into his cabin as Toby jumps and barks, happy to see us.

Noah picks me up into his arms as he shuts the door behind us with his foot.

He sails us into his bedroom as laughter bubbles from my chest. No sooner does he flip the lights on than a scream works its way up my throat and I do a rather inglorious dismount from his arms.

Sprawled naked on his bed in breathless anticipation is an all too familiar blonde bimbo—Cormack Featherby. And as soon as she spots me, she pulls the comforter over her body in haste.

She scoffs. "Excuse us, Landy. This is a private affair."

I glance to Noah and close my eyes. "I'd better get home to Pancake and Waffles." I offer him a sweet kiss on the lips and leave him to clean up the feather-headed mess in his bed.

Some things seem impervious to change.

Cormack is one of them.

CHAPTER 15

S tay away from Noah or else!
I stare at the note pinched between my fingers far longer than necessary. The paper it's written on is creamier than my nighttime moisturizer. And if its gold embossed monogram *CF* hadn't tipped me off as to who sent it—the perpetrator who handed it to me would have. I glance across the counter at Cormack Featherby.

She pranced right into the Cutie Pie Bakery and Cakery after her Swift Cycle class per tradition, and Britney hops by her side trying to get a gander at the note in my hand. I flash it her way and Britney hoots so loud you'd think it was something far more exciting than a foreboding message.

"Did you just threaten Luella?" Britney slaps her hand over her knee. "Oh goodness." She digs the tips of her pinkie fingers into the corners of her eyes to keep from crying. "Cormack, you are too much today. First the rant about Noah kicking you out on your naked rear end and now this? You're lucky Lacy hasn't slapped you with a restraining order. Don't you think it's time you let sleeping dogs lie?"

"Oh, I did." Cormack's lips twitch with what I'm guessing is rage. "I stepped right over Toby as I made my way into that bedroom."

Huh. Not once has Toby not greeted me with an enthusiastic running, jumping, pet-me-over-the belly hello. I guess he, too, is just not that into her.

I slide the note back across the counter. "I don't need this, Cormack. And I'm not staying away from him. Like it or not, Noah and I are embracing our marriage." I leave out the part about it being a temporary stronghold, per the instructions from his therapist.

She rolls her eyes. "It's a fake marriage. I know all about it. Hazel told me herself she thought you were serious so she finalized the paperwork for you."

It's true. Hazel Wellington took over her sister Amanda's event planning company in haste and was desperately trying not to mess up when she messed up royally and filed the paperwork making my union to Noah ironclad in the eyes of the law.

"It might have started off that way, but Noah and I have had a change of heart. We're taking this seriously, and so should you. Look, I realize that you've fallen hard for Noah again, but maybe this is a good time to set your sights somewhere else?" *Like the south of France*, I want to say.

Brit nods as her ponytail swings back and forth. "I'm sure there's a wealthy count, or an earl, or even a loaded commoner that might strike your fancy—or your appetite for financial destruction." She chortles and I struggle not to chortle right along with her. "Excuse me, ladies. I need my coffee." She scoots down to the register where Lily takes her order.

Great. Never would I have guessed that Britney would become the voice of reason. And furthermore—that I would desperately want her to remain in my presence and act as a buffer between Cormack and me.

"Or how about an older gentleman whose tax bracket is in the next galaxy?" I offer. "My mother is hosting a singles mixer next Saturday night that will be crawling with silver foxes."

Cormack leans in hard, her eyes narrowed to tiny celadon slits.

"Listen up, Lana. Noah Corbin Fox and I are destined to be together. A very prominent fortune teller gave me that delicate information not long after my last divorce was final."

Last divorce? Oh, heck, I don't want to know how many divorces she's racked up.

A heavy sigh expels from me. "Listen, Cormack. My name is *Lottie*," I enunciate each syllable. "And I'm sorry to break it to you, but I don't need to listen to whatever that charlatan who made off with your money may or may not have you believing. And I don't need to listen to your threats. I'm not backing down on this."

"Oh, okay," she balks, nodding like a bobble-headed doll. "So you get Essex *and* Noah? And what about the rest of us, Laraine, or whoever you think you are?"

I'm about to tell her that I'm technically not with Everett anymore but don't have it in me to verbalize those words. Everett is still very much tattooed over my heart.

And as if on cue, that tall, dark, and ornery judge walks right into my bakery with the twitchings of a naughty smile.

He steps over and nods to the two of us.

"Lemon, Cormack."

Ha. She doesn't get a surname delight like I do. I can't help the pettiness. Cormack is sawing over my nerves *and* my sanity right now.

"Everett, you are a sight for sore eyes. Are you ready?"

"As ready as I'll ever be. Any hint as to what this might entail?"

I crimp my lips. "No. This is a complete surprise. Are you still game?"

Earlier today I dug deep into the internet trying to find a Julia Wright in Newport, Vermont, and although it wasn't easy, I managed to track her down to an interesting location. Suffice it to say, it will be a blast from the past for me, but I'm not entirely sure how Everett will handle it.

"I'm game, Lemon. I'm up for anything, and I say bring it."

Cormack gags. "What about me? Essex, please explain to your fiancée that she can't be engaged to one man and married to another."

He grimaces a moment as he looks her way. "Actually, Cormack, I see that scenario play out more than I care to admit down at the courthouse."

"Speaking of courthouses." I slide the creamy parchment toward Everett. "Feast your eyes on this little piece of evidence."

He picks it up and shakes his head. "Cormack, you do realize that if anything happened to Lemon, this would be admissible in court. I'd advise you to keep all your threats verbal." He winks my way. "Spoken words are a heck of a lot harder to track, especially if the one who heard them wasn't around anymore."

My mouth falls open at his obnoxious sense of humor.

Cormack belts out a husky laugh. "I can always count on Essex to have my back. Watch out, Lemon Tart. If you don't remove your claws from my man, I am coming for you." She takes off in a fury, and I watch as she stalks down Main Street.

"You do realize you didn't help."

"Not helping is half the fun. Besides, she's about as harmless as a housefly."

"And just as annoying."

His brows bounce. "You ready to take off?"

"Only if you let me throw a few cupcakes into a box for the ride over. I still love to feed you."

"I'll take what I can get."

I box up a half a dozen of my friendly ghost cupcakes and thank Lily for watching the shop for me. She already agreed to do so this afternoon.

Everett and I get as far as the entry when a familiar looking husband comes in bearing a bouquet of blush pink roses that look as delighted as I feel.

Everett's chest expands. "Noah, if you hurry up the street, you can still give the flowers to your girlfriend."

I nod. "I'm sure she'd appreciate them. She's having a rather rough day."

Noah's cheek flickers with a hint of amusement. "These are for my bride." Noah extends the flowers as if they were a peace offering. "I'm sorry you had to witness any of that in my bed last night."

Everett's lips purse a moment, and I can feel the zinger coming before it ever leaves his mouth.

Everett leans in. "When you have to hand-deliver an apology bouquet after a night in your bed, it's time to consider a different kind of therapist to frequent. You do realize there are women who specialize in upping your game. They're found at Red Satin after dark."

Noah shakes his head, his eyes never leaving mine. "I don't need another woman."

"Thank you, Noah," I say, graciously accepting the flowers before turning to Everett. "We found Cormack naked in his bed last night. It was an adventure I wasn't up for, so I left rather abruptly."

"And so did she," Noah adds. "So where are the two of you off to?" Any enthusiasm he might have had begins to wane as he takes a moment to scowl at Everett.

"Newport," I tell him. "I have a credible lead as to where I might find another one of Pastor Gaines' victims, and Everett was kind enough to volunteer to come with me."

Noah shifts his gaze to Everett. "I'm sure he was." He nods his way. "Do you think you'd mind sitting this one out? I'd kind of like to go on a covert op with Lottie sometime. I hear she's pretty good."

A quiet laugh rumbles through my chest. "That's because you got to experience it firsthand last night."

"Touché."

Everett scratches at the back of his neck. "I'm fine with it."

He tries to hand the box of cupcakes back my way, but I stop him.

"That's so you don't forget me." It comes out with a twinge of sadness.

Everett bows down and gifts me a wet kiss on the cheek before whispering, "And that's so you don't forget me."

He takes off, and I try my best to scrape my heart off the floor.

Noah takes up my hand and offers a pained smile. "Are you ready?"

"I'm always ready for you, Noah."

CHAPTER 16

*N*ewport, Vermont is a bustling lakeside community that is rife with old-world charm and its fair share of stunning fall foliage.

"I haven't been here since my father was alive," I say as Noah drives us down a major thoroughfare. "It's so beautiful I just want to feast my eyes on everything at once. I love feeling like a tourist."

"I'm glad I get to share it with you, Lot. We should talk about traveling one of these days. We never did get an appropriate honeymoon."

He waggles his brows and my mouth falls open at the romantic prospect.

"Let's do it. Is there a city that Cormack has been banned from?"

He belts out a laugh.

"Why are you laughing? Most people fear the boogey man. I fear a Featherby popping up from under the bed."

He groans, "You're right. It hits way too close to home for it to be funny."

I decided to leave out her ridiculous threat for now. I don't want to ruin this fun trip with any more talk of that nitwit.

"I'm glad you're here with me, Noah." I point up ahead. "You'll want to turn left at the end of the block and our destination should be right there." I didn't dare tell Noah what he was in for. I had a hard enough time imagining Everett doing this with me let alone Noah.

Keelie and Lainey have all but sworn off my antics for the rest of the haunted month, and Meg is swamped at the "studio" as she calls it.

"I'm glad I'm here, too. I've been meaning to steal some serious alone time with you. I guess you can consider this our first official date night—or afternoon as it were."

"Oh, I love that. Can we still have date night once we have a gaggle of children?"

"Only until we get to twelve."

"Twelve!" I swat him on the arm and we share a laugh, but as soon as we make the left, Noah grows morbidly somber.

"Oh no," he moans as he pulls into the first parking spot he sees. "Why does Everett get mimosas on Lake Champlain and I get this?"

I try my best to stifle a laugh. "If it makes you feel better, I asked him first."

"Sadly no, it actually makes me feel worse." He winces over at the enormous roller skate spinning in the sky. "A roller derby?"

"Yup. Owned and operated by Julia Wright herself. I checked the social media account of the place and she's practically in most of the shots. And seeing that she's super active, I'd say our chances of speaking with her today are pretty darn good."

"Can you speak from a full body cast?"

"You're a riot," I say, hopping out of his truck.

Noah takes a deep breath while looking at the sign. "The Roller Space Case." He shakes his head. "Let's hope they have good pizza."

Noah and I head into the oversized brick building with its floor-to-ceiling windows and old cracked vinyl floor entry.

The sound of wheels softly whirring in the expansive basin to our right, accompanied by the scent of—Noah guessed it—pepperoni pizza gives this place a nostalgic appeal. Back in the day, my mother used to haul us girls out to Ashford when they still had a roller rink and we'd fly around that track as if our lives depended on it. How I miss those storied days when my father sat on the sidelines eating a slice of stringy pizza, cheering us on as if we were Olympians. And we sure felt like we were.

Noah points over to a large neon sign. "Haunted skating the entire month of October."

"Ooh, sounds like Julia likes to kick it up a scary notch."

The bored teen at the reception area perks up. "Did you say Julia?" Her hair is long and shockingly pink. White cordless earbuds hang from her ears, and it reminds me of the time my mother asked why the girl in front of us in line at the movies had cigarettes coming from her ears.

"Julia? Yes, actually, I did."

We step over and she slides a couple of liability forms our way, which Noah begins to diligently fill out. I happen to peer at the names he's jotted down—Corbin Fox and Kenzie Fox. Our middle names and a brand new surname for me. I like the idea of trying it on for size.

The teen taps into her phone. "Did she give you a discount?"

I'm about to refute the frugal error when Noah nods.

"Yes, she did." He taps his hand over the twenty-dollar price of admission per person, and I can't help but chuckle.

"Sure thing." The girl knocks ten percent off the price and takes our shoe sizes before reappearing with a pair of his and hers skates. "Julia is in the rink if you want to say hello. She's the Grim Reaper."

A forced laugh bucks from me. "Julia is always the Grim

Reaper." I shake my head at the girl as if I had a clue as to what I was talking about.

She wrinkles her nose. "So you heard?"

"Heard what?" I lean in, suddenly hungry for what the teen with the cigarettes hanging out of her ears has to opine about.

"About a year ago her husband disappeared." She says that last word in air quotes. "People think she offed him, but she insists he took off on his own. But really? The pastor of New Way Church just up and leaving his wife like that? They were so in love. And he was so nice. Always smiling. He never had a bad thing to say about anyone."

And, sadly, not a word she said surprises me.

"Does Julia have a bad thing to say about anyone?"

She laughs, exposing a retainer in her mouth that runs across her teeth in a thin silver line.

"Julia is insanely nice. Emphasis on insane. But you know that. Anyway, the town gossips think she went bonkers and mowed him down and buried the body—thus the Grim Reaper costume. Julia has been a good sport about it."

"Sounds like it."

"Have fun," she chimes as she tends to the next customer in line.

"Wow, Noah, who knew she'd prove to be a wealth of information? Maybe Julia did kill Pastor Gaines. It just took her a while to track him down."

"If she did, I'd say she was tenacious. And I'm not ruling it out. But one thing I've learned as a detective is that popular opinion isn't always the best route to follow." We get to the benches next to the refreshment stand and Noah pats me on the back. "Have fun, Cupcake. I'll watch from the stands."

"Oh no, you don't."

"Come on, Lot. I'll test out the pizza for you. On a scale of frozen Frisbee to Mangias, I'll give you an honest readout."

"Very funny, detective. But there might just be a delicious reward of another variety in it if you don those slippery shoes."

His evergreen eyes press hard into mine and my insides bite with heat.

"That's one challenge I can't refuse."

Noah and I put on our skates and head down to the rink, with me gliding happily along and Noah hanging onto the guardrail for dear life as if each step were about to launch him off a very steep cliff.

We hit the whirling masses, mostly teenagers screaming at one another while looking at their phones. The rink itself is sparsely lit by way of an illuminated disco ball. There are cobwebs over the ceiling and large fuzzy spiders hanging from the walls. Most of the kids are dressed in costume, and the music blaring from the speakers sounds as if it should be gracing a haunted inferno.

I take up Noah's hand and we're off, slowly, painfully slow.

"Noah, you can walk faster than that. Just relax and try to have fun. It's totally okay if you fall."

"It's totally okay if other people fall. I happen to have a gun just inches from precarious places on my body. I'm liable to shoot off my baby maker if I take a tumble. And if I do, we can kiss our baker's dozen goodbye."

"Thirteen?" I muse, and no sooner do I say the number than a sparkling black cat materializes perched on Noah's shoulder.

"You rang?" He looks around the establishment, managing to look bored in the process. Come to think of it, Thirteen always looks bored.

Noah looks to his left. "He's on me, isn't he?"

"Yes," Thirteen muses. "Try not to dislodge me on the very first fall. I happen to enjoy being eye to eye with a beautiful girl."

"I'm blushing," I tease. "And you're just in time. There's a Grim Reaper in here somewhere I plan on interrogating."

An older blonde comes our way wielding an oversized plastic machete, and I gasp at the sight of her. And, instead of remaining calm and staying in my space, I step out in front of her and we both spin out of control.

"Lottie?" Noah calls out as he rolls away. "Where are the brakes on these things?"

Thirteen lets out an adorable roar. "Never mind him. Do your thing, and I'll make sure the bumbling detective doesn't lose a limb."

Especially not the baby making limb, I want to add, but I'm too busy flailing.

An arm steadies me, and I gasp all over again.

"Did I scare you?" She blinks those all too familiar blue eyes my way.

Have I mentioned Pastor Gaines has a type? Dear God. Come to think of it, Mitzi did share the same fair skin and hair, same sparkling blue eyes. Wow, Pastor Gaines had to look far and wide to fulfill his fetish for blonde widows with some serious cash in the bank. Little did he know he was about to hit zippo with my mother. She's not loaded.

"No, actually"—I struggle to catch my breath—"you just look so much like my mom it caught me off guard. I've been missing her." I add that last tidbit in hopes to elicit a bout of sympathy.

"Oh dear." She clutches at her chest as if the thought touched her—and that's exactly how my mother would've reacted in the very same situation. "Come here." She pulls us off to the side. "How long has it been since you've lost your mother?"

I open my mouth to correct her but decide to go with it.

"It's very recent. This last summer." Something tells me I'm going to have to dodge lightning bolts for the rest of my days for pretending that my mother bit the big one.

"That's not that long ago at all. They say it takes a full year just to get out of that fog grief lands you in."

445

"Oh? Are you familiar with it? Have you gone through a similar loss?" Not that she'd grieve someone she killed.

She hooks her powder blue eyes into mine, and my stomach cinches because it really does feel as if I'm with my mother. Elaine and Mitzi might have passed as sisters, but this woman right here is Miranda Lemon's long-lost twin.

"I'm painfully aware of loss—just not the kind you're dealing with." Her lips quiver a moment the same way my mother's have been prone to do. "I'm not sure if you're in the know, but it's no secret my husband walked out on me last year. People actually think I *killed* him." She holds up the plastic machete. "Thus the irony in my choice of accouterments. But don't worry. You're not speaking with a killer. Although if I found him, I'd gouge his eyes out with my own bare hands. I wouldn't let him go so easily."

"No gunshot to the chest, huh?"

"Ha! Not on your life."

I make a face because I find this Miranda knock-off to feel mighty credible. "Can you tell me about this man? Why would he take off on someone as kind and pretty as you?" I mean that.

"Greed." She glances over her shoulder. "I'm only telling you this because I think you need to hear about some other people's troubles. Maybe it'll help take the edge off your own." She tilts her head as she softens her gaze over me. "I'm not sure why, but you remind me so much of my own daughter. Anyway, Stephen —that's my husband. We had a good marriage. He stepped into the picture shortly after my first husband died, and I fell hard for him. It's as if he knew all the things I needed to hear, and I lapped it up like a kitten to milk. We were so happy—deliriously happy. He had a small church he started up, only about fifty in the entire congregation, but I believed in him. And, of course, I had the equestrian center." She glances down to the floor, and I can see the shame building in her eyes.

"Had?"

She nods. "People think I sold it because I wanted to, but that louse I married took off with every red cent I had in the bank. I didn't want to lose my home. It's the home I shared with my previous husband. That would be another loss I couldn't have dealt with. So, I decided to sell my share of the equestrian center I inherited along with my sisters. Thankfully, they both bought me out. And with the money, I had enough to pay off my mortgage. With the rest, I bought this place. It was in foreclosure, and I brought it back to life all by my lonesome." She shrugs. "It was old and rundown, had seen better days, and didn't have much hope. The last owner took off on it out of the blue. I guess you could say I saw a lot of myself in this place. Stephen took off one day out of the blue himself and left me in a pile of rubble, too." She sighs deeply.

"Have you ever thought of trying to hunt him down?"

"Are you kidding?" She narrows her brows my way. "Now you listen here, young lady. Any man who walks out on you is not worth chasing."

"Not even if you plan on prosecuting him?"

She winces. "And eat crow in front of family and friends? I'm too mortified to tell them how much he swindled me for. And I ask you to kindly not repeat a word."

"Absolutely not." How interesting that the common bond between poor Julia here and Elaine Gilmore is that their pride stands in their way of reporting his crime. I bet he played on that as well. Stephen Gaines is a master manipulator, and he knew exactly who he was targeting. "I'm sorry you went through all that. You wouldn't mind if I gave you a hug, would you?"

She presses out a sweet smile. "I think it might make both of us feel better."

I offer her a warm embrace, and she squeezes me hard just the way my mother has a propensity to do.

"Take care," she says, rolling away backward. "And don't be a stranger!" She takes off like a bullet, and I spot Noah and Thirteen up by the café and swim upstream like a salmon trying to get to them.

"How was it?" Noah asks.

Thirteen hops off his shoulder and lands smack onto the pizza. "Yes, what juicy morsels did the reaper have to share with you?"

"It's the same story we've heard before." I shake my head. "And none of those women wanted to report him in fear of the social consequences that would befall *them* of all people. This is just heartbreaking to witness. I wish there was some way to go back in time and wring his neck."

Thirteen lowers his head. "I'm so disappointed," he growls it out in sorrow before dissolving in a vat of sparks and stars.

Noah and I take our time finishing up the pizza.

We head over to the front desk and return our gently used skates, and the girl with the shocking pink hair doesn't even bother looking up from her phone.

Noah wraps an arm around me as we make our way into the brisk autumn air.

"I've never had an investigation with so little leads, so few suspects that I actually want to pursue." I pull him in and look up into those brilliant green eyes. "What are your thoughts, detective?"

Noah hardens his gaze at the roller rink. "I'm starting to think we're heading in the wrong direction entirely."

"Can we search his office? His home, maybe?"

"I can get a search warrant for both, but it's against protocol for me to bring you."

I bite down hard over my lip. "What if I broke in? You can be my lookout. Come on, Noah. I'm good. I could put this together —*we* could put this together." I don't want to say it out loud, but depending on who killed Pastor Gaines, I might not want to turn them in.

"I could lose everything, Lottie."

"You won't. I promise. If it looks as if someone is coming, feel free to arrest me. I won't protest."

He closes his eyes at the thought. "I'm not arresting you." He opens the right side of his jacket, revealing the tip of a silver cuff partially tucked in a pocket sewn into the lining. "Not for real anyway."

"Ooh. Does that mean this bad baker is about to get put into restraints?"

"I show. I don't tell."

"Fine. I'd much rather you take me back to Honey Hollow than to anywhere Pastor Gaines might have gone. I'm not sure I'm that interested in digging around in this investigation any longer." A thought comes to me. "Listen up. I'm about to give you a hot tip, detective. I think I'm about to break and enter into the cabin across the street from my home."

"And I'll be right there to arrest you." His dimples dig in.

"I knew you had a naughty streak in you."

"What can I say? You bring out the beast in me."

We hop into his truck, and Noah takes off for Honey Hollow as if he were on the chase for a common street criminal.

The truth is, we're both on the chase, and whoever did this to Pastor Gaines is about to have their luck run out on them. As much as I'd like to submerge the case, my thirst for justice keeps corking it up to the top.

But when the killer's luck does run out on them, something tells me I'll have a hard time turning them in for their crimes.

Once we get back to Country Cottage Road, I end up keeping my end of the bargain and breaking into Noah's cabin. And Noah ends up keeping his end of the bawdy bargain and lands me in handcuffs.

"I've always thought you were arrestingly handsome," I pant as he bolts the door behind us. "Cheesy, I know."

A crooked grin flickers on his lips. "I suppose this is a good

time to tell you I'm also an FBI agent—Female Body Inspector."
He winces. "Cheesy, I know."

"It looks like I'm at your cheesy mercy, detective. I suppose you'll have to inspect away."

And inspect away he does.

Suffice it to say, a perfectly legal lusty time is had by all.

CHAPTER 17

A lemon-yellow glimmer of sunshine, the first light of day, greets me as I get to the bakery in the morning.

It's Saturday, the day that Noah, Everett, and I agreed to head to counseling together later this afternoon. And then after that trauma is over with—tonight my mother is entertaining an entire hoard of horny gray panthers and silver foxes at the big senior soirée her new boy toy Topper Blakley talked her into.

Not that they're official.

After he got wind of the homicide charges pending, he took a full step back from any kind of a commitment. Something tells me he draws a hard line at assassins. Not that my mother is an assassin. Although it does sound rather impressive. And considering her first victim was a bona fide louse, I'm profoundly dazzled by her marksmanship abilities.

I hop out of my car and head to the back of the bakery. No sooner do I get the key into the door than an enormous cracking sound emits from my right, and I look up just in time to see a weathered old oak tree crashing down in my direction.

A viral scream gets lodged in my throat just as I press myself up against the building and a couple of branches graze my back-side—but, for the most part, I'm no worse for wear.

I turn around, only to find the bulk of the trunk smashed over the top of my beat-up Honda.

"No, no, no!" Great. As if people don't think I'm cursed enough, I almost got crushed to death by a tree of all things. My God, if I had just been a foot back, I would have gotten clobbered right into eternity!

I take in a ragged breath before heading into the bakery and sending a group text to both Noah and Everett.

And as I suspected, they both arrive in record time. What I didn't expect was for them to arrive together. I let them in the front, and Noah wraps his arms around me while Everett takes off to inspect the damage.

"Geez, Lemon." Everett can hardly squeeze his way out the door. "It's like the tree was coming for you." Once he's through to the other side, Noah and I join him. They take off to inspect the tree at the base, and I hop over an entire obstacle course of branches and leaves to get to them.

"Well?" I carefully navigate my way in their direction. "What's the verdict? Termite rot?" Wow, if it is, it'll be up to me to tent all of Honey Hollow since Nell practically gifted me the neigh-borhood.

Everett and Noah exchange a glance.

"What? What is it?" I say, trying to get a better look.

Noah takes a step back, and I look to where Everett is crouching with his hand over a flat stump.

"What is that?" I say as I inspect the seemingly clean break.

Everett gives a quick look around. "Someone took a saw to it," he says, getting back on his feet.

"A *saw*? You mean someone was out here? They deliberately tried to kill me?"

Noah shakes his head. "They most likely sawed it last night.

And—if we're going to go the sinister route, they waited for you to show and kicked it over."

"Oh my God." My adrenaline spikes all over again. I press my hand to my chest, only to feel my heart trying to kick its way out. "Cormack," I pant. "She did this."

Noah's eyes grow wild with disbelief. "What makes you think that?"

"Because she threatened me. You saw the note, Everett. The woman is dangerous. Noah, I demand you arrest her."

"*Lottie.*" His brows narrow as he pleads with me to reconsider with this tone.

"Don't you *Lottie* me. That nutcase almost did me in."

He whips out his phone. "I'll ask where she is."

"She's obviously hiding in the bushes." I shiver as I struggle to warm my arms with my hands.

Everett wraps an arm around me, and immediately I'm heated by his body.

He sighs. "Noah, you call your girlfriend. I'll get Lemon out of the cold."

Noah scowls up at him as Everett and I hightail it back inside the bakery.

"Everett, you believe me, don't you?" I ask as he wraps his arms around me once again. His blue eyes are the only color in this monochromatic early morning world.

"Lemon," he says it sweetly enough. "I'm not sure she has the dedication to come out in the middle of the night in the freezing cold to saw an oak tree in half."

"You'd be surprised what a great motivator hate can be—and she does hate me." I make a face at him. "All right, traitor. I'll go make you some coffee."

And I do. I make both Noah and Everett my special pumpkin spiced lattés and pull out an array of cookies left over from yesterday while I go bake a fresh batch of everything. As much as

I tried to convince them that I was fine and that they could certainly go back to bed, neither dared to leave the bakery.

By the time I pull out a fresh batch of pumpkin spiced muffins for us all, the morning crew rolls in.

Both Lily and Keelie step up and examine the three of us.

Keelie starts in on an obnoxious string of giggles. "Why does it look like Noah and Everett just rolled out of bed and had a rigorous workout?"

Lily smacks her on the arm. "Why do you think?"

"Oh!" I shake my head as I do my best to swallow a mouthful of muffin. "No, they were moving a tree out back just a little while ago. I thought it smashed my Honda in half, but it turns out there's just a tiny dent over the top of the car."

"Moving a tree?" Keelie's voice drops an obnoxious octave. "Is that what they're calling a threesome these days?"

Lily's lips cinch a devious smile. "If there was a tree involved, I guess it was a foursome."

My mouth falls open. "I'm awfully close to pelting you both with muffins. And Keelie, the reason I asked if you could help out at the bakery tonight is because I have a huge order of cupcakes and cookie platters that I need delivered to my mother's senior soirée."

"Ooh." Lily bucks. "I almost forgot to tell you. She called last night before we closed and doubled the order. She wants to have some treats for the guests of the haunted house she's hosting as well."

"Great," I say. "It looks like there will be a fright in every nook and cranny of the B&B tonight."

Lily zeros in on Noah. "So when are you arresting Miranda? Or is she getting a pass because she's your wife's mother?"

Noah glances to Everett, and I wonder if they've already discussed the dicey legal waters we've ventured into.

"I don't see her as a flight risk." Noah glances my way. "And I don't have all the necessary evidence to make the arrest."

"You will." Lily nods. "Sorry, Lot, but face it, your mom has a propensity for offing her boyfriends. I think Mayor Nash escaped a fire."

"Or dodged a bullet," Keelie adds.

I shake my head at Noah and Everett. But I don't say a word that might protect my mother's questionable honor.

Do I think that my mother had it in her to kill a man in cold blood?

I don't think I want to answer the question.

SOON ENOUGH IT'S AFTERNOON, and both Noah and Everett have come back to the bakery after leaving a couple of hours ago. They're both showered and dressed to impress—our *therapist*. Okay, so maybe a tiny bit of their hard work was for me.

The three of us drive out to Fallbrook and straight to Dr. Frankie Allen's office where we head right in, single file.

She turns around, her hair in a messy bun, her merlot-colored leather jacket is fitted, and she's wearing a pair of crocodile textured heels in a matching shade of burgundy. Her smile quickly morphs into a gasp.

"Well, as I live and breathe. Essex, you dirty, dirty dog!" She holds her arms open and he falls right in.

Noah leans over. "Did she just say Essex?"

Mother of all things holy.

How is this possible? I mean, I realize that Everett got around, but really? Our therapist, too?

She's rocking him in her arms like a baby, her fingers wandering up and down his back like she's conducting some kind of tactical assault.

"Everett," I hiss without meaning to. Oh heck, I meant it.

He pulls back and nods her way before taking a seat next to me in the big comfy chairs she has set out three in a row.

"Well"—her cheeks are ruby with color as she takes her seat in her enormous leather chair—"I was not expecting this surprise." She looks to Noah. "You neglected to tell me your stepbrother was the infamous Judge Bed 'Em and Leave 'Em Baxter."

So she does know him—in *that* way.

I shoot him a look for amassing such a reputation to begin with, and his lips flicker like flames too stubborn to give a real smile.

"Yes," Noah muses. "That would be him. And he is, in fact, the man who decided to interject himself between Lottie and me."

Everett leans in to get a better look at him. "Lemon chose me."

"Lemon?" Dr. Allen all but swoons as she wrinkles her nose my way. "Isn't that just adorable? Oh, how I miss your nicknames, Essex." A hearty giggle rips from her and she sounds like a donkey braying. "Of course, my nickname was for behind closed doors only." More braying.

I glare at Everett a moment.

And why are we here again? To repair my relationship with Noah or to tear what Everett and I have left to sexual shreds?

Dr. Allen straightens in her seat, her hands folded in front of her. "So, Lottie"—she's doing some oddball fidgeting with her eyes as if trying to get me to look at Everett without moving her head—"you've had a fair sampling of the two. I can see now why all the indecisive behavior. Noah, you'll have to understand that Lottie is in a peculiarly difficult position. Both you and Essex are wrought of a very high caliber. I'd go as far as suggesting that this is an impossible decision."

Noah shifts uncomfortably in his seat. "Lottie has chosen. We're moving on with the marriage."

She balks, "For two months."

"At minimum," he corrects. "It could take up to six."

I can tell Noah is rooting for seven.

Everett sighs as if bored with Noah's efforts to maintain me as his legal spouse. "I can move it along, and I will."

"Ooh!" Dr. Allen shimmies her shoulders as she giggles. "Don't you just love a man in charge, Lottie?" She sighs, never taking her eyes off him.

Noah grunts, "I have a team of deputies at my disposal."

Dr. Allen gives him a quick wink. "And don't think for a moment that doesn't drive the bakers wild." That throaty giggle reprises itself. "Isn't that right, Lottie?"

"That is correct." I pat Noah on the knee.

Dr. Allen shudders as if coming to. "Let's get down to business. Speaking of which, Lottie, did you and Noah get down to business?" She pops a pair of glasses on, and they promptly glide right down her nosy nose.

I use all of my mind power to glower at her.

"Yes," Noah whispers as if prompting me to admit it.

I clear my throat. "A lady never tells."

She looks to my right. "And Everett, how does that make you feel?"

"Oh, come on," I balk. "How do you think it makes him feel?" I'm fighting mad all of a sudden. If I were her, I'd move because I'm about to flip a table.

"It's okay, Lemon." Everett picks up my hand and offers a sweet kiss to the back of it. "I completely understand. You're married. Noah is your husband. This is something the two of you wanted before I ever stepped into the picture romantically."

"Oh, Essex." Dr. Allen picks up a brochure with her picture on the cover and fans herself with it. "How chivalrous of you. Are you currently dating?" She presses her lips together as if she were hopeful he wasn't.

"I'm on hold until Lemon fully makes her decision. I'm confident she'll choose the best path for the both of us."

"For the three of us." Noah's voice sounds strangled.

Dr. Allen frowns his way as if he was ruining her mojo with the good judge.

"Noah"—she offers him her full attention—"how does it feel having Lottie back fully?"

Noah picks up my hand and warms it with his, those emerald eyes hooked to mine. "It feels amazing. It feels as if my life has kick-started again and I have the one person I longed for back in my arms. I feel complete with you, Lottie. I feel as if we've already started our family. You're my family."

My heart melts—every last part of me melts into a puddle hearing Noah proclaim his love for me that way.

"And Lottie?" Dr. Allen opens her beak once again, and I'm really starting to get irritated with her. "How do you feel?"

"I'm sorry, but I refuse to eviscerate Everett. I'll tell Noah how I feel when we're alone."

Everett takes a breath. "Lemon, please, I don't mind. I know you have very deep feelings for him or we wouldn't be sitting here. You were with him first, you gave yourself to him in an intimate way last year, and you firmly believed the two of you were altar bound—the first time. Please don't hesitate to let him know how you feel. Remember, it was me who implored you to take this marriage head-on. I'm not going to fall apart simply because you declare your love for him."

I bite the inside of my cheek hard. Of course, Everett knows all the right things to say. He's a judge for Pete's sake. He says all the right things for a living.

A ragged breath pumps from me.

"Noah"—I turn his way, and my eyes blur with tears in an instant—"my heart belongs to you in ways I simply cannot explain. When our lives blew apart last February, I honestly tried to find it in me not to care for you anymore, but my heart didn't allow for that to be an option. I'm in love with you, madly in love, and I can't help myself." My body goes rigid as I feel the weight of Everett's stare over my back.

"Come here." Noah pulls me into a hard embrace. "Thank you for sharing that with me."

"Very good, Lottie." Dr. Allen sighs. "Now I'd like for you to do the same with Essex."

I shoot her a look for being so liberal with her first name privileges.

"*Everett.*" I give her the side-eye before turning to him fully. "I am truly, madly, insanely in love with you." I shrug. "I can't help it. When Noah and I split in two, it was you who helped put back the pieces of my heart, and I'll forever be grateful to you for that. And, as it stands, although I'm fully committed to my marriage with Noah, you still hold a very special place in my heart—and not one part of me wants to evict you from it. You know parts of me that no one else has ever seen."

Dr. Allen titters, and I tap my fingers over my mouth.

"That's not what I meant."

She motions for me to face forward once again.

"Noah"—she hitches her head toward Everett—"please let Essex know how you feel about him."

"How long do we have?" Noah smarts before leaning forward to get a better look at his old stepbrother. "Everett." He offers a slow blink. "We've had our fair share of disagreements. I've wronged you in the past, and you were right to be angry with me. I stole your first love right from under you. It was a stupid adolescent move, and I'll regret that forever. And when you came back into my life—through Lottie, I instantly feared you were after retribution. I couldn't blame you for being attracted to her. But I could blame you for actively pursuing her while we were still together, or so I thought." Noah presses a remorseful smile my way. "I understand now you were just a very good friend to Lottie. And once Lot and I took a step back in our own relationship, you were right there ready to fill my shoes. Again, I couldn't blame you. I wasn't half the gentleman you were."

Dr. Allen nods. "And now? How do you feel about Essex today?"

Noah clears his throat. "Today, I'm grateful for you. It's

because of your encouragement that Lottie and I are able to pick up where we left off and see where this could lead. And I'm in full agreement with you. I only want what makes Lottie happy. If it's me, I'm thrilled. And if it's you"—he takes a hard breath—"then I will accept her decision and wish the two of you the best." Noah's shoulders sag at the prospect. "But above all, Everett, I'm thankful that we've reached a place where I can once again call you a friend."

Dr. Allen claps, and I offer my own meager applause.

"Noah, that was great," I say, wiping a tear from my eye.

"Essex?" Her lips expand. "Your turn."

Everett sighs hard as if this was something he wasn't anticipating nor did he wish to continue. I say join the club.

He looks to Noah, those blue eyes settling in. "Noah, when you and Alex came into my life, I thought finally—the universe is making all the wrong things right. I had my wish for a brother fulfilled twice over. After about a week, I realized my error," he teases. "But in all seriousness, having the two of you around made me feel complete. Losing my father was tough, but having a new family was an amazing gift, and I didn't take it lightly. So when I discovered that you decided you knew what was best for me—in regards to Cormack, I was livid with you. I swore I'd find a way to sell both of your kidneys on the black market. And I was privately learning jiu-jitsu in an effort to kill you swiftly in your sleep."

"Everett"—a nervous giggle bounces from me—"refocus."

"Right." He wipes his face with his hand. "Noah, bottom line. You survived my wrath. When Lemon came into my life, I found something unique in her that I've never had in a woman before— a friend. And as time went on, I knew my heart wanted more. I laid out my feelings for her and she graciously thanked me for doing so, but assured me the two of you were on the right track. Later that month, Britney showed up and blew all of your good plans out of the water. And just like that, Lemon and I fit. But in the interim you and I grew to be friends once again. I knew she still had feelings for you, so making sure the two of you either finished what you started or ended on the right note was crucial. I love Lemon." He pauses while staring hard at Noah. "And I'll be honest. That's not going to change."

Dr. Allen whimpers while fanning herself all the more.

Heck, in a moment I'm about to join her.

"But—I love you, too, Noah." Everett flexes an all too brief but genuine smile. And just like that, I explode into a million confetti hearts all over the room. "And that's why I'm doing this. Not for one other person would I have done this. But I'm doing it for you —because you are still my brother."

"Oh good Lord up in heaven." Dr. Allen tips her head back as we both indulge in a deluge of tears.

"Everett"—I hop over and fall onto his lap, pressing my lips to his as I pull him into a hard embrace—"that was so beautiful. What a sacrificial heart you have. I'll never forget those words for as long as I live. It was truly the most touching moment I have ever witnessed."

"Lottie?" Dr. Allen clears her throat.

"Yes?" I glance around and Noah's gaze is wide and hard.

"Oh right." I hop right back into my seat.

Dr. Allen motions for the three of us to stand. "I think Lottie had a brilliant idea. It's time to share a heartfelt embrace."

I pull Noah in and wrap my arms around him hard. My husband. My everything. Noah truly is just that.

Noah and Everett exchange a rather manly embrace—that's more of a pat on the back than anything.

"Homework." Dr. Allen bears a wild grin our way. "Noah, you're to treat Lottie to something special, something romantic, something unexpected that will change her views of you. Think outside the box."

"I look forward to it." He gives my hand a squeeze.

"As do I." I dot a quick kiss to his cheek.

"Good. Noah, you have another assignment. Essex, this includes you as well. The two of you are to go on a male bonding expedition. Something isolative that will give you both some quality time together and room to share your thoughts with one another. Agree?"

"Agree," both Noah and Everett chime in unison.

Noah nods his way. "How about I take you to Hollyhock when we get a chance and you can help me check out that lodge I'm looking to purchase."

Everett tips his head. "I'd like that."

Noah mentioned to me a few weeks back that he was looking to make a lucrative investment, something he could pass down to his children one day—*our* children. The thought warms me all the way to my toes.

"In that case, enjoy the rest of the weekend." She pulls a pin out of her bun and her red hair falls wildly all around her. "Essex, you know where to find me if need be."

"So unprofessional," I mutter under my breath as we file out of her office.

Everett looks from Noah to me. "Anything else I can do for you, Lemon?"

"Yes, as a matter of fact, there's something the both of you can do for me. Be my date for the senior soirée. I have a feeling those attending my mother's geezer-fest shouldn't be left unsupervised."

Everett raises a brow. "Sounds to me like it's time to party."

Noah gives a sly smile. "A room crawling with single women? I wonder how many women will call you Essex?"

I'm beginning to wonder that myself.

CHAPTER 18

"*E*ssex!"

The first giddy granny we see says his proper moniker right out the gate.

"Mom?" He pulls her into a quick embrace.

And that right there is the only exception to the coital rule—with the other only exception being his sister.

The B&B is brimming with bodies, young and old as it were. As soon as we finished up in Fallbrook, we hardly had enough time to load up all of the cupcakes into the back of Noah's truck and hustle them to my mother's celebratory version of dueling banjos—haunted silver banjos as it were.

I've just set all the cupcakes and cookie platters in place—in the conservatory for the silver set and in the dining hall for those who paid to have their socks frightened right off of them. I've already seen Greer running around with her head in her arms, looking mildly visible to the naked human eye, and about a dozen different people marveling at my mother's special effects.

Little Lea has Thirteen tucked under her arm and they're roaming the halls kicking people in the shins and biting them.

Winslow looks awfully dapper in his ghostly duds and he's

463

holding a pitchfork and jabbing it at random. The guests are so riveted by the floating garden tool that they've actually tried to pry it away from him. But seeing that Winslow was once a farmer right here in Honey Hollow two hundred years ago, he's hanging on to what's rightfully his.

Carlotta, Brit, and Cormack are conducting the haunted house tours—an odd trio if ever there was one—but I don't mind one bit that my mother is enlisting the aid of her regular boarders.

Carlotta trots my way while Cormack accosts Noah. And Brit heads over to Everett as they share a laugh—probably because he's filling her in on our last adventure.

"Listen, Lottie—" Carlotta pulls me farther out of earshot in her zombie-like costume, her face painted so white there's a hint of a blue cast. The dark circles under her eyes look menacing— and, shockingly, she looks a lot like I do at three in the morning. "Your mother has crossed the line this time."

"Does she have the toilet paper running in the wrong direction again? I've threatened her in the past. The toilet paper runs over—or she's out."

Carlotta takes a moment to swat me. "This is not about toilet paper. It's about human waste—as in a literal human. You can't let her see this Topper person. He's a whopper, all right. He's bad news, you hear me? Whatever you do, you need to make sure it stops! And it ends tonight, Lottie." She picks up her enormous gray tattered gown and looks to the throngs of tourists bursting through the doors, wide-eyed and smiling. "Now if you'll excuse me, I have to scare the pants off a group of high school students."

"Wait!" I yank her back by her bustle. "You can't just leave me hanging like that. What's the matter with the guy?"

The chandelier goes on and off, and a riot of screams ensues from all around. The lights start to dim once again, and this time they stay that way. Perfect. I was hoping the universe would remind me why I liked living in the modern era once again. Lord knows if we ever had to revert to candlelight we'd burn the town to cinders.

"Later, Lottie. I've got little Lea angry with me, and that's one brat I need to make nice with." Carlotta stalks off, and I opt to join Everett and Brit over Noah and his psychotic concubine.

Brit purses those pillowy lips of hers my way. "Sounds like no progress was made today, Lancaster."

I inch back, unsure of how the alphabet soup got so far. But I'm in no mood to try to figure out Britney, so I go with it.

"You're right," I say. "It turns out, Dr. Allen is one of Everett's coital castoffs. She was hitting on him hard."

She snorts. "She was hitting on Noah pretty hard when we started out, too. But I set her straight."

"You told her to knock it off or else you'd flip a table?" I knew I should have sent furniture flying.

"No. I gave her a lifetime pass to the Swift Cycle gym I planted down the street from her office. Believe me when I say her face turned colors."

"Ha! Don't worry, Brit. I'll bring a box of my impossible-to-resist chiffon cupcakes the next time I head her way. I think we make a great team in that respect."

She cranes her neck past me. "Someone else thinks she makes a great team with your husband."

I turn around to see Cormack trying to climb Noah as if he were Mount Olympus as Noah does his best to remove her from his person.

"That's it. I may not have a table to flip, but I can flip a blonde just as easily."

No sooner do I dig my claws into Cormack's shoulders than Everett plucks her away and sends her back to her post at the distal end of the B&B.

Noah takes my hand. "I'm sorry, Lot. Maybe I should get a restraining order."

"Why? So she can break it? *Please*, she's unstoppable." I lead us toward the kitchen. "I'd better make sure any surplus of cupcakes I brought are put into my mother's refrigerator."

"I'll help."

And sure enough, my friendly ghost cupcakes are beginning to melt into white gooey globs. I slide all of the boxes down the island as Noah fits them into the fridge in various patterns as if he were playing a skilled game of Tetris.

The back door begins to open slowly, and I head over in the event one of my mother's guests has turned themselves around.

"Hello?" I open it wide and my breathing ceases. My brain can't believe what my eyes are seeing. A scream evicts from me at the top of my lungs as I shut the door in a fury.

Noah dashes over and pulls me close. "What's wrong?"

"The door," I pant. "I saw him. He was there."

"Who was there, Lot?"

"Pastor Gaines. He was tall and dressed in a suit and that smirk on his face he always wore, and even his eyes looked as if they were laughing at me."

"Stay here." He bolts that way and whips the door open, peering out at the darkness. "There's no one out here, Lottie. Do you think you could have...you know"—he winces—"seen a ghost?"

I suck in a never-ending breath. "My God, if my powers have grown in such a way that Pastor Gaines of all people can haunt me, then I don't want anything to do with them. I'll be turning in my supersensual card to the first paranormal agency I can find."

"Come here." He pulls me into a strong embrace. Noah's rock-hard body adheres to mine, and I don't want to let go. I don't want to be a part of this night any longer.

"Let's check on my mother and then get out of here." I run my hands down the front of his shirt. "I'd love to bring you back to my place." I shrug. "I miss having you there with me."

"Then that's where we'll go." He lands a sweltering kiss to my lips.

Noah and I race next door to the conservatory brimming with a sea of gray—and oddly, these people all look just as good if not better than any of their younger counterparts I've come across.

The women look amazing with their skin glowing, their grins stretched from ear to ear. The men aren't so bad either with their fancy suits, their winning smiles. Everyone has a drink in their hand as laughter and the din of cheery conversations abound.

I'm in awe of every single soul in the room. They've lived great lives and they're still going, healthy and strong, classy and elegant, looking for love right here at the—

My eye catches the sign hanging from above the back door —*Welcome to the Third Annual Swingers Soirée.*

"What?" I spot Miranda Lemon yucking it up with a group of dicey looking men, and I make a beeline for her. "Can I borrow you for a moment?" I pull her to the side without waiting for a response. She's donned a tight black dress, so short I'm entirely convinced she's donned the top to a pantsuit, which is suspiciously missing its lower half. Her hair is curled and winged back circa 1980, and she has a swath of bright red lipstick on—always my favorite shade on her—MAC, Ruby Woo. Honestly? Is there any other color?

"Would you let go?" She plucks her arm free. "In the event you're unaware, I bruise easily."

"So does my ego. What are the fine people of Honey Hollow going to think once they find out you're hosting a porn convention *and* an exorcism on the very same night?"

"They're going to think I'm fun, Lottie!"

I suck in a quick breath. *"Fun?* Mother, are you even vaguely aware of what a swinger is?"

"Yes." Her brows narrow as if the idea stymied her. "It's a group of people who like to have a swinging good time."

"Good grief. I'm going to go with the fact you really don't

know. It means you like to swap—and exchange partners. As in *eww*, that's disgusting!"

"I don't want to swap. Topper and I are officially together now." Her voice curls in a sexy snarl that makes my stomach churn. "I'm his date tonight."

"Of course, you are. How else would he play this perverted game? Only I bet he's not going to swap you. He's simply going to add to the equation!"

She waves me off. "Oh, Lottie, I know he is. In fact, he introduced me to two other very wealthy men who are interested in taking us out for drinks!"

Good God. I can't.

"And what exactly do you think their intentions are with the two of you?" I had to go there. If you're going to connect the dots, you should always start at the beginning.

"We're going to further discuss our favorite positions on things." She stops abruptly and glances around as if slowly coming to.

"Brace yourself, Mother. They weren't talking politics. The entire lot of them wants to take you to bed!"

She fans herself with her fingers. "Your father always said men were wild to have me as their own. They'll just have to eat their hearts out. I belong to Topper now."

"No, don't you get it? Topper wants them all to have you at *once*."

Her mouth falls open. "You mean? The three of us?" Her jaw roots to the floor. "Oh, Lottie, now you're just being silly. Head on over to the bar. Topper arranged to have a signature drink made for the party. It's called a trilateral delight."

There are no words in the human lexicon to describe how I'm feeling right now.

"Fine," I say. "I didn't want to do this, but I'm going to have to rat you out to Lainey and Meg." I take a picture of Mom smiling under the raunchy signage and shoot it over to my sisters.

Meg is the first to respond with an emoji that's laughing so hard it's crying.

I flash it at my mother. "She's still typing."

We'll put her in a nice home come morning. Lock her in the pantry for safekeeping tonight, would you?

"See this?" I say with a touch of satisfaction. "Meg thinks you're a danger to yourself and you should be restrained."

Mom lifts a brow. "I'll agree to the pantry so long as Topper can come with me."

Lainey texts back an entire sea of expletives, and I'm a bit slower to share my sister's disdain with her.

"You girls are impossible." She waves me off as she looks around. "Wait a minute. That's Marcia. She's Richard B's girlfriend, and she's leaving with Carlisle." Her fingers gravitate to her lips. "And isn't that Betty? Wasn't her husband of fifty years here? What's she doing kissing Mr. Riley? He has a very attractive girlfriend who is twenty years his junior."

"Face it, Mother. You've got an entire roomful of partner swapping deviants who think you've just green-lighted their philandering behavior."

"Oh dear," she moans as she looks around. "We need to get these people out of here. If the citizens of Honey Hollow find out about it, they're liable to run me right out of town!"

"And straight to Leeds where they think you belong." I glance around for two of my favorite studs. "Hang on."

I spot Noah and Everett with their arms folded tightly across their chests standing a safe distance outside of the conservatory.

I speed over in a flash. "Quick! We need to help my mother get these people out of here."

Everett shakes his head. "I can't risk getting my picture taken anywhere near that banner. I've got a career to uphold."

"Same here," Noah pipes up.

"Well, how in the heck am I going to get them out of here?" A wild panic starts to build in me at the thought of the senior sect pulling an all-nighter at my mother's B&B. A thought comes to me. "Noah, clear the room so we can get back to my place."

Noah charges past me and whips out his badge, holding it high overhead.

"You have two minutes to vacate the premises or you're all under arrest!" His voice roars so loud, the echo circles the room twice.

And just like that, a silver blur takes over as the room drains from its every orifice.

Noah comes back with the look of a man who's about to get lucky, and he is.

"Good work," I say. "Even the bartender has abandoned his post."

We say goodnight to my mother and pile back into Noah's truck.

"Would you mind running by the bakery so I can pick up my car? I'll be needing it in the morning."

"Sure thing."

We stop off and Everett offers to drive along with me.

It's so cold in my Honda, I apologize ten times before we ever leave the alley for dragging Everett into the Ice Age with me.

"You need a new car, Lemon. One you can start remotely and have it nice and toasty by the time you get inside."

"Like yours?" I tease. Everett's car has enough bells and whistles it could run the space station.

"Like mine."

I take the turnout of the alley a little too fast, trying my hardest to make the light at the end of the street.

"Slow down, Lemon. Arriving alive is still the right option."

"You bet," I say, pumping the brakes, but nothing happens. "*Everett?*" My voice hikes in a panic. "Everett, the brakes aren't working!" I slam the pedal to the floorboard over and over again.

"Lemon, watch out!"

A horrific crash erupts as my front end wraps itself around a tree, and just like that, the windshield explodes as Everett bursts right through it. My head slams against the steering wheel and the world grows increasingly fuzzy.

She's done it. Cormack has finally managed to kill me, and unfortunately for Everett, she might have offed him, too.

CHAPTER 19

*T*hirteen stitches.

I'm sensing a theme here.

Thankfully, Noah decided to follow us and was able to call for an ambulance. After a visit to the emergency room, both Everett and I walked away with ugly bruises. Everett also sustained cuts to his arms, which he used to shield those aggressive good looks when his seat belt failed, but, none-theless, we're still at a few stitches apiece—thus totaling the unlucky number. I have three stitches along the right side of my forehead, and Everett has ten running from the corner of his lip to his jaw on his left side. The scans they did showed no signs of brain swelling for either of us, and for that I'm extremely grateful.

The doctor suggested someone keep an eye on the two of us for the next few hours, so I spent the night at Everett's to keep an eye on him and Noah slept on the couch. Yes, I slept with Everett, but we did just that, sleep. Well, he slept. I listened to his steady breathing all night while plotting a murder of my own.

If Cormack thinks she's going to get away with this, she is sorely mistaken. First the tree? And then cutting my brakes? She is certifiable! But then, I've known that all along. Of course, neither Noah nor Everett dares to believe it.

They actually defended her.

Defended!

I'm quick to push it out of my mind. Once I start dwelling on it, my blood hits an instant boil.

Besides, now that it's clear Cormack has her sights set on me, I've been on guard all week. And there have been incidents. The sack of flour that nearly decapitated me from the upper rung of the delivery cart in the alley? Cormack. The metal pole that seemingly came out of nowhere and tripped me on the way down my porch yesterday morning? A total Featherby move.

But most disturbing was the mysterious basket of apples that was waiting by my door when I got home last night. They had a stamp from Grand Orchard on them and a simple note that read *Enjoy!*

Normally, I would have been ecstatic to have the treats. Fresh apples this time of year are my absolute favorite. But I couldn't shake the vision of Cormack injecting them all with cyanide, so I promptly took the whole thing and threw it into the trash bin in the side yard.

Almost a week has passed since I wrapped my car around a tree. It's Halloween, the night of the Monsters Ball at the Evergreen Manor, and I've been making a steady stream of deliveries. I've worked tirelessly over the last two days baking around the clock to make sure there would be enough to fill the ridiculously large order Naomi put in. On the final trip, Everett helps me pull out the last few boxes of cupcakes and lock up the refrigerated van. It's the van he gifted me almost a year ago after I helped clear him off the suspect list after one of his girlfriends—and I use the term loosely—was killed. I was in a competition to win one of those refrigerated beauties when I came upon the suspect, and sure enough I hunted her down. I burned my pie and lost to a longtime rival, but the killer was brought to justice.

"Let's get these to the kitchen, Frankenstein." I can't help but giggle. Everett has opted to forgo a costume. Instead, he looks dapper in his business attire that he wears down to the courthouse. But those stitches on the side of his face give the appeal of Dr. Frankenstein's monster—and I have to admit, it's a sexy look.

"They come out tomorrow, Lemon. So do yours."

"Don't I know it. I feel like a patchwork doll each time I look in the mirror. Hey? You don't think Cormack will try to finish me off tonight, do you?"

He winces as we enter the kitchen of the Evergreen Manor through the back door. You can hear the din of voices, what sounds like a cast of thousands coming from the main hall.

The parking lot outside is filled to capacity, but thankfully there's valet so no need to worry about stumbling around in the woods trying to get here.

"I talked to Cormack." Everett sighs.

"You did?" I practically shriek the words at him. Cormack has been wisely avoiding me. That is, when she's not busy planting booby traps in an effort to do me in.

"Yes, she came by the courthouse yesterday afternoon and we went for coffee."

"Coffee? At *our* coffee shop?" Okay, so the fact it's ours is a bit of a stretch, but the coffee shop next to the courthouse is where we met. It might have been a bit of an inglorious meeting, what with me trying to ram him in the crotch with the top of my head. Initially, there was a bit of a trip and fall trauma that resulted in a difficult time getting up, but it was a memorable meeting nonetheless.

"Yes, Lemon. At our coffee shop." His lips twist as if he were remorseful. "I'm sorry. But I spoke to her about the incidences that you—*we* found concerning, and she categorically denied any involvement."

"Of course, she did. Every killer that I happened to have

apprehended this last year categorically denied having anything to do with their crimes right before they were caught. You of all people should know that every suspect sings his innocence."

And just like that, Thirteen materializes over the elongated island flooded with far too many sweet treats. Naomi really did over order. She never was good at math.

"Good All Hallows' Eve," he purrs.

"Good evening, Thirteen," I say quickly before turning back to Everett. "So I suppose you're just going to believe her word over mine. Nice to know where my credibility lies with you."

"You have no evidence."

"You have no evidence she didn't do it!"

"*Ohh*," Thirteen yowls. "Who is the infamous she?"

"*She* is a witch," I hiss and Everett's eyes enlarge at my seemingly uncalled for outburst.

Noah walks through the back. "Knock, knock." He comes over with a crooked grin. He's dressed in jeans and a crimson varsity football jersey with the number thirteen in large gold letters, and I can't help but smile.

"Hey, princess." Noah stalks over, looking far too handsome for me to keep my hands off him for too long. "You look great. You look like a queen, and you are. You're my queen. Are you up for the romantic day I have planned for us tomorrow?" He lands a quick kiss to my lips and lingers for a moment.

Noah has yet to make good on Dr. Allen's suggestion to do something wildly romantic with me, but he assured me he was cooking up something big.

"You can bet I'm looking forward to it. And, for the record, I'm a fairy," I say, plucking at my pale green skirt. There's a silver bodice up top and small iridescent wings strapped over my back. "Meg furnished the costume for me. She says they have an entire cache down at Red Satin. I opted for something more demure than the other offerings she suggested."

"You opted wisely." He leans in and whispers, "Save the wings. I've got plans for them later." He nods to Everett. "What's with the tension?"

"Cormack," Everett says her name quietly as if he were afraid he might conjure up a demon. He's not that far off.

Noah tips his head back with a knowing look on his face.

"What?" I peg him with a look that suggests he needs to cough up answers and do it now.

"Everett told me about his meeting with Cormack. It sounded like it went well. She said she didn't do it."

"Noah, you are legally obligated to side with me. I'm your wife. Why are you so quick to believe Cormack all the time?" I glower at Everett who looks as if he's about to burst out smiling at the thought of Noah and me having a spat right in front of him. "I'm talking to the both of you. I'm sick and tired of the two of you defending her honor and overlooking the fact I nearly died multiple times at her twisted hands. I should take that note to the Ashford's Sheriff's Department. Maybe they'll believe me. Or has she infiltrated the ranks there, too?" I stalk off.

"Hey"—Noah calls after me—"Lottie, wait. Come back."

"I am leaving. And I ask that neither of you follow me."

Thirteen trots on ahead as we make my way to the reception desk. The Evergreen Manor could easily engulf my mother's B&B at least four times over.

Fun fact: It was once home to a colonial era earl who thought a supersized estate would be enough to bring all the pretty maids to the yard. And I'm betting it worked. The outside has a stately appeal with its large oversized Grecian columns that stretch to the sky and the ironwork that scrolls along the balconies. The inside is opulent with a homey feel. It has twin staircases that twist to the second level and the ambiance is that of a fancy hotel. The granite counters are lined with pumpkin vases brimming with sunflowers and there are cobwebs and fake spiders and cutouts of witches and ghosts in every nook and cranny. But it's the people who have caught my eye.

Every costume imaginable is pouring into the lavish ballroom to my left. I see the bride of Frankenstein, whom I'm sure will try to snag Everett for herself—at least if she were sane or single.

There are tons of beautiful girls in costumes with the too short, vamped up, glammed up versions of everything you can imagine from nurses to fairy-tale princesses. The men are either monsters, vampires, or dressed as some version of a sports team.

I head straight to the front desk where Naomi is dressed like Maleficent, the wicked fairy from *Sleeping Beauty* who proclaims herself as the Mistress of All Evil. I'd say it suits Naomi. Her dark hair looks as if it were freshly dyed, so very, very dark it looks as if you could fall right into it like some time-traveling portal.

She's speaking with a tall woman with cinnamon-colored hair, older, about my mother's age, her orange lips twisted with what looks like rage. Come to think of it, they seem to be having a rather heated conversation. The woman is dressed as a mummy right up to her neck, and I must admit, the gauze is wrapped so amazingly well it looks as if it's a body suit of some sort. For her sake I hope it has an escape clause for restroom use.

I clear my throat and Naomi glances over, their voices suddenly mute and it quiets the environment around us substantially.

"I'm all done laying out the desserts in the ballroom, and I have an enormous overstock in the kitchen. I'll be here all night, so I'll make sure the dessert tables are amply supplied."

Naomi ticks her head back. "Thank you."

The cinnamon-haired woman steps over. "Trisha Maples. I'm the manager here at the Evergreen Manor." Her lips pull tight in a line as she extends her hand, and I apprehensively shake it.

Manager of the Evergreen? I'm pretty sure that's Naomi's job.

"Lottie Lemon. I, uh"—I glance to Naomi, trying to see if maybe the woman misspoke—"I'm the owner of the Cutie Pie

Bakery and Cakery on Main Street. I provided all the baked goods for the evening."

"Perfect. You were next on my list."

Why do I get the feeling this is a hit list?

She closes her eyes a moment too long as if putting me at ease. "The Evergreen is hosting a friends-giving charity event early next month. It's fifty dollars a plate, and a large portion of the proceeds will go directly to feeding needy families in the area. Of course, all of Honey Hollow is invited, so we'll need to have plenty of pumpkin pie on hand. Could you provide those for us?"

"Absolutely. I'd be thrilled to help out with the event in any way I can."

"Perfect, just put together an invoice and have it sent directly to me. Apparently, I'm the only one that can understand numbers around here." She turns to glare at poor Naomi. And oddly enough, I do believe this is the first time I've ever referenced my salty cousin as poor Naomi. Usually, it's poor me for being in her presence. She moans as if to acknowledge this. "Did I hear you say Naomi ordered far too much dessert for the evening?"

"No, I didn't say that."

"I distinctly heard you mention an enormous overstock in the kitchen." She shifts her narrowed gaze to Naomi. "This is a prime example of why I'm needed here. I'm a numbers girl, Naomi. And I, unlike you, know how to make them work. I'm off to see the gratuitous spending for myself." She heads toward the kitchen, leaving a scarf of heavy perfume in her wake.

"What's going on?" I take a step forward. "I thought *you* were the manager of the Evergreen Manor."

"I thought I was, too." She glares hard in the direction Trisha took off in. "I called my boss and he assured me that Trisha is not taking over my position. He says she's the district manager of the chain. I'm not sure I'm buying it. She's gunning for my job just the way Lily is gunning for my boyfriend."

A scoffing sound emits from me, and I try to play it off like a cough. "Have you and Alex taken that next step? You know, making it official?"

"About as official as that fake marriage of yours. I heard you spent the week in bed with Everett."

"It wasn't a week." I hold my breath for a moment. "Okay, so it was three days, but Noah was right there with us and I had to make sure Everett didn't die in the night. He took a nasty fall out my windshield."

"Noah was with you, too? *Eww.*" She sweeps her gaze from my head to my toes. "Or should I say *ooh.* I'm sure they both cater to your every need and desire. Who would ever think our little Lottie would grow up to be such a Lolita? Oh, wait—*I* did. You've always been easy, Lottie, but my God, two men at once? And you don't even hide it."

"There's nothing to hide."

"There wouldn't seem to be to a loose woman like yourself."

I'm not going to fight her on this. I know what she's implying isn't true. "You're just jealous, Naomi."

Thirteen hops up onto the counter between us, his body glowing a strange purple hue, and a part of me wonders if that's some sort of supernatural costume he's donned for the evening.

"Somebody knows something," he growls. "Something is afoot. I'm not sure what."

Naomi steps around the counter until we're just about nose to nose. "I am jealous, Lottie." She crimps a sarcastic smile with those dark crimson-stained lips. "Are you satisfied? I'm jealous that you have two grown—seemingly sane men warring over you. That they can't seem to breathe without you, and that they even share the same airspace despite the fact they can't stand one another half the time. They sacrifice a piece of themselves and their egos all in hopes that you'll choose them. And what do I get? I get to be on the other end of the deal. I get to war with my own best friend over a man I would die to be with. But then, she's no best friend. If she truly cared for me, she'd back off and let Alex and me have the future we deserve."

"I'm sorry, Naomi. I can't imagine how difficult that must be. But you and Lily are like sisters. Surely you can figure this out. And if I were you, I'd figure it out fast. It's only going to erode your friendship a little more each day."

"What friendship? Once Alex and I tie the knot, I'm never speaking to Lily again. The only reason I'm even pretending to tolerate her is so that Alex doesn't think I'm being petty."

Someone clears their throat from behind, and we find Alex there looking dapper in a suit.

"Good evening, ladies." He pulls Naomi into his arms and lands a kiss to her lips. I'll admit, it's a little unnerving to witness considering he looks so much like Noah.

She blinks up at him. "And what are you supposed to be? Let me guess, my naughty prince? We can go to my room in a bit, and I'll let you show me exactly how naughty you can be."

He laughs as if it were funny and not at all the siren song Naomi meant for it to be.

Alex opens up the lapel to his jacket and flashes a silver badge our way. "My brother lent me his old badge, so the both of you better behave or I'll have to take you into custody."

Naomi titters like a schoolgirl. "I won't behave. I promise." She holds out her wrists as if she's ready to be cuffed right now.

He nods my way. "How's the case, Lottie? I just talked to my brother and he says he's stumped. But then, I don't expect much out of him to begin with." He gives a little wink.

"Noah is right. Honestly, in all the months I've been investigating cases, this one has proven to be the toughest. Sure, there are suspects, and boy, did each and every one of them have a great motive, but nothing seems to be clicking. I think I just need one strong shred of evidence to propel me in the right direction."

He shakes his head sympathetically. "I'm sure it'll come together. Have you tried talking to his family?"

"I wouldn't know where to begin. Noah mentioned the body was unclaimed at the morgue."

Thirteen twitches. "He has a sister and a brother."

I take a deep breath. "I know." I nod his way. "One of his exes mentioned that Pastor Gaines did have a brother and a sister. Pastor *Gaines*." I roll my eyes for even saying the name. "He was a fraud through and through."

Alex pats me over the shoulder. "Review the footage on Main Street once again. Who knows? You might see something new."

"Maybe."

Trisha the mummy manager comes back just as Alex and Naomi head into the ball. There will be no fun for Trisha this evening, I suppose.

Noah and Everett emerge from the hall to my left, and I make a face at the two of them without meaning to.

Everett says something to Noah before offering me a polite nod and heading into the ballroom. Noah strides in my direction, the beginnings of a dangerous smile curving on his lips, and even though I'm a twinge angry with him for not siding with me, I suddenly feel the need to steal him away into the nearest dark corner.

He wraps his arms around me and lands a kiss to my lips.

"I'm sorry. How can I make this up to you?"

For a moment I get lost in those glowing green eyes. I'm about to suggest the dark corner, but my mind makes a left.

"Can you show me the footage from the bakery that day?"

His brows swoop in low. "Yes. After the party. I just saw Lainey and Forest head in dressed like salt and pepper shakers. And there's a rumor Meg has reprised Madge the Badge."

"Ooh, that does sound like costume gold, but I think I just need to settle my soul a bit."

"Let's do it." He pulls out his phone and leads us to the exact dark corner I had in mind. Noah fiddles with his phone until the footage pops up. Noah has just about everything related to the case accessible by phone. "Here we go. This is about fifteen minutes before the murder occurred." Noah has the speed adjusted so that it's time lapsed just enough to avoid monotony.

"There he is," I say as my adrenaline kicks in. "Pastor Gaines and my mother. That striped sweater sure makes him easy to track," I muse as they whirl their way through the crowd comically. "My mother was so angry with him for following her around—at least until they got into my office." I avert my eyes at the memory of my mother getting busy in there with him.

"I remember." Noah points to the screen. "And here they are talking to you, and there they go into the bakery."

"And there's the infamous food fight," I say, almost amused this time. It's taken me the entire month to forgive Meg for starting it to begin with.

"Here you are!" a high-pitched voice calls from behind, and we turn to find Cormack dressed in a short beaded dress. A cradle-like cap is pressed over her blonde locks as strings of pearls grace her neck. The heels on her feet have to be at least six painful inches tall. Cormack makes a stunning flapper, and here I look as if I belong in a cartoon. "Guess what, Big Boss? Have I got a surprise for *you*." She struts over, weaving one leg over the other dramatically. "You have to come outside to see it."

"Let me guess?" I tilt my head, my voice filled with a homicidal level of sarcasm. "A wood chipper with my name on it?"

"I'm not speaking to you, Loretta. I'm talking to Noah. *My* Noah." She gives a wink his way.

"Lottie, I—"

"Go," I say, taking the phone from him. "I want to review this a few more times anyway."

Noah leans in. "I'm going to make things crystal clear. I'm letting her know we're over," he whispers lest she actually hears him.

Noah takes off, and I land my focus right back on the footage taken from the day of the murder.

Thirteen jumps from the floor to my shoulder, and I let out an audible *oof*.

"You do realize you can control your heft," I grunt, and just like that, he's lighter than air. "Thank you."

"Let me see the footage," he purrs into my ear, and I hold the phone a little higher. "Ah yes, I tried my best to lap up those cupcakes gone to waste. You should look into arresting the woman who caused the carnage."

"She's my sister, and Carnage is her middle name."

"I like her already."

"Look at this. The street is filled with every style of ghoul and tool, much like tonight. And there's Pastor Gaines again. This is the second time he's coming in." I blink back. "Only he's not wearing that striped garish sweater. He's wearing a leather jacket and that baby blue shirt underneath. I remember wondering why the wardrobe change, but now that I can see what a malfeasance that sweater was to begin with, I can totally understand the need to stop everything and burn it." I sigh as I turn off the footage. "I'm sorry, Thirteen. I'm officially done with this case. Not only do I lack any real leads, but he was a terrible person. If Noah can't catch the perpetrator, then the killer just might go free forever. I can't help you anymore. Maybe it's best to let sleeping dogs lie."

Thirteen digs his claws into my shoulder as he arches his back, letting out a hair-raising meow before using me as a springboard and running all the way into the ballroom.

"What in the heck was that about?" I'm about to head in that direction when a man dressed in a black suit and a black felt mask covering his face partially like the Phantom of the Opera walks through the door. He pauses and does a double take in my direction before offering an eerie, all too familiar grin and acknowledging me with a nod.

He melts into the crowd that's feeding into the ballroom, and I freeze. I can't breathe. Something about him felt sinister, pure evil. A feeling I've gotten before from Pastor Gaines himself.

That couldn't be him. Noah is sure he's in the morgue.

Here it is, All Hallows' Eve, and I'm pretty sure I'm being haunted by the scariest ghost of them all.

Just my rotten luck.

CHAPTER 20

*T*he ballroom at the Evergreen Manor pulsates with strobe lights as the music filters in through the speakers, a touch too raucously loud for my liking. The room is thick with bodies, all of them moving and grooving, and it feels as if I've just been thrust into a sea of limbs. There's no hope of me ever finding Noah or Everett in this mess.

The Monsters Ball is in full swing, and the magic of Halloween night has cast its spell over all of Honey Hollow.

A blonde Cinderella, dusted with glitter from head to toe, makes her way over, and I can't help but crack a smile at my best friend.

"Keelie, you are ridiculously adorable," I say, pulling her into a quick embrace and her sugary perfume stuns my senses. "And you smell like cotton candy."

"It's not cotton candy. It's your friendly ghost cupcake. Bear and I were sharing one in the laundry room in the back and—"

"And I'm going to stop you. Have you by chance seen Everett or Noah?"

"Not Noah. But I saw Everett. I didn't get his costume." Her lips tug to the side the way they do when she sees something she wants to gobble up. "What's he supposed to be anyway?"

"The usual—a sexy beast." I crane my neck over her shoulder, hoping to see him.

"Isn't that the truth. Speaking of missing people, have you seen my sister? Lily is on the warpath, and I really need to warn her. You'd think as her twin, I would know where she is at all times."

"Last I saw, she was on her way in here with Alex. But then, she is dressed as a wicked witch for all practical purposes. Who would ever think you were twins?"

We laugh it off before Keelie gets sucked back into the undertow of the crowd.

A sparkle of light ignites at my feet before darting through the sea of bodies.

"Thirteen," I say as I do my best to follow him. I stagger my way out of the ballroom, and in an instant my eardrums soak in the relief from all the boisterous noise. I'm holding two phones, one of which is Noah's, and I take a moment to frown at it because I'm wishing it were him.

Who knows what Cormack wanted to show him out front? She probably had a net ready to trap him.

I glance around for Thirteen, but there's no sign of any supernatural presence.

"*Boo!*" an eerie female voice shrills from behind, and I jump as I turn around, ready to strangle whomever it is for scaring my wings crooked, but it's not any person I could send into eternity. This soul already happens to be there. "*Greer!* Don't do that to me. I nearly had a heart attack. I'd kill you if you weren't already dead."

She chortles away as if it were hilarious.

"What are you doing here?" I ask as I look around for signs of that wily cat.

"We just finished the last haunted house tour. Your mother is closing up shop and heading this way, so we thought we'd join in on the fun, too. Winston and Lea are in the ballroom checking out the costumes, and I saw a fairy out here so I thought I'd say hello. Imagine my disappointment when I realized it was just you." She gives a giggle and a wink.

"Funny."

"How's the investigation going?"

"It's not. I've got five suspects and nowhere to go with them."

"I bet one of them is the killer, Lottie."

"I bet one them is not—or if she *is*, I don't really care. I quit the case."

She inches back a notch. "Now we both know that's not allowed."

"Lucky for me, no one ever flung a rulebook in my face."

She shakes her head emphatically. "Tell me about the suspects. Maybe I can help untangle this knot?"

"Fine, but believe me when I say the only way out of this one is to cut it loose." I sigh as the suspects rotate in my head like an all too sparse Rolodex. "First, there's my mother."

She nods. "Who went on record to say she could kill him just shortly before he was gunned down."

"How do you know that?" It happens to be true, but still.

"I was there, remember?"

"Okay, but she didn't kill him. And if she did, I am totally turning a blind eye—which oddly enough, I think I'd do with just about any of the other suspects. There's Mitzi Underwood, the socialite from Fallbrook who looks suspiciously like my mother. He married her, took all her money, and split town. There's Elaine Gilmore from Lake Champlain who looks exactly like my mother. He married her, took all her money, and split town. Her daughter, Rachel Kane, who does graveyard tours in Ashford. She actually had the cookies to put a hit on him a couple of years ago, but nothing came from that—unless her useless hitmen were having a latent reaction, which I doubt. They took her money, and that was that. I'm still considering erecting a monument to her." I sigh. "Then there's roller derby queen, Julia Wright. She happens to be a replica of my mother. He married her, took all her money, and split town. Are you sensing a theme yet?"

She wiggles her nose as if an offensive odor filled the space between us. "I smell a rotten egg."

"Stephen Gaines was worse than that. Anyway, I'd better find Everett and Noah. We had a bit of a tiff."

"The three of you?"

I give a guilty nod, and she titters.

"How adorable. Your first big fight as a threesome."

"We are not a threesome. That sounds fifty shades of wrong."

"That sounds fifty shades of delicious to me." Something in the ballroom catches her attention. "I'd better get back inside. Little Lea was threatening to pull off a real decapitation tonight, and I hear screaming." She floats right through the wall, leaving me all by my lonesome with no Noah, no Everett, and no real suspects—not that I care about that last part.

A thought hits me as that conversation with Keelie echoes through my mind.

"Oh my God. If I'm right, then Pastor Gaines wasn't killed by any of the suspects."

Thirteen runs in from the door that leads outside, heading this way in a dizzying array of otherworldly light as if he were malfunctioning.

"Lottie"—he runs in a circle around me—"do not follow that man anywhere."

"That man?" My feet carry me down the hall toward the opened door, and I stick my head out in search of *that man*, whoever he might be.

And then I see him, just a breath away—and yet the truth still feels just out of my grasp.

"It's you," I say, stepping out into the icy Honey Hollow night.

The sound of the Monsters Ball behind me dies off like a dream quickly fading.

"It's me." He sheds that ever-expanding grin as he closes the distance between us and I attempt to run, but it's too late. He's wrapped his arms around me with what feels like superhuman strength. "*Gotcha.*"

The phones drop from my hands as I struggle to break free.

He's got me indeed.

*J*t's dark. It's cold. And it's Halloween night.

Have I mentioned I'm in the arms of a madman being traipsed off into the woods below the Evergreen Manor? Coincidentally, I live on the other side of these woods. Country Cottage Road is just on the other side of this thicket, and I can practically feel the false security that my rental home affords.

How I wish I were home. How I wish I were having my toes chewed off by a swarm of snakes. How I wish I were anywhere but here—my body and mouth restrained by this entity who I'm not even certain is human anymore.

I bite down hard on his hand and taste blood.

"Now, now." He laughs as he lands my feet to the ground, his chest pumping hard against my back letting me know it was too strenuous for him to go on like that. He's getting weak. I can use that to my advantage. I glance to the thicket of evergreens we're enveloped in as the dappled moonlight fills the gaps, looking for anything I can use as a weapon. We're standing on a severe slope. One wrong move could send either one of us toppling down.

Thirteen appears, roaring and growling as if this monster could hear him.

I twist against his powerful hold on me and knock my forehead to his so hard I'm convinced I heard a skull crack—with my luck it would've been mine. I pick up a fallen branch no bigger than a baseball bat and hold it between us.

"Lottie, be careful!" Thirteen warns, but I'm too mesmerized by what I'm seeing.

The moonlight slices over his features, confirming my greatest fear. That dark hair, those dark laughing eyes, his perennial smile. Pastor Gaines, Stephen Heartwood, whoever he is—he's alive and in the flesh.

"You're not dead."

A deep laugh rumbles from his chest. "Of course, I am. The coroner has my body."

"No." I shake my head. "He doesn't. He has your brother's, doesn't he?"

He closes his eyes a moment before a small laugh erupts within him.

"You see, Lottie. This is exactly why I needed to come back. I knew you wouldn't let this rest. If anyone at all were to foil all my hard work, it would be you. And that is why we have to die together."

"You're not killing me. But you killed Jack, didn't you?"

His eyes grow large. "You know his name. I knew you were good and how I wish you weren't. But you were already onto me, weren't you? Do you want to know how I knew that? Those calls you had your boyfriend make last month to the references on my application with the church, they tipped me off. Because they were all me."

"Last month, Amanda Wellington was about to go to the sheriff's department because she knew something. She figured out you were a fake—and that you were nothing but a con artist and a thief, didn't she? I bet you were thrilled when she died."

"No. I loved her. And yes, she knew." He shakes his head at the thought. "She had become dangerous to me, and if someone else hadn't taken care of her, I would have been forced to. But I'm grateful that didn't happen. I loved her. I did."

My heart sinks. "But you knew your number was up so you concocted a plan to off yourself. And that explains why you came back to the bakery that day wearing entirely different clothes and didn't seem to recognize me. It wasn't you at all. You lured your poor brother there. And by the way, your brother had better fashion sense." I shake my head. "I'm sure you think it's a shame you didn't have a chance to marry my mother and drain her bank account the way you did the others."

"I wouldn't have done that to your mother. I loved her, still do. She changed me. I'm not that man anymore. However, with you around, I would have had to pay for my sins regardless."

"Then why kill your brother? Why didn't you just kill me and be done with it?"

"Lottie!" Thirteen says it like a reprimand.

"Don't you *Lottie* me. You knew he had a twin and you didn't tell me?"

Thirteen bucks his head back. "I thought you knew!"

Pastor Gaines looks around, wild-eyed. "Who are you talking to?"

"A cat by the name of Thirteen. Sound familiar?"

He inches back, his face rife with disbelief. "I once had a cat by that name. How very strange."

"Want to hear something stranger? It *is* your cat. He's here to help solve your brother's murder. And now that it's done, he wants to see you behind bars."

Thirteen postures. "Now, I didn't say that—but I do believe it to be true."

"Ingenious, killing your brother with my gun." Poor Ethel, who is still being held against her will in some lockbox down at the Ashford Sheriff's Department. "You're a fraud in every sense of the word. It's not a surprise you didn't even use your own gun."

A dull laugh bounces out of him as he pulls something from his waistband and I can see it for what it is—Ethel's carbine cousin.

"I had my own, Lottie, but once your mother provided it from seemingly thin air, it felt like fate." He points it right at me. "I tried other ways to kill you, the tree, the brakes. I tried so many times to hurt you, but you proved impervious to my schemes."

I suck in a quick breath. And all this time I believed it was Cormack.

Cormack, who all but kidnapped Noah tonight.

"Oh God," I whimper. A thought comes to me. "Wait a minute. You married Noah and me—you married my sister and Forest." I shake my head in disbelief. "Are you even ordained to do that?"

"It was perfectly legal. I assure you. Anyone can become an ordained minister. In fact, a copy of my certificate is on record at the church."

"Yeah, under your fake name." Great. Lainey and I have just been stiffed with marriage certificates that could have just as easily been plucked from a Cracker Jack box.

"*Lottie?*" someone shouts my name faintly from a distance and Pastor Gaines waves the gun at me.

"It's time, Lottie. Say your final prayers. You're about to meet your maker."

"Thirteen," I pant without daring to take my eyes off the gun. "Go back to the ball, find Carlotta, and tell her I'm in danger. Tell her where I am, and who I'm with. She'll know what to do."

"*No,*" Thirteen yowls it out with an attitude.

Pastor Gaines twitches his head to the left. "All right. Enough of this insanity. It's not working with me. But I will give you points for trying. Your mother always did maintain you had a remarkable imagination."

I glance down at the surly cat who has suddenly decided to cop an attitude.

"What do you mean, *no?*"

His fur is glowing a dull shade of purple once again, and it looks majestic with the sparkle of dark stars that seem to be forever trapped in his fur.

"I mean no, Lottie. If I leave, he might kill you."

"He might kill me if you stay." My fingers grip over the stick in my hand. From my peripheral vision I can see Pastor Gaines squinting and bending over as if trying to get a better look in the direction I'm focusing my attention, and I take advantage of it.

I launch the stick in an upward swing as hard as I can muster and knock the gun right out of his hands. It flies off to the right and down the embankment before lodging against a boulder.

He shouts in pain as he grips his hand, and I take another upward swing with that stick and hit him hard and swift in the cookies.

Pastor Gaines lets out another cry, this time far more hair-raising than the last as he bends over to nurse his wounds. And then I go for the gold. I swing that branch as if my life depended on it and strike him right over the temple with all I've got. A sickening crack—the sound of a vase breaking is all I can relate it to —pierces through the night and Pastor Gaines falls to the ground with a thud.

Thirteen hops over his back and sniffs around his neck.

"Oh dear, Lottie. You've done it. It's over. Justice has been served."

"You don't mean..."

"Yes, I do, in fact." He lies down over Pastor Gaines' back. "Oh dear, Stephen. What has become of you?"

"Lottie?" Everett booms from the top of the slope. Before I know it, his arms are wrapped around me and I point down to where Pastor Gaines lies motionless over a bed of pine needles.

"It's okay. It's over." Everett dots a kiss to my cheek. "It's all over now."

And it is.

CHAPTER 22

$\mathcal{E}$verett called the sheriff's department, and the entire area was swarmed with deputies within minutes. Detective Ivy Fairbanks showed up and cleared me to head back to the party before I caught my death.

Everett and I hiked back up the hill and did just that.

It's sweltering hot in the ballroom compared to the near frozen air of fall. Not to mention the fact Everett has an arm wrapped around my waist with a death grip. He's vowed to stay with me until we find Noah.

Mom comes bopping up to us, dressed as a bride of all things —complete with veil and a round bouquet of blood-red roses.

"Oh, Lottie, you are adorable! How did you like those juicy apples I set on your porch yesterday? My horticulture club took a field trip to the orchard, and I thought of you. I'd like a fresh apple pie if you don't mind." She gives my cheek a pinch, and I don't have it in me to tell her that I just killed her ex-boyfriend. Even if she wasn't that into him those last few days, I don't think the news would bring her any joy.

"The apples?" I guess it's good to know she's the one that gave me the apples and not Cormack. A part of me is actually

495

starting to feel sorry for the featherheaded Featherby. I've accused her of so many horrible things. But then, she has successfully kidnapped my husband for the night, so I suppose we're even.

"Oh, never mind the pie. How do you like my costume?" Mom's shoulders bounce with glee. "I'm a bridezilla." She gives a cheeky wink.

A tall man with a shock of white hair and one of those seductive phantom masks sneaks up behind her and wraps his arms possessively around her waist.

Mom jolts before turning and laughing. "You nearly gave me a fright!"

"I plan on giving you a real fright later."

My chest bucks with disbelief. "Excuse me?"

Mom waves me off. "It's just Topper. Don't worry, Lottie. We're not serious. We're just fooling around." She dances off with him as if they were a two-person conga line, and soon enough bodies are attaching themselves to that crazy train.

"Just fooling around?" I look to Everett. "That's exactly what I'm afraid of."

"I wouldn't worry about her too much. Let's get Noah." Everett takes me by the hand as we begin to weave through the haunted looking crowd.

Everett and I look high and low for Noah and finally give up. I lead him to the back of the facility where we pick up the phones I dropped earlier, both mine and Noah's, and a thought comes to me.

"Call Cormack. Tell her that wherever it is she's hauled Noah off to, it's time to bring him back to his wife."

At least I hope I'm Noah's wife. I'm not sure I quite believe anything that man said. You can bet I'll be charging over to the Honey Hollow Covenant Church looking for that certificate of ordination. It will break my heart to have to tell Lainey that the pastor who married her was a fake.

"Good idea." Everett whips out his phone and calls, but she doesn't pick up.

"Figures. She's knee-deep in a Fox, and there's no way she's wasting a single second of it." I guess that's better than my Fox being knee-deep in her. Noah would never do that to me in a million years.

That long line of cheats from my past comes back to haunt me.

Like I said, Noah would never do that to me in a million years —I *hope*.

Meg runs up with her dark hair ratted all the way to heaven and heck and a pair of bright yellow contacts in her eyes with a line for a pupil. Her outfit looks like something Wonder Woman might wear if all her uniforms were at the laundromat. Both her red metallic bustle and her bikini bottoms are dotted with blue and white stars. She's wearing flesh-toned tights that make her legs look rubbery, and it all has a nightmarish appeal that I think she's actually going for.

"You look great," I say, but she's too busy looking behind us and waving someone over.

Hook runs this way and wraps his arms lovingly around my sister's waist, but he doesn't even say hello to Everett and me. In fact, he looks darn right distressed. He's wearing a baseball hat and a raglan jersey with the word *COACH* printed across it in all capital letters.

"What's the matter, Coach?" Everett pulls me in close as if he wanted to protect me.

Lainey traipses up in that confining costume she's ensconced herself in. She's holding the hat that's supposed to be the top of her peppermill. Her bulbous stiff dress looks adorable on her and even gives me a sneak peek at what she might look like one day when she's with child. A part of me wants to ask if she's with child now.

She grabs ahold of my hand. "Lottie, I'm sorry. Forest is down

497

the road at the corner of Crest Field and Country Cottage Road. He says you need to come quickly."

Before I know it, the five of us are in Hook's truck as he speeds us down the twisted road in haste and parks off the shoulder.

The entire area is inundated with people. There is a fire truck, an ambulance, and at least a dozen patrol cars.

Everett and I jump out of the truck and he navigates us into the heart of the melee.

Up ahead there's a small sports car smashed against a sturdy old oak and it doesn't look good for the driver. Medics swarm both sides of the vehicle, shouting to one another as if time were of the essence.

"Everett, what's happening?" My adrenaline kicks in hard, and I can't breathe.

"I don't know, Lemon. But we're about to find out." He points to my brother-in-law, Forest, who's headed this way. Forest is a fireman, and he's got his yellow pants on and his white T-shirt is covered in what looks like crimson grease.

"I'm sorry, Lottie." Forest shakes his head. His eyes are glossy with grief. "We're doing everything we can for him. Cormack is going to be fine. Just some minor abrasions."

"You're doing everything you can for *him*? You mean..." I stagger toward the wreckage. The twisted steel is illuminated under the strain of the moon, and just beyond that lies the blank darkness of the woods. I spot Cormack's blonde mane resting as she sits in the driver's seat. There's a dark head of hair slumped to the side of the passenger's seat as a group of firemen tries to pry the door open with the jaws of life.

"*No*," I shout so loud half of them turn my way.

Everett collapses his arms around me so tight it feels as if he's trying to press me inside of him.

"Lottie," a still, tranquil voice, deep and startlingly familiar, echoes from the right, from the dark, dark woods and I propel from Everett and bolt that way.

"*Lemon*." Everett chases after me, but he doesn't have to run far because I freeze as soon as I get to the lip of the woods.

Standing before me in a spasm of shimmering light is the ghost of my gorgeous, sweet husband, Noah. A spray of stars spins beautiful and serene in what was once his earthly frame as he holds out a hand to me.

"Oh, Noah," I moan at the sight of him before running over and collapsing my arms around his ghostly body in a firm embrace.

"Lottie," he says my name sweetly, just above a whisper. That pained look in his eyes lets me know he's less than pleased with this horrific outcome. "Everett will take care of you. He will love you as ferociously as I do. Lean on him. I love you, Lottie Lemon." He takes a full step back just as Everett takes up my hand. "I love you both. Goodbye, Lottie. Goodbye."

*NEED MORE HONEY HOLLOW? Find out what happens to Noah and Lottie! Pick up Pumpkin Pie Parting (Murder in the Mix 15) today!

The unthinkable has happened, and I'm left to reel with a profound level of grief that I haven't known since my father died. Throw in a ditzy llama, a snow lodge, and a murder, and you'll have a recipe you never want to share at the Thanksgiving table. One thing is for sure—Noah and I will never be the same again.

Santa Claws Calamity

Bow Wow Big House

Murder Bites

Felines and Fatalities

A Killer Tail

Cat Scratch Cleaver

Just Buried

Butchered After Bark

A Frightening Fangs-giving

A Christmas to Dismember

Sealed with a Hiss

Country Cottage Boxed Set 1

Country Cottage Boxed Set 2

Murder in the Mix Mysteries

Cutie Pies and Deadly Lies

Bobbing for Bodies

Pumpkin Spice Sacrifice

Gingerbread & Deadly Dread

Seven-Layer Slayer

Red Velvet Vengeance

Bloodbaths and Banana Cake

New York Cheesecake Chaos

Lethal Lemon Bars

Macaron Massacre

Wedding Cake Carnage

Donut Disaster

Toxic Apple Turnovers

Killer Cupcakes

Pumpkin Pie Parting

Yule Log Eulogy

Pancake Panic

Sugar Cookie Slaughter

Devil's Food Cake Doom

Snickerdoodle Secrets

Strawberry Shortcake Sins

Cake Pop Casualties

Flag Cake Felonies

Peach Cobbler Confessions

Poison Apple Crisp

Spooky Spice Cake Curse

Pecan Pie Predicament

Eggnog Trifle Trouble

Waffles at the Wake

Raspberry Tart Terror

Baby Bundt Cake Confusion

Chocolate Chip Cookie Conundrum

Christmas Fudge Fatality

Murder in the Mix Boxed Set (Books 1-3)

Murder in the Mix Boxed Set (Books 4-6)

Murder in the Mix Boxed Set (Books 7-9)

Murder in the Mix Boxed Set (Books 10-12)

Murder in the Mix Boxed Set (Books 13-15)

Murder in the Mix Boxed Set (Books 16-18)

Murder in the Mix Boxed Set (Books 19-21)

Mystery

Little Girl Lost

Never Say Sorry

The First Wife's Secret

Romance

Just Add Mistletoe

3:AM Kisses (3:AM Kisses 1)

Winter Kisses (3:AM Kisses 2)

Sugar Kisses (3:AM Kisses 3)

Whiskey Kisses (3:AM Kisses 4)

Rock Candy Kisses (3:AM Kisses 5)

Velvet Kisses (3:AM Kisses 6)

Wild Kisses (3:AM Kisses 7)

Country Kisses (3:AM Kisses 8)

Forbidden Kisses (3:AM Kisses 9)

Dirty Kisses (3:AM Kisses 10)

Stolen Kisses (3:AM Kisses 11)

Lucky Kisses (3:AM Kisses 12)

Tender Kisses (3:AM Kisses 13)

Revenge Kisses (3:AM Kisses 14)

Red Hot Kisses (3:AM Kisses 15)

Reckless Kisses (3:AM Kisses 16)

Hot Honey Kisses (3:AM Kisses 17)

Shameless Kisses (3:AM Kisses 18)

The Social Experiment (The Social Experiment 1)

Bitter Exes (The Social Experiment 2)

Chemical Attraction (The Social Experiment 3)

Feisty Kisses (3:AM Kisses, Hollow Brook1)

Ex-Boyfriend Kisses (3:AM Kisses, Hollow Brook 2)

Secret Kisses (3:AM Kisses, Hollow Brook 3)

Naughty By Nature

Escape to Breakers Beach

Breakers Beach

Breakers Cove

Breakers Beach Nights

Escape to Lake Loveless

Beautiful Oblivion

Beautiful Illusions

Beautiful Elixir

Beautiful Deception

The Solitude of Passion

Someone to Love (Someone to Love 1)

Someone Like You (Someone to Love 2)

Someone For Me (Someone to Love 3)

Young Adult Romance

Melt With You (A Totally '80s Romance 1)

Tainted Love (A Totally '80s Romance 2)

Hold Me Now (A Totally '80s Romance 3)

Paranormal Romance

(Celestra Book World in Order)

Ethereal (Celestra Series Book 1)

ABOUT THE AUTHOR

Addison Moore is a *New York Times, USA TODAY,* and *Wall Street Journal* bestselling author. Her work has been featured in *Cosmopolitan* Magazine. Previously she worked as a therapist on a locked psychiatric unit for nearly a decade. She resides on the West Coast with her husband, four wonderful children, and two dogs where she eats too much chocolate and stays up way too late. When she's not writing, she's reading. Addison's Celestra Series has been optioned for film by **20ᵗʰ Century Fox.**

For up to the minute pre-order and new release alerts

*Be sure to **subscribe to Addison's mailing list** for sneak peeks and updates on all upcoming releases!
**Or click over to the WEBSITE
AddisonMoore.com**

✦Follow Addison here for the latest updates!

✦Follow Addison on **Bookbub!**
✦Like on **Facebook**

***Want to chat about the books? Hop over to Addison's Reader Corner on Facebook!**

Feel free to visit her on **Instagram.**

Made in the USA
Las Vegas, NV
30 July 2022

52447620R00296